Morrigan's DAUGHTER

PATRICK J. FITCH

Copyright © 2019 Patrick J. Fitch
All rights reserved
First Edition

PAGE PUBLISHING, INC.
Conneaut Lake, PA

First originally published by Page Publishing 2019

ISBN 978-1-64628-802-1 (pbk)
ISBN 978-1-64628-803-8 (digital)

Printed in the United States of America

Who can find a virtuous and capable wife? She is more precious than rubies. Her husband can trust her, and she will greatly enrich his life. She brings him good, not harm, all the days of her life.
—Proverbs 31:10–12

Here's the smell of the blood still: All the perfumes of Arabia will not sweeten this little hand. Oh, oh, oh!
—*Macbeth* (Act 5, Scene 1)

Is the Goddess of War in Celtic Mythology who traverses the circle of life from birth until death. The patroness of wrath and revenge, she incites warriors to bravery and instills fear into her enemies.
—Morrigan

Chapter 1

THE "RONK"

Iraq War veteran Ronan John "Ronk" McShea graduated from North Catholic High School north of what now is the Three Rivers Stadia complex in Pittsburgh, class of June 1992. His parents belonged to the same North Side Catholic parish as Steeler founder Art Rooney Sr. and were proud to say they were one of Art's apostles. His father, John Patrick, retired prematurely from the Edgar Thomson Works of U. S. Steel near Homestead, Pennsylvania, in 1980 with back injuries sustained on the job and needed the use of a cane but managed a wide circle of friends at the Black & Gold Tavern just blocks from the confluence of the three rivers. The hit the steel industry took from foreign competitors in the '70s left their favorite professional sports team as the only remaining steel in town. The downshift was abrupt and brutal for the McShea clan. It was the end two decades of a century, a slow erosion from steel's heyday in 1890 when nineteen mills dotted and flourished in the greater Pittsburgh area. Now the medical industry and Allegheny County's eight major colleges and universities supplanted what was once the dominant employer in greater Pittsburgh.

The transition from steel to cyberspace occurred abruptly in the 1990s. By the year 2000, the Edgar Thomson Works, the Clairton Coke Works, and the Irvin Works in West Mifflin today outside of Pittsburgh were the only remaining plants left—a sad museum of industry past. They're still in operation, but the neighborhoods surrounding them suffer the odium of rust belt decay. A valley that was once the crown jewel of the industry is a relic of years long gone. Now "God, Corps, and Steelers" formed his trinity of commitment for both father and sons. The steel industry remains a mostly melancholy memory.

Like his father, a Korean War infantry grunt Marine, Ronan elected to join the Marine Corps after an uninspired four years at Penn State where he graduated with a pedestrian 2.2 GPA and a bachelor's degree in civil engineering. His primary loves in undergraduate school were "boilermakers" (a shot of Imperial whiskey with any brand of beer) and any woman willing to disrobe for recreation. Despite its reputation for academic excellence, Penn State's isolation in the middle of Pennsylvania also makes it quite the party school. Just ask the now dying *Playboy* magazine. Even today it still lists Penn State as one of the top ten drinking schools throughout the spectrum of Americana. Ronan's "frat boy" carousing and behavior displeased his orthodox Catholic mother, Maureen Eileen McShea. But she surrendered to the reality and prayed she didn't get one of those late-night calls from a local police department to bail her son out of jail or identify him on a slab at the Allegheny County morgue. It's one of those painful visions parents never entertain.

Yet they all fear its reality. It's the phone call they never want to hear.

That gestated Maureen's line etched in stone: drunk and disorderly or pregnant girlfriends got no bail or sympathy from his mother. She knew full well the foibles of fraternity parties and the hold it had on young men with unrestrained testosterone. Even in high school, Maureen reluctantly tolerated his beer drinking and carousing around the house with his three brothers. But Mama McShea's boys knew not to flaunt the house rule.

"Beer only, no whiskey and no overnight guests—male or female! I do not want to find some drunk adolescent passed out in our living room or in the front yard."

She delivered the message in myriad ways to her four sons. Her rules left no exclusions.

Even the most pious of parents often make real compromise. She would concede his exposure to alcohol abuse reluctantly as an immature rite of passage. She didn't like it but worked around it. Most mothers have more insight into adolescent behavior than the pop psychologists of the world. They deal with it daily, not in one-hour sessions at $150 to $250-plus.

His dating choices, however, left her unanimously unimpressed with the concrete caveat: "Do not darken my door, Ronan, with some of those sorority sluts for whom you seem to gravitate. When you finally grow up and can keep your trousers tightly zipped, then your father and I will gladly welcome your dates to our home. Until then, do not shove your venal transgressions under my nose. I raised you differently."

But college and time away from the strictures of home told a different story. Most parents knew and, like the McSheas, chose selective amnesia when it came to their own children. Sometimes the boilermakers became a depth charge where you drop the whole shot glass into the beer glass. Net effect was still the same: a high-octane draft beer. He spent summers in the Corps Platoon Leaders Class from freshman through junior years. Then armed with the baccalaureate in 1997, Congress conferred a commission on him in 1998 at Quantico, Virginia, and later trained him as an artillery officer (gun grunt). He served in Iraq twice before finally leaving active duty in 2008 as a battery commanding officer. Although he originally planned to serve twenty years and then retire as a Marine officer, a "short round" scuttled his career when he confronted his regimental commander in 2003 about an ill-advised order to move his artillery battery then north of the FEBA (Forward Edge of the Battle Area) just south of Bagdad during what he called the second Iraq War. The colonel ordered Ronan's 3rd Battalion, 11th Marines battery north. Ronan declined with a cogent argument that such a movement was imprudent, premature, lacked sufficient intelligence data, thus too fraught with peril to the mission. He genuinely felt his unit was in danger since the whereabouts of Iraqi Imperial Guard ground units then was too fluid. He was a quality artillery officer with the sapiens of one more senior.

He declined the order.

An angry exchange ensued, replete with extended, colorful dialogue that Captain McShea lost along with a relief of his command followed by the perfunctory, tepid fitness report by the regimental CO. Said report shredded his career inclinations and torpedoed his elevation to major. Prompted by the commission severance check of $65,000, Ronan opted to retreat home and began life anew in his hometown but retained a commitment in the Marine Corps Reserve.

With his Penn State pedigree, he, nonetheless, had no problem snatching a coveted open slot with the Army Corps of Engineers. So he began a Federal civil servant as a riverine supervisor for the dredging of the rivers and adjacent tributaries in Western Pennsylvania and northern West Virginia. As such, he would spend four to five days per week on dredge barges throughout the area as liaison for the Corps with the private dredging companies contracted to do the work and keep the channels clear for barge and riverine traffic. He loved the environment that reminded him of his time on active duty but also savored the lack of senior supervisors onboard the tugs that allowed him freedom to work and no chain of command harassment or second guessing. Senior supervisors didn't embrace the river stints, sometimes fraught with danger and long periods of boredom. Life aboard the tugs and barges that did the dirty work had no appeal for his chain of command. It wasn't a three-star, four-day journey to a river resort. More often it was wet and cold, subject to the fickle of Western Pennsylvania weather, October through May. Each season had its own collection of challenges. All he wanted were the attaboys that came from senior civil servants for jobs well done.

As long as they left him alone, his sarcastic Irish temper and disdain of hierarchy remained contained—Ronan on water, bosses on land. What a concept!

The towboat crews for the cleanup barges, however, had comfortable accommodations, and the shipboard cooks were excellent. At this point, Ronk still nourished a modicum of hostility toward any authority that had no time "on the river." He dubbed his bosses "dry dock pussies" for their fear of the water and the daily hazards onboard the towboats. The exquisite shipboard cuisine and open weekends, however, were logical choice for Ronk, devoid of what he called the cretins of bureaucracy. Couple that with the paid myriad down days with inclement weather, it allowed him the luxury of extended onboard reading time, as threatening weather always preempted dredging. When the weather was angry, so were the rivers and all their tributaries. Rain, snow, and wind often staunched the daily work agenda. Ronk loved the job—good money, time to himself. Like his parents and most of his youthful family and friends of cross-generations, they gathered at the B&G for everything from wakes, weddings, and Steeler football to a post Bar Mitzvah celebration held for the son of his longtime friend, Daniel Stein, also a Marine officer veteran of Iraq and Afghanistan.

It was there at the B&G that he re-met and re-pursued his now wife, Kathleen O'Rourke, at age twenty-nine. Married in 2000, they proceeded to add three more to the family's fire team. Although both he and Kathleen graduated from North Catholic High, they never socialized in high school, as she then found both him and his friends contemptibly boorish, vulgar, and vain. That was all with good reason.

The high school male vanities nicknamed her Katnip because of her flowing red hair and angelic undercarriage at six feet zero that attracted a host of salivating high school acolytes who badly wanted to date her, undress her, and recruit her into the wide world of indoor sports. Sometimes they had no whiff of class or sophistication, even with an alleged Catholic upbringing. They were coarse, naïve, and crass. It was just part of the standard high school milieu.

The phenomenon that Catholic schools, both high school and elementary, began to recruit a majority of non-Catholics, Jews, and even a sprinkling of Muslims began in the '90s. That continues today. Parents appalled by the disarray in most urban public schools, Pittsburgh included, gravitated toward religious schools that, at least, had a modicum of discipline and deference to Christianity or Judaism.

Kathleen and Ronk were likely the last of a third generation of North Catholic graduates exclusively Catholic. Today the graduating classes would be peppered with a minority of other Christians and Jews with parents in flight from the public systems.

Although she tolerated no lapses of respect from any of the assembled gentiles or Jews in the school student body, Kathleen heartily rebuffed their sometimes profane advances, usually with blistering commentary of their sexual and social deficiencies.

Kathleen could give as well as take with equal intensity. Her other derogatory nicknames among the rebuffed ones were Alley Kat or Red Pussy. But protective of their family jewels, the high school dimwits rarely uttered them to her face.

Katnip was also a nickname she detested heartily but later tolerated when they married. It became a private joke between them not to be uttered in public; otherwise, she would cut off his red hair exploration, both north and south. Once, one of the lesser North Catholic male juniors used the moniker Red Pussy at a school dance in front of a six-pack crew of his homies during her junior year. That was a classic wrong move. The ensuing groin kick crumbled him and messaged the rest of the boys in their class. Although the school chaperones threw her out of the dance, the boys got it. But her parents did not. They were less than amused, particularly with the follow-up three-day suspension from class imposed by Fr. Charles Kaminsky, the school principal. Amidst it all, Kathleen was unrepentant, and Papa O'Rourke even admitted that it was the first time he ever directed a litany of profanity at a priest for which he refused to apologize.

"The son of a bitch deserved it," he said to Maureen. "He's a wraparound asshole."

Her silence cued concurrence.

No one in the junior class, however, ever again used the term in her presence. It didn't stop the ruminations of their dirty minds, but the insults were nevermore verbalized publicly. They didn't want their gonads crushed.

She also initially described Daniel Bernstein, a fellow Marine Iraq veteran, as the "most Narcissistic, Neanderthal prick of a male to walk the earth since Attila the Hun." It was thus a hard roll of the eyes and swallow for her when Ronan anointed Daniel their best man at their Catholic nuptial Mass.

"How's Father McCann going react to a Jew as your best man?"

"Does it really matter?" Ronk replied. "Weren't Joseph, Jesus, and Mary all Jews? This is the twenty-first century. I thought we'd buried that shit along with the demise of the Flat Earth Society."

Daniel Bernstein was an acquired taste for Kathleen. His penchant for the reversion to frat boy was sometimes a hard swallow, but she relented, and it never became an issue again. She conceded that despite his sometimes noxious personality, he was also a gun grunt (artillery) Marine Corps officer like Ronk, so he possessed some modicum of the civil. But he was an arm's-length hug with cringe to touch.

Daniel, moreover, was a religious chameleon who fit into almost any Judeo-Christian tradition from Orthodox rabbi to Baptist telepreacher. At the heart of it, he was an aspirant comic in the style of Don Rickles so he could mock anyone of any faith and did so with great verve.

Several Stein jokes at the rehearsal dinner put the issue to rest. They included a collection of blue ones from his circumcision repertoire, packed together as part of Ronan's proposed bachelor party. Although it made a couple of the bridesmaids wince, he unsheathed them and garnered some appropriate laughs. Daniel managed to keep the event on the fringe of PG-13 so as not to alienate Kathleen.

"God, my mother's here!" she whispered to Ronk. "Can't he just tone it down a bit? Daniel needs a lesson in boundaries. If he doesn't, I'll give him a .40-caliber vasectomy."

The dinner menu was superb, but the Stein dessert left an aftertaste that would linger for years.

Never comfortable in a city environment, the O'Rourke-McSheas some four years later bought and re-invigorated an old farmhouse in Butler County directly north of Pittsburgh. Its nineteenth-century charming exterior required almost $50,000 of interior renovation that consumed the next five years of their marriage. Like many country homes, the rustic appeal needed an update from space to plumbing. Yes, it was a labor of love, and they began what seemed a normal lunge into family with their children—Katie, Sean, and Seamus—in a very rural motif on what used to be a fifty-acre farm. That was the setting in spring 2018 when both their lives took an auspicious left turn on a gloomy April Friday evening.

It all changed on the Southside of Pittsburgh in little more three minutes, punctuated with just four gunshots.

Chapter 2

KATHLEEN

Stop-N-Go is a chain of detritus strewn throughout mid-America from Pennsylvania to Kentucky. They hock everything from gasoline to sanitary napkins. They're ubiquitous, banal, and never remind you of a pastoral walk around Walden Pond. Yet they are as intrinsic to the economic engine of success as toilet paper and now LED light bulbs. Oil in twenty-first-century America is still the king of transit and will not abdicate that slot despite the wailings of the New Left, New York banshees of green energy. Alternate energy models gestated by the whiz-bang undergraduates from Carnegie Mellon University and Cal Tech to MIT have assaulted the primacy of petroleum. But oil's demise will not broach expiration until after the year 2200. Function cedes to reality. Try heating your home on a January day in Montana entirely on green energy or driving from Los Angeles to New York in lieu of flying!

Get a grip, lefties. Black Gold is still the king. So sorry, Al Gore! Don't junk your Learjet quite yet. Just maintain your hypocrisy.

Maybe solar will put Ford and GM out of the internal combustion engine business. Maybe it will in the next century. But Kathleen and most of her peers doubted its arrival much before 2050 at the earliest, the recent dire Federal warnings notwithstanding. The imagined alternatives are just not ready to assume primacy.

We likely have more than a dozen years left. Good luck, New Yorkers, retrofitting all those buildings. It might happen sometime later when her red locks camouflage some gray with the help of some color in a bottle, but not now. Sanity trumps fantasy. And not tonight when her Blazer was thirsty.

These lurid gas Meccas, dinky (and often dingy) islands of most everything ingested by road warriors and the automobile, still rule the day. Where else can you go to get beer, Tylenol, condoms, and Hershey's chocolate all in one fell swoop? Nothing like the wonders of American capitalism! Just ask the Cubans or the Venezuelans about the stocks at their local convenience stores.

Often she saw as many variants of condoms as cigarettes on the back rack of product. But the store subtly reeked of foul scents that mimicked stale to lurid. Those ranged from urine to oil. Restrooms can be free-fire zones for filth in exotic scents. So the paradigm is the same from Maine to Oregon, separated only by name and quality of restrooms. This one was as mediocre as most. Grab a seat and hope your bottom doesn't take something home with you that will require further medical attention from an ob-gyn or urologist. Kathleen actually had athletic leg strength sufficient to elevate her glutes and urinate from a distance. It was a trick she employed often in Europe after a college graduation trip through Europe where she found public French toilets the then height of misery, more often just a hole in the floor of the john.

She did it often in the desert, well trained never to touch the toilet seat or the desert sand.

Now it was just pump gas, pay, empty bladder, shoot home.

It was the same sublime irritation with Ms. Kathleen O'Rourke-McShea. She had been in cleaner Porta-Potties in Iraq. Like most women, she wasn't a clean freak, but she expected at least minimal accession to said in Western Pennsylvania, what she once called "a genuine modicum of cleanliness, just like I demand in my own home." Thus she recoiled at the indifference to sanitation in public restrooms for women often manifest throughout her hometown of Pittsburgh and beyond. Indifference to it could bring her temper to boil.

"You don't to have to abide by dirty restrooms. It's particularly galling to women," she once railed to Ronk. "Remember when we took the kids to Disney World? Their toilets and baby-changing stations and sinks are always impeccably clean. They tend to it. It's one of the waning, great things about everything Disney—the clean! There's just no damn excuse for foul in the restroom. Even McDonald's takes better care of theirs. I've relieved myself too often in sand over there in the heat of the Middle East to put up with it here. Men don't seem to give a damn, but we both have already fought the battle of E. coli and camel dung. I ain't toleratin' it here."

As gas stations go, this Stop-N-Go was reasonably clean, well kempt, and free of graffiti, as was this one on West Carson Street. The snack rack was your standard five rows with four shelves of the junk cornucopia of fat foods, sugar, and carbs, along with emergency household sundries—you know, the coronary attack snacks that your family doctor warned you to avoid, from diabetic cupcakes to potato chips. The overpriced carbohydrates keep thousands of cardiologists in business. Eat it today, wear it tomorrow. The snack rack is a cardiologist's dream. It keeps them in business and fattens their wallets. Vapor lock follows years onward with coronary artery disease.

Despite generations of education, some habits don't change. Stents and bypasses are still the order of the day. As Sonny & Cher Bono once crooned, "And the beat goes on."

So avoid you don't. Most Americans are part of the crowd that succumbed to the advertising and ignored the warning until treated to a ride on a gurney at the reception doors of some emergency room. Kathleen was not one of those. She was still lean and mean, even after three kids and the perils of a middle-class diet. She remained supremely more Marine than porcine. Her women peers at Securitas, Inc. held her in high esteem and awe because she worked out daily when there in the company gym, just like she did on active duty. She was a company role model, especially for the flock of young interns hired who looked to her for guidance and inspiration. She didn't disappoint. Like most Marines, she could inspire as well as demand. Women on her staff in McLean, Virginia, actually created a T-shirt that proclaimed, "Be like Kat: Sweat," with the paradigm of a woman doing squats with a barbell of hundred-pound weights. It sold more than two hundred copies to staff members and outsiders in support of a local Girl Scout troop in Alexandria.

She lived what she preached.

After filling her Chevy SUV outside, she went inside to pay and noted the lack of cash in her purse. So it was "plastic time" at the cash register. Fifteen gallons at $2.10 per, she handed the bored attendant her debit card. He ignored any social exchange, processed the card, and handed her the requisite receipt. She signed it. Then came the query.

"Where are your restrooms?" They were not obvious to the casual customer.

The attendant initially pretended to ignore her. She was not in his purview of acceptable life-forms tonight. You know, just a woman. His disdain resonated through his beard and clenched teeth. She persisted, this time slowly, slightly louder and with articulate, syllabic precision. Kathleen was not your reticent, stereotype, middle-class mother.

"Where...are...your...restrooms, please?" Her piercing look demanded an answer. He answered, deliberately averting her stare. "Just around the corner of the ice bins over there," the attendant said, "to your left." Kathleen caught the "dog" part of his sneer and assumed he intended to mean "bitch." His indifference was cultural. After all, wasn't she just a female, not quite worthy of his extended wisdom? The cultural, condescending attitude seeped out with oozing dismissal. Not worth his time! He really felt humiliated here in America to have to serve women, but he needed the work and swallowed his pride daily. It wasn't like home where what he said was domicile law. At work, he had to defer to women customers. He hated it but he liked the minimum wage money more.

She tried to ignore him, but he was such the stereotype. Although accustomed to it in the business world, she still found it offensive yet not worth picking a fight over every slight indignation. You could spend all day in business correcting insults and sneers. Now in somewhat of a hurry, she turned away from the three other customers, two men and a woman, nondescript in toto until the next five minutes. Her bladder called. Her mind was elsewhere.

Outside she did notice a light sprinkle—rain on the way. Maybe, she thought, more to come later.

Checking all three stalls, she moved into the cleanest of the three on the western end. She then hung her purse on the door coat rack, dropped the paper ass gasket into place, hiked her skirt, dropped her red laced panties, and then heaved an audible sigh of relief as she released a pint of Starbuck's overpriced coffee, readjusted the panties and skirt, and then flushed. Contemplating what to pick up for family dinner, she abruptly froze. What she heard were three distinct voices yelling very loudly, followed with the report of four low-caliber gunshots. She exhaled perceptively. Now transfixed, the purse remained just beyond her immediate grasp. This was what military combat vets call an "Aw, shit!" moment. It's when the body chokes a rational response. Her immediate reaction was to freeze, the natural response to an unanticipated threat. It was the paralysis of fear just before the adrenaline rush.

Outside the clerk wailed in what seemed like an angry exchange in a language she didn't recognize with the two male customers she previously ignored. The yelling swelled and then ceased as they incoherently screamed in tandem with a third voice. Then the four shots reported that pre-cursed the eerie aftermath.

The dark of silence!

Police reports later identified the original exchange as parsed with Farsi or Arabic and English. Now finished, Kathleen instinctively stood, awkwardly reset her skirt, put her low-heel pumps in her large purse, drew her weapon, remained still, and listened. The two men were ranting at each other. "What about that other customer, that woman?" She thought, *I thought there were three of them.*

The four gunshots, she correctly assumed, signaled an armed robbery in progress. The subsequent quiet confirmed it. Her mind raced through the choices of what next. Her first instinct was to run to the source of the gunfire, but the math of a three-to-one exchange cautioned sobriety. She thought better than to pick a fight against a superior crew that she might not win.

The adrenaline shaking began as her mind raced through possible scenarios after she drew her Walther PPK and cell phone from the purse. Without premeditation, she put her cell phone in the chained cover around her neck, dropped the lid, and backed onto the toilet tank. Muscle training took over. She thumbed the safety to the Off or fire position. What next? Then what seemed like a vacuum eternity of about a minute passed, and the restroom door squawked open. A soprano level, feminine voiced person raised the curtain on the ascending act. The odor of the room birthed the stillborn chill of fear.

"We checked your registration, Mrs. McShea," she intoned, "as you have the only other car at the pump island. So come out quietly and we won't hurt you! We already have the money."

The hollow words reverberated like cascading marbles on slate. Kathleen's world morphed to ice. The shake of the adrenaline rush accelerated in earnest but then subsided to calm control.

Noting the plural "we" of the threat, Kathleen assumed the worst. *There were three...I think!* Unconsciously she started to hyperventilate, and her blood pressure elevated. They knew her name. They obviously went through her Blazer's glove box.

How? When? What the fuck? Oh God, what the hell else did I leave in there? Think! Think! Suddenly came the realization. *Oh shit, my (company) Heckler & Koch!*

Now her weapons training and full-throated adrenaline kicked into gear. She became a biological animal. Calmly stepping down from the tank with her Walther PPK, she crept to the open corner of the stall and unhooked the stall latch. The door opened, lurching inches outbound. She peered through the door crack and assessed a blonde Teutonic woman of similar height, dressed in leather with a large Glock handgun.

"Don't move, you fucking bitch," the target commanded, but those were her last words on earth.

Kathleen responded, sans remorse, dropped to one knee, and pumped two rounds into the offending assailant—a textbook double tap, center chest and head. She'd done exactly as trained on multiple military ranges. The blonde Aryan slumped backward and bled profusely as she only managed one round through the ceiling. She gurgled through her throat as Kathleen's second round punctured her left carotid artery. She was still alive at that point but slowly fading with seconds left. Less than a minute later, she would be dead. Her dropped Glock spun toward the dual sinks. It clanged with a steel thud. Kathleen had neutralized the threat. It was all very clinical, the by-product of years of training. But the clinical rarely deals well with the aftermath. Watching a dying, bleeding body is not an event most humans ever witness or savor. It's unnerving and rattles even the most well trained. The blonde's eyes resonated fury that pierced Kathleen's most dark Irish soul.

Once you've crossed that line of human termination, you can never return. Your past is now etched in stone. Your future will have an eternal, brazen image of death. You either grow from it or allow it to destroy you.

Kathleen had crossed the line. That moment was seminal but gave no hint that she would do it again, at least four more times within the month.

Still shaking, she exited slowly away from the stall and slid onto the dank floor with her back against the adjacent western wall. She drew her knees to her chest, instinctively dropped the magazine in her Walther, ejected one round, re-inserted the magazine, cocked another round into the chamber, and pointed her weapon toward the restroom door. Safety still off, overcome by the sudden influx of adrenaline and secondary sugars, she began sobbing uncontrollably, weapon at the ready. Then almost unable to do so and in a nervous, livid rage, she pulled out her cell phone with her left hand, shaking profusely, and stumbled through a simple 911 call that seemed an eternity to complete.

Chapter 3

THE GREEK

Yusuf (or Joseph as he preferred) Tsakrios was native to Pittsburgh but sported a very different pedigree. He grew up in a working-class Southside household that gave tribute to Mediterranean ethnic cultures. Although his surname was Greek, his Palestinian mother remarried after leaving home during the UN mandate for the creation of Israel in 1947 with then infant son Yusef. He vaguely remembered his birth father's name and didn't much care. How she made it to Pittsburgh with him was family lore wrapped in facts enveloped within sheer fiction. It was an after-dinner discussion, but the story always changed, morphed by the narrator. So Joseph had virtually no accurate memory or feeling as an adult for the yearning, romantic fantasy of Palestine that his mother portrayed. All he remembered was her hatred of Jews. Her anti-Semitic rants, however, left him unmoved. It had no meaning for him and his stepsisters. The vista of his worldly panorama barely stretched across the rivers that defined downtown Pittsburgh, the Golden Triangle. The lure of the old country had no allure.

"Why," he once asked his mother as a child, "would you want to go back to a place with no bathrooms, cars, or running water?"

A hard slap to his face at age eight for posing the question ended his quest for ancestry answers. Joseph, thus, became completely indifferent to family heritage. It was an early version of "Don't ask, don't tell, and don't expect to be told."

Widowed at a young age, Aisha Boutros met her second husband, George, through a mutual friend in Pittsburgh in 1950. George owned and ran a bakery shop on Pittsburgh's Southside on the main drag, Carson Street. Joseph acquired his four younger stepsisters during the 1950s. It seemed to him as a child that his mother was always pregnant and daily complaining about it. Although his stepfather's name was imposed, he had little interest in the family bakery. That, he felt, was work relegated to women.

What attracted him, and toward which he gravitated, was the numbers and illegal gaming racket thriving on the Southside amid the steel mill workers then flush with money during the steel boom years of the 1950s. Inundated with worldwide orders, the mills worked three shifts per day. The mills were 24-7. Money and Iron City beer flowed freely even at 6:00 a.m. when the night shift got off work.

Life was abundantly good for the United Steelworkers They expected it to last per saecula saeculorum, like a trip to heaven… forever. The optimism and vibrancy of steel continued for another three decades until it all dissipated by the 1980s. The end was brutal.

At twelve, Joe became a "runner" who would collect the numbers slips from bars and restaurants and deliver them to Big Al Lyshinski at a local pool hall for $2 a run after school. Guys would lay bets on the closing Dow Jones average at 3:00 p.m. and, if you picked the right number, you'd double whatever your bet was. Then Big Ski, as he was known on the street, hired Joseph to retrieve the numbers bets from sundry drop spots on Carson Street (in paper bags, thus the colloquial bagman) from the betters. They wrote their names on the back of the numbers slips. The number you bet was not duplicated. Big Al only published a limited sequential list of numbers that used the previous day's Dow Jones as the median. Fifty percent of the numbers were higher than yesterday's closing, fifty percent lower. There would be only a bag per tavern or bar. Big Al would thus pay out only one bettor per location. He pocketed the rest.

Joseph never drew the suspicion of police because of his age. It was bagman on a bicycle? What's criminal about that? And it was the perfect cover. Beat cops knew the scam but often couldn't be bothered with low priority gambling busts. Besides, what's a little sidebar kickback among friends? Particularly if they had a cut of the action!

The numbers racket was tolerated, low priority in those days. There was little public passion to suppress it. It was the Eisenhower years. The war was over, so no one died laying down cheap bets. The clichés Iron Curtain and the Cold War were an accepted fact of life, along with bomb drills in school where kids dived under desks, giggled, and laughed at the adult rendition of nuclear war. The Red Scare of Sen. Joe McCarthy made front-page news, not petty gambling on the then seamy Southside.

There are things to worry about and there are things to ignore. So life continued with more relevant priorities!

Lyshinski created other betting game variants of numbers, and the tavern patrons eagerly plunked money down in the multitude of bars and taverns that still dot Carson Street today. One-armed bandits were still illegal then. Today those bars have a plethora of games on terminals connected to the Internet.

You've come a long way, baby! Undercover gambling is now mainstream.

Add that to the Rivers Casino that now punctuates the Three Rivers confluence on the Northside and you have the ongoing tradition of sublime indifference to gambling, petty or otherwise. Las Vegas came to Pittsburgh—and stayed! Promotion for the casino is now mainstream, along with Iron City beer and the plethora of Allegheny County car dealerships.

As long as those tax receipts proliferated, gambling was not on the list of capital sins in 2018. Numbers slips are now just an archaic memory. The receipts now flow to the Commonwealth of Pennsylvania. For Joseph, however, it certainly beat collecting two-cent deposits on pop soda bottles for pocket change and had much more prestige. Later at the then South Hills High School, Joseph discovered the more exotic wonders of pandering and convinced four girls of his senior class that contract sex certainly beat working at the local Kroger's or A&P as a grocery bagger or baggerette. By the end of his senior year, the five entrepreneurs were raking in more than $1,000 per month by graduation day in June. No one suspected, as

Joseph kept his business stable of friends for hire completely away from the high school. He screened all the phone appointments through a pay phone near his stepfather's bakery, and the four girls always worked in safety pairs with their clientele on weekends with adults contacted through the gin joints on Carson Street. Meeting sites were a problem, but Joseph solved that. He manipulated one of his stepfather's fleet of panel bakery trucks, swung a weekend parking deal with one of his buddies who worked the Wharf Parking Lot on the Monongahela River, picked it up on Friday, and kept it there through the weekend. Return: Sunday night. His crew outfitted the back with a double-bed Sealy Posturepedic and—voila!

Open for business: nine to five, Saturdays and Sundays only.

They were on a roll with a young pimp and four girls ready to shake their moneymakers. Cash only, no credit! Debit cards were not yet in existence.

"Remember," Joseph told each of them sternly at their grand opening weekend of business, "always use rubbers when you fuck these guys and collect the cash up front. The one not performing holds and hides the money. If you get pregnant or contract VD, it's on you. So keep your pussies clean and no fucking when you're on your periods. Okay?"

"We don't have control over that, Joseph," classmate Darlene Whitson reminded him. "We'll let you know when the monthly arrival occurs so we can coordinate. Let us handle it. Okay? And don't place any stupid demands on us. It's hard enough with all the damn excuses we have to make to our parents. Maybe you don't have that problem with yours, but our parents are nosy. We're girls, you know. The rules are different at home than for boys. Besides, the guys you send us mostly just want head, so we can cover it even on our periods. You got it?"

"Yeah, I got it! Just check in with me after first period lunch on Friday before each weekend so I can make the appointments."

"Remember, I get 50 percent."

The adolescent Joseph was hardly a paragon of class or morality, but the girls were equally amoral. Money defined everything, and they all liked it. It was stashing the moneymaker mattress and returning the truck Sunday night that was originally their primary business problem. But that was the advent year of rental garage spaces now universally popular, adjacent to a nearby bar that provided the solution. Mattress secured Sunday night for resurrection the next Friday. The girls provided clean sheets and dirty minds. Joseph took care of the sheet cleaning at a Southside laundromat.

The dirty minds remained intact.

The numbers racket and sex: a seamless bond sealed in high school heaven. The five of them flew under the radar for almost a year before, during and after graduation. Neither stepfather George nor his mother seemed to notice...or care about the apparent largesse of cash that Joseph always seemed to have. Money was the currency of Tsakrios family life and acquisition of said silently applauded. His high school business only fortified his attraction for life's underbelly.

That was his audition into the warehouse racket at age twenty where mentoring by the local mob boss, Nick Scardelli, only fed Joseph's ambition to make it big, fast, and with ruthless abandon. Abandoning hookers.com long before the Internet as fraught with too much police exposure, he dissolved the enterprise and eventually invested his money in multiple coin-operated laudromats over the next two decades. He then added two restaurants and a small Southside bar called the Lunch Bucket since that was one of the stops on Carson Street frequented by cops where he once previously laundered gambling proceeds. The beauty of laundromats and restaurants was their business models rested on cash and a host of phony receipts. Although it required hours of manual labor, counting cash or coins by hand was tedious but devoid of receipts that might track the crime. The numbers (betting) portion of his business expanded dramatically in the '60s and '70s with the explosion of sports betting and the introduction of harness horse racing to Pennsylvania. Although local county and state district attorneys tried to shut down both him and Lyshinski for years, Joseph's attorneys and his much slicker CPAs outmaneuvered the best Allegheny County and the commonwealth could muster. They just had better book cookers. The local culture ignored most gambling transgressions, as the abuses of prohibition were still fresh in the minds of older adults. Tolerating it was far less lawless than the gargantuan effort needed to suppress it. The hush money paid to sundry law enforcement types was effective, just a normal business expense, and he kept police agencies at bay for years. Besides, the temptations for cops in the '50s were legion. A little side money supplemented the relatively meager salary in those days of policing. The wages of sin for Joseph pointed to prosperity and an upper middle-class home on the fringes of town.

Now he lived very comfortably in the North Hills in an inauspicious but large five-bedroom house on two acres that bordered on the exclusive community of Fox Chapel. He finally married Veronica Ronzonelli, a woman twenty-five years his junior in 1996, and they had twin daughters, Christina and Maria, both now seniors in high school and students at Oakland Catholic. Although now a millionaire approaching his seventieth birthday, he was the epitome of low profile, with one exception—he had both a driver/butler and a bodyguard that fit the gangland stereotype: large, well dressed with limited personality and major-league attitudes.

Both lived off campus and remained virtually invisible in public, except with Joseph.

The family had four cars, but the Mercedes was Joseph's. When he ventured out with his prize Kraut, it was the only time you would see the three together. The driver, Elmer Moran (whom Tsakrios nicknamed Fudd), was a longtime petty hood and Vietnam infantry vet who loved the easy cash money The Greek dispensed, along with the fealty demanded with it. Fudd neither intruded on his boss' business nor the nuance of what he thought was a strange marriage.

"Shit, man," Fudd once told friends. "Veronica was a sophomore in high school when she first met him. That's just wrong. He was in her panties when she was a minor. I don't care that she married him when she was twenty-five. She'd been *stupin* him since high school."

Tsakrios was unfazed. "Just shut up, do as you're told, and take the cash."

The bodyguard, Eric Laudergast, however, was a much more serious breed of predatory cat. No sense of humor and serious as a coronary thrombosis, he held a seventh-degree black belt and a marked proficiency with small arms. He honed most of this talent with a lengthy stint in the South African Army at the time the white apartheid regime collapsed prior to the ascension of the African National Congress and the ascent of Nelson Mandela. He then began a peripatetic trail around the globe, as he saw no more future in the new South Africa. Three years thereafter, he eventually emigrated to the United States via Australia and found his way to the entrails of Pittsburgh's sleazy side via the trucking business in the strip district. Joseph hired him at the onset of the Iraq War at a time when his businesses were thriving and disgruntled business associates seemed legion. That was particularly true of some of the underpaid law enforcement on his payroll for whom a thank-you fifth of Canadian Club was insufficient as a Christmas bonus. Eric was, in Joseph's words, "six feet four inches of life insurance!" Although neither of them had an extensive criminal record, they all rode the rail of "should have had," beginning with extortion and assault. Tsakrios did indeed have an astute team of lawyers that he paid handsomely. His staff's primary role was intimidation with class and taste, a description wholly appropriate.

It was with his driver and his life insurance policy that intersected with Ronk McShea that fateful Friday evening in Homestead at almost the same time as Kathleen sent a slimeball Aryan-Amazon to the afterlife fifteen minutes before on the western end of Carson Avenue.

It was a strange intersection of coincidence, fifteen miles and a lifetime apart, that would bind them all in a maze of sin in which they would all wallow.

Chapter 4

AFTERMATH

"Drop the weapon," Hughes screeched. Kathleen sat there with an incoherent stare, mind miles away in semishock. The cop stood above the dead woman's body, trying not to step into the blood pool, and repeated the command, this time an octave higher. *Maybe she's hard of hearing?* he thought. *Or was she literally deaf?* He fell into the rookie cop mode. In truth, this was his first month on the job, and he was scared to death of the unknown that came with the call. His hand shook violently. It was his first dead body, and training seemed inadequate to assess the woman seated against the far wall.

"Drop the damn weapon! Put it on the floor, kick it away, and on your feet," he repeated with an emphasis on each word. "I say again for a third time. Put the goddamn weapon down. Any further moves and you're toast. Do you want me to shoot you?" he said with his standard .40-cal pointed directly at Kathleen's head. Which one was more rattled was a close call.

She, however, had it more together than the hovering cop. With a piercing look of disgust, she slowly placed the smoking Walther to her right, pushed it away, and watched it slide toward the shaking, very nervous Officer Delbert Hughes.

"The fucking bitch tried to kill me!"

She glared at him. He returned the favor.

"That remains to be seen. On your feet!" he ordered. "You're under arrest. Turn around and put your hands behind your back."

"She tried to kill me," Kathleen screamed again to a patently bored and unsympathetic, agitated Hughes.

"Then you have nothing to worry about, lady," replied the rookie uniform. "Just do as I say and we'll sort it out. Get up!"

Hughes yanked her toward the sinks, cuffed her, and then moved Kathleen toward the door when in crashed his patrol car partner, Bobby Burnett, pistol drawn, poised to fire.

"Hey, Hughes," Burnett began, "what the f—" He trailed off, retracted his firing position, and almost tripped over the body. "Another fuckin' stiff? This is a banner night, Delbert, a two-fer. Who the hell's this babe?"

"Maybe the perp, who knows," said Hughes. "Check the weapons on the floor. Just clear 'em, tag 'em, and wait for the homicide gurus," he said with some obvious annoyance. Burnett's regular partner, Matthew Kelly, was home on family leave in Brookline after the death of Kelly's father-in-law. So Burnett was stuck with the rookie Hughes for at least another three shifts. Burnett saw it as a sort of babysitting with inexperience that could get you killed. Rookies were a hazard with which he did not want to deal. Now he had a rattled rookie, a dead body, and he suddenly was the senior cop on site.

"Can I put my shoes on first?" Kathleen snarled. Hughes searched the purse still hanging on the toilet privacy door and dropped them at her feet. Now cuffed, she slid into the pumps. Hughes grabbed the purse from the stall and her by the arm.

"Okay, let's go. Outside!"

Burnett stood nearby and just rolled his eyes. His thought went unsaid.

"This rookie is a walking can of worms. Please, God, do not pair him up with me again. He's more likely to get me killed than any perp."

Kathleen stumbled outside arm in arm over the body with Hughes in tow to the now expanding convocation of six police cruisers and a very redundant EMT crew with an ambulance, no customers and no place to go. The fire battalion, lights still flashing, was the last entrée without a raison d'être on scene. That's the perverse beauty of dead bodies. Almost always the threat to police is moot and mute when the homicide guys actually arrive. It's part of the reason homicide detectives like the job. If truth be told, it's the safest in the department. At the other end of first response, Burnett had teamed with Kelly for more than eight years and only had two occasions to draw his service weapon. This was just another body to process without the threat of death to the attending cops. He just didn't like working with newly minted rookies.

Now crack an Iron (pronounced *Arn*) City Beer. Welcome to coroner time.

The convention met quota with Detectives Joe Duffy and Mitch Schubert who roared into the last remaining parking space at the less-than-cozy confines of the corner Stop-N-Go with their standard four-door undercover Ford as unobtrusive as combat boots on the bride at a Russian Orthodox wedding. Kids on the street could spot them two blocks away. Just like Sergeant Trumpke! Drug dealers, delinquents, and taggers could smell them from a mile beyond.

"Such a deal," Duffy quipped. "The uniforms do all the scut work, and we get to process the two dead jagoffs inside and never have to draw down. Eh, what a country! What a job! Cue the comedians. I luv' it! Looks like a long, long night. Unlike McDonald's, I ain't quite lovin' it. Rustle up more sarcasm."

"Yeah," Mitch yawned, "ain't it a joy but look at the upside—lots of overtime. It's summina do!" Translation: something to do. Pittsburghese is a nascent Pennsylvania dialect peculiar to the western sector and eastern Ohio.

Both newly arrived cavalry flashed their badges and moved inside.

"Anyone else hurt?" yelled Duffy to no one in particular. And no one in particular answered him.

Dismissive attitudes of the uniforms for any detective still permeated some elements of cop culture. They thought detectives were sometimes lazy while they operated in the violent milieu of the immediate crime scene. They respected the mutual hierarchy and coveted the promotion but only rarely socialized. This was just the business required to keep the peace. Street cops all prefer regular, predictable shifts. Homicide is, however, by definition, open 24-7. Clients rarely make appointments, and homicide cops often lose hours of sleep. The 2:00 a.m. phone calls to report to work were the rule rather than the exception.

Schubert scored the nickname Piano Man at the precinct, not because of any family ties to the famed composer but because of his girth, height, and part-time undergraduate job in college at Pitt as a piano mover. It paid well but did not bode well for aging, adult vertebrae. Now married at thirty-eight with four kids, he relished the plethora of overtime, but his deteriorating back precluded the business of piano moving on weekends.

Five mouths, large mortgage, big bills! Overtime money motivates.

Mitch also qualified as Steeler large at six feet and six inches and 280 pounds who barely fit into the confines of the standard police SUVs now favored by the Pittsburgh Office of Public Safety, an enlightened hybrid of emergency services that included police, fire, and ambulance functions.

Duffy, on the other hand, did not share Mitch's overtime addiction. Still single at thirty-six, Joe hated those 2:00 a.m. phone calls that often interfered with his active, erotic night life. Homicide obviously infringed on his woman time and even more often drove them away. They could see the biblical handwriting on the wall with Detective First Grade Joseph John Duffy: never home, a man on extended adolescence, with multiple personal weapons in a profession replete and riddled with divorce, even with pay at just under $79,000 per annum.

Schubert tonight, however, was in a particularly dark mood. Duffy picked up on it and queried Schubert as they exited their prowl car.

"Hey, Mitch," Duffy said, "is everything all right at home? You seem a little distracted tonight and are obviously not on your game. Is everything cool at home? You seem inordinately unhappy."

"Yeah, J. J.," Schubert replied. "It's nothin' that can't be fixed. She's into a weird space that I don't understand that's almost menopausal. And she's only forty-two. Now she's into that Chinese topography thing."

"What?"

"She thinks that cooking and fucking are two cities in China. Maybe that's all part of, as she says, the change."

"Oops, sorry I intruded," Duffy said. "I don't think I can help you there, particularly with the cooking part! I'm worthless in a kitchen."

"I'm very sorry for your loss. That sounds like martial counseling time. Geez, Mitch, I don't think I qualify as a marriage therapist."

Duffy, however, was not the counselor Schubert needed. He was taken aback by Schubert's sudden admission of trauma on the home front, but he himself was not what you call a good long-term marriage bet. His advice on marital discord had limited credibility. Homicide was rife with too much testosterone, too much time away from home, and a constant horde of feminine temptation.

"It's been real and it's been nice!" intoned one of his many trysts at her recent exit in anger, "but *hasta la vista*, Jose!"

One of the nondescript uniforms securing the scene held the door for Duffy and Schubert and then calmly pointed to his right.

"The first one's on the deck behind the register. The other's in the women's head."

Joe noted the description used for the restroom as the "head" and the "deck" and correctly concluded that the uniform with the nametag "Olflaski" must be a US Navy or Marine Corps vet. On the floor lay the body of an olive-skinned man of Middle East origin with at least two apparent bullet holes in his upper torso.

"Does he have a name?" Duffy asked. "We haven't touched the body," said another one of the uniforms. "We was waitin' for yunz guys to do your magic," he said with salivating, dripping sarcasm that cops do so well. "We was waitin' for dis 'n' dat from the coroner guys. But yunz guys have that special touch! Be my guests."

Pittsburghese everywhere!

Yunz is the Pittsburgh vernacular for "you all" or the Southern equivalent of "y'all." In this case, the "yunz guys" were Schubert and Duffy. Translation of "dis 'n'dat": this and that!

"Another goddamn yinzer on the force! When will these dinosaurs of language disappear?" Duffy grumbled as he leaned over the counter, moved carefully around, and began searching the pockets of the now deceased clerk for a wallet or ID.

The editorial evoked no response from his partner, Schubert. Duffy then pulled a set of the perfunctory medical gloves from the breast pocket of his tweed sport coat, snapped them on each hand slowly, and then knelt and tilted the body onto its right side where he found the wallet in the left back hip pocket. The victim had $17, a Pennsylvania driver's license, a Visa card, a membership to a strip club in the Hill District, and a couple of photos of what appeared to be family.

"The vic is forty-three-years-old, lived in Mt. Washington. His license identifies him as Samuel M. Khalifa. Wadda wanna bet his middle name is Mohammed?"

"That's original," Mitch replied. "And what if I told you I don't care? Get on with it!"

As it turned out later, however, Khalifa's middle name was Mikail, the Arabic translated as Michael. So Samuel was a Christian, not a Muslim. Confirmation came from the cross hanging from his neck.

"My bag, I blew it," Duffy said. "Kill that stereotype. Remember Gorbachev, Russia's former big cheese? It's spelled the same way! And it looks like he has family, too, like a wife and two kids."

"That's had now, J-J," Mitch replied, using his preferred nickname for Joe. "Our clerk is now a tragic part of human history here on the entrails of culture on the Southside of"—he paused for effect—"the Burgh!"

"Don't quit your day job, big man. Performance art is not your future and comedy definitely not your strong suit."

"And when I make it big on stage, you, Mr. Duffy, will get no free passes to my Tony Award ceremony."

"So here we are, drenched in original but very bad comedy. I don't see the vic laughing. This shit never changes. Only the funerals that follow with their stock parade of mourners!"

"Duly noted, you plebian! And you still ain't getting any free tickets." Now Schubert was in full acting mode. "You pig shit Irish have to pay full price."

"But that's the part I don't like about this job," Mitch continued, again to no one in particular in the room. "Why didn't they just take the damn money and run?" After a pregnant pause, what remained was an inattentive, disinterested audience of cops with no ovation. Duffy turned to the uniform nearby and said, "Bag this, please," as he handed him the wallet and the cross and then moved toward the second body in the restroom.

"We have the restroom shooter cuffed outside, if you want to interview her," another of the uniforms yawned. It was near the end of his shift. He was obviously marinated in end-of-shift boredom. Both Duffy and Schubert appeared not to hear. Actually they chose not to hear. So they politely ignored him and his ensuing rhapsody of dull conversation.

The next step was to shift their attention to the restroom.

The blonde body of apparent Nordic descent in the restroom had no identification except a quality neck tattoo of undetermined origin carved on her previously stunning six-foot-plus torso. Neither Mitch nor Joe recognized it nor the shooter, but they were impressed with her ability to handle a large handgun.

"Big broad...with a Glock," Schubert said, "that's one badass mama! She's taller than you, might have kicked your ass or mine into the middle of next week, J-J." *And now, she's oh so thankfully dead.*

"If that's the shooter outside, she's good. One to the chest and another to the head and neck! Wish some of our own could shoot that well. She'll put most of our dawntawn (downtown) guys to shame on the range," Duffy said as he again slipped into the local vernacular.

Entry wounds are typically small. The mess was at the exit on the floor and an adjacent wall. After a cursory scan of the body, they decided to let the coroner's lab rats deal with that one. Moving to the outside, Duffy approached Kathleen standing next to her Blazer and then ordered Hughes to uncuff her. Hughes lifted a hand to protest when Duffy calmly interrupted.

"Is this your first murder scene, Officer...Hughes, is it?"

"Yes, sir, it is. I was just following protocol, sir!"

"Well, protocol this, *mi amigo*—just unhook her. I understand and I got it."

"But..." Before Hughes could finish the sentence, Duffy raised his left hand in dissent.

"Please just do it. We got this."

Now unshackled, Duffy went through her purse on the hood of her SUV and pulled the wallet, a cosmetic kit, lip balm, checkbook, and a wallet with the driver's license and her concealed weapons permit.

"Kathleen O'Rourke-McShea," Duffy repeated slowly with a fake Irish brogue. "That's quite a handle, lady! At least, you had the good sense to remain Irish by injection. I presume you shot the blonde honk on the floor in there?"

"Yes," Kathleen replied, still shaking, now firmly irritated at Duffy's flippant, condescending tone. "You still use a checkbook? What a dinosaur you are. This is cute obsolescence. Do you hate iPhones?"

"Up yours, detective! Your attempt at humor is juvenile," Kathleen shot back. "The Walther is mine and you can check the concealed carry for verification. I have an iPhone only for and at work and...I want my weapon back!"

"In due time," Duffy said. "Tell me what happened. You just *happened* to be at the right time in the wrong place for Ms. Nordic Hitwoman, Ms. Kathleen O'Rourke-McShea, right?" Duffy's lingering sarcasm with the rolling of her name again seeped to the surface but still found an unreceptive audience.

Exasperated, she turned, flipped her hair back, braided it into a ponytail, and turned toward him again, fire in her eyes.

"Okay," she said, exhaling countersarcasm. "Listen up one more mellifluous, fucking time! Your binary ninth-grade education is plainly visible. Pay close attention, Officer... What is it on that badge...Duffy? Oh, there's a surprise. Another Irish cop! What's your story, Duffy? Couldn't make it with the fire department? They require that you be in shape, but the diocese could still use another couple of priests. I understand they have an excellent health care plan and you don't normally get shot at and altar boys you can boink on the side."

"Oooh, the lady has fangs! Touché, madame! You need to go to Reconciliation to clean up your nasty mouth. My pastor at St. Catherine's of Siena in Beechview will be glad to hear your confession because you seem to cross the entire spectrum of foul. Your mother must be very proud of you."

Kathleen then patiently went through the sequence of events for the second time, just as she had with Hughes, now filtered with contempt for the redundant pace of questioning. Her real unspoken thought was, *God, this cop's a complete jerk! Where do they get these harbingers of vanity?*

"Well, someone or somebodies know who I am and where I live, as they obviously went through the glove compartment in my car and took everything, including my mail. Then the dead bitch addressed me by name."

"Oh, really! Hughes didn't note that," Duffy said as his countenance, demeanor, and approach suddenly shifted from flippant to real. His mood abruptly turned from flippant to hardcore, dead serious...all in a warp second.

"That changes things."

But that twere not all the dead bitch found.

Chapter 5

HOMESTEAD WARF

Even Mercedes lusts after petroleum, the diesel variant. Joseph's prized Kraut was a diesel junkie that required numerous hits during his weekly schedule of business. It had an addiction to the black heroin, as Fudd called it, at fewer than sixteen miles per gallon. So Moran pulled the four-door black German S-Class sedan onto the Homestead GetGo fifteen minutes east of the Burgh just after the Carson Street heist at its sister station west. Business concluded in Mount Oliver, they were headed toward Joseph's deceptively modest estate in Fox Chapel. Although lavish at first glance, it was never garish. Tsakrios was acutely aware of his high visibility with law enforcement. He didn't need to punctuate his lifestyle with a domicile that reeked of money to attract further attention from the alphabet soup kitchens of the IRS and FBI, ATF, etc. Obsequious was his choice: hidden with no public attention. *En espanol, es escondidio*!

Moran proceeded to fill the tank.

It was Friday about 6:00 p.m. and Ronk had just debarked from the tug moored next to a crane barge with its cargo of riverine trash near Monongahela City where his father was born. There were two barges of trash from almost fifteen miles of river. He declared it a good week of mud moving, along with the added bonus that they'd found and retrieved two stolen cars dumped and/or drifted into the channel. Local police loved those retrievals. Steal the ride, dump it in the river. Chances of prosecution: minimal. Cops were happy just to clear the caseload. These two thefts came from Munhall.

Ronan then delivered his weekly work summary to the Corps substation via his Federal iPad and went to his truck for the drive home. The report was curt, very succinct, reflecting his military writing style. It looked like a five-paragraph order: 360 tons of woodland trash removed that included sundry household items from toilets to furniture...and the two vehicles. The reception barges were full. The computer aboard the tug could exactly calculate the volume and weight of the trash, along with the draft of both barges in front of the towboat and crane. The river, sadly, was all too frequently the dumpster of the sideways citizen crowd. Kathleen saw the dumping behavior as an all too appalling modality of degenerate modern culture. The Mon was something of a semipermanent ecological disaster. The required cleanup was constant.

Ronk, however, knew it as job security. If you dumped a stolen car in the river, eventually the Corps of Engineers would have to retrieve it as a navigation threat. It was criminal behavior that precursed job security.

The Mon's history was also infamous as a cemetery of stolen and parked wrecks. Residents who carelessly left their vehicles too near the waterfront overnight sometimes awoke to a missing ride. The Mon's satanic, swirling undertows act much like open ocean riptides. They can suck down a vehicle or body and swallow it vertically into oblivion. Ronan fervently remembered a story his father told him about a B-25 that crashed into the river January 31, 1956, with a crew of eight who took their crippled plane that night into the water that Sunday at the end of a military reserve drill weekend. They barely missed crashing into the famed Homestead Grays Bridge yet managed to land on the water's surface just south of the bridge near the Yougiohenny (pronounced YOCK-A-HAY-NEE, accent first syllable) River. Witnesses on the bridge said the aircraft, with a wingspan of 157 feet, allegedly floated for eleven minutes and then finally slipped away, never found as the river claimed the bodies of two of the crew. Likely they succumbed to hypothermia in water approaching freezing that time of year. Their bodies eventually surfaced downriver.

But the aircraft didn't.

The Mon is one of thirteen rivers in North America that flow almost directly north with runoff from the northern West Virginia tributaries and creeks. Six of the crew survived despite the frigid water temperature. Controversy swirled about the bomber's contents, so a private entity of historians, the B-25 Recovery Group, applied in October of 2016 for a dredging permit from the Corps of Engineers. It was one of those Rod Serling *Twilight Zone* moments with which Ronk was fascinated as a kid. Fifty years in the river. Wonder who would find it? Even though he loved the river work, he knew that the Monongahela River was now both a giver of life as a remarkable fishing venue and a crass undertaker for swimmers and the inebriated. It is forever dangerous and never to be trusted, particularly when the water temperature dropped precipitously after November.

The plane has yet to be found, although the search group thought it was buried near a rock quarry now under forty feet of river mud.

Every year on New Year's Day, a group of local fanatics led by a steelworker, now deceased, named Gus Brickner would do the polar plunge into the Mon with a coterie of his friends, some very lubricated with Imperial Whiskey, Iron City Beer…or both. Today the traditional still holds with a newer generation of nutjobs but closer to the Monongahela Wharf in downtown with fire department lifeguards and swims lasting fewer than five minutes.

Nobody drowns. Hypothermia staved off.

But they still had, however, the requisite complement of whiskey and beer with their morning bacon and eggs.

Ronk also knew that issuance of a Corps permit for the search put him right in the middle of both overtime and "point of contact" controversy. He was about to become the Corps' point man, essentially the information anvil for local media to hammer. He remembered the conspiracy theories that swirled about the missing plane and the attendant paranoia about UFOs during the Cold War. Conspiracy swirled everywhere. Was the plane on a secret mission?

Did it have nuclear weapons? And all this paranoia predated the advent of the Internet. It was the hyperactive stepchild of the Cold War.

Now three years later, the plane was still missing.

He ignored multiple phone calls from the onslaught of reporters from the local press corps pursuing narratives about the crash from the story morgues of the only newspapers then in town, in 1956: *The Pittsburgh Press*, *The Pittsburgh Post-Gazette*, and *Pittsburgh Courier*. The latter of the three catered to a predominantly African-American audience.

"Let some public affairs hack handle this," he once told Kathleen. "What dose guys want (as he would deliberately slip into Pittsburghese) is to use me and the tug to carry their water on this Boy Scout expedition. It's too damn dangerous to have these amateur plane hunters and reporters near the boat. I don't want the liability. Let them handle their own assets and float on their own gear. They're not part of any public agency or primarily trained in riverine procedure. I don't like it."

His Corps federal chain of command, however, saw a public relations bonanza and handed him a scorched poker of lead man, in football parlance, a lookout block for the assembled electronic and print media just before the quarterback was about to suffer a sack for a loss. If anything went south with the recovery, Ronan was the anointed hit man, the poster child to take the fall and the crux of the blame for oversight or failure. The blame game was one played by most Federal agencies very well. And he was in the V-ring on the rifle range. Nobody wanted to touch this project with a ten-foot pole... or a nine-foot Swede. It was too fraught with hazard. Thus, Ronk was not pleased or assuaged by Corps HQ in Pittsburgh as their designated scapegoat on site. Having survived numerous artillery shellings in Iraq, he knew the drill. Top-down supervision had someone to blame at the bottom of the food chain.

"It's kind of like being in the butts at the rifle range," he once told the tug's captain. "Stick your head above the protective concrete barrier and you might catch a terminal chunk of incoming lead." The butts were protective barriers below the line of fire where they raised and lowered the paper targets to score and alert the shooters downrange from the two-hundred-, three-hundred-, or five-hundred-yard lines at the rifle range. It was all quite safe unless you were stupid enough to stick your head above the barrier. There was an old myth that circulated among Marines that famed commentator Walter Winchell's son had done just that and caught a round in his brain bucket.

"Was it true?" Ronk asked. "Who knows? But it was myth morphed into legend. So why spoil the beauty of a thing with the inconvenience of truth?"

Both Ronk and Kathleen had concealed carry permits from the Commonwealth of Pennsylvania. Kathleen chose Walther PPKs at home as the most efficacious choice as sidearms for their homestead. She and Ronk both liked the weight of the pistol design and they had plenty of interchangeable ammunition for both. Although both qualified with Beretta 9mms and .45-caliber pistols while on active duty, the semiautomatic seven-round Walther .22s were lighter, easier to conceal and handle. So Walther made the cut as the weapons of family choice.

The .44-magnum mythology of Clint Eastwood's *Dirty Harry* film series is only appropriate for a very large, heavy, or tall shooter with big hands that could handle the recoil and "maybe" hit their intended target. A .44's closest cousin is a canon, and it's as noisy as a .357 Magnum, although in the hands of a weekend amateur it might qualify as useless.

Kathleen's company H&K also qualified as a hand cannon, but the Walther's home was normally in her purse. The H&K resided in the glovebox of the Blazer. It was her backup weapon as she rarely dressed in pantsuits sufficient to conceal an ankle, waist, or shoulder holster for the H&K when at work.

Although Kathleen was tall, she only weighed 142 pounds, while Patrick at just below six feet remained a svelte 210. The fired Magnum bullet is incredibly loud, emits a terrifying flash, but is often inaccurate in the hands of amateurs. Said amateurs would be better off throwing rocks at an intended assailant.

Nota bene: Cosa Nostra (aka mafia) hitmen almost always used .22-caliber pistols, light and effective at close range. It is an upfront and very personal weapon of execution, easily hidden and almost always with noise suppressors, not silencers. It roams about the body with post contact. What starts at the head might wind up buried beneath the ribs. And contrary to the raging controversy about silencers and bump stocks that arose after the slaughter in the summer of 2017 in Las Vegas, they're simple to make. All you need is a small coffee can and pack it with steel wool. Then secure it with sufficient duct tape. That will easily muffle the sound of any execution, although silencers as portrayed by the *ignorante* of the press and film media don't truly exist. They muffle the sound of the fired bullet, but there is some noise. It's just contained within a small radius.

Walther .22s are much more practical for personal defense. Besides, the Swiss Walther was the preferred weapon of Bond… James Bond.

In addition to a gun safe, the McSheas also had four Mossberg 500s posted at various points throughout their Butler home at night when the family was there. Mounted inside closet doors at night, they were always fully loaded and within reach on both floors—two upstairs, two down. They returned to the safe in the morning when the parents were not home.

Their philosophy was wholly consistent with the warrior creed of the Marines: an unloaded weapon is no more germane to home defense than a sack of nerf balls. These, Kathleen often noted, were tools, just like farm implements with a relevant purpose in a threatening environment. Their mutual lines of work were both hazardous, she more so than Ronan's. She only had to draw down during her seven-year career with Securitas once on behalf of a client but had never yet to fire. It's always best to avoid arriving at that point in personal protection. Kathleen knew expended ammunition and discharged bullets precursed a mountain of postmortem paperwork to avoid at all costs. Several trees would die to justify the firing. Better a live client with no blood, manacled on the hood, than a dead derelict with a questionable past.

The last task on the morning plan of the day, every day, was to secure Moss and friends in the safe and anchor three of the first-floor doors with jammers and then exit the fourth back door on the first floor. Although neither had any interest in hunting, they both were conversant with weapons of all types from rifles to shotguns. "Walther and Moss," as Kathleen once said, "were the homestead, household butlers." Rufus and Jake, the family dogs, supplemented the family security team. Jake was a Belgian Malinois and Rufus a big, goofy White Lab with a monster bark you could hear for miles. Jake retired after three tours in Afghanistan with the Marine Corps and accorded a Purple Heart, courtesy of a Taliban bullet. He was particularly protective of their three kids and the babysitting Alvarez clan. Jake treated them as his puppies. Military veterinarians extracted the bullet from Jake's left shoulder in 2013, but the latent damage impaired his movement just enough to force his service retirement. Ronk jumped at the chance to adopt him when his unit dog handler received a replacement.

Since his arrival on the Butler homestead, several friends approached and preemptively tried to touch the kids without his canine consent. That was when Ronan and Kathleen would caution one and all that such adult behavior was a mistake. Jake gently but forcefully reminded them that permission to hug or touch their kids required permission from "higher canine authority." He would sit next to the child in question, bark gently, but never growl with adults he didn't know. The trick was to come under Jake's jaw, not from above, which all dogs perceive as a threat. Once assured that you liked him and he trusted you, you could touch his charges. If you broke the rule by coming at him above his head, Jake would stand and move between the adult and whatever child you approached and sit perfectly still.

"The next move was yours," Ronk once cautioned an inquisitive neighbor.

Don't make the wrong choice. A growl was sufficient warning. Don't push the perimeter of the envelope. Jake had no sense of humor. Remember, he did three tours in Afghanistan and retired a gunnery sergeant. He was a scout sniper dog in which the Corps invested more than four hundred hours of boot camp training and eighteen months in actual combat. *Caveat canis*! Jake never bit anyone, nor was he ever grossly threatening but always assertive with strangers. Kids the age of the O'Rourke-McSheas all had the requisite security clearance. Their childhood friends were all part of the kid platoon. Besides, Jake and Rufus love to play with any balls the kids would throw and were also adept at a game called toy hideaway with the collective of the McShea and Alvarez kids. They all learned at an early age to take care of what was theirs, or their bodyguards might hide the items throughout the property.

Sean and Seamus lost a lot of toys on the family acreage.

Both dogs were about five years old, thus qualified adults, who were always on watch and on duty. The house and property were their post. It was the safest and most secure homestead in Butler County.

For another five days.

Chapter 6

EVIL LURKS

"I saw her. Some miserable slut, the one with the Blazer, just shot Ursula," Snake said. "I want her ass. She will die slowly and painfully. We gotta go back. The bitch killed my Ursula. She's got to pay."

"No," Wiley said as he backed the battered Ford out of its parking place and gunned it west on Carson Street. "We're first goin' home. We gotta get the hell out of town. Do you realize what you just did? We were just there for the cash and you had to lose it. Shit, you just killed the damn clerk, you idiot. You didn't have to do that. Now we're on the hook for that worthless dead piece of shit. For what? The cash register money? So just shut up, will ya! I need to think and you ain't helpin' it. Why did you do that? It wasn't the plan."

Like all good criminal cowards, they abandoned their partner, Ursula. They couldn't spell the term "collateral damage," but she was it. Ironically, she was the smartest of the trio, the one who concocted most of their sideways schemes. Now the most together of the trio was dead, and the descent into panic was in full swing. No time to mourn the dead. That wasn't within their range of empathy. It was time to get away as quickly as possible. Snake was enraged, but Wiley was collapsing into total dysphoria. What should have been a simple robbery became a homicide gone badly. Both of them were the epitome of stupid married to inept.

They saw. They stopped. They went.

Now they'd graduated to felonies, and the Stop-N-Go was their diploma awarded on a cheap stage on Pittsburgh's Southside. Murder became their valedictory. They were just too rattled to pick up their diplomas. It augured poorly for their limited future that was about to take with them on the long road to prison.

"Shut up, Snake. We gotta get the hell out of town. Just think about that for a while," Wiley yelled. "You've been using too much of that damn crank. You need to get off that shit. You ain't thinkin' straight. Ursula is dead. So what? There's no description of our truck out on the scanner yet. Concentrate on getting us out of town back to Tri." *Tri* was Wiley's truncated colloquial for Triadelphia, West Virginia, where they lived in a neighborhood called the Pickle Patch, a quiet biracial ghetto that welcomed peripherals and "transitionals" of all stripes, colors, and backgrounds. It was the kind of recruiting ground from which the French Foreign Legion liked to cull, a ghetto comingled with a barrio on a mountain of white trash. They fit right into its lowlife cesspool of citizens. Triadelphia actually had a real community years before when the then Route 40 National Road was the main drag between Pittsburgh and Wheeling, West Virginia. That was usurped and bypassed with the new Interstate 40 that effectively became its death knell off-ramp. Like myriad other towns bordering the interstate system, Triadelphia became just an economic fringe scab, a travel afterthought. The interstate and the New 40 became its grave maker and de facto epitaph. What used to be was contemporary corrupt history. And so it was the same with Triadelphia as with two of its least prominent citizens.

The police scanner on the truck's floorboard squawked furiously about a host of things but not as yet the next appendix to their resume of crime. They still had time to escape.

Murder and robbery were new additions to their long rap sheet and degrees of malevolence. But ex-cons like Snake and Wiley were accustomed to the hue of the chase since they were teens. They stoked their delinquency teen years ago with petty crimes like cow tipping and mailbox baseball right after they got their drivers' licenses. Wiley's high school buddies would start out on a late-night run with a truck and a couple of baseball bats. Driving at high speed down the complex of country roads in the Ohio County area, they would attempt to whack mailboxes off their stands. It was a great laugh for them all. The cow tipping was more serious. To push an animal on its side, even though it would upright itself, ruined the milk production of a dairy cow and infuriated farmers. Farmers vented their frustration with both the Ohio County sheriff and the West Virginia State Police.

But Snake and Wiley had a great time with it.

Their ignorance, or wisdom, however, was as deep and shallow as Middle Wheeling Creek. Vandalizing or destroying mailboxes is actually a Federal felony. Teenage stupidity sometimes knows no bounds. Postal inspectors frown on the sport.

They even had a scoring system for how badly they could trash one. Two whacks were a double and three a triple and a home run if they dropped the box onto the ground. Most of the time they hit singles depending on how fast the driver of the truck approached. With another friend, one would drive and the other two intrepid criminals would be in the bed or the passenger side of the vehicle. Once in a while, they would strike out but irritated enough of the residents to clamor for law enforcement to abate their serious juvenile game. It was not a kid game to the locals or police, nor was it to the Federal postal inspectors assigned to quell their behavior.

What they didn't realize was that said activity was a standing invitation to marshal the combined efforts of the US Postal Service investigators, the Ohio County sheriff, and the West Virginia State Police. That put an almost immediate stop to their teen criminal spree with a state trooper lying in ambush over the same route they took the week before.

They were never accused of possession of too many smarts.

Their third Saturday night run thus launched their baptism into the state juvenile detention system at sixteen. As per the aforementioned, they were classic juvenile delinquents on the road to adult convictions.

Released on probation at eighteen, they both graduated to petty theft and finally to house burglary, simple assault and muggings, from truckers to old ladies. But it was their inability to unload what they stole that led them to enroll in the state prison system. Their lack of sophistication about how to fence made them low-hanging fruit for every cop in the West Virginia panhandle. By the time they entered the adult criminal court miasma in 2002, they began their undergraduate course work in prison after they tried to sell a rented garage of stolen items ranging from hunting rifles to specialty car wheels to undercover members of the state police.

The state troopers even asked them for receipts before they fitted them with the manacles of joy.

Guests of the state they thus became until 2012. The troopers were moreover even more than happy to Google extended reservations for them, all expenses paid, meals and lodging included with lengthy probation periods to follow as guests of the state. The old prison joke was that they were now graduates of Moundsville Tech where the new and improved state prison had supplanted the old. New building, better kitchens—same cast of characters!

Marketing was not their strong suit, so it was onward to a refresher course in criminal behavior. Thus it was no surprise they both became cellmates and spent the bulk of their twenties confined for sundry felonies, both malevolent and benign. If you came to prison as a petty thief, you left with the tools to become a major thief. Prisons gestate criminal graduate students. Rarely do they hone future Nobel Prize winners.

Previous encounters with the law were mostly crimes of property that left no dead bodies. *No más*! The criminally erudite pair also had a slew of pending warrants they collected like treasured baseball cards. The Pickle Patch gestated three generations of these inane, lightweight criminal types. Police knew where to scour where cheap burglary and theft suspects resided. It was almost like the neighborhood had neon signs for cops: "Here they are, search here! No warrant needed. The stolen shit is right out in the front yard." And it was their home. It was a police-friendly neighborhood to clear pending cases.

"Where da criminals?"

"Oh, over there in the Pickle Patch. Follow the trail marked 'Single-Digit IQ Road.'"

Wiley began to panic, but Snake seemed only obsessed with nailing whoever killed his girlfriend. Unlike his friend, Wiley, he was barely literate and likely read at a seventh-grade level. He could barely decipher the back of a soup can label and, thus, qualified as a true Pickle Patcher. Not astute enough to buy a GPS, Snake nervously sifted through the wad of papers taken from Kathleen's glove compartment and a Western Pennsylvania map. Wiley was almost hyperventilating and exceeding the speed limit. Skirting around the West End, their eventual choice of escape routes was to drive west on the parkway toward the Pittsburgh International Airport and drop south on I-79 to I-70 and slip into their hillside house they rented in the West Virginia panhandle. It didn't help their pursuit of elusion and evasion with their choice of the white trash, twenty-year-old Ford pickup ugly as it ran with metallic squeaks and moans that screamed old age. The registration was in the name of Wiley's married sister, a regular multicolored bondo special—dull red with those streaks of blue-gray bodywork yet to be repainted, screaming for an Earl Scheib moment. Its color was as subtle as a prolapsed hemorrhoid, but it ran well and Wiley was topping it out at seventy-five. It was just enough not to attract police attention. Seventy-five, you're fine! "Eighty and you're mine," said the state troopers.

"How much did we get out of the register? We're gonna need some gas soon. Count it up."

Snake quickly counted the bills.

"It's $214," he snarled. "I ain't going back to the joint, Wiley. I just ain't. We gotta lie low…but I do want to meet this O-row-ke-mac-she and hurt her bad. That bitch killed Ursula. We got her pistol, too, from the glove compartment. It's kind of a bonus, so we can get rid of ours. Hers is some sort of German brand with a big clip. Looks like fifteen rounds! I can't pronounce it, something like Hector and Cook."

Snake's seventh-grade education, like leeching pus, often painfully oozed to the surface, again confirming why he matriculated in prison, not at Carnegie Mellon. He couldn't even correctly read her name but he had her phone number from business cards, home address, and a collage of her bills. Now even one of her company-issued handguns. He, too, was hyperventilating like a nine-year-old on Christmas morning. Included in the collection were some pictures of her kids and Ronan, plus her bank statements, all wrapped in a fury of blind hate. Kathleen later regretted the sloppy oversight of leaving the items in her glove compartment. After all, she was in the security business, and the mistake of oversight in her own vehicle placed her and her family in mortal danger.

Even the best of security professionals make mistakes. This oversight had done just that. Fortunately, after sin, there's always redemption.

Wiley and Snake now had potential for violence: excessive; predictor for success: minimal. But their cerebral and criminal, corporate limitations always trumped their next moves and countered all logic.

Dumb percolated to the surface.

Snake wanted to cross the Ohio and veer north toward Butler County. Wiley's spectrum of imagination was barely double digit, but he was the Lone Ranger to Snake's Tonto. Their collective IQs hit minimal room temperature, although Wiley was closer to a something more normal than Snake. Their collective incompetence would be their undoing some forty minutes later. Just like their mailbox gig, they would go to jail. This time, however, it would be to the Mound where a five-foot-three, 140-pound Wiley had a pending future as a prison butt buddy.

"I want that bitch low and slow. Cross the river, Wiley! We gotta finish this...*now!*" Snake punctuated the command with the .38-cal to Wiley's neck. "Okay, man," Wiley said, "but what ya gunna do when we get there? What the fuck's the plan? And by the way, don't threaten me again, Snake, or you and your mama will get an ass whippin.' Understand? Take the gun away...before I get really angry."

Snake relented.

"Left turn when we get there, onto I-79!"

"No, asshole! Not now, Snake, we gotta get outta town and regroup. Take your head out of your ass. Think with your head, not your dick. We can't go after her right now. We're too toxic." Wiley slapped the gun away from his neck.

"Toxic? What the hell does that mean, Wiley?

"What the hell is *toxic*? Don't swear at me."

"It means we're goin' south. Goin' home first. Got it? So don't give me any more shit. We'll go home, lie low, and see if this hits the news channels and papers, so just chill. Man, we gotta be out of sight for a while. We both got records, and you know they're going to be lookin' for us. So just shut up and let me do the thinkin'."

The now less than dynamic duo, not Batman and Robin, was about to transmogrify into Crackheads on Steroids. Snake had the guns but Wiley the wheel. Wiley and patience prevailed. His IQ was also several multiple digits higher than Snake's, so the cooler-headed Wiley turned south onto the parkway through the West End near McKees Rocks and veered south toward the state line, a mere forty-five minutes away on I-70.

Snake would have to wait on his vengeance trip that would never come to pass. His boarding pass for that flight cancelled, and the pilgrimage to the Mecca of revenge slipped over the horizon. Their descent into the swill of crime was about to become a comedy skit…but draw to a dismal conclusion with their choice of further crime targets. Their Triadelphia crime wave was about to compound their Carson Street stupidity. Their choice of victims would become their PhD thesis in felony of the stupid.

They would flunk the test.

Chapter 7

WRONG PLACE

Fudd remained with the vehicle while Laudergast and Joseph went inside. They needed diesel for the erstwhile Mercedes but little else. The Afrikaaner flashed his very Armani wallet while Joseph drifted to the drink lockers for some bottles of water. The store had your standard, mind-bending array of choices. It was Iron City to Perrier and everything in between. Standing there, his mind drifting toward home, he noted the domestic breeds of American beer for which he had no taste, along with a mental check-off to stop at the state liquor store near Fox Chapel for something more akin to his taste, like Chivas Regal, very high-end scotch. He then parked three large Perriers on the counter adjacent to the cash register for himself and his staff. Laudergast put a very crisp $100 bill on the counter. It was the first large bill she'd seen all day and dutifully dropped it into the floor safe behind the cash register.

Ronk approached the same GetGo Mart on Waterfront Street in Homestead minutes later, parked facing the building, and took the far left of the eight-space parking lot. After climbing from his now semi-antique F-150 of 1989 vintage, he exited and moved around to the passenger side and then dumped his backpack from the bed to the front seat with his river quota of weekly laundry, along with a second set of work boots onto the passenger side floorboard. He didn't bother to lock it, as he deemed there was little of value to steal.

It was a safe bet. His truck had all the class and persona of a toxic waste dump.

And who wants to steal muddy work clothes? he thought. *That's why God invented Walmarts. No locks needed.*

That visual was an accurately astute observation. Thieves with any semblance of taste wouldn't go near it. The truck reeked of obsolescence and an ambivalent past.

Now it was time for a quick six-pack of Rolling Rock and a gallon of milk. In certain neighborhoods, he would have locked the truck tighter than a frog's ass in the Mon. Certain classes of thieves will steal anything, even a Ronk wagon.

Here, what the hell, he thought. *It'll only be a minute.* Then he remembered his Walther in the glove compartment and locked both doors by hand.

Now it was the end of the work week, so he ignored the two scruffy men exiting the jeep from the parking slot to his right. Both were well over fifty, sporting potbellies and encroaching gray hair. They were a time warp straight out of the 1960s. Their most noteworthy features were their ZZ Top beards, the jeep itself, and the odor of rotten fish that permeated both them and their ride. It was time for the carwash and the shower with a wardrobe change. He made the obvious assessment that they were not members of the Homestead Chamber of Commerce. Aside from Ronk's visual perusal, nothing about them was either remarkable or appealing.

His indifference gestated the tactical mistake of ignoring them.

That would change in Homestead minute, a full forty seconds faster than its New York counterpart. Ronk slammed the passenger side door with a loud clank befitting the truck's age, history, and pedigree, locked the doors, and then went inside.

Ignoring the signs that the fishermen were somewhere between unremarkable and sinister was a lapse of judgment. His mind was elsewhere, somewhere in Butler County, thinking of a naked redhead and what the evening agenda might be. That compounded the error. Moving toward the dairy case, he was stooping to retrieve milk and a six-pack of Rolling Rock when commotion erupted at the cash register.

"Hands up all you assholes where we can see 'em! Make a wrong move and your ass is dead. Yunz jagoffs, back away from the counter. Same for you bitch! Now open the register."

Obviously they were locals, yinzers with a bad attitude and no class.

The ZZ Toppers instantly morphed from fishermen into armed robbery connoisseurs. One packed a revolver, the other a pistol. The ensuing surreal scene was neither a suave approach nor something out of a smooth Tarantino film. But the barrel ends of firearms seldom are. The fishermen became the opening act of an egregiously bad play, and they weren't singin' the "Tube Steak Boogie" or "Gimme All Your Lovin." Blood drained from Ronk's face.

"Aw, shit," he whispered aloud. "Where's my weapon?"

Then he remembered.

Right where he left it: in his truck's glove compartment, as secure as a bottle of Wild Turkey bourbon at an AA meeting.

The two thieves now had a riveted, coerced audience of Tsakrios, Laudergast, and the woman store clerk. Fudd was still outside at the pump station. They had temporarily forgotten about Ronan at the dairy case, but the second dirtbag had a sudden infusion of recall.

"You in the back, jagoff, upfront. Now!" one of them screamed. "Put your hands up where I can see 'em. No funny business. Get up here or we'll wax your fuckin' ass too."

The one time, Ronk thought, *I need my weapon…and it's twenty yards away. Fuck it!*

The second topper then moved toward the dairy case and pointed his gun directly at Ronk's head. "Move up here…now. Didn't you hear us the first time? This ain't *Sesame Street* and I ain't Big Bird."

Laudergast had handed the woman clerk the century note moments before, a new, crisp, bright picture of Uncle Ben. She ran the perfunctory magic marker over the bill to assure its authenticity and groped for the change in the register after she dropped the big bill in the floor safe. She was supremely shaken with the task of counting change from the large bill. Her hands shook violently. Change accepted, the Armani returned to its designated spot in the interior right pocket of his overcoat. Then it was suddenly hands up for all. The second intruder repeated the command again with an added tagline.

"Clear the register, bitch!" He handed her a small canvas bag. "All the money in the go bag…now! That includes the change and the hidden $100s under the change plate. You got it? And open the safe too."

"I can't," she said with a quivering voice. "I can only drop money through the slot. I can't open it."

Pointing toward Laudergast, he waved his pistol at head level.

"Make a move and I'll air-condition your skull. We've done this before, so don't make a move that will end your day.

"And empty that classy wallet onto the counter. We'll take that too."

Although not exactly an original Oscar-award approach, it effectively paralyzed the now hysterical attendant, a middle-aged woman with fading orange hair tethered to the nametag Julia. She began to scream.

"Shut up," ordered the two now distracted fishermen in unison and pointed their weapons momentarily toward her to emphasize their irritation.

That distraction was all Laudergast needed.

The Greek and Laudergast had stepped back from the counter until the South African furtively managed to extract his hog leg .44-magnum perched under his left armpit. Seconds later, he unholstered and placed one round each into the two foul-smelling robbers with shots to the upper body. Death was instant. The loud reports of the two shots reverberated for at least a city block.

Magnum pistols are notoriously loud and can be heard for miles. The double report seemed loud enough to alert an entire zip code. But this convenience outlet, next to the river, did little to muffle the shot sounds, amplified by their proximity to the open water. But what also travelled well were the screams of the clerk, and she was in high-pitch, piercing mode.

The shorter of the two dropped first near the counter, while his cohort crashed backward onto the tobacco rack near the cash register behind the counter as the clerk elevated the decibel level again. She stumbled toward the door of the back office, dropped to the floor, and continued to wail. The robbery threat faded to neutral, but now the problem was her unacceptable noise level.

In a literal flash, there were two on the floor, both very dead, hemorrhaging blood with a very hysterical clerk. The situation wallowed with agitation. Fudd ran into the store, correctly assessed what happened, and rushed back to the Mercedes to restart the engine.

Laudergast grabbed Ronk and shoved him toward the door.

"Move, asshole, and get into the Mercedes," Laudergast ordered Ronk at gunpoint, followed by the Greek. "You're comin' with us. Gimme your keys, I'll bring your truck."

Ronan tossed the keys to Laudergast and turned toward Tsakrios. "What the hell's goina on? I'm no part of this. What the hell do you guys want?"

"Now you are, my friend. Please do not provoke either of my employees," Joseph said. "They will drop you in a heartbeat faster than a bad habit. You did notice the fate of the two little pigs that interrupted us with their very bad, discretionary choice."

Now they had Ronk's full attention.

"But we will be deeply appreciative of your silence, and I thank you immensely for that, but we can't have any police intervention. We'll give you your truck back. We disappear. You disappear. Just shut up and do it. This ain't no goddamn field trip to Kennywood Park."

Then Tsakrios turned toward the cringing clerk with his pistol pointed menacingly. "You never saw us, understand? We were never here. Don't call anyone for five minutes and get real stupid when you talk to the local pork patrol. Silence is golden. Otherwise, my associates will be back and they won't be happy. You'll never need another dye job 'cause you'll be quite dead. Do you understand? Don't say a fuckin' thing."

She meekly whispered, almost inaudibly, "Yes!"

Then he returned his attention to Ronan.

"Same goes for you."

"But…" Ronan protested.

"Like I said before, give Laudergast your keys," Joseph intoned. "You were never here either. But we have to go for a little ride. Then we'll decide the next course of action."

Laudergast! Wonder what kind of an ethnic name is that, he thought. *Must be some sort of European, but what about that strange accent?* Ronk couldn't initially place it.

Since his Walther was also in the glove compartment of his truck, it was, at this point, a useless condiment in a three-course argument, as Laudergast and Fudd had the heavier artillery. Tsakrios had a small revolver and Ronk only his good looks and now rapidly fading bright smile. His cerebral ceded to panic. His heartbeat elevated with anxiety. Blood pressure shot up, and he was hyperventilating.

Commands at gunpoint motivate. Ronan had seen enough dead bodies in the Middle East to last a lifetime, so he correctly assessed that Laudergast was the real deal as his accented South African English marked him as mysterious, unpredictable, and serious as terminal carcinoma. Ronk tried to place where he's heard the accent before.

Then it hit him: that strange, malicious character in one of the *Lethal Weapon* movies with Mel Gibson and Danny Glover where the actor was the bad guy. Intimidation with this Afrikaaner was his apparent role here. He played it well, and Ronk was not about to challenge it.

"Grab the water bottles I dropped," Joseph yelled as all three moved with Ronan now in tow, motivated by the menace of the Laudergast hog leg and the Tsakrios .38. Ronan stumbled as they went to the Mercedes, but Laudergast grabbed and dragged him by the arm. He had been shot at before and awarded a Purple Heart for a minor shrapnel leg wound in combat, but his emotions were now completely off-kilter. Gunshot wounds were not supposed to kill you outside of Iraq, least of all near your hometown. His emotions furiously were trying to unravel what was happening and what was about to happen without success.

He was suddenly thrust back into combat mode.

"Laudergast, take the truck," Joseph barked. "We'll lead you over the bridge. You know the route, but we're going to take a sidebar with our guest."

And just what was that sidebar? Ronan thought. He started to tremble slightly, trying concurrently to retake control of his thought process.

Laudergast opened the back door of the sedan and shoved Ronan inside and then went to Ronk's truck. It started easily, although it was loud and fringe obnoxious. In California, it would qualify as a gross smog poluter. He put it in gear and swerved to follow the Mercedes driven by Fudd. As they started toward and over the Homestead Grays Bridge, the fleeing vehicles sped cautiously toward the North Hills very carefully at no more than five miles over the posted limit over the famed bridge. Joseph had slid into the back seat on Ronan's left. His revolver was pointing and menacing.

Seated next to Joseph in the back seat as Joseph was about to explain it all, Ronk's cell erupted.

It was Kathleen.

"Don't answer it!"

"It's my wife."

He punctuated the command with a wave of his snubnosed .38 just below Ronk's left ear. It was a gesture fraught with the appropriate malice. No response required.

Ronk caught the gist of it very clearly. He said nothing.

The cell rang, rang, and rang…a third time. Then it immediately went to voicemail.

Chapter 8

THE PANIC

Kathleen dialed two more times. Still no answer! That was so not Ronk. He always answered for her. She slammed the phone onto the passenger seat and swore in disgust, more fear than impatience. The raucous noise was amplified with the arrival of the coroner's autopsy van that cops nicknamed the Cyril Wecht Meat Wagon. Sammy Khalifa was going to the autopsy slab in style in a ride he really didn't deserve. The attribution paid homage to Pittsburgh's high-profile forensic pathologist, both an attorney and medical doctor, widely known for his criticism of the pathology report of President John F. Kennedy. He was and remained a very living legend. Wecht thought the feds botched it. That suspicion still lingers today. To his credit and reputation, Wecht never relented or retracted his blistering critique. His argument counters few alternates, except the ossified summary of the Warren Commission. Wecht's pointed attack of the pathology report and the commission's findings faded into history and legend that years onward will still summon credence.

Cop humor is always dark, but most of the time, it's veraciously on target. A career parade of dead bodies and a lifetime of maladroit criminals make most cops very cynical. Dark humor is their therapy. Their jokes and sarcasm so convey and reflect. Unlike the nature of most business, cops deal daily with the two percent of humanity who trespass and break the fifth and seventh Commandments on almost a daily basis. Barabbas, et al. are still among us, even with thefts from the collection plates of sundry churches and synagogues.

The real root of all evil encapsulates the seventh Commandment: "Thou shalt not steal."

The assembled Friday tavern revelers across and on the south side of Carson Street expanded the curiosity bubble. Drunk and disorderly prevailed. Uber drivers held a convention for those too inebriated to drive. Her phone speaker was barely audible, overwhelmed by the abrasive noise level of police and fire vehicles plus the swelling crowd of early inebriates. Welcome to Carson Street on a Friday night, home of the St. Patrick's Day Pub Crawl. Tonight was just a preview of what happened every previous March 17, an ode for publicly sanctioned drunken excess. Conversation broached calculus limit, decibel level breached 90. Soon the Pittsburgh police will be out with the "potty-and-pee patrol" circa nightfall when they would embarrass and confront dozens of young women with full bladders from the barrage of Carson Street taverns with limited seating capacity electing to micturate on the streets and alleys of the Southside. There the P&P patrol would be there to remind them not to drive home under the influence and issue tickets to the inebriated young women and men relieving themselves in public. Cops hated it but were forced to do it after multiple complaints from bar owners.

"Oh, and by the way, sign this ticket and your court appearance is noted at the top."

Peeing in public was not yet a felony, except maybe in Singapore, but it did give you a permanent police record about which you could tell stories at cocktail parties years later. Lizzie Borden had the lock on murder, but "Micturating Michelle" held the patent on public relief. Likely those stories would fade into the bad memory bank when the women in question had inquisitive children.

In common street parlance, the whole milieu was pure unrestrained noise. But all the while, her runaway imagination ebbed and slid toward grim scenarios. Her concerns were multiple zip codes away. She was still running on residual adrenaline.

Duffy's persistence melded to distraction, for her inventory of action needed next. She was about to declare Duffy a public nuisance pain in ass and wished he would just momentarily shut up so she could think.

And go away. She wasn't into the binary attention mode.

"Listen," he continued, now on the verge of yelling, "we'd like you to add a written statement and interview you tomorrow at the Public Safety Office. You can have your attorney there, if you want, but as of now, you are only a material witness to multiple felonies. We…I mean…we need your help on this."

She momentarily turned away, stared north, and exhaled perceptively. With her back to him, she threw her hair away from her face, braided it in a ponytail with one of the many she kept in her purse, and then exhaled, pivoted, and hissed.

"Tomorrow's Saturday, Duffy. That's not my priority, De-tect-ive!" She spit it out with a long, slow pause on the second syllable. "Right now, I don't know if your two scumbag suspects are on their way to Butler or having coffee in my kitchen. Maybe they killed our dogs. Or do they have my babysitter and kids as hostages? I have some priorities here that exceed the dead bitch and the store clerk who posted their premature obituaries. Got it?"

She turned away from him again.

"Fair enough! I understand the concern. I'll alert the Butler County Sheriff's Office to dispatch deputies to your home, assure that the kids are okay, and stay there with them until you arrive. Okay? It's the best I can do right now."

She didn't answer, which Duffy took as an affirmation. He turned away to make several phone calls.

Kathleen dialed again. Still no answer!

She wanted Duffy to disappear. Then she wanted to follow.

The incident site plus the convention of police now was just a deposit fading into bad history. The prescient threat, she now believed, was in Butler County. Maybe the two slimes who killed the clerk just wanted to get out of town. But they had everything in the glove compartment from her vehicle registration to her phone bill, and they now had her H&K. She breathed heavily again, trying not to succumb to nausea. Her military training told her to stop and calmly assess the threat. She felt naked without her primary weapon and angry at her omission not to lock it in the glovebox on the way home. But Kathleen's maternal instinct fought against what seemed like a groundswell of mistakes. It was all so surreal.

"So can you come into town tomorrow?" Duffy said. "I'll even come in on my day off to guide you through the process. It shouldn't more than an hour."

She dropped her head in evident disgust.

"Duffy, you're not married, are you?"

"No, I'm not!"

"I can see why. That's patently obvious. You need housebroken, first with a woman who will mollify your obnoxious attitude. You project it like a fifth of Jameson. It fries me! You possess all the sensitivity of one of the local massasaugas (mass-ah-SA-wahs). Just like them, you're on the endangered species list! Call me in an hour after I get home."

"A what?"

"It's a Canadian Indian name for this two-foot rattlesnake that ranges from Iowa to Pennsylvania, originally named after a river in Ontario where they were first found there by the Brits many moons ago, probably about the time of the French and Indian War, circa 1760."

"Never heard of them!"

"Take a trip to our local zoo. They're indigenous here, along with our local copperheads and timber rattlers that sometimes make hiking and hunting around here dangerous.

"We have them here throughout Western Pennsylvania, even in Allegheny County, but they're thankfully rare. They're even on the endangered species list protected by our environmental zealots. You know, the environmental fanatics over at the EPA! There's a breeding couple of them at the Pittsburgh Zoo. Maybe you should visit them sometime in the herpetology den. You might find some long-lost relatives, maybe a cousin or two down the family tree."

"Ooh, slice and dice me! Sarcasm galore! Have I really made that poor an impression?"

Duffy threw up his arms.

"I'm just doin' my job here, lady, so gimme a goddamn break! You're bustin' my ass, and I'm really just tryin' to help."

Grabbing her purse from the hood, she moved to the driver's side and onto the seat, inserted the key, and detracted the front passenger window. Duffy sighed and said, "Okay, you are not at this point, I repeat, not a suspect. All right? But we have to process your personal weapon as material evidence. We will then return it to you. When and if you go to the PSO tomorrow, you will also be fingerprinted to separate your prints from those on the Glock. Understand? It just protects you, me, and the department from any accusation of impropriety. We'll also file a complete criminal incident report.

"Understand?"

"And what is that mysterious 'due time,' Mister…Duffy, that time frame you mentioned earlier? I'm dubious. I've been fingerprinted more times than the aggregate population of the Allegheny County Jail. The FBI and the Canoe Club (USMC) have me on their Most Printed List at the Hoover building in DC. Get my prints from them. I know you're a contemporary troglodyte, but they do that sort of ID thing now electronically. You know…with those little Internet gremlins in cyberspace. Then match those to the prints on both weapons. I never touched the blonde honk's Glock. My Walther will have one round in the chamber, three in the hole and the ejected shell casings on the deck. The dead honk has the lead, one between her tits and another between her runnin' lights. So now go do your goddamn job! I'm going home to secure my family's safety."

She hissed it out, just like a snake, with another thick drool of venom at which she could be so professionally adept.

Ronan often saw her that way when she slipped into what he called the red-headed-roid-rage. It did not happen often, but when it erupted, it was volcanic. Thankfully it was a moveable feast, seldom seen on the ecclesiastical calendar.

"This is supremely irritating, so there will be no trip to the PSO until I get my kids to safety with my parents in McCandless Township. I need to go…*now!* Got it? We can continue this little parley tomorrow after that happens. Here's my business card with the cell number."

She was slowly tiring of his professional persistence. It was mutual. He so the same of her!

But he had to remind himself. She apparently really was a combat veteran. She still had the Marine Corps Reserve ID, along with her driver's license and a legal permit to carry. What he didn't yet know was that she was an intelligence officer still in the active reserves, proficient with small arms, a certified third-degree black belt, and a resume married to an obvious attitude rife with impatience. It was time to call a rain delay of the game, shut down the high hard ones, and go into extra innings tomorrow. With the conversation now stilted, he pressed the pause button.

She reached into the SUV's console and extracted a small leather case with Ronan's Federal business cards on the perfunctory Federal template shared with several million other Federal bureaucrats. She handed Ronan's card to him through the passenger side window, along with hers. It had the Corps of Engineers logo in the upper left corner, the Pittsburgh office address, and phone, along with their home landline number, a quaint relic of the '90s.

If Ronan was a criminal on the lam, he was hiding in very plain sight, Duffy thought. *Who the hell still has landlines? This crew is straight out of dinosaur central. Even twelve-year-olds have iPhones.*

Both cards summarized Duffy's material witness contact information with the tactical touch of a shillelagh. This was no normal middle-class country woman with a middle-class husband with a middle-class home in middle-class America. Her husband, Ronan, was a Federal no-nonsense riverine rat with missions broaching daily menace on an unforgiving waterway. He was also a combat vet likely with at least a Combat Action Ribbon, so he presumed what level of security clearances they both held and guessed they both had TSs (top secret), maybe something beyond. He also assumed they were both proficient with small arms.

Duffy's assumption would later prove ever so correct. She struck him as a woman whose hard exterior was very real and not a façade or shell cover for something empty. Cynical as ever, Duffy thought her card should change the title consultant to something slightly more lethal.

Kathleen O'Rourke-McShea
Security Consultant/Weapons Training
Securitas International
McLean, VA 24517
(412) 977-1745

Like weapons trainer was a good cover title. But she impressed him as someone more viper than consultant.

But this was not the time to ask. Securitas International he knew about, and they weren't only just consultants, and you didn't hire them just to guard the bingo receipts at the parish Friday fish fry. Their clients ranged from corporate executives to government officials outside the penumbra of Federal protection. Most of their staff members were ex-military and packed with vets from both the Iraq and Afghanistan wars. Their calling card was competence married to deadly proficiency. They did not come cheaply. Don't ask if you couldn't afford it. Protection on the cheap was not the SI calling card.

McLean, Virginia, moreover, was not a neighborhood replete just with amateur UFO hunters. Serious spooks and John Laws lived there. The local voting rosters featured a maze of stone-cold Federal professionals with a swath and panoply of interests, clients, and clout from firearms to cyberspace. Most of those were Federal agents associated with agencies with names in the Federal lexicon unknown to most of the general public.

"Thank you for your help," Duffy concluded. "I'll talk to you tomorrow. Is 9:00 a.m. okay?"

"Yes, we'll be there," she said. "Both of us!"

Now it was time to retrieve Schubert and compare notes.

Kathleen dialed another three times. Still no answer! "Something's wrong. This is so unlike him," she blurted out to herself and an empty interior. "Ronk, where are you, baby? Where are you?" she screamed aloud as she fumbled through her purse for the keys left there by Duffy. Her mind was racing, although she knew she needed to slow down to think more clearly.

"Please answer the phone...please! You're beginning to scare me."

The terse, curt flash on the screen shot a spinal chill up her back. No signal! She succumbed to panic mode and began to tear up with emotion.

"Something's wrong. Stop and slow down!"

"Hail Mary, full of grace," she began aloud, "blessed art thou among women and blessed is the fruit of thy womb, Jesus. Holy Mary, mother of God…pray for us sinners now and at the hour of our death. Amen. And please, Mother of God, protect my family!"

Now she began suddenly to shake and sob uncontrollably, this time with an angry intensity. She had once again descended into a biological animal, an *ens biologis*, fearing the potential loss of her entire family. The tears almost impaired her ability to drive. She then anchored her purse on the back of the driver's seat, put the Blazer in gear, and drive she did.

She veered north and with ferocious abandon. Speed limit be damned, along with all those who threatened her homestead.

Chapter 9

THE KIDNAPPING

"Again, don't answer it," he said. "In fact, hand it to me. Then tell me, what's your name?"

Ronk surrendered the cell phone as Joseph still had what appeared to be that petit, six-shot revolver of unknown origin poised at his midsection from Joseph's beltline. Unlike the movies where unloaded revolvers might fool a movie audience, this one was quite loaded, with shells fewer than two feet from Ronan's thoracic trunk. Little guns kill just as well as big canons. A well-placed .22-caliber to a vital organ is just as lethal as a Sharps rifle with a .45-caliber shell at half a mile.

"Again, what's your name?"

"Ronan McShea."

"What do you do for a living?"

"I'm an engineering supervisor for the Army Corps of Engineers working out of Monongahela City with dredging contractors."

"So what's that mean?"

"I supervise mud and debris removal in the main channel of the rivers that includes obstructive cars, trees, and debris. It's an ongoing process, fraught with debris in the river not obvious to the naked eye. It's a year-round evolution. The trash from seasonal storms moves rapidly through the undulating current northward and creates shipping hazards year-round, especially near the elevation locks adjacent to the dams. We have to remove it with our subcontractors, and it's a year-round process. I'm the Corps engineering supervisor on the lead tug with every dredging operation."

"Very impressive," Tsakrios said. "So I presume you're a well-educated man?"

"Penn State, class of '97, civil engineering!"

"Is it a tough job?"

"It can be. It requires multiple approaches from geometry to sonar. The river currents shift the junk constantly. River depth must be at least thirty-five feet in the main channel. God proposes, we dispose...of stuff that impedes traffic. It's kind of like the cleanup crew after the St. Patrick's Day parade, except more hazardous and dangerous, but I like it."

Then he shifted the conversation.

"So why are you doing this? I'm not part of any of this. Let me out and let's pretend this didn't happen."

Tsakrios wouldn't answer. Joseph then gently tossed the cell phone onto the front passenger seat and began his soliloquy. "I have no beef with you, Mr. McShea. Never met you before and never want to see you again. I'm a businessman who just cannot abide police scrutiny. The two slimes my associate sent to Jesus or hell or whomever they believe is God cannot be connected to my family or business. Understand? It's nothing personal."

There again, Ronk thought. *There's that description and perversion of the word* business.

His fear level suddenly elevated.

"Where do you live?"

"Butler County, off Route 8, south of the city. I was just on my way home from work, just minding my own business, when I met you."

"Well, here's the plan since you witnessed the 'incident,' as I call it, and you've seen our faces. First, pull out your driver's license and throw it onto the front seat next to my driver."

Reluctantly and slowly, Ronk complied and drew the license from his wallet. That done, he paused. "Now, the wallet!"

Ronk acceded again. Wallet with the extracted Pennsylvania license, now with both tossed onto the front passenger's seat.

"Okay, what now?"

"We will take you to a pre-arranged, designated spot in the North Hills and watch you go down a steep hill approximately seventy-five yards away from my vehicle. You will exit sideways through the back passenger door and proceed down the revetment and you walk away. When you are sufficiently distant, we will then disappear…forever. You then will climb back up the hill, and your truck will be parked roughly one hundred yards downslope to your right. The truck will have your keys, driver's license wiped free of prints, wallet, and your phone on the floorboard. Then you will never see us again. Am I clear?"

"Yes!"

"Should you get some strange attack of conscience and notion of justice to sing to the FBI, be apprised the tentacles of my business associates may reach out and touch you and your family unlike anything AT&T or Verizon can. We now know who you are and where you live. The rest of your vital information will be easy. So *do not* contact police and do not mention this day to anyone else. Do you understand?" He was quite emphatic as he jammed the revolver into Ronan's ribs.

"Roger that!"

The rest of the ride was devoid of conversation. Ronk tried to quell his fear with silence and development of a plan of escape and evasion. Nothing at the escape and evasion course at Quantico prepared him for this. He tried to squash his fear without much success.

It didn't work. His mind went into hyperdrive to devise an escape plan because, at that point, he had little faith in Tsakrios's words.

Approximately ten minutes later, they turned onto I-279 north, traversed another thirty minutes more, turned off on a marked exit he didn't recognize, and proceeded to zigzag through a neighborhood visually foreign. He tried to inventory neighborhood landmarks: churches, stores, unusual houses, parks, anything unique. The buildings were all amazingly generic, boringly similar to most suburban squalor. Nothing stood out. Least of which was the CVS Drugstore they briefly passed. They all looked the same. The environment was the universally bland complement of brick and mortar, patently suburban and droll.

He recognized none of the topography and just knew they were somewhere north of the Allegheny River. They finally approached a long hill that curved northeast for about a mile and then stunted west/southwest at the apex.

The rain had slowed to a mist.

The Mercedes eased onto the shoulder and waited while Laudergast went over the rim and took Ronan's truck further down the grade. Tension oozed. Driver, Tsakrios, and Ronk pressed the agenda. Was this a drop-off point or an execution site? Pregnant silence was the backdrop. Then what seemed like an execution minute later, Joseph exited on the driver's side, stood by the car's trunk, and ordered Ronan out through the right shoulder side of the Mercedes.

Ronan feared what might be next but logically summoned his military training instincts for analysis.

They haven't blindfolded me like standard procedure for the kidnapped or hostages, but we're also obviously out here on a main highway with lots of traffic and potential witnesses. They also don't seem to care that I saw their faces, he thought. *That's a negative. But if I lunge for this guy coming out of the back seat or his honcho driver, I'm probably collateral damage since they obviously are familiar with the whacking thing in whatever their business was.*

Ronk knew what the word implied. It just underscored the tension of the moment and its implications.

Logically he likely could have taken a man only slightly larger than he and almost twice his age by force. There was, however, that sobering little detail of the sidearm and those "udder guys." It would be a five-to-one firefight against the well-dressed businessman, the driver, the hefty bodyguard, and Smith and Wesson revolver with his hog leg firearm friend in the three-man entourage. As a practicing Catholic and third degree Tae Kwon Do black belt, his fear wasn't the personnel. It was that prescient and salient memory of the bodyguard's beast of cannon that he saw put two very large holes into two unsuccessful career criminals. He was especially leery of the bodyguard, the shooter. You know, that other guy with the odd accent and bad attitude! Ronk further noted that Tsakrios was dominantly right-handed as he stood upright at the edge of the slope over the hood of the car. No advantage for McShea there. The boss man had a direct bead on him. He wished the "boss" was left-handed. It would diminish the distance of a takedown in close combat and give him an edge.

Yet he instantly opted against it.

Assessing the disappearing evening sun to his right, he faced almost directly east. His visual reconnoiter of the 360-degree landscape affirmed they were just below the road's crest, but the five-degree slope away was open with limited vegetation. New spring grass had just begun to bloom along with the sundry foliage left by the Commonwealth of Pennsylvania on the slope. It had been obviously graded professionally, so he surmised they must be on a commonwealth four-lane highway judging by its center concrete median barriers devoid of parking space for the number one lane. Hardly a place for a public execution! Harking back and summoning his basic school hand-to-hand training, he further guessed he could traverse the slope to its base and zigzag it in about twenty to thirty seconds.

If he really intended to whack me, why was the driver still in the vehicle? he thought. *He and the other guy both wielded weapons of low-caliber mass destruction, but the guy with the revolver wielded the immediate threat. And he was obviously the boss, and this was right out in the open, much too public for a whacking, particularly since the ongoing heavy traffic was an invitation for multiple witnesses.*

Odd place to murder someone, he thought, especially at rush hour. That gave him, he thought, a new, slight edge.

"Get out," Tsakrios ordered.

So he anchored his left foot on the road shoulder, without comment, and bolted downward right, aided in large measure by the flexible desert boots he wore daily on the river with an Iraqi-Afghani pedigree. Soft and resilient, they had good soles and history with a ground-pounding "grunt" resume.

He kept running, combat zigzag, and kept waiting for the shots reports. There were none. His uncontrollable heavy breathing was quite involuntary. Although still well-conditioned, he was shaking violently. The expected shots never arrived.

He flung himself onto the ground, facing uphill about thirty yards away. No Smith &Wesson, no gunshots, just a screeching vehicle breeching the crest and disappearing. Combat caution dictated he move laterally southwest along the slope for another thirty yards before moving back to the road for which he yet had no name. It's called envelopment in infantry jargon. He walked to the crest and another ten minutes beyond. There on the northeast side was his truck, not locked, not burned, no vandalism with all four tires fully inflated.

What the hell? he thought again. *Who the hell are these guys? This is beyond weird. I think I literally dodged a bullet, but now I am truly pissed off.*

"What's next?"

He slowly pulled the driver's door open. It creaked loudly of its old age. Inside the driver's side, his keys, license, wallet, and cell phone were on the driver's side floorboard. Phone first. He opened it up and tried to dial Kathleen's number. No response! They'd taken the SIM card, so the phone was dysfunctional and impotent. It was as worthless as North Korean currency at a Federal Reserve Bank, now just a paperweight. Without it, he felt naked, right here in bumfuck North Hills, somewhere in Pennsylvania. The trio had snatched it, thrown it away, or destroyed it. So now he succumbed to an almost inaudible hoard of cursing, summoned with no audience. The litany of foul ended with a loud, screaming soliloquy: "Okay, gentlemen, whoever the hell you are! Now you've really chapped my leather hide. I have a certifiable case of the red ass and I'm coming after you. You just fucked with a supremely irritated Marine. You're now the prey, and I'm the predator."

Next on deck: the aforementioned "What next?" On the passenger seat lay an unsealed four-by-nine business envelope. He opened it very carefully.

And there it was—a money cache, a full two inches thick. He gasped at the envelope but wouldn't touch the money itself, just reclosed it and laid it back on the seat. *No screamin' shit! This augurs poorly*, he thought. *And where the hell exactly am I besides somewhere north of the Allegheny River with a wad of cash that isn't mine? Okay, time to look for a gas station and directions. Gotta get home!*

The Butler County Sheriff's office days later said the stash of currency was $10,000 in nonsequential $100 bills without any viable fingerprints. His office had a US Secret Service detail pay them a visit upon notification of the apparent hush money and certify that the money was valid, not counterfeit. They would identify which mints printed the bills but not how they were collected or bundled.

"If you didn't know or couldn't see or identify who put it there or...why," said Butler County Chief Deputy Andy Malone, "and no one claims it within thirty days, the money is yours. And you won't get any hassle from the Secret Service. It doesn't look counterfeit, and the bills aren't sequential."

Somehow, Ronk thought, it had a Garden of Gethsemane ring about it. Thirty pieces of silver updated. More trouble than it was worth, a veritable migraine of currency.

"Guess it gives a new variant on a theme," he said to any audience, "to the term Judas's money."

The money stayed with Malone in the Butler Country evidence locker. Then it did become what Ronk feared: cash that pointed toward conspiracy. Was he a victim or a coconspirator?

Hush money or bait, he thought, *this has a stench that runs from here to the Denver mint.*

The next dilemma percolated to the surface: enter the FBI. Kidnaping is and has been a mandated Federal offense since the Charles Lindbergh case in the '30s. So like it or not, the FBI and he and were about to become very well acquainted.

And Ronk knew how little they delved into spurious humor.

Chapter 10

BLACK IRISH

The shift roll call briefing finished just before the 911 call pealed through Homestead Police Headquarters. The outgoing dispatch was succinct, terse in cryptic cop fashion: "Shots fired, two down at the GetGo on Waterfront."

"Murphy, Johnson," the dispatch officer crackled and turned to them. "You're on deck, Murphy. Git some! It's a new day with new slime down at the wharf."

"Oh well," Murphy replied with his normal nonchalance, "it's another day with another couple of knuckleheads to fill the shift. Savor the overtime. It's steroid for the pension. God bless the spectrum of stupid criminals. They keep us in business. And they're great for my de facto commonwealth retirement fund."

Detective James Patrick Murphy was a cop with an aspirant obsession to become a stand-up comic. Most of the time, he was more comic than cop. Eddie Murphy was his hero melded to George Carlin. He meshed the two personae into an array of ethnic characters he invented in high school. He was, in fact, the epitome of the class clown. Very early in ninth grade, he discovered he had the knack and the ear to mimic ethnic voices married to characters in his repertoire. He could be Paddy O'Meara, very Irish cop; Johnnie Walker, the Anglican uptight preacher; or Hans, the raging Nazi stereotype. Later he added Giuseppe, the Italian parish priest, and Manuel, the Mexican chef. You just didn't know which of his cast of characters would answer the radio call. It worked for the girls at Taylor Alderdice High, his alma mater, one of whom gladly modified his virginity status in his junior year. His parents were less concerned about that than the late hour he came home at 3:00 a.m. after the date with an older senior girl, Melanie Moore. They were more concerned that he returned home with the family car still intact. His social agenda was secondary. She had, however, just lifted his status from virgin to participant in the back seat of the family four-door, '64 Chevy Malibu, much to his pleasant surprise. Melanie almost always got what she wanted. That continued on her way to Carnegie Mellon U where she majored in math and a plentitude of men. She could count and, by her senior year, had both a bachelor's degree and more than fifteen undergraduate men on her conquest list, along with a treatable case of gonorrhea. Murph's parents presumed the obvious but never brought the subject to the dinner table. They presumed it was just a rite of passage that didn't jack up their auto insurance rates.

His comedy routines, however, played unusually well for the cops in Homestead. He was entertainment central. The dispatchers (all four of them) became quite adept at countermimicking Murphy and often bled into Murphy's UN village of characters with injected humor over the airwaves to sometimes very morose and gruesome crime scenes. What surprised strangers the most about this twenty-year-veteran cop, who could make them belly laugh, was that he always left them with a wry smile.

"Well, Murphy," one dispatcher once asked, "who's on duty today? I'm fond of Manuel and I marvel at how you do all those accents. I'll bet the girls all loved you at Alderdice." Murphy just smiled. The compliment required no response. He accepted it with grace.

Then he paused momentarily as he checked his sidearm. Unlike his younger cohorts, Murph still preferred the classic 1911 .45-cal. "I think I'll have to develop a Russian…name him Boris the Tourist. I think the staff is too bored with the current crew in my play of life."

James P. (Patrick—it really was his middle name!) Murphy was very African American, originally from Augusta, Georgia, and raised a very Southern Baptist. All you had to do to unlock his jailbreak, cell block of voices was to ask Murphy about his Irish background.

"Well, you know, I'm really black Irish," he would intone, always with a very serious demeanor. "It's actually a Spanish racial strain developed during and after the Spanish Armada against Sir Francis Drake. The Spaniards would arrive on the coast of what is now the Republic of Ireland, looking for the multitude of oak trees that then populated the island for ship repair and creation. Oak was the preferred timber used in shipbuilding during that era of the Armada. The Spaniards eventually denuded most of the west coast of the island to support the fleet. Ecology was another four hundred years away."

But that wasn't all they denuded.

"Their first question: where da' the oak trees?"

"Followed by the second question: Where 'da women?"

"They were denuded next."

"So," Murphy said, "I have relatives from Madrid to County Cork. You know what sailors throughout history want right after chow."

Then the tale would expand. And it wasn't a short story, more like a three-act comedy romp. Murphy loved to play his roles on unsuspecting members of the cop fraternity, particularly over the phone with those of Caucasian persuasion who had not yet met him. His imitation of the Irish brogue was impeccable. His favorite holiday was the High Holiday, March 17. You'd think he originated in Dublin, born and raised. The later visual would always stun newcomers who met him for the first time.

"Really? Black Irish? Really?"

"You're shittin' me?"

And that would cue five to ten minutes of vocal imitations that would enrapture any audience within earshot. Occasionally, reality intruded. This was one of those times.

"I got the shotgun," Johnson shouted. "You got the keys?"

"Yeah, let's hit it," Murphy said.

Detective Emmet Johnson had become Murphy's closest cop friend over the years. A preponderance of ex-wives will do that. The scourge of the three exes supported Johnson's descent into Dante's ninth tier of marital hell through the treachery and havoc of three marriages about to torpedo his encroaching retirement. All three women had court orders that took a swath from his diminishing retirement account. It was your basic 401(k) public trough at which fed the bank accounts of all three. His three kids (one from each) were all now adults, so Johnson had jumped off the child support train, but all the women were still healthy, vibrant, and threatened to live to ninety-five. He had thirty years on the force and now with an albatross of former spouses and three alimony payments each month for three to five more years. He was in court-ordered purgatory. With that much time accrued on the job, he could conceivably retire with 75 percent of his monthly base salary paid into the Pennsylvania Service Employee Retirement System. For Johnson, that was a service credit of his base salary slightly more than $64,000 per annum.

"That's BC, however," Murphy often reminded him…in front of their peers. The tease was brutal.

"Before conjugal payouts!"

The three formers extracted an aggregate $1,154 per month from his paychecks, so he was addicted to overtime. His now diminishing and monastic bachelor lifestyle depended upon it.

"Don't you wish one or two of them would just quietly die?"

Murphy was often relentless and guilty of piling on, as goes the football cliché.

"Yeah, God, please quietly take anyone of the three! Or take all three," Emmet once said. "They're killin' me slowly with court-ordered paper cuts."

"Well, Emmet, I guess you're going to have to work 'til you're seventy," Murphy once said with a very sardonic smile. "I can get you a second job at the Pittsburgh Playhouse. You need the cash, don't you? And they need security for the ticket receipts."

But today Emmet was in no mood for the onslaught that he fully realized was his own fault, but Murphy's daily reminders were no longer quite that funny anymore. Wife number 3 laid a sob story on him over the phone just minutes before the shift about the woes of their twenty-year-old son who needed "more tuition/book/computer fee" money for the next semester at Waynesburg (State) University.

"He's an adult, Delores. Haven't you expanded his vocabulary to include the word *job*? I mean no screamin' shit, woman," Emmet continued. "I don't have it and you damn well know why. He's going to have to grow a set sometime, get out there, and pay for some of it himself. Life begins. You do him no favors with pampering. So have him get another student loan!"

Murphy waited by the car, leaned over the car hood, and grinned broadly. But the conversation evolved, or actually devolved, even more rapidly. You could hear Delores Johnson from ten feet away. It ended loudly and badly. Johnson threw his cell phone onto the prowl car's dashboard in disgust, turned and put the shotgun into the trunk, and then peered at Murphy. He had *the* look. He was a brother in a very foul mood and in no mood for counseling.

"Shut the fuck up and get in the car," Johnson said. "You ain't my pastor or CPA!"

Murphy put his hands up in mock surrender. No mocking. Silence was the order of the day.

Since Murphy knew all three of the Johnson women, they were a fertile garden for his spectrum of jokes. He had an entire routine around the three that mimicked a three-act comedy routine, and he was always trying new material on Emmet. It was at times blindly hysterical. But this morning was not one of them. Ten minutes later, lights flashing, speed limits dismissed, comedy ceded to raw reality. Off they sped, lights and siren, just like the movies. It was just another day on the banks of the Monongahela with no beach and the drab overhead of the Pennsylvania spring. Spring there brings rain and postpones the arrival of the sun most of the time until mid-May.

The scene at the GetGo qualified as a trip to the zoo of human behavior. The uniforms had barely secured the location when street people and brothers of the street began to congregate and impede. Murphy jumped out of the car, assessed the rabble, and took charge. It was like a script extract lifted from *The New Centurions*, Joseph Wambaugh's first foray into fiction.

Slipping deliberately into his black Southern sheriff routine in front of the gathered trolls, he slammed the prowl car door. "I'm only goinna tell y'all this one time," he bellowed. "Get the fuck back beyond the taped area and let us do our job, or you might be spending the weekend with us as guests of the city. And you won't like our accommodations. There ain't no room service and not much toilet paper. And you likely won't like your new roommates, some of whom might want to become your special friend."

Murphy was sufficiently imposing at six feet and two inches, 220 pounds, with a Pittsburgh Steeler cornerback attitude and packing that nasty .45-caliber motivator. When the peripherals and morning transitionals moved back sufficiently, Murphy singled out one of the young, macho wannabes in the crowd.

"You want to be the first, ma man," he said to one of the young crowd members who flashed some gang signs and copped an attitude. "I got plenty of cuffs and lots of room at our bed-and-breakfast. I ain't playin', so get your ghetto ass back."

Murphy's comedy routine was on the bench. Detective James Patrick Murphy was now "the man," and you best pay attention. He visually perused the entire crowd. The *look* was sternly menacing. They slowly got the message and began to dribble away. Disperse is the proper police parlance. Heed or be accorded some Homestead Prime Time. The Homestead police on site wanted no interference.

Entering the GetGo, the scene was one of clutter, worthy of a murder scene replete with all the blood and spatter it could summon. Bonnie and Clyde couldn't have done it better. The cigarette rack had exploded with blood and dead flesh, but the cleanup would have to wait. Murphy and Johnson were not in a hurry.

Pistols holstered, out came the medical gloves.

"Okay, Emmet, wadda we got?"

"Judging from the beards, it looks like that little ole band from El Paso, Texas…ZZ Top."

Murphy couldn't resist.

"Yeah, but where's the drummer? Guess these guys won't be doin' the 'Tube Steak Boogie' anymore. Those are two very large holes. Twenty bucks or lunch says it was a .44 or maybe a shotgun pellet. It should be easy to find the expended rounds in the wall behind the counter.

"I presume the banshee behind the counter was the clerk?" Murphy then said. "She looks completely freaked. What we have here doesn't look like much of a helpful witness." Julia, the clerk, was with one of the first uniform officers from the responding unit, apparently giving the running narrative of the ZZ Toppers. As they approached the bodies, Johnson noted the pungent obvious. "Damn, these boys must have been swimmin' and fishin' in the Mon," Johnson said. "They smell like week-old carp. They're really nasty-ass white boys."

"Maybe they are carp." Murphy smiled. "Do carp wear ski masks?"

"Anything else, numb nuts?" Johnson quipped. "No time for jacked-up humor. I ain't in the mood. Let's just get it done."

"Just one of the fringe benefits of the job," Murphy shot back. "Dead fishermen and overtime! Just cash the check. I know you're fond of those."

"Well, let's leap into it. I'll take ugly fisherman number 1 and you take ugly fisherman number 2 now impaled against the cigarette rack behind the counter."

Division of labor settled, they began the tedious process of searching the bodies, identifying them, and constructing the scenario with a very rattled clerk with a high drift factor.

Act II, scene 3! Murphy and Johnson went to work.

"Damn," said Murphy. "That's one big mutha of a hole. And the one in the wall's even larger. My money's on a shotgun. That's an ugly way to go!"

Meantime, Tsakrios, Inc. et al. motored northward with a very reluctant passenger.

Chapter 11

HOME FRONT

Like a host of places between the Allegheny Mountains and the Rockies, Butler, Pennsylvania, is mostly a very vernal community quietly under the thumb of the Great Lakes. Whatever windchills descend from Canada always clobber Butler. July is celestial; January is glacial. The thirty inches of snow that normally arrive before New Year's Day and the Catholic Calendar Feast of the Three Kings are not aberrant phenomena. The weather in Butler County may encompass many extremes. But one word would describe it from year to year: consistent.

"You gotta be part Canadian to live here," Ronk once mused. "Beautiful summers. It's just that damn winter thing. It just never relents. Either you love it or reluctantly tolerate it."

Winter is officially an acquired taste. Ronk had a longtime college friend from San Clemente, California, who was a surfer and later moved to the snowbelt of Chicago and loved it. Ronk wasn't sure that his buddy, Tom Cruise, was likely a couple of sandwiches short of a picnic, as Ronk didn't like winter that much. He embraced it, but it was the isolation it imposed that he loved the most. Winter demanded retreat indoors if you were a snow paranoid. It became the perfect excuse to avoid the social perfunctory of church and flee to the refuge of bars, saloons, or taverns.

Longtime Butler residents, however, cherished the proximity from urban America despite the predictable ritual of the always angry winter. Rest assured, as beautiful as there is a Butler summer, there was always the reality check of December, January, and February. Can't stand the humidity of July? Check in again on Groundhog Day with the chosen, terrified groundhog always crowned with the nickname Phil.

"Don't they have to tranquilize that animal every year?" Kathleen once asked. "Handling by all those humans must throw some of the groundhogs into shock. It's Punxsutawney Phil on downers. They make the animal a junkie just for public display once a year."

Yet Butler County had all the swath of extremes and four seasons to match. Spring and fall are glorious. Sometimes, however, that's small consolation by the advent of the New Year.

"Butler County ain't Cleveland," intoned one local wag, "and we ain't a suburb of Pittsburgh, sixty minutes away. Not urban, not rural. We're Butler and, when you live here, you'll know why."

Kathleen and Ronan knew exactly why.

It was within striking distance of both Cleveland and Pittsburgh but distant enough all at the same time. Access to the culture south is and was optional, but they savored the monastic isolation of the woods, the quiet so absent down the entrails of I-279. The summers were green, lush, and very often soaked with rain. Contrast the winters with sometimes bone-chilling cold and average temperatures that fluctuated within the lower fringes of Fahrenheit. The adjustment to climate required a human commitment with which to deal with it all. Living there meant knowing the joys and extremes.

Esteban and Cecilia Alvarez also cherished the solitude and opportunity to emigrate from Sonora, Mexico, and suffered the indignation of Pennsylvania winters some twenty years before. Now both thirty-six, they were members of the same Catholic parish as the McSheas where they first struck a familial relationship at parish functions that led to Cecilia's hire as the de facto family nanny. Esteban had a ten-year history with the local, thriving Alpaca farm where he was now the senior foreman responsible for the four-hundred acres and 1,500 herd of the Peruvian cloven animals owned by the Evan McIlhenny family. He had grown up on a ranch in the Mexican province of Michoacán, so he naturally transferred his ranch skills north, although he would freely admit that the cold was a major adjustment. Mexico to Pennsylvania requires a major change of perspective for all new arrivals, even those so previously acculturated elsewhere.

Alpacas had a South American, Peruvian pedigree from the high Andes, so cold weather was a minor shift for them in Pennsylvania. Their prized fur is legendary. The Butler Alpaca venture modestly profited well enough with New York connections that allowed the McIlhenny Farm to retain Esteban and four other ranch hands to care for the seemingly docile beasts whose fur made sleek outer garments and an ongoing profit. The business was steady, and the Alvarez family grew with it. Their own three children meshed well with the McSheas, and Cecilia buttressed both households with a range of skills from home maintenance to cooking and transit for the kids' multiple activities from music lessons to soccer. The two families forged a dynamic for all six of their mutual progeny.

Ronan's job with the Corps meshed with Kathleen's sometimes erratic security gigs that included personal protection for business executive and lesser government officials enamored with themselves. They were the bureaucratic swamp dwellers insufficiently high on the Federal food chain to be accorded taxpayer-paid security but exposed enough to invite assault by some Federal-hating, whacking, semisociopath nutjob. Thus the need for personal security!

The Butler domicile was therefore a transit hub with any one of three adults in charge, the parents or Cecilia. Often even one or both McSheas were either out of town or dealing with personnel crises at work that demanded attention.

"When you're the boss," Kathleen once said, "all the problems and company headaches land on your desk. It's not like you can just shovel it away, but it obviously does interfere with family life."

Ronk had less of it on the river, but Kathleen often fielded a barrage of problems from both her home office and Securitas Headquarters in McLean. Security threats were myriad and required forward thinking. That's what made the staff at Securitas, Inc. a vaunted commodity.

That mandated the McSheas schedule Friday nights through Sunday as absolutes for family, but their professional slates made them sometimes missing in action at home during the workweek and occasional weekends. The Alvarez solution was to integrate the activities of the six children made economic, cultural, and domestic sense.

Cecilia, additionally, added the asset of fluent bilingual Spanish education for Seamus, Sean, and Katie. After four years, McSheas 1, 2, and 3 were much more Spanish conversant than either of their parents for the time they spent with her, Raul, Alejandro, and Maria Alvarez. Seamus (James) was the oldest child who absorbed the nuances of Spanish most rapidly and would often blurt out Spanish phrases in his seventh-grade class designed only to disrupt.

He was thirteen going on felony.

The Alvarez kids even taught him some of the "dirty" words. He loved being the class agitator, so he used them frequently. It was fortunate that Sister Evangelista either didn't know them or, more likely, ignored them as the expected behavior of a McShea kid. Their proclivity for delinquency was part of their McShea DNA. Older faculty remembered Ronan well, although not always fondly.

"They must take after their father," Sister Patricia Marie O'Dorn once said. She was a young, recently professed member of the Sisters of St. Joseph, and originally from Cork County, Ireland. Her brogue was still heavy, sometimes difficult to understand, but she expected intense discipline and attention in her fifth-grade classes. Angels they were not, but Sister Patricia had an array of tricks, both positive and negative, to control rowdy students like the McShea kids. Most kids responded well to her charm and demeanor, but Sean was often accorded added attention from Sister Patricia for an array of classroom misdemeanors.

Discipline and attention—she would get neither from the McShea brothers and had them both, just two years apart that often required ongoing parental discussions with school staff.

But Seamus's most famous interruption was during a penmanship lesson during an earlier spring in fifth grade when Seamus was ten (yes, Catholic schools still did that!) where the girl in front of him had this very long pigtail. Temptation overcame. The devil was in the room. Seamus couldn't resist. But it was likely only a venial sin, nothing so mortal as to send him to the basement of sin reparation.

He very furtively dipped that pigtail into the inkwell on his desk. You know, those old desks with the fold-up top and the hole on the left rim for the ink bottle. Having sufficiently soaked the pigtail in ink, the girl classmate suddenly noticed the intrusion, jumped up, shrieked in panic, and began running around the room. Sister Evangelista, then his fifth-grade teacher, was appropriately appalled and removed him from the room to the nurse's office across the hall.

Ink spots everywhere sparked the cyclone disorder of the moment: chaos objective attained, fomenting group hysteria.

But it also garnered him a trip to Principal Sister Martha Mary Dermott, a call to Kathleen, and a sullen trip home where Kathleen lit up his derriere with a ping-pong paddle used only once with the McSheas when they were much younger. Kathleen dragged Seamus by the ear into the house and looked at him sternly in the living room with unusual, elevated anger.

"Don't move, wait here! I'll be right back."

It was that "right back" part that both boys knew what was about to happen.

Back she came, armed with said paddle, grabbed him by his shirt collar, pulled up a chair, dropped his pants, put him over her knee, and administered ten swats—one for each year of his life to his bare bottom. The sting and the red had a lasting impact. She "let it all hang out."

"Don't you ever do that again, Seamus Patrick McShea! If such happens again, we'll double it."

"Yes, ma'am," Seamus weakly replied.

Both fighting tears, she commuted his sentence to room restriction where he quietly cherished his ability to sow classroom disorder, miss the remainder of the school day, and completely irritate both the nuns and his mother. It was all part of his master plan to spawn disorder. Venial in abstraction, the sin was almost comical.

As she banished him, she turned away, fighting tears of restraint, snuck a low chortle to the now empty room, and prayed!

"Sweet Jesus, thank you! He's just like his father. Just like Ronan. Please save him from the truly unsavory in life. Please don't make this the opening pattern of something truly criminal!"

But Seamus did have to absorb the taunts of Sean and Katie as they pranced around the house that night, singing, "Seamus got the paddle! Seamus got the paddle! His buns are flaming red-ed! His buns are flaming red-ed!"

Seamus, nevertheless, did appreciate the privacy retreat of his family's house, as he knew the Alvarez kids had to a share three bedrooms and a single bathroom on the McElhenny farm where privacy was truly a premium. With their own second bathroom, at least the spats to control the toilet and shower space were minimal. That was unlike his fifth-grade friend, Patrick Gilronan, who had seven sisters, and he was the eldest of only one of two boys.

Morning fights for the kids' bathroom in the Gilronan house were legendary, and their narratives were grist for the grade school rumor mill. Their peers giggled incessantly at the stories, true or false.

"You mean you have to stand in line to pee in the morning? How horrible," said one of Patrick's classmates. She was appalled. "I can't do that. That's gross! Don't invite me to your birthday party."

"I used to lock the door," one of his sisters, Noreen, said, "and wait for my mother to come. Then I could sit there and listen to them scream at me from outside. But I could pee in peace. Then our dad took the lock out."

"Well, what did all of you do then?" Seamus asked.

"We peed faster! If we didn't, Dad would hide the toilet paper."

"God, your dad is evil. Don't tell my dad and give him any ideas. No toilet paper. Ooh! That's really awful."

"But then, one day," Noreen said, "he was really, really mad at us and took the door to the bathroom away. We all had to wait in line for our younger sibs to pee without a door for a week. One morning, I didn't make it, so I just peed in my pants...but it got me to the front of my sister's line. They were grossed out and left."

Seamus thought the Gilronan household was the sequel to *The House on Elm Street*, a horror film restricted by his mother. She didn't want him to have it, but he conned his grandfather O'Rourke, the ever-soft touch, to buy him a copy that he shared secretly with brother Sean. He and Sean tapped Grandpa for a host of forbidden videos. But hiding the forbidden CDs was the problem. They sometimes disappeared, just like their anatomically correct magazines. Whenever Kathleen said no to something, Seamus and Sean would lobby Grandpa but never tell their parents. Grandpa was the soft touch, but Kathleen suspected.

"Dad, did you get that Game Boy for Seamus or Sean?" she once asked her father.

"No, dear. It must have been your mother. Ask Eileen."

Kathleen knew the truth, but she couldn't dissuade her dad or paddle him. But she did patrol the boys' rooms on those rare days when she was home and they were at school.

She also still remembered a transgression with her own dad when she was seven years old. It was not a fond one. He lit her up with seven bare-butt swats that she vividly recalls even as an adult. It was the first and last time she ever crossed Papa O'Rourke. At this point, she couldn't even remember why. With kids that age, it must have been trivial. She loved him dearly but knew where not to tread, just like she laid down the marker with her two sons. Katie thus far had no swatting excursions with either parent. Kathleen's unwritten rule was the entry to the Swat Club terminated at age ten. She knew the leverage with teenagers was more effective with activity restraint. At sixteen, the leverage was access to transportation, car keys, and dating.

The brothers kept their Grandpa secret away from Katie because they knew she would rat them out to Kathleen. Katie was the self-appointed conscience of the house and always alerted Kathleen to her brothers' transgressions, spying upon them incessantly, and was willing to tattle them out to the parents. And she was moreover an unrelenting tease when the brothers paid visits to Swat Club.

The transformed McShea two-story farmhouse was typical of those built the previous decades before World War II—two stories with only one bathroom for the whole family, almost always upstairs near the bedrooms. Multiple bathrooms were not in vogue when the fifty acres actually housed a family farm from the Great Depression until almost 1970. Bathrooms in those days had only two functions: bath and relief. They were not for adult recreation. The McSheas added two more bathrooms, four bedrooms, three baths (one downstairs), and a modernized kitchen—middle-class Nirvana!

Rambunctious kids, magnificent dogs...what could go wrong?

They all were about to find out. Wrong is like the contemporary Mayhem guy who pitches insurance for Allstate, a major, national insurance company.

You seldom see malice and evil coming until it overwhelms you.

Chapter 12

FRANTIC NORTH

Kathleen kept calling as she sped north away from Duffy, the dead assailant and attendant cacophony of noise. Unable to raise Ronk after three attempts, she shifted focus and called Cecilia at her home, spewed the details of the evening, and asked her to keep the three McShea kids until she arrived. The threat was real, but she hadn't completely assessed how real. She broached panic but didn't want to convey that to Cecilia. Keeping the kids wasn't a problem, although Cecilia was indeed appalled by the circumstance of her delay.

"You actually shot her?" she kept repeating. "Were you hurt? *Espero que la pendeja esta muerta*, Kathleen."

"Oh yes, she is, Cecilia, quite dead! Don't worry about that, but please, don't tell the kids yet. I haven't been able to contact Ronk but I'll be there within the hour. Don't alarm the kids with any of the details yet. I want to be there to explain it all."

"Shall I go check on the dogs?" Cecilia asked.

"No, that's not necessary," Kathleen replied. "Don't go near the house until I contact Sheriff Malone, okay? I don't know whether it's safe to go near the property yet. The dogs are savvier than you think, particularly Jake. Strangers had best think twice before approaching him. Sheriff Malone will have deputies driving by."

"Are you okay?"

"Yes, I'm fine. Just keep the kids with you until I pick them up."

"*O Dios mio, mi amiga...si, si, si!*"

And no, Kathleen thought, *I'm not fine but, the Alvarezes don't deserve this. This isn't their gig. I've just stumbled onto a pile of dung that doesn't need to affect them.*

Her next call was to Sheriff Andy Malone. As a sidebar to her employer, Securitas International, Kathleen had a working relationship with the Butler County sheriff as at least two of their high-level clients also lived in the county, partially out of the need for privacy but likely for more secure domiciles removed from urban cauldrons, easier to secure and defend. High-profile targets, sometimes out of paranoia and abject anxiety for security, crave isolation. That didn't mean they were the proverbial village idiots. Threats were often real. Never treat them as cavalier. The corporate executives on her client list knew and understood the threats of the world in which they traveled. And it sometimes included a wide swath of nutjobs and career criminals with evil intent.

Kathleen and Ronan were thus now on a first-name basis with the sheriff who was also a member of the same Catholic parish. Malone retired from the Pennsylvania State Police Department in 2010. Members of the Butler County Republican Party then persuaded him to run for the vacant office of sheriff in a special election after the sudden death of his predecessor, Abe De Walt, that same year. Only fifty-five, DeWalt was in the middle of his four-year term of office when a debilitating stroke sidelined him. The special election promoted Malone to fill out the expired term, and he easily won a full four years in 2012, followed by a third in 2016. They became friends with Malone via the parish council, and both Kathleen and Ronan had his private cell number.

She rang it up.

The terse three-minute conversation was all Malone needed. He contacted the night watch commander immediately thereafter. The station clock above the entry broached midnight. Two minutes later, Deputies Robert Correy and Wayne DeSantis were on their way to the old farmhouse that the McSheas called home, no lights or siren. But they knew the stipulations of threat from the evening briefing.

"Roger that, 10–4."

Malone's mandate was stealth mode. He talked to deputies via their private cell phones in the prowl cars so as not to publish the dispatch over the open police channels. The plethora of insomniacs with no life in Butler County, augmented by police scanners, was a literal pain in the ass for Malone's deputies. Newscasters and ne'er-do-wells often beat his deputies to crime and accident scenes. The interference that provoked complicated prosecution and sundry civil suits in auto accident cases. Cell phones were actually liberating for them. It enhanced the privacy of their conversation they wanted hidden from the public. Corruption of technology works both ways. Criminals, cops, and journalists all work both sides of that street.

"No on-air broadcasts right now. Use your cells," he said, "until this situation clears."

"Free press, my ass!" he once said to his chief deputy, Tom McLaughlin. "They're more like a pack of local jackals we must endure, especially that little moron, Seth Moreland, of the *Butler County Eagle*. He thinks he's Clark Kent. What an annoying little prick he must have been as a kid. He's a small-town Chihuahua who has no sense of propriety. Never trust him. He couldn't keep a secret if you shoved it up his ass to his larynx and ignited it with C-4. Always tell him the bare minimum required by law. He must have been one of those annoying little Occupy Wall Street pricks while he was at NYU. How the hell did he wind up here?"

"Don't know, Chief," McLaughlin said. "Maybe he couldn't get a job anywhere else. Most newspapers don't pay shit to their youngest journalists. They're basically indentured servants. Butler is low-hanging fruit for journalism rookies like him with inflated egos. Next step up from here is not the *Washington Post* or *Wall Street Journal*. Whatever the *Eagle* pays him probably is just above minimum wage for scribblers, but we may have to tolerate him for several more years. He doesn't like Butler, and much of Butler feels the same about him. Somebody in another town will scarf him up. The journalism business is peppered with transients. He's under thirty, so it's likely he'll be gone in three years. Millennials are completely transient. He has no particular affinity for Butler, so color him gone. He'll be replaced with a shitbag of similar sentiment."

"Yeah, hopefully soon! I'll kick in for his going-away party." Malone sneered. "Maybe he'll move to uptown Scranton or Wilkes-Barre. Let those irrelevant hicks deal with him."

"Okay," said McLaughlin, "how do we play this? We've only got twelve deputies for the shift, and I'm wary of solitary deployments after dark. So it's two per car. I think that's prudent unless you direct otherwise. I don't think we can just sit on their house with something like a stakeout. We don't have the weekend manpower, but a continuous drive-by should suffice."

"Right, we can't do it," Malone muttered almost incoherently. "We've got almost eight hundred square miles of county with more than 186,000 people… That's correct, isn't it? We have only thirty deputies that include six detectives. That's fifteen per shift…sometimes! Tom, that's a load to cover these eighty-six boroughs and townships, much less Butler itself. We're stretched and everyone in county administration knows it, but their priorities for security only surface during disasters. Too bad some of those prized wizards at Homeland Security don't appreciate it. Although I sympathize with their dilemma, protection is scattershot for the general public. Apprise the McSheas of our coverage and let's pray for luck. I believe both of them have concealed carries and neither one is among the meek who will inherit the earth. But they'll likely have to rely on their own devices. I don't think Kathleen's two Stop-N-Go amateurs are the impending problem. It's that pinprick collection of hoods that apparently kidnapped Ronk who scare me. They didn't seem to care that Ronk can identify him and remain alive to testify. That's brazen in-your-face, scary shit and should give us all some sincere moments of pause. That guy, what's his name again? Tsakrios, Sackrios, some goddamn Greek name? Pittsburgh PD seems to know him well. That means so does the FBI. I'll bet he's a borderline sociopath. I don't care how well he dresses."

"Have any of our guys talked to the FBI or the agent in charge of the Pittsburgh field office? I think his name is McArdle."

"No, McArdle retired two directors ago. They brought in another new guy last month named Wendlestadt. I haven't met him yet. He apparently was in the San Francisco field office. Guess it's time we got acquainted."

Conversation came to an abrupt conclusion as Malone's secretary barged into his office. Amy Dodd had office seniority, and Malone ceded it to her. Closed doors, private conversations yielded to Ms. Dodd. She'd been there more than forty years since some time after the LBJ administration and was not about to take any crap from whoever was the elected sheriff. The sheriff's office was her domain. Sheriffs came and sheriffs went.

Dodd remained.

And she made that abundantly clear to whoever was new and duly elected. She was mildly abrasive, but Malone trusted her loyal, but blunt in-your-face approach.

"The FBI on line number 2 for you, Sheriff! Do you want to take it?"

"No shit, Tom, we have the Fed's attention for a change. Think they'll send two of their newest vestal virgins up here to backwater Butler for defloration? We'll see! We don't do baptisms, and every one of them I've met so far has no sense of humor."

"Yeah, Mrs. Dodd, I'll take it.

"This is Sheriff Malone. How may I help you?"

Two very curt minutes later, Malone dropped the phone in the old cradle.

Butler County still revered elements of the precellular past. The cradle was still the phone king in Malone's office. His cell phone was only a backup.

"Guess what, Tom? Our Federal brethren are already on the way. And I'll bet their chariot of choice is impeccably clean."

"I wouldn't have it any other way for our overbearing Federal peers."

McLaughlin chuckled loudly. "Twenty-dollar bet, boss—Ford or Chrysler. Both spotlessly clean on the taxpayers' dime. Four doors! Feds don't do two doors unless they're undercover."

"Obviously four doors," Malone said. "Feds have no other kind. And I'll take the Chrysler with two agents, at least one of whom is part of some deplorable minority. Isn't that the new 'in vogue' adjective since the tsunami of Trump? Their newest rage in that office is Hispanic, but it might be an asset here with the growing Mexican population. Hope he or she speaks Spanish."

"What about gender—male or female?"

"Okay," Malone said. "I'll go with a Ford and two agents, one female, and let's make at least one of them either Black or Hispanic. What's your choice for this magnificent Andrew? You've lost the last two bets, so choose wisely, Thomas."

"I'll go with one standard, older white senior agent and one young female, any ethnic."

Neither one would collect on the bet. The pool of uncollected office bets would expand to $160.

The surprise was mutual. The arrivals were two females—one the very African American Creole Amanda P. Vedros from Lutcher, Louisiana, and the very Mexican American Alicia Contreras-Garcia, raised in Albuquerque. Both were in their late thirties, each packing the standard Federal .40-cal sidearm, along with the standard Federal Bureau of Imbeciles imperious attitude. They might laugh and joke, but they do not play. Malone, McLaughlin, and Dodd had seen this movie before, and they were immune to its persuasion.

After introductions, Deputy McLaughlin retired to the adjacent room near the dispatcher with Amy Dodd. Together they began to snicker.

"God help us," Dodd said. "Feds are so predictable. I've been here since LBJ, and it's still the same pattern of approach. Their playbook is so predictable, even since 9/11. They get it right about 70 percent of the time, but the choice of recruits seems etched in stone. It's abjectly depressing! The names have been changed to protect the innocent, but their newly minted seemed pumped out like robots."

"At least, these two may dress with a sense of professional style," McLaughlin said out loud. "Maybe we have a new generation of agents that have some personality, unlike most of those middle-age Caucasian guys that infected the bureau for so long. I think they used to import them directly from Utah, stiff, overnourished, and with limited imagination. Maybe these women might add an element of class."

"Maybe," said Dodd. "But don't hold your breath. Remember, they're still the FBI. And to paraphrase Ronald Reagan, they're here to help! Ain't that sometimes a damn, fucking laugh!"

And Ms. Dodd rarely devolved into vulgarity.

"Yeah, just like the IRS. Never met a Federal hack job I completely trusted," McLaughlin said. "They always arrive with a straightjacket of preordained rules that run from here to Erie. And they harbor no input or alternate suggestions from us minions in the field.

"No kidding! Some things never change. I have limited expectations that this will be different."

McLaughlin heaved a long sigh and returned to Malone's office. "Which room shall we use for our Federal guests?"

"Bring 'em in here. It will jack up their applause meter to think the highest elected law dog of the county is deferring to them. We won't even need prayer rugs and have to assume the position. They're lying to us and not telling us everything they know about their investigation of McShea's kidnapping, so why should I share what we know without some reciprocation. We're just the backwater, hick department, don't cha' know? So don't offer any juicy evidence tidbits unless they offer something in return. Besides, they didn't send their senior guys. Farm country is not their forte. They think they've got the lock on urban crime. Invite them in and we'll pretend to be the country rubes they think we are and play the role of their lackeys and junior cohorts in criminal investigation."

Malone stood and moved toward the large southern-facing window to his office. Kathleen's crime scene was more than an hour distant and a day ago. He thought momentarily and chose his response carefully.

"Again, Tom, some things in life never change. Life does have some requisite immutable. The FBI is one of them. Bring in our honored guests, and we'll all tell each other lies that none of us believe."

Chapter 13

GOIN' SOUTH

"Okay, the kids are at your parents. Cecilia's notified and it's almost midnight, so what's next? No bad guys in sight yet. Is it time for canasta? Or do you have something else in mind?"

Kathleen had just slipped into her favorite blue chemise, moved behind Ronan, put her arms over his shoulder, and laid her head just behind his right ear. Since boss man and boss woman were now home, the canine sentries were off duty in the far quarter of the room. They quietly rolled over and went to sleep. Rufus hit the snore button in less than two minutes. It's what dogs do.

They knew what was coming. They'd watched it before with sublime canine indifference.

"Humans! This is why they need us. They spend so much time just messing a well-made bed. It doesn't matter whether they're five, fifteen, or thirty-five."

The dogs had seen it many times before, yawned, and went back to sleep. They knew what was next on their agenda. It was pure human boudoir. Their reaction was the same: abject boredom. Since solitude is a rare commodity for parents with multiple children, Kathleen was not about to let the warranty expire on her next move. Privacy was a prized commodity without children when you have some hours to yourself for a change. The immediate threat seemed suppressed, and their overpowering emotion was exhaustion.

"Well, Malone will keep at least one of his cruisers within range out there, at least until dawn Monday morning. The dogs are inside, weapons are all upstairs, so all we have to worry about is a firebomb downstairs. So what do you think? Is it pink piccolo time for Kathleen Maureen O'Rourke-McShea?

"Oh, sweetheart! What an epitome of the downside you've become. Have I corrupted you that much? That's either your Irish cynicism or depression," he said.

"But nothing quells dark humor like seduction. Please, we both need to sleep. This day's been too long. Is it really playtime? It's almost the next day."

"That's why you're the gun grunt and I'm the intelligence officer," she cooed. "I set the flares out near the two gates and tied them to the remote on the upstairs computer. The 14s are next to the doors on each deck with eighteen rounds in each mag, so we're set for the night."

He turned to her in sudden disbelief. "But what about the flares?
"How many?"

"Two each at the north and south gates on trip wires roughly thirty meters apart. They're tied to the upstairs computer and will ring the buzzer alarm if they're tripped."

"What? Woman, are you out of your bleepin' mind? You've just violated about ten Federal statutes and the fireworks haven't even started? What are you doin'? You aren't licensed for flares. I'd better call Smokey the Bear to come and arrest you."

"No, I'm not and I also didn't tell you about the case of pop-up flares I have from Securitas, did I? They're quite legal. You vulgar, grunt types know them as jack-off flares.

"They are here to protect the home front, dearest, along with the most erotic boy I fantasized about from high school, even though you were too dumb then to realize it. Besides, Jesus will forgive me. I have a license for these toys. If we pop them, they will alert us to any intruders. Securitas International isn't the national home for retired Girl Scouts. Remember for whom I work. The licenses for them are in the office safe, along with our will and other papers. You just haven't looked at them recently. It's all quite legal. If I die first, you'll need to know where they are and that they'll need to be returned to the company. They will make no noise about how or why you obtained them. They already know.

"You cool with that, m'luv?"

"I am because I have to be. I married you for the whole package, mind, spirit, body, and your ascendant criminal intent. It's just sometimes you mimic the extremes between Catherine of Siena and Joan of Arc. But I surrender when your Joan of Arc climbs aboard and demands attention."

"Fear not, my dear," she intoned as her flowing red hair enveloped him, and she pressed him to the southern wall of the room. The declining chemise retracted further, off the shoulder, and fell to the floor as she pressed closer to his rib cage and pinned him with the frame of her body. Her hands were now further south onto the small of his back and sliding toward happy valley.

"God, I love your chest hair. it's so Andy Garcia!"

He offered slim resistance. Why resist? It's what men love most.

"You know, you have me at a disadvantage here," he stuttered as her six-foot frame slithered toward him against said back wall. Ronk was actually slightly shorter than she at five feet ten. She shuffled closer. She had him off guard. He was in the middle of an ambush, mildly blushing, but she sported a sheepish grin. She was in her stalking mode and loving it. He was, in fact, the target downrange, and she had a lock on the V-ring.

Travis Tritt had it right in the exit number from the film *My Cousin Vinny*. This wasn't the Bible Belt, but Kathleen still had a body made for sin and was about to bring directed fire support on target in artillery parlance. The Sixth Commandment was about to take a beating. They were saved by the exclusionary clause of sin that allowed deployment of sheer lust upon those very happily married.

"You could make Samson shave his own head," he exhaled, "and become a Buddhist monk! Your Delilah is pure nymphomania."

"And you *relish* it, my dear. Don't deny it. Now do as Mama says. Move this formation and your delightful ass east. I'll take care of the undressing part."

Four wardrobe moves later, shirt and jeans involuntarily, and slowly removed, left Ronk in his birthday suit, craving with delight. She was indeed right: Ronk panted with conspicuous anticipation.

"What is this?" she whispered in his ear. "No underwear, Captain? You're out of uniform! I will have to impose a more detailed personal inspection later. Might require medical gloves! We can't have your amorous body parts so exposed around those raunchy river women with whom you cavort daily.

"I love and have devoured every minute of your now famed admiration for more than fifteen years, twenty-five counting the ogling of your adolescence," she continued. "But also know this, all men are easy—food and sex! And you're my favorite man and have come oh so far from your odious high school days. And Penn State didn't clean you up either, but I love you in spite of your notorious array of sluts in undergraduate school. Remember, I knew about your male slut reputation even before we dated. And your mama filled me in on all the salacious details that I didn't know from our mutual alumni at North Catholic, so don't give me any of that innocent altar boy routine. You're the father of three now and obliged to fill the recreational needs of your horny wife. So see to it, Marine! That's an order. You're now on the menu. I'm hungry. And I'm the only diner. And tonight I'm dining a la carte. It's time for you to ring my happy bell. So do as the good major commands. Refuse this order, and I may have to arrest and restrain you with my newly purchased velvet handcuffs and confine you to my mattress brig."

"I do, did, and will endure the yoke of fidelity for your marital affection!" he stammered. "Proceed with your enhanced interrogation!"

"And as a reminder, if you didn't notice, *Captain*, I still outrank you as K. M. O'Rourke-McShea, Major, USMCR, your favorite field grade. No more cavorting with junior lieutenants on drill weekends or that hot new gunnery sergeant number in C battery. That little bitch Mendoza had best not be on your radar. *Comprenez-vous, mon amour?* She's now divorced, I understand, and on the prowl, so you damn well better not be the prey. The major doesn't share. You're off the market, just in case you have erroneously advertised otherwise with less competent women. Messin' with my man is a mortal sin. The penance will be heavy with a long stint in purgatory."

"Penance for whom? Me or the offending female?"

"For you, it may be confinement to quarters, shackled to this bed. For her, it may be a Sharia-style public flogging that will suppress her vile and wicked ways with her selection of a married target. You're taken. Never forget it."

He was now giggling with soft laughter. Things were now rising on his Panama perimeter, and Kathleen was not about to take no for an answer.

"Do you want me to salute now or later? Should I stand at parade rest? Or are you writing up a charge sheet for fraternization? It's a little awkward right now with the southern movement herein."

"Not now, Captain! I have another fire mission for which I will issue a five-paragraph order."

She continued to press against Ronk further away from the wall nearest the master bath door.

"On your back, Marine! That's an order. You have been derelict with your erotic duty watch this month. My period ended last Tuesday, and my estrogen level is off the chart. Yet you have done nothing to quell it. That's dereliction of duty, Captain. See to it!"

His resistance slowly dissolved to hot butter as she moved him onto the bed with slow, deliberate gusto.

"Never mess with your wife on a mission nor one with a legitimate black belt," she drooled, "especially if that woman also is CO of your domicile! This ain't the BOQ (Bachelor Officers Quarters) with multiple choice selections of raunchy women on deck. Furthermore, the reconnaissance report of your northern sector notes two switch signals hidden among your plethora of chest hairs. And I really like your hair. But I'll have to check further with a mine sweep of the nipples that have surfaced. They may be triggers to further IEDs (Improvised Explosive Devices) lurking and yet unseen just south of the beltline. You must be quiet and remain totally immobile as I disarm the two systems. Just consider me the mine sweeper."

But Ronk was only *reasonably* quiet. He just continued to stutter incoherently with delight. He was about to receive what every committed husband cherishes the most, and it wasn't a basket from the Easter Bunny. He was about to receive a major league Lewinsky.

"And I'll have to sweep the target area, as I suspect there is a gun emplacement in the battery that I must neutralize. So remain still, as you were, while I finish the necessary reconnoiter."

Two minutes later, Kathleen arrived at mission objective.

"Now I'm the cowgirl and you're the saddle. I think I'll have to mount. Remain still as I grab the saddle horn."

The parapet was poised to fire, but Kathleen mounted into position and lowered it fewer than five minutes thereafter. Site secured. She rolled over with a Cheshire grin, as she so enjoyed catching him off guard. That's much of what she loved about him. That stud of a frat boy dissolved and surrendered to her coerced charms every time she whipped out the seduction package.

And despite her teased warning about straying too far, Ronk was not about to order out for tacos when he had carne asada at home. Captain Ronan James McShea surrendered to the ennui, faded into an overpowering surge of calm, and then rolled over onto the southern side of their bed and fell into an intense nap. Mission accomplished. She looked at him and suddenly clutched him with intense passion.

"I love you, baby, but duty calls," she quietly crooned and ceremoniously covered him, retrieved the chemise, and moved through to the three other bedrooms, carefully noting potential firing positions. The pistols and shotguns arrayed in all three were all fully loaded and locked into place near one of the windows in each.

Jake immediately jumped up from the southwestern corner of their bedroom, followed, and gave her a startled, stern canine look consistent with his Belgian Malinois DNA.

The dogs were abnormally quiet throughout Ronk's prenap sedation.

"What's up, boss?" His tail now was not wagging, and she was not the normal, cheerful morning mother of three. Jake, the Afghan vet, sensed the danger; he was trained for it.

Both he and Rufus anticipated the pending agenda. Rufus was the corporal to Jake's gunnery sergeant. This was not their normal duty hour, and chow time was still hours away. Now they shifted into silent military mode: tails down, heads bobbing from side to side throughout the second floor, and noses locked and loaded, alerted to anything that smelled danger. Serious threats lurked to the south of their Butler homestead. The K-9 unit fell into serious combat mode. Kathleen, however, was not quite so sure but prepared to do whatever was necessary to protect their home. She directed them throughout each room on the second floor. They discerned no adverse scent. They finished in Katie's room.

There she stood near the window, overlooking the yard.

And reflected!

This was already a weekend fading in which she killed one. The haunting memory was still fresh. The year in Iraq and the seven years with Securitas still could not numb the past forty-eight hours. She relived it all in the pit of her stomach.

Moving into the adjacent bedrooms, Kathleen stood in front of the window, overlooking the front yard, still dressed only in her birthday suit draped by the chemise with a Mossberg 12-guage in hand. She feared what she knew was to come next.

The Greek would attempt to assassinate her husband. That was his only way to avoid trial and conviction. Terminate the star witness—of that she was sure. She exhaled heavily and once again started to quiver. She dreaded what was the necessary next.

As she sat down on Katie's bed, the tremble returned, along with the tears that slowly erupted and quietly began to fall.

And she kept repeating.

"This will not stand! This will not stand…this will not stand."

Then the tears became a fully formed volley.

Chapter 14

THE INTERVIEW

The aroma of freshly brewed coffee cued reveille, and Ronan slowly reached and checked his watch: 0603. Kathleen was downstairs on her cell with Duffy; she didn't seem happy. The conversation was loud, punctuated with staccato profanity.

"Not a good sign," muttered Ronk to a room devoid of audience except the dogs as he groaned his way to the master bath. Even the bath mirror offered no solace.

"Good morning, Marine. You're still ugly! Even Jake thinks so."

Then the phone call from downstairs caught his attention. With the exception of their midnight rendezvous, Kathleen's normal speech banter turned tart. Her anger was that profound, although she realized her sudden coterie of verbal excess might need some reconciliation time, as Catholics now call Confession. Ronk noted a lot of shits in her phone exchange. She even threw in an occasion "goddammit.' The venial swearing sins were piling up.

Yeah, that's about right, he thought. *It's time to get real! Shower first.* Jake and Rufus stood guard outside the master bath. But he also remembered, as the flow of the warm morning sun swarmed into their bedroom, why he was so in love with the redhead who distained him in high school but watched him from afar.

"*Nota bene*, life's not so bad despite the external array of threats."

Turning to the Oracles of Butler County, to which the family sometimes referred to Rufus and Jake, he proclaimed, "But isn't she the most impressive female you've ever met?" They both barked in agreement. The vote count outside the shower was 3–0. They anointed her said title by unanimous consent. Rufus was a white Lab, so he'd agree to anything that might warrant a dog treat.

Today's descent, however, into hardcore reality would feature cops and Feds of all stripes. Kathleen had a date with Duffy and Ronk with the FBI. They hoped the ad hoc cop convention could do this all at once together at the same location—at least, that's what Duffy promised. Although it remained unspoken, they both harbored doubt. There was just too much subliminal, professional jealousy among the three competing agencies. Even the imposed integration of effort post 9/11 never quite extinguished the chafing that local police departments felt for The Feds, a phrase used with subliminal, sometimes spiteful, dismissal. It was leftover of generations of turf wars and jurisdictional jealousy. Kathleen confronted that often as Securitas, Inc. and frequently dealt with the twenty-three sundry Federal agencies with independent arrest power from the FBI, US Marshals, and the Secret Service at the Department of the Treasury. They all groveled for a piece of the action and sometimes impeded one another despite the penumbra of cooperation imposed by Homeland Security.

First Kathleen called her mother, apprised her of the situation, and asked to keep their kids at least until Sunday night so they could sort out the tsunami of law enforcement about to engulf them. Eileen O'Rourke knew the Alvarez home location and assured her daughter that they were on the way from McCandless. She followed with a second call to Cecilia and reiterated her warning to stay away from the McShea homestead until the "all clear" sounded and apprised her of Grandma's arrival.

Homefront plan of the day was to disarm the trip wires and flares around the gates and then lock Jake and Rufus outside on the property. They had door jammers on three of the downstairs exterior exit doors and triple locks on the front door and back kitchen door. All had triple-pane windows, so burglary was a challenge but not impossible. Every action has an equal and destructive reaction.

The collective precautions were a thwart to uninvited amateur house guests, but professionals not so much. The best burglars alive, Ronk once said, were firemen with all the toys to both "break and enter, rescue or steal." And he always noted that firefighters bragged about their ability to enter any building under any circumstance. "Yeah, out there to serve and protect…or maybe loot."

They had all the implements of rescue or snatch.

"Yeah," he once mused to the then Butler fire chief, "the very guys you trusted with your life and most prized possessions were also the world's most adept house burglars. Ain't that some screamin' irony! Name a building that firefighters with their truckload of tools couldn't breach this side of the Great Wall of China. Hint—there are none."

Firefighters have all the functional utensils of destruction designed for entry and mayhem. Twenty minutes later, the McSheas had the flares, the two M-14s, and the house secured, along with the shotguns in the weapons safe just off the living room. They then allowed themselves a short delve into Pittsburghese.

"D'd jeet yet?" (Translation: Did you eat yet?)

She replied, "No, jew?" (No, did you?)

"Eat'n Park or Denny's?"

"Whichever yunz want!"

"Then let us go to morning chow first haste!" Ronk said. "I think this day is going to take more than high-end caffeine to endure. My story is stereo, and I'm not sure they're all going to believe it. There are just too many coincidences, and cops don't believe in those."

"Relax," she replied, "I've got this pig-shit Duffy under control. It will be the Federal Bureau of Irritants who will make the day long and irritable. We were both involved in two separate major felonies at the same time on the opposite ends of the city. That defies credulity, and when they discover our military history and clearances, we may be looking at career colonoscopies from all of them."

"Just what I wanted"—he laughed—"anal intrusion to start my weekend."

"Well," she retorted, "I believe you already got what you wanted for the weekend."

"Yes, ma'am, I did indeed, and I am so grateful for said. You made yesterday night a savory memory after that drive-by with death."

Her next call was to Detective Duffy who confirmed the 0900 appointment. Duffy's late night at the Stop-N-Go precluded any other social assignations, so he seemed as tired as he really was. Friday night was long and arduous for both the Pittsburgh and the Homestead PDs. It was the same for the McSheas. Duffy assured her there would be a gathering of the clan, anxious to hear their *Tale of Two Cities*, fifteen miles and two extended monologues apart.

"Now breakfast. Denny's okay? It's the first off I-79."

"Yeah, let's do it!" she said. "It's gonna be a grand slam morning, so we may as well eat well. Lunch with Duffy's Pittsburgh crew may be the ALPO special, where we may lose whatever's left of our appetite."

Thirty minutes later, they headed south on I-79 in her Blazer. As much as she loved Ronan, his truck always smelled like some giant variant of yard fertilizer, forty-weight oil, and dead fish…with good reason. He liked it that way. It was a genuine man-truck junk wagon, a sort of off-limits, battered hulk where women dare not tread or sit. The vehicle was definitely not suitable for necking or pubic exploration. Unless you were totally desperate, it also appeared un-"theftable." No self-respecting car thief would be found dead in it. It repelled men and women equally. Half the time, he kept the keys in the ignition, even in public. Ronk joked that it was worth more stolen that it was sitting on the street. Everyone he knew agreed, including Kathleen, but that didn't mean she would ride shotgun in it. It was antique married to white trash. And Kathleen was neither a redneck woman nor a white trash broad. Neither description fit Ms. Kathleen Maureen O'Rourke-McShea. She exuded class. He exuded reluctant warrior. But when necessary, she could impose the requisite blue streak of pain upon anyone so deserving.

Her citizens' band handle should be "Handle with Care."

Thus, the choice of transit of this AM was her Blazer. That was a no-brainer.

Pittsburgh's police department has six districts throughout the city with its headquarters in District 2 on Center Avenue, two blocks from the Monongahela River. Years ago, the then Public Safety Building was really a nonhostile takeover of the site of the old Baltimore and Ohio Railroad. The B&O was now on the history rubbish heap of rail companies long gone but whose rights of way are now part of the gigantic CSX system. The interview site where Duffy was to meet the McSheas is a modern brick building replete with everything a modern cop shop has to offer—big rooms, little rooms, a battalion array of desktop and portable computers, lots of commotion, and a couple of ad hoc detention cells.

The McSheas arrived at 0850; the Duffy show resurrected at 0855.

"I guess Sheriff Malone notified the FBI, and one of them will be here too. This Duffy's an okay guy but so predictable," said Kathleen. "Local cops all work from the same tedious script of investigation. They're addicted to it by training. I guess it works for them, but it's too constricted a management style for me." Together Duffy led them to a large room with an audience of multiple officers from the city, commonwealth and Federal agencies, eight badges in all. Kathleen was unimpressed. Ronk was mildly intimidated.

"Well, who gets first shot?" Kathleen said.

"I do," said Duffy.

"But first let me introduce your husband to Senior Agent Ralph Oliver of the local field office of the FBI," Duffy said. "He and his team will interview Mr. McShea, along with Detective Murphy from Homestead and Lt. Steve Royce of the Pennsylvania State Police, a city stenographer, and a sketch artist with a laptop computer down at Room 117. A second FBI team is going north to meet with Sheriff Malone." Ronk bailed on the names after Murphy. It was a crew that only confirmed his suspicion that a long, long morning was not only ahead but replete with redundant, hostile, and irrelevant questions.

"Why use a fire team," he quietly whispered to Kathleen, "when you could do the same with a squad or platoon? These guys have the vapor lock on overkill. This Greek guy must be high on their Valentine's Day Hit List."

After the perfunctory round of handshakes and name exchange, Ronk knew he'd just met at least eight people, all of whom were already etched in oblivion and only one who made any positive first impression: Detective Murphy. Duffy he knew about. Murphy was easy to remember, but Royce and the women just sort of blended into the background, museum tan of the surrounding room walls.

Duffy invited Kathleen to an adjoining room and left Ronk with the remainder of the investigators. The stenographer and the sketch artist trailed and began to set up their equipment. Kathleen duly noted the room was likely meant for VIP visitors. The six cherry, leather-cushioned chairs around the Kentucky oak table reeked of high-end leather. Cop royalty met here, not the derelict knuckle-heads arrested for any assorted panoply of crime. The corner coffee table also had its own very Keurig coffee machine with real china and saucers, unlike your tacky throwaway Styrofoam cups.

Before Duffy could offer, Kathleen raised her hand with a "No thank you" at the offer of more caffeine. She could tell that another bladder break was soon on the horizon and excused herself to excrete. That left Ronk and the remaining law dogs in a mutual staring contest. Ronk prevailed.

"But I will take bottled water, if you have it, just as she left."

The refrigerator below magically came to life at Duffy's manual behest, displaying three rows of Dansani and the remaining spectrum of Coca-Cola products. He extracted one each for the assembled four. Duffy politely took their opened bottle caps, dropped them in the attendant wastebasket, and sat down with his battered notebook, noting the date and time of interview with a backup tape recorder next to it.

When she returned, it began.

"Okay, did you get any kind of look at the two guys who offed the clerk?"

"No," she sighed, "they were both nondescript white guys with heavy brown jackets and watch caps. I never looked into their faces, as I had other things on my mind."

"Could you give me an idea of their height and weight, for example?"

"Well, they were both shorter than I am, and I'm six feet, so I'd guess between five-eight and five-ten."

"Did they have any distinguishing features, say, a limp, a prosthetic, scars, beards, moustaches, tattoos? If you remember, that would be helpful. Anything at all?"

"There was nothing else that I could see, no!"

"Did any of them speak?"

"Not to me, just the bitch in the bathroom. The three of them briefly conversed with one another, but I didn't hear it and ignored it."

"So you couldn't tell if they conversed in English?"

"The dead mama spoke with a heavy Northern European accent, Duffy, but they could have been speaking Aramaic and I wouldn't have known. What the hell! They were then not within my scope of acceptable life-forms until that estrogen weasel intruded upon my micturition break."

"Your what?"

"Forget it, you wouldn't understand!"

The ensuing pause incinerated under a thick cloud of sarcasm lasted all of ten seconds.

"Like to pee, Duffy, as in urinate, excrete! The noun is spelled differently. The verb is 'to micturate.'"

"Oh, okay! So I learned somethin' new today. Please, again, I'm just tryin' to work here, so kindly cut the overbearing, demeaning sarcasm."

"Okay! I relent and apologize."

"Did the blonde woman follow you into the head?"

"No, it was only after I was in the stall and until she called me out."

"When were you first aware of her or the other two perps?"

"The gunshots, Duffy! That was my very first hint, don't chya think? I mean something was obviously sideways, Detective. Remember, I wasn't exactly seated on the john at the fifty-yard line at Heinz field. I was seated with my panties down around my ankles. It's a pretty damn vulnerable position. That was my focus—the two shots! Not the two scumbags in the store."

"How long after you heard the gunshots did the woman appear at the door of the head?"

"About two minutes later."

"Is that when she called you out by name?"

"This is getting redundant, *mon frère*! We already went over this last night."

"Yes, my dear Irish rogue!" Sarcasm returned; Duffy could do it too. He then turned to the stenographer and the sketch artist.

"You likely be better used with Agent Oliver and Detective Murphy, so go to Room 117 and let me know when you're done there." The two women ever so quietly exited.

Duffy waited until the door closed to resume. "You never made visual or conversation contact with either of them until just before you shot blondie?"

"Third time around, Señor Duffy! Same answer. No! Maybe you ought to talk to the coroner's autopsy guys. They'll be interviewing her as we speak with scalpel and scissors and other sharp objects. She likely has more answers in death than I can provide in real life. Remember, one to the head and the second to the chest… right between her magnificent tits."

"So you noticed the size of her breasts?"

"It was a little difficult to miss. But she was much taller than Dolly Parton."

The late night and Kathleen's full frontal, blunt style left Duffy with little else to ask. No one apparently saw the dead woman's cohorts or their getaway vehicle. The light rain took care of that. Only the dead body held any remaining forensic evidence.

"Okay, Mrs. McShea—or do you prefer Miss?—I have no further questions right now. I thank you for coming in for the visit."

"Neither. I actually prefer Kathleen…or Mrs. O'Rourke-McShea, if you must. Since the average American spells at about a ninth-grade level, they usually concede and call me Kathleen."

"I heard your partner yesterday call you J-J. So is that a nickname?" she asked?

"Nah, it's just an abbreviation for Joseph John."

"Well, Duffy, that's as Catholic as St. Patrick's Cathedral on March 17, so Detective Joseph J. Duffy is about as green as you can drench in an Irish coffee. I notice you have no discernible Pittsburgh accent. Did you grow up here?"

"Yeah, but I guess I missed the vocal branding. It annoys the hell out of me. It's audible ignorance!"

"It still comes through occasionally," she said, "but you're not a true yinzer. But I have one last order of business—my Walther!"

"The lab processed the prints last night, and yours matched your weapon, so we will return it to you downstairs in the property room with minimal paperwork."

"And what about the dead bitch's Glock?"

"It matched her prints with her grip, so your story is absolutely true."

"Well, no screamin' shit, Joseph John Duffy, was there ever any doubt?"

"No, there wasn't, Kathleen, and I apologize if I so inferred last night. I was just following protocol."

"Well, your protocol lacks a certain modicum of common sense, but I accept your apology. It needs revised. You were just doing your job, and I was pushing the envelope of good taste. I do that a lot. Ronan has the patience sometimes of a Benedictine monk, and last night was very stressful. You don't expect to have dinner conversation with your spouse that begins with 'How was your day, honey?'"

"Aw, not bad, I just blew some dirtbag bitch away with a double tap…and now I have to clean the damn thing—my weapon, that is."

"You two are indeed an unusual couple."

"My line of work suggests that the Federal idiots with Ronk would not want to have me in the room with them for the interrogation. How long might this take?"

"Don't know but I will check in with them. Meantime, we have a more comfortable lobby down the hallway where you can wait. It's sometimes used by the department heavyweights and the chaplain to deliver bad news. But it beats the hell out of the main lobby replete with the lower quadrant of human life."

"I'll be in touch," he concluded. His frustration with her attitude only matched hers with his. Like chess, it was a draw. Game called on account of rain. Neither one gave an inch, and it wouldn't be their last sortie.

Then it was onward home to the crisis looming that would become a firefight.

I don't think we're quite ready for this, she thought, *but here it is.*

Chapter 15

RONK'S TURN

Agent Oliver led Ronk to the room without windows at the end of the hallway. It reeked of stale air that belied the fact that the building was a universal "no smoking" government venue. The in-your-face posted signs throughout were hard to miss, but compliance was apparently perfunctory.

This must be a voluntary policy. A bunch of folks here obviously ignore it. So much for strict policy enforcement! Someone in the health department should cite these guys, he thought. *I guess policy oversight is also optional.*

It just buttressed his contempt for any bureaucracy that seemed to get in its own way from Iraq to Upper Saint Clair.

Oliver repeated his own introduction with a pro forma of the same for the two junior agents with him, both of whom had laptops and seated themselves at a long table behind and to Oliver's left. One was a woman, the second a man, both of whom sparkled like all FBI rookies with the requisite business suits or blazers, not yet tailored—tactful but not tacky. The second woman was apparently a stenographer, appropriately dressed down in business parlance. Post introduction, Ronk had already forgotten their names. They had no nametags. So why care to remember? Between them, they couldn't have counted much more than sixty birthdays. They were obvious spanking-new Federal rookies, but you have to start somewhere in any venue. These two were at the bottom of the food chain and career ladder. The only way forward through the totem was up. They had at least twenty more years to retirement and the semi-largesse of a civil service pension.

Ronk chose to ignore them.

It was obvious that Oliver was the "big dog" and they were the "lapdogs," not to get off the porch and speak unless so ordered by Big Barker. He laid his briefcase on the table, pulled out a folder of some sort, cleared his throat, and began.

Thus spoketh the senior canine.

"So you allege you were kidnapped by these three guys who also killed the two would-be robbers at the GetGo in Homestead on Wharf Street yesterday?"

"There is nothing alleged about what happened," Ronk replied. "The two of them tried to rob the convenience store, and the big guy with the handgun blew away the two would-bes, as you describe them, with a very loud .44-cal something. There are two very dead fishermen down at the coroner's office on somebody's slab. That I know."

"How do you know it was a .44?"

"The only thing louder than that in a confined space is a one-niner-five artillery piece. So yeah, it was a .44. Trust my guess on that. The slugs you extract from both of the victims will so match."

"So you appear to be familiar with said weaponry?"

"I was an artillery battery commander in Helmund Province, Afghanistan, but you already know that, smart-ass, since you ran a background check on me and my wife and have my Corps OQR (Officer Qualification Record) in front of you. That's an inane question. So don't fawn on me with feigned ignorance. Get to the point. The Homestead Police Report is also in the file you're holding, along with the transcript of the conversation I had last night with the Butler County Sheriff. All the details are there. So why are we doing this again?"

"'Cause I's likes to hear the story myself," Oliver said, slipping into a mock urban vernacular, "just to check the elusive subtext of da events myself. Bore me again with the necessary and sometimes nebulous details. I'm's a detail junkie."

"Elusive subtext?" Ronk stammered. "There was nothing elusive about it, Agent Oliver. You jackin' me around, so excuse me if I'm a little impatient and more than mildly irritated."

What we have here, Ronan thought, *was another Federal knucklehead with an attitude. Do they pump these jagoffs out like $20 bills? Apparently! This guy is one classic piece of work.*

"We can begin with the beginning," Oliver said, "and don't omit any of the lurid minutiae. I like stories that bristle with the full amplified context. Consider it an FBI obsession that I share with other members of the fraternity and just be patient with my approach. Please tell us the story again."

Again Ronk thought, *What a vain, miserable jagoff! He really thinks he's the reincarnation of Elliot Ness.*

So Ronk went through the entire scenario again for what was now the third time. Oliver interrupted not once. It was like reading a script during a rehearsal walk-through. He seemed to already know the ingratiating details and asked no questions. This rehash was apparently just to see if Ronk was lying, misconstruing or deliberately editing any aspect of the original story. Forty-five minutes later, the interview abruptly terminated.

"That will be all. Thank you, Mr. McShea. We'll call you if we need further confirmation or clarification. But please stay for a while and work with Ms. Avery on the sketches of the kidnaping suspects."

"What's the real agenda here, Oliver?" Ronk shot back. "If you've been watching these guys for the better part of a decade, don't you already have their photographs? I just don't believe you. They ain't Goldilocks or the Three Bears but three very serious criminals."

Ronk's question apparently merited no response. There was none. Oliver was done and he expected Ronk to just comply without objection.

Further confirmation, Ronk thought, that dis guy is the prototype Federal anal aperture. This trip was a waste of time!

The chief agent and the stenographer then gathered their stuff and abruptly left. Oliver picked up his very antique Federal briefcase, frayed but functional. The junior varsity agents followed in lockstep. But thirty more minutes with Avery showed she was much more attuned to detail and ran through a logical list of questions to create real-life renditions of Greek's two henchmen. He was impressed with her approach. Tsakrios's face was very public and well known about town, so his identity was easy. It was the hired hands about whom Avery pressed Ronk for details. Her work was truly professional, and the end product caught Ronk pleasantly off guard with its accuracy. He was impressed. She was a model of precision and laser focus with questions. Seeing the pictures evolve on her computer laptop was almost eerie. Such quality work and attention to detail appealed to his engineering instincts.

The productive thirty minutes gestated a litany of questions for facial nuances. At the end, Avery created creepy, dynamic profiles of both Laudergast and Fudd, almost suitable for framing that were as accurate as a posed photograph.

He just sat there for a long minute, amazed, and then watched as she packed her gear very slowly and deliberately. The door had closed quietly after Oliver as Ronk remembered the JV team never said a word during the entire forty-five-minute episode. Only Avery asked for specifics of the suspects' descriptions.

What a two-act play, he thought. *Do they rehearse this script? Or is it really spontaneous?*

Then without comment, Avery again asked Ronk to confirm the newly minted faces on her screen. Ronk nodded affirmatively. They were sufficient renditions of the kidnappers to please and dazzle all concerned law enforcement. Very quietly she closed the computer, picked it up, and abruptly left him alone and with the same nonchalance as Oliver. It was just her job. Personal interaction was secondary.

The silence of the door latch returned the room to posted terminal quiet. Period, end of sentence! Ronk stood, did a 180-degree visual survey, and railed aloud.

"Well, so much for extended damn interrogation. Have a nice day, Avery. It's been a real treat, Oliver. But more treat than real. *Hasta la vista,* babies! So kiss my denuded Irish ass," he pondered aloud to the now vacant audience. "What the hell was all that about?"

"Except for the sketch artist, we could have mailed this stint to all a y'all over my cell phone."

It was just summa do on a Saturday morning. Since he wasn't sure where Kathleen was with Duffy, Ronk dialed up his favorite redhead. One ring sufficed. She was obviously and equally unhappy.

"We're still exhuming the details from this thing with Pittsburgh's finest. I'll meet you in the front lobby when we're done here. It should only be a couple more minutes."

Wrong she was on the timeline. The "couple a minutes" painfully dragged into another thirty until she appeared with Duffy in tow. Her facial expression said it all as she seemed to sneer at what she said was "the most ponderous, unnecessary process of the decade." If redundancy was the order of the day for the Pittsburgh Police, they had it stocked in triplicate.

Once is not enough. Redundancy is revered throughout the annals of criminal investigation.

"I couldn't tell if Duffy actually forgot last night with all the noise and chatter or posing to ask me out on a date. He floats between professional and flirting about everything from the incident to the weather and women's fashion. It must be some sort of conversation, cop diversion technique. I didn't think it made that much sense. He also took copious notes, but I don't think I added anything to the narrative. It was like we were talking in circles, like last night never happened. What about you?"

"Speaking of extraneous conversation, Oliver has the lock on it'," Ronk said.

His questions were drawn from a script with which I guess they berate every Federal witness or suspect. Then it ended almost as suddenly as it began. He just got up and left with nary a word or a goodbye. Not even a cordial "Au revoir" or "Thank you for coming in." He just suddenly closed his briefcase and hit the hatch. The rookies never said a word until Sketch Mama asked me to describe the Greek's sidekicks, particularly the bodyguard. They certainly all have a defined lack of social graces and seemed terminally bored with the requisite Federal script.

"The Homestead cops both seemed to have a keener sense for detail than Oliver," Ronk added. "They were the ones who focused on the shooter's name earlier with me that I thought sounded like 'Louder' something or other. Oliver just sort of blew past that tidbit. Murphy honed onto the accent as it suddenly dawned on me later that it was like the bad guy in one of the *Lethal Weapon* movies. Wasn't he supposedly a South African Afrikaner or something? That's how he sounded, but Oliver didn't seem to care. Murphy did and seemed much more attentive to the nuance of the accent. Maybe it's because local cops deal with more diverse local, ethnic populations. Oliver just seemed to be filling out a form, and I suspect he wasn't quite convinced it was a kidnapping. He was just puttin' in his shift time and seemed more anxious to salivate over the money in the envelope I gave to Malone. Maybe he wants to beat the Treasury and Secret Service to the punch. The whole scenario reeked of professional jealousy, but I presume we're now free to go home."

"Yeah, I think we've exhausted Duffy's limited spectrum of imagination," she said. "I'm less concerned about blowback from the parade of lower life-forms I met last night. The two with the blond honk don't concern me as much as the guys who kidnapped you. They have no fear about recognition and are obviously unafraid to exact reprisal. That's what we need to worry about. I'm sure my company H&K will show up in some future crime somewhere, but Securitas will require ten pages of explanation plus the police report about how their handgun is now in the wind. It's a damn good thing they like me. Lesser employees might be canned over such a transgression. They have a latent paranoia about lost weapons, sometimes even worse than cop shops. Lost weapons used in future crimes portend civil suits from victims either shot or injured by any loss of stolen or lost handguns that the company owns."

Kathleen's intuition would prove fatefully correct. Forget about the Triadelphia country amateurs. The well-dressed mobster was the one to fear. Cops and security pros like Kathleen did not like or trust reality that seemed to coincide. No cop anywhere believes in in the random occurrence of crime. What was the mathematical probability of random confrontations by a married couple at the same time on a Friday night…fifteen miles apart?

Two felonies with no seeming connection, yet now they were parcel of the same nightmare. Random intersections of vile are something cops don't believe. But the first order of business, Kathleen thought, was to address the threat level of the Triadelphia derelicts. Their innate ineptitude, however, was the seed of their own demise. Her fears dissipated later that day when they met Sheriff Malone that afternoon. Threat dissolved to comic relief.

"Let me tell you a tale," he said, "about which even my deputies doubled up laughin' their asses off when they heard about your two characters."

And so Malone began.

"Dumb is its own reward. Stupidity is the valedictory of the criminal class."

Chapter 16

FORTUNA REDUX

Exceeding expectations, the paperwork with retrieving Kathleen's Walther PPK was no big deal and, in fact, startled both of them with its pristine efficiency. Two forms, two signatures, driver's license, and her concealed carry got them away from the property clerk obviously fat-packin' it toward a civil service retirement. His nametag was F. Remminschneider, but his first name could have been Fatuous or Fatigue and almost didn't quite fit the nameplate. No wonder the evidence locker was in the cellar of the building. It was more like the banishment basement. Like most evidence lockers, it was drab and packed with bins in caged rows somewhat organized alphabetically back to 1936. What the mice and humidity hadn't destroyed remained mostly unattended for decades as the mildew and spiderwebs would attest. The reality was that cold cases that had no DNA may as well be a lost gnostic Gospel of the first century. Cases before 1990 with the active advent and use of DNA had limited detective curiosity. Prior to then, it was true: crime does pay. Old murders waned with time and rarely closed after the first year, so no cop with any testicles or pubic hair of any merit wanted to work there. It was a morgue without bodies presided over by one lone-badged cadaver masquerading as a live human being.

So it evolved to become the perfect place to park a nonperformer like Remminschneider. He made meter maids look like Popeye from the film *The French Connection*. Somehow the Pittsburgh Police

Public Relations Department would never have him as their spokesman...or spokesperson. Disaster would portend if they let him in front of a microphone.

So they didn't and he was banished.

"I guess this is where cops go to do a little purgatory time," said Ronk. "He seems totally disinterested in his job. He must have fubared with someone else in the chain of command. That place oozes misery. Out of sight, out of mind, I guess, and that's where they want him." (*Fubar* means 'fucked up beyond all recognition.')

But her mind was an hour north.

"Is your weapon in the Blazer?" she asked.

"Yeah, with two extra clips...just in case!"

"Okay, so it's off to see Randy Malone, and maybe that second virus of Feds Oliver promised to meet us. This is going to be a grand bleu weekend. I'm emotionally exhausted already, and this whole procedure just grates me. Ain't exactly a weekend to remember, just one I'd love to forget. But the nightmare has just begun."

The interviews had a predictable termination of conclusion before the lunch hour. After all, this was Saturday. The overtime apparently wasn't that highly prized by the sundry scions of law enforcement. Everyone in attendance seemed anxious to motor out to some other real appointment of consequence. So they hustled back to their Butler homestead, stopped at the northern front gate, and parked the Blazer just outside. Quietly they exited, no door slamming, and fell into combat mode using only hand signals as they broached the house roughly thirty yards apart from one another. Ronk slowly opened the north cattle gate. It squeaked, much more loudly than they wanted. No conversation, weapons drawn.

"Remind me to WD-40 this damn thing," he said.

"Consider yourself reminded," she replied.

Ronk moved to the east and just to the south of the secured kitchen door while Kathleen moved to its north. As quietly as possible, Kathleen isolated the three keys to the door and the two deadbolts vertically arranged above and below the knob. Starting with the lowest, she unlocked all three, although the seated retraction of the deadbolts sounded to her more like low-volume jackhammers. The grimace on her face punctuated it.

"Ready?" she whispered.

"As I'll ever be, Major!"

Ronk pushed the door open, but a loud clank interrupted as one of the metal dog dishes was in the way and banged its way across the floor.

Aw, shit," they both exhaled in unison.

"No dogs," Kathy said. "Bad sign! They should have heard us by now."

Into the interior they crept, casing it just as they both trained at Quantico, weapons swung laterally left to right and vertically up and down. Kitchen first, followed by the laundry room. They moved to the spacious dining room, same for the adjacent family room and office. Since they rebuilt the old farmhouse after sifting through a maze of Department of Interior regulations and mandates, they had to replace and widen the stairway to the second floor. No longer did the stairs creak. They were tighter than a frog's ass in the Mon. The master bedroom and Katie's room were impeccably neat. Just about everything else was in place. Not so those of their two sons. Seamus and Sean had bedroom bunkers that qualified as extension campuses of the Allegheny County Landfill. The persistent, sometimes incessant, parental harping had thus far little effect. Their pre-adolescent sons were deaf to their pleas.

"It's a cross we both have to carry," Kathleen once said to Ronk. "Maybe we'll rack up some points in heaven later for patience. God, were you that much of a slob when you were in high school?"

"No, my dear, I was supremely organized and inspection ready at all times."

That drew the obligatory stare of disbelief and sarcastic laughter.

"My dear, sometimes it seems you've dragged the blarney stone back from the old sod. You're so full of shit! Your eyes are earthen brown. Are you really going to go with that? I know you better than that."

Ronk's eyes were actually hazel.

"You doubt, my darling! Our sons must have taken after you. My sister had the habits of a homeless derelict, so females can be just as slovenly too."

Both their sons, however, did qualify as prepubescent slobs, and Sean would be the first to brag about it, even at the dinner table when the subject of cleaning up their rooms often came up for family discussion. He was quite proud of the fact that he could inventory and account for everything within his living quarter. He also knew it needled both of his parents incessantly, so he took some perverse delight in the eternal parental torture of bedroom chaos.

That precursed the parental compromise: Doors closed at all times and no locking out the adults. Seamus violated that directive two years before by locking his doorknob at one point with one of the extra door jammers Ronk purchased for nocturnal door security downstairs. He wanted privacy for his "reading time" and sex education interests. Wrong move on his part! All it did was tick off El Jefe and spur him to action.

Ronan had a mild paternal fit, just short of rampage. It was one of those enlightened times he did so without profanity or obscenity. He was actually more restrained with his children than Kathleen. When provoked, she would give them the full Monte of her temper. Dad was actually the softer touch. Both boys knew the drill and often played off one parent against the other, depending how glaring the affront or offense. They were not so different than most of their peers, just slightly more polished at treading volatile water.

After the aforementioned door jamming, both doors to the boys' rooms magically disappeared and spent the next month in the rafters of their large family barn that doubled as a garage. And there was no trolling the Internet in the family room, and their mandatory school laptops were safely secured every night in the gun safe.

Lesson learned the hard way. Wi-Fi to the bench!

Kathleen also regularly patrolled both rooms and, at one point, found a sampling of classic *Hustler* magazines ingeniously hidden behind Seamus's dresser. He apparently shared said booty literature with his eleven-year-old younger brother that introduced both of them to things they had not yet seen, like the wonders of female pubic hair.

"Do you think mom has some of that?" Sean once asked his older brother as they were fixated on an old copy of *Hustler*.

"Mom's classier than that. She shaves," Seamus replied. "So she only has a little bit."

"Well, how do you know? That's gross! How did you know that?"

"I saw her getting out of the shower a couple of months ago. I saw it all. It's red just like the hair on her head."

"Dad will kill you if he finds out."

"That's only if you tell him. And I'll kill you if you do. But I'll show you sometime if you keep your mouth shut."

"Better yet, I'll tell Mom it was you who peeked. It'll be your ass with the belt rather than the ping-pong paddle."

And Sean then ran out of the room.

Seamus didn't even bother to camouflage or hide his prurient interest. The "literature" laid in the open, even if it offended his mother. Lascivious interests were right there on top of his bed without pretense or shame. But Kathleen did presume certain proclivities of teenage boys. After all, she went through the crucible of high school prurient interests and knew all about adolescent male curiosity. It's a little different, however, after you've birthed your own. It wasn't theoretical anymore.

Now a mother, she was mildly conflicted about what to do next, the standard conundrum felt by every generation of parents. She opted to ignore the obvious lewd interests and consult Ronan.

"Should we make an issue about it?" she asked Ronk. "It isn't like they can't get at this stuff on the Internet or have some adult buy it for them at the local 7-Eleven, even with us on watch for it with the filters and screens on the Internet."

Later that issue became an incident forced upon her in a leering way.

"Not unless they graduate to something more perverse," Ronk responded. "They're great kids in every way that we know. Maybe we should just let it ride and be thankful that all they're into is naked female anatomy. I might sweat them if they had copies of *High Times* or do you remember *Blueboy*? Or even something more sinister on the Internet? There's some strange stuff out there, so let's just let it slide and monitor some of this rancid social media crap. That's at least one issue out of the way. But we better talk to them about it, or they'll find out elsewhere. If we harangue them about it, it will just drive them underground. After all, haven't we discussed nocturnal missions, masturbation, and all that relevant sex stuff? Do you notice seminal remnants in their pajamas or shorts in their dirty laundry? And Katie is not even yet at the menstruation stage yet, is she?"

"Yes, there are seminal remnants in your sons' pajamas and underwear. It's noticeable in their laundry, probably just like their dad, Ronk, but I'm not going to make any noise about it. After all, when we were in high school, I just presumed all you guys were into it, wanking away. And incidentally, so was I! I checked in with a lot of confession time over that. Penance once was a whole rosary. That was with Father McCabe. I never went back to him. He even lectured at me. It was just humiliating and embarrassing. Over masturbation? What a jerk. Grave moral disorder, my ass!

"As for menstruation, that's a little further down the road," she sighed. "I just like her to hear it from me and not from anyone in her Girl Scout troop or some twisted little wench at school. Girls that age can be nasty, particularly now with social media, so we have to be alert. I know when it first happened to me I was frightened, as my mother didn't tell me much in advance. Little girls should know all about that, I think, beginning about age seven or eight at the latest. I'll let you know when to start buying tampons. If I wasn't around, how would you handle it? A lot of single fathers have to do that. Doug Williams seems to have handled it well with his three daughters after the death of his wife, so you may also have to address it... not that I'm planning on checking out soon."

"We have enough on our plates right now, so let's change the subject. Now back to reality," Ronk said. "Just don't die on me. There's too much paperwork. Besides, that's why we have wills with all that there. And you know how I hate paperwork! But where are the dogs?"

After clearing the second floor, it was a return to the exterior and a quick sweep of the garage/barn. Still no dogs! They began to call. After five minutes, both came back with their tails wagging as if to say, "Welcome home, y'all. Where y'all been?" Jake had something in his mouth and he came to Ronk and dropped it at his feet with tail furiously wagging.

It was a small drone, not one that either of them had seen before, about the size of a model airplane. Still intact, it had what appeared to be a small camera in the plane's nose cone. It was a toy with sinister implications and application.

"What the hell is this about? This is a ten on the creep meter," he said aloud.

"Hey, Kat, go back inside and get some of those medical gloves in the laundry. We gotta take this to Malone. This doesn't smell well. Who the hell is spying on us? It must have some sort of pungent order or scent for Jake to pick it up. I'll throw it in the bed of the truck. You follow in the Blazer. This is weird!"

And off they shot to the sheriff's office.

But the spectrum of events was about to get weirder...and life-threatening!

Chapter 17

THE WARRANT

Oliver's abrupt exit from the Pittsburgh Police HQ had little connection to bad manners or anything dubious about the purported crime. He was already on his cell phone with his staff followed by a quick digression to call Agents Amanda Vedros and Alicia Menendez-Garcia on their way to Butler.

"Call in all staff immediately for a meeting at 1500. That means even the janitors. This is all hands on deck. I don't anticipate any problem with the warrant, but we need to make a smooth, sudden entry to preserve any evidence the Greek may try to destroy. Get a full complement of agents so there's no chance of him moving or destroying any relevant documents. Anticipate having to quell any resistance from the wife and daughters, so make sure we have at least two of our female agents there to body search the wife and kids. I don't want any hint of inappropriate or sexual harassment complaint from that notorious gang of lawyers on Greek's payroll. Anything that even smells like inappropriate must be quashed."

"Sure thing, Chief, I'm on it," came the terse reply from Agent Bill Brody, Oliver's, the de facto third in command.

"Roger that!" came the affirmation. "And, Bill, I'll need the requisite signatures by 1700 so we can execute the warrant around dusk so we'll know they're home."

"Boy, I'd like to be a witness to that shit storm," said one of the agents on the conversation periphery. "Judge Mulvehill losing his cool to ask for a pen to sign a warrant during his Saturday golf game at Oakmont. For a raid on Sunday? That would be a hoot! Maybe we can catch that one on somebody's cell phone. I'd pay money for that image. It might make YouTube's top ten of the week! Maybe this isn't such good timing for warrant execution."

But Oliver was still on the phone and ignored the professionally offensive comment with earshot. He and the JVs pulled out of the police visitor's lot and veered back across town to the regional field office at the 3300 block of East Carson Street. It was almost midway between the robberies of the Stop-N-Go and the GetGo. Transit time from there to both sites: fewer than twenty minutes from HQ to either destination with lights blazing. It was almost part of the patina in a neighborhood crime spree. But Oliver wanted the Greek's scalp badly. That took immediate priority. The connection to both robberies would meld later.

"This guy Tsakrios has been a Teflon Don for more than thirty years," Oliver said to the two junior agents in his ad hoc audience. He wasn't even sure he remembered their names. They both graduated from the Quantico FBI Academy less than a month before. They were so new to the Pittsburgh field office that Oliver had yet to give them the one-on-one welcome interview, "This is how it goes down with the boss." He only knew them by nametag. The ink on their orders to report was still fresh and laying on his prized cherry office desk. Their job now was to speak only when told to do so. Now it was time to listen.

"He's so old-fashioned he's slicker than a cat shittin' on tin roof. We've been trackin' him for years, but the locals have only hung a couple of misdemeanor beefs around his neck, never a major felony. He puts none of his records on his home computer, scatters his money around in a variety of accounts and at least three overseas of which we know. So how does he communicate with his criminal clients and never get intercepted? Wanna know what the chief thinks?"

Blank stares followed from the JVs, the FNGs as Oliver once called them. It was a hangover from his Army time as an eighteen-year-old in Vietnam in 1970 to 1971 as the war wound down. *FNGs* was a slang, derogatory term for new arrivals who didn't know their ass from their elbows. They were the fuckin' new guys with no experience and enough naiveté, aka stupidity, to get someone else killed by their own ignorance and poor attention to detail. "Yeah," said both of the rookie agents with no name in unison. "Boss man, speak!"

"How about using the US Postal Service? Just write a letter."

"Yeah? Really?" one of them said. Oliver still didn't remember his name, so he continued to bore onward with his exegesis.

"We don't know to whom he writes and can't even intercept them before they arrive. Imagine some Federal judge wailing on the poor Fed prosecutor two days out of law school, just trying to make a living, posing the argument that stealing private mail between two private citizens is really appropriate due process. His or her ass would get scorched and crucified on the cross of at least four Amendments—one, four, five, and six."

"Right, we have to get hold of his mailing list."

"I don't know, Chief, that's riding the rim of 'fruit of the poisoned tree.' Club Fed, Long Beach, would be making reservations for us instead of him. I'd prefer that instead of Gitmo."

"Just a thought! But we're here and let's gather the assembled multitude with ideas better than mine."

Ninety minutes later, most of Oliver's FBI ad hoc task force Pittsburgh crew of twenty-eight was seated and attentive. Small talk "twited" and tweeted to a minimum, the sudden call to orders left most of them in "civies' without the mandatory suit and tie. The exclusions were two women agents just back from maternity leave and a third from his honeymoon in Tahiti. Most of the remaining wore "warrant service clothing" replete with body armor and the identifying outer jackets with the FBI logo. All had their backup ankle weapons. Agent Al Gormley even went so far as to have a double backup, ankle, and small of the back. He strapped his .40-cal to his right side. Gormley was a throwback to the '70s where some agents' eccentricities were just quietly overlooked.

He was left-handed and had a Heckler & Koch in the small of his back and a tidy little .38 on his right ankle. Over his thirty-five years as an agent, he perfected an ambidextrous shooting style, along with a raucous attitude. "You can never have," he once said publicly, "too much ammunition or too much pussy!"

Although the public comment was mostly ignored in front of a team of his assembled peers, the crack earned him a written reprimand and a three-day suspension for unprofessional conduct. His then partner, Janice Sobrinski, asked Oliver to keep her paired with him as she admired both his unconventional attitude and his uncanny ability to shoot well. It also helped that she was a committed but quiet lesbian, a pairing not quite made in heaven but worked well together. They just like to order off the same menu, and she just didn't give a damn about his sometimes crass, unsolicited comments. He just seemed to revel in vulgarity as part of his core personality. As long as he could keep her and other agents on task and kill bad guys proficiently, she wanted Al as a lifetime partner.

The PowerPoint presentation in the office theater began exactly at 1501. Slides and pictures of Tsakrios, his life history, his compendium of crimes, were ready to surmise. They had an entire book on him that began more than forty years before.

Agent Oliver began with the perfunctory biography that lasted almost twelve minutes. "Tsakrios's enterprises are semi-legendary around here," he began. "For those of you new to the Pittsburgh field office, he has been into gambling, money laundering, and extortion for years. He was even into prostitution as a kid. If it involves money, his fingers are on it. But he's never graduated to physical violence or a palpable felony. Everybody in the DA's office knows the Greek. He's an eel to prosecutors. He just slips away. They've charged him with everything from racketeering to jaywalking but take notice that he's living in Fox Chapel.

"Years ago, retired head Steeler Coach Bill Cowher used to be a neighbor. He acts like the model citizen, goes to church, attends the parish bingo night, and pays his taxes religiously, at least those the IRS can track. But this is, I think, his first big fuck-up, so execute this warrant carefully. Accrue and catalogue all relevant evidence by the book. That includes any and all letters, even ones to Santa Claus, Mrs. Claus, the Easter Bunny, or Bugs Bunny. Remember, he allegedly kidnapped a Federal employee with two of his employed dirtbags who took out a couple of would-be robbers in Homestead.

"He didn't get to be near seventy with no joint time by being completely stupid.

He's polished and cunning with a battery of attorneys on payroll. The attorneys may even beat us to the courthouse. So don't let anyone blow this by being inappropriate or overly aggressive. I want this to stick. Let me or Agent McPherson do all the interrogation and make sure you segregate the wife and kids from him."

Then the phone rang. Oliver put the call on speaker.

"This is Agent Dana, Chief. Judge Mulvehill is in the steam room of the Oakmont Country Club with Judges Weiss and Ring. Do you want me to barge in?"

"Forget what I said before. I'd luv to have you do that, but it would tick off Mulvehill. He's cranky enough normally, and we'll need him again. Anyhow, make sure he's away from Weiss when you flash the warrant. Weiss is a *nebbish* with an ACLU pedigree. I don't need him running interference. Get Mulvehill alone. Okay? As soon as he signs it, get your ass back here by 1830. If you can't make it back here by then, meet us at the residence. We'll execute the warrant at exactly 2100."

The next item of business was the Google map of the Tsakrios property.

Agent Christopher Doherty came forward to present the plan of execution.

"Here's the aerial of the house. It's two stories with a basement and attached three-car garage. There are three doors on the first floor, one exit in the front from the basement, and one off the southern deck to the second-floor hallway. We'll have a drone circling overhead to alert us to anything above our heads. Agent Toby Miller is here and checked out on the drone. He'll be behind one of the approach vehicles on the net and will only intervene if he spots an immediate threat to us as we approach. His code name is Dragonfly, so if you hear 'Team, this is Dragonfly,' do not blow him off. What he transmits may save your life.

"There are also two decks on the opposite ends of the house, but each has no exit. The two decks have no stairs to the ground. They are not part of the original floor plan, and I don't know how Tsakrios got his occupancy permit when he built them. Maybe we can ask the county to tack on a fire code violation, but that will have to wait until after Monday. Plus they have two large Dobermanns that I presume are not stranger friendly, so I've enlisted the K-9 unit from the state police Troop D post in Butler to assist. Their dog, Wrangler, will be there with us, along with at least one of their search and rescue dogs.

"Please do not shoot the dogs, either his or the state trooper's. We don't need dead canines to muddle this raid. I get enough nasty letters from the governor's office and PETA. Don't need any more on the pile. When you hit the house, go first for his office on the west end of the first floor where we believe he has both a gun safe and a wall safe. The search warrant covers both of them."

Oliver's loud, booming voice then punctuated the end of the brief. "Saddle up!"

Out in the adjacent parking lot, door slamming and the racking of shotguns opened the symphony of clatter. Plan enunciated, the platoon of twenty-eight crossed the rivers with lights and attitude. Raids like this with overpowering firepower seldom got anyone killed. None of them wanted the mountain of paperwork even remotely associated with the death of a suspect or agent.

Oliver was one of the agents at the Waco disaster years before when Janet Reno was attorney general. He was eminently aware of the possibility of disaster and didn't want to see his own career end in an inglorious blaze of ignominy. So the convoy began the short pilgrimage at what would prove to be a long, exasperating night with garbage bags full of stuff with alleged evidence.

The noise of the predawn intrusion included the two screaming daughters and wife, barking dogs, and an angry Tsakrios. The bag collections continued unabated for almost six hours. They scooped up everything but the Dobermanns' tootsie rolls.

But the aggregate collection of stuff the raid alleged to be evidence would not sway Judge Mulvihill. Au contraire, it just ticked him off. The collection was insufficiently arrayed to convince the already irritated jurist. He hated interruption of his Saturday golf games, even by family, so the Oliver raid offended him grievously despite the fact he signed the original warrant. It was ego versus ego.

Oliver's ego went down in flames.

So Monday morning, it would also put Tarkios back on the street in fewer than thirty minutes. Mulvihill's Irish temper would prevail with a smackdown and dress down of the Federal prosecutor. All for naught? Maybe naught, but it frustrated the FBI. Frustration seeped from the bench to the courthouse doors. No one would walk away happy…except the Greek and his phalanx of attorneys.

Chapter 18

COMIC RELIEF

The twenty minutes from their farmhouse to Malone's office wound erratically through Saw Mill Run. Today it had none of the of the usual weekday afternoon traffic. Greater Pittsburgh was not yet Southern California, so Fridays were still a traffic respite in Butler County.

That, however, threatened to change in future years as the rush to develop north of Pittsburgh became the rage.

As Kathleen drove the Blazer, Ronan took the truck with the strange model airplane that just screamed of danger. He first called his parents and then hers, rebriefed them on the situation, and asked them to scoop up the kids at Cecilia's. Kathleen's parents got on it immediately. That was one problem postponed and one threat alleviated. Now they wanted to address the more ominous one: the kidnappers and the apparent connection to the little drone on the property. Welcome to 2019 and the bizarre world of technology. It was a "What the hell is that?" moment!

Malone seemed happy to see them. He savored their friendship and trusted their instincts and treated them like they were all in the same line of work.

"Good afternoon, McSheas. Welcome back to my humble work abode and do I have a tale for you," Malone said even before he offered coffee.

"We've got one for you too," Kathleen said. "And Ronk has a magnificent toy in his truck, but I digress. You first!"

"I think your Pittsburgh brethren *caffeined* us out when we were there," Ronk followed.

Ronk broke the silence as Malone poured two more cups.

"You have a jovial grin, Randy, so this has got to be good."

Kathleen accepted the "bad cop, shop coffee" offer more out of deference to Malone's hospitality. She, too, was up to her esophagus in hype and caffeine. Thus she offered only perfunctory sips on what purported to be hot coffee. It wasn't high grade, but she pretended to drink some, leaving her low-gloss peach lip balm on the rim. Lipstick on Styrofoam always wards off male cup poachers. Maybe Ronk would drink from it, as he enjoyed the taste of any residue of her body. To others, a lipstick cup was the ring of caution: "Do not touch; female poison within."

"Please be seated. This parable will warm even the coldest depths of your hardened Irish hearts," Malone began with the dripping sarcasm at which cops are so adept. "And I think it will solicit a laugh or two."

Okay," Ronk continued, "I'm up for a laugh, considering the last seventy-two hours. So far, the weekend has been less than stellar. We need a break. Drone onward, Sir Galahad, Knight of the Realm of Butler!"

"Well, it seems Kathleen's half of the weekend trauma is essentially dead. The threat there is gone. Here's the almost hysterical background," Malone began, suppressing a smile, "that put every deputy here into the laugh mode. It confirms the law enforcement bias that some criminals are complete and utter morons. I mean dumber than a Punxsutawney Phil. My tale picks up on the border of the Commonwealth of Pennsylvania and the breakaway colony of West Virginia near the forgettable town of West Alexander.

"It seems the two dimwits whose partner Kathleen killed had the misfortune of a highway encounter that would effectively terminate their sordid, criminal careers. They made penultimate mistake of picking on the wrong victims just south of the commonwealth line on Interstate 40. There was a disabled car on the shoulder of I-40 just as you cross southwest into the Middle Wheeling Creek valley below within the West Virginia Panhandle. As bad luck and pure fate would have it, the two women standing by it were waiting for an AAA rescue truck. Don't know what was wrong with it. It doesn't matter at this point, but the two women were cops!"

Then he paused for silent effect.

"Why is that interesting?" Malone grinned and waited.

"Okay," Kathleen said. "I'll bite. What's the punch line, Randy?"

"What they didn't realize was that Emma James and Rosalie Parks were both cops, both armed and on their way to Olgebay Park near Wheeling for an excursion that included sharing the bed linen."

"And you know this how?" Kathleen asked. "And why is it germane?"

"I know Emma personally and have worked with her on numerous search and rescue operations, particularly during deer season when there is no dearth of dumb asses who think they're Jeremiah Johnson and either accidentally shoot themselves or one another. Sometimes they suffer from hypothermia because they dress like it's still Labor Day. But most of the time, they or hikers just get lost. You know, doing the abjectly stupid stuff! Emma is a twenty-year sergeant with the DuBois PD with the search team that features two trained German Shepherds. She's really good at this, particularly the tracking, a vaunted commodity for them with the number of cases they always have during the fall and winter. She has a couple of teenage boys from a prior marriage but is politely open about her adopted lifestyle. She switched teams sometime after she hit forty. She's a stellar cop, and her ex seemed like a complete prototype dolt. I met the guy twice and I think he's a truck driver with a gear box that constantly shifts into low. But his third gear doesn't shift upward. I don't know what she saw in him in the first place first, but she truly is good with their two boys. They're both on their way to become Eagle Scouts. So high kudos to Emma! Rosalie, however, is a junior patrol officer at Grove City, and I think she just went through a nasty divorce, probably because of the connection to Emma. But she's still in the closet."

"Why is it, Randy, that cops are such gossip magnets? I mean, who cares?" Kathleen said. "I'm just glad she's an adequate shot. Range qualification trumps everything else for me. What happened next with the dirtbags?"

"So to continue," he said, "when our metastasized 'duogonites' of virtue approached the two, Emma was on her cell phone, presumably with the tow truck on the way. Rosalie saw one of the two approaching with a weapon poised to fire. So she immediately drew down on him and dropped him, although sadly he'll survive. Too bad he just didn't die at the scene and leave the Ohio County coroner to deal with it. He has a bad left shoulder wound, but here's some further good news. He is now a guest at the Ohio County Jail."

"*Duogonites*? Did you just coin a new word, Randy?" Ronk asked.

"He just did," Kathleen said, but Malone ignored the tease.

"We are waiting here with bated breath!" Kathleen followed. "What else?"

"The West Virginia State Police have your Securitas weapon and they already know it's yours, so that's not a problem, but you will have to retrieve it in person, and that will require a trip to their barracks near Wheeling where it's in their evidence locker. Mrs. Dodd has the phone number for you. They'll also want you to identify the two for a quickie extradition to Pennsylvania. We cops are always ready to send another jurisdiction's bag of shit back to where it belongs. They so reciprocate for us. It's sort of a police slimeball reciprocity."

"Well, I obviously needed the weapon since it's a company issue, but my employment visibility requires some anonymity here, and I'll do a line-up thing. I prefer, however, just to identify them by photo," Kathleen said. "Testifying at trial is obviously a different discussion, but until this threat to Ronk dissipates, I prefer my face gets no public attention for our collective family safety. When is the arraignment date for Tsakrios? If he's bent on vengeance and taking Ronk out, it will be soon. I'd like to move the kids out of the way, so kindly work with me on this."

"And then there's this matter of the annoying little shit reporter from the Butler Eagle, Seth Moran."

"Well, he'd better eat his Wheaties," Ronk intercepted, "because if Jake perceives a menace or threat to the property, he should think twice about trespass. The dog will only charge on trained commands, and they are in Flemish, so 'Here, boy' or 'Good dog' from a stranger might arouse more than pacify him, even if he's smart enough to pack a bag of doggie treats like leftover bacon. The reporter better call first. Otherwise, we may have a situation, particularly if he climbs over the northern front gate. Jake thinks it's a military boundary like those compound gates he guarded in Afghanistan. He recognizes only the motor hum of our vehicles and those of the Alverez clan. Maybe we should alert the editor and owner of the Eagle not to send that punk Moran on a snoop mission. We don't need any further legal hassles. We're up to our ass already.

"But Jake's not the biggest threat," he continued. "It's Kathleen. I know from witnessing an old school dance at North Catholic. She can crunch a guy's gonads into cottage cheese in an accelerated heartbeat. He'd best call first before showing up. Kathleen does not like surprises."

"My dearest Ronk, husband, lover, and father of my children! Remind me never to hire you at Securitas as my public affairs officer. You have no sense of public relations. I am not that violent. You do have a penchant for hyperbole. I only crush gonads now attached to scumbag criminals."

"Oh yeah, Kathleen, it's a point well taken," Malone said. "I'm fully aware of your range of skills and I'll address it with Harper Gough, the publisher and senior editor. But you know he's going to insist on access to both of you, so I'll slow-walk our response. This is a story with a local angle so they won't relent. The local slant is their circulation draw that gooses the wild lead above the fold."

"Yeah, rah-rah First Amendment," Kathleen clamored into the exchange, "except when it threatens real lives and property. Make it plainly clear to Gough that it's not the dog he should sweat, it's me. I can slap that pusillanimous prick Moran into the middle of next month and never leave a mark. We don't need the aggravation. This is a serious threat, and local press hounds had best not put my family in danger."

"Okay, Kathleen, don't go all commando on me," Malone joked. "There's no need for demonstration of your black belt proficiency. I love you, Kathleen, but please don't bitch-slap this little *smecle*."

Then he paused.

"Except when there's a need for violence…appropriately applied!"

He said this with a wry smile, knowing full well that Kathleen was maybe one of three women in Butler County who could back any play about which she bragged. Her black belt was not a joke. It was the same with the company for whom she worked. But she was very much the disciplined, calm, meticulous mother of three—that is, until provoked. Note the example of the animal world. When mama cat is lying in the sun, watching her cubs play, life is good. Threaten her kids with something like hyenas and the abstract turns real. Malone just wasn't sure how far she was willing to stretch the bounds of law and good taste, and he sincerely didn't want to find out. As much as he liked her, he recognized the aura of danger surrounding her was not a myth or legend. In some states, her hands could classify as deadly weapons. She and Ronk were both Marine to the core, she almost more than he, and not averse to quelling violence with extreme counterviolence. It's just the way they're trained, and they are not the Boy Scouts or Girl Scouts going to a jamboree at Valley Forge.

"Please don't do anything for which I'll be forced to arrest either one of you. That is not something I yearn to do. So please? I realize you'll only likely call until after we need the coroner, so kindly give me a break."

"Awe, we wouldn't do that to you, Randy," she teased. "We want you to wade into retirement blissfully, not in a wheelchair. We're just your friendly country, backwater, neighborhood watch couple proficient with small arms."

Then she paused for effect with her eternal admonition…and sighed!

"The unwritten sign on the front gate should say, 'Enter at your own risk! The dogs bite and so do we.'"

Malone swallowed hard and grinned. "Kathleen, can't you just tone it down just a little?" But Malone also knew not to pull the pin on that grenade. It just might blow off half your face. Like his deputies, the McSheas were the real deal. Both of them were combustible and sometimes unpredictable to strangers. As much as he liked the two of them, he never forgot who they were.

And he had to remind himself incessantly that they were the friendlies, not the enemy.

That would manifest before the conclusion of the spring solstice. Her later range qualification on their homestead would confirm what Sheriff Randy Malone already knew.

They countenanced no unwarranted home intrusion. And the Butler County coroner and his staff graduate students would soon entertain three formerly healthy adult bodies on his autopsy tables for his neophyte interns.

The three guest cadavers would succumb to gunshot wounds, the third from multiple body traumas to the head and neck yet to be determined.

But his face was badly mangled. Identification would have to be by fingerprints or DNA.

"Oh, I almost forgot," Ronk said. "The dogs found this drone on our property. It's in my truck. What do you want me to do with it? I'd just as soon give it to you."

"And I'm going to give it to our two rookie FBI agents on their way here to visit us all here in backwoods Butler. They love to play in the DNA pool, so stick around and we'll all get acquainted."

Chapter 19

BAIL CALL

Federal Courts open promptly for the public at 7:30 a.m Monday through Friday, excluding Federal holidays. But if you arrive early, you might miss anyone on Uncle Sam's payroll but Federal agents and marshals. It's essentially an early coffee break until sometime around eight fifteen. Civil servants move at a snail's pace. It's as precise as a four-step diaper change. Movement is lava flow. They define their work pace as deliberate, although the general public grades it more like pure sloth.

What you won't see in the early morning are the absent black robes of most judges who saunter into court about 10:00 a.m. If they are meticulous, they must wade through a mound of paperwork before they even doff their judicial robes. What you will see are just all the ancillary staff, sometimes pretending to move piles of files from table to table to create the impression of movement. Like theater, it's performance art. Very *kabuki*!

Judge Mulvihill was less than happy that Monday morning, anyway, when he read and examined the array of less than stellar evidence gestated by the warrant he'd signed after the interruption of his Saturday golf game. Oliver was in the gallery as well as Stephen Weinstein, the rookie Federal prosecutor who presented the case for indictment. It was a quick précis of fewer than five minutes.

Mulvihill was neither amused nor impressed. He'd already read it and had perused the mountain of purported evidence for almost forty-five minutes.

"Mr. Weinstein, I granted your office and Agent Oliver enough leeway to garner evidence of at least five multiple felonies, and this is all you gleaned from the search of the Tsakrios' house? I've just spent most of the early morning wading through this inventory of drivel, and this is all you found?"

"The government believes with this inventory that there is enough evidence presented to hold Mr. Tsakrios without bail, Your Honor, particularly his bank records."

"Is the alleged kidnapping victim free?"

"Yes, Your Honor, he is at his home near Butler."

"So the alleged victim was released and came home with a purported $10,000 in what the government claims is hush money? Is that correct, Mr. Weinstein?"

"Yes, Your Honor."

"And you further note that Mr. McShea turned those monies over to the Butler County Sheriff. Is that also correct?"

"Yes, Your Honor, but Mr. McShea was abducted without his consent at gunpoint. He did not go with Mr. Tsakrios voluntarily."

Tsakrios sat at the table to Weinstein's right with his phalanx of four attorneys and just stared ahead. He and they were all decked out in the standard $1,200 Brooks Brothers' shark-skin suits led by a lead attorney Randy Shankle of Jessep, Overfelt, Franklin, and Jay, LLC.

Big-time firm, big-time clients—most of whom were on the leeward side of the law. One of their most notorious clients was even what they flippantly called a post office special in the early 1990s with a roster slot on the FBI's Most Wanted list. Tsakrios wasn't quite there yet because he obviously hid in plain sight and had no penchant for overt violence.

Shankle was ready to pounce, but Mulvihill persisted. He often prattled onward incessantly, especially when he was under the influence of prosecution incompetence. This morning, it was a droning marathon supplemented by supreme impatience.

"I'm going through your compilation here, Mr. Weinstein, and the evidence of RICO racketeering is measly and weak. That concerns me. Also, did Mr. Oliver's team also arrest the purported coconspirators of the kidnapping and assault cited in the warrant? Where are they?"

"No, sir, Your Honor, they are still at large with arrest warrants outstanding on both."

"Okay, so given the aggregate stock of evidence, particularly from the robbery in Homestead where the clerk seems unable to identify anyone but Mr. Rogers and the Kardashians, what do we have here? Given Mr. Tsakrios's stature in the community, what does the government recommend?"

"We recommend no bail, Your Honor, and that the court bind Mr. Tsakrios over for trial."

"Mr. Shankle, your turn."

"Thank you, Your Honor. Defense counsel believes that this inventory of defamatory charges does not support pretrial confinement. They are inconsistent with an accused with a stellar reputation in the community and no prior felony arrest record. He deserves release on his own recognizance. Mr. Tsakrios's high public profile poses no flight risk, and he is anxious to appear in court to fight these scurrilous charges. Besides, the address on the warrant was wrong. They targeted the wrong house."

Weinstein jumped back into the fray.

"May I remind the court that the primary charges include kidnapping and assault with a deadly weapon. It was the right address, Your Honor. It was, in fact, Mr. Tsakrios's home. The clerical error is peripheral. We recommend no bail for Mr. Tsakrios, along with pretrial confinement, and the same for the eventual arrest of his accomplices."

"And no, Mr. Weinstein, you may not remind the court. And the citation of the wrong address is not peripheral, just in case you forgot that in law school. Precision is essential to any warrant. Unreasonable search and seizure is still core to the Bill of Rights. Do you remember that part of due process, or did that slip into your lost curriculum file?

"This is a tenuous case at best, poorly written. Did you assign the brief on this warrant to your interns? Both you and I went to the same Duquesne law school some twenty-five years apart, but I believe we both took the same bar exam. So please don't patronize the court. This compilation of evidence is paltry and weak. It is, in part, as my grandfather O'Neil would say, replete with blarney."

Mulvihill had the theatrical Irish penchant for sarcasm, and he was laying it on thickly.

Down came the gavel.

"I'll grant bail at $2.4 million! And, Mr. Tsakrios, don't even think about leaving Pennsylvania. This is the primary condition of your bail. Go to church, make medical appointments, but remain hunkered in your home in Fox Chapel. Do you understand? Otherwise, I will revoke it."

Tsakrios smiled and humbly replied, "Yes, sir, Your Honor."

The whole drama lasted a mere seven minutes.

"Thank you, Your Honor," Shankle said and turned to confer with his colleagues and defendant. Oliver stormed out of the court gallery in semi-disgust, followed by Weinstein. The ensuing hallway conversation was testy to the extreme. The gavel may just as well have slapped Weinstein across the face. Both he and Oliver had just sustained a groin kick from a judge normally friendly to the office of the Federal prosecutor.

"What the hell was missing from that?" Oliver demanded. "Shit, we have his guy dead to rights on kidnapping and assault, even if the rest of it was window dressing."

"Well, you want to know the real reason?" Weinstein shot back. "Maybe if your guys had waited until today to ask for the damn warrant and not rousted Judge Mulvihill from his goddamn golf game Saturday, we might have had a better outcome. Mulvihill's court calendar percolates with pending felony cases, especially some of this crap with a local ISIS cell. So you managed to irritate and shave the remaining Irish off his receding hairline. Way to go! It's never a good idea to push the hostility envelope during a Federal judge's off-duty hours. Where the hell did you guys learn this warrant technique? And did you have to manhandle his wife? Couldn't this all have waited until today? This case is now in peril because of the timing of the execution of the warrant."

"There were exigent circumstances."

"And what might those be, Agent Oliver? This victim, what's his name…McShea…came to you on Saturday morning. Didn't Tsakrios allegedly tell him to keep his mouth shut, and didn't McShea give up the purported hush month to the Butler County Sheriff? That's exigent? A little patience and a better search might have convinced Mulvihill not to grant bail. I mean Tsakrios is a rich son of a bitch, and he'll make bail in cash or property deeds to the court by the close of business today. Sometimes you FBI guys run where walking would suffice. Get those goons that the Greek allegedly brought with him, so maybe we can get his bail revoked. Otherwise, we have to live with it. Get off my ass and go do your job."

"Okay, Stephen, we have a problem."

"No screamin' shit,' my friend. We can probably nail him on the kidnap and assault charges, but you better dig on the racketeering. You know the drill. Yeah, Tsakrios is a known criminal quantity, but a jury needs supportive facts, not arithmetic suppositions. Juries are rarely populated with intellectual elites with an Ivy League pedigree. Their eyes will bleed into nap with this array of evidence."

"That's your job, goddamn it," Oliver groused. "Don't put that on my agents. I thought Federal attorneys had all passed the bar. What the hell do you have on your staff, law school interns from K-Mart?"

Weinstein pivoted and walked away. "No," he said as he stormed away, livid at the insinuation that his staff was inept at the insinuation of incompetence. The senior FBI agent of the Pittsburgh Field Office had just ruined the rest of his day.

But paybacks are a beach on which sometimes you're forced to lie on, depending on your undergraduate obsession with English.

What Weinstein really wanted was to welcome Oliver to the New York minute. It was on the tip of his tongue, but he showed remarkable restraint. He swallowed the F-bomb.

So he didn't unload on Oliver. He just fumed and ignored the obvious insult. "Later," Weinstein said. Conversation terminated.

Still enraged, Oliver went for the only remaining weapon in his holster: the .40-caliber cell phone. He dialed his office and began braying to one of his junior staffers. It was a one-way monologue. Now it was the young agent's turn to shut up and listen to the bevy of instructions spit out at mach speed.

"Rework everything we have on Tsakrios, from his juvenile record to parking tickets. Talk to his tailor. I want to know if he dresses left or right. Contact Welch over at the IRS. Then ring the bell on his CPA. Recheck all his business licenses he's acquired over the years. Then see if we can crack his Swiss accounts. Certainly our computer geeks in DC can do that. Got it?"

"Yes, sir," came the tepid reply from somewhere in the bowels of the Carson Street FBI.

At the other end of the court hallway, the mood was much more avuncular with Tsakrios and his legal staff.

"Okay, George," Shankle began. "This is one of the most restrictive bails I've ever seen with caveats longer than a John Holmes erection. So you need to go to the court clerk now and outline every dime of the bail money or the property secured before the close of business today. Understand? And can you cover the bail?"

"Yes, I've just called my CPA, Capelli, and he'll be here within the hour with the requisite docs."

"Very well," Shankle said. "Don't exit the building without me until we've assured the court that you've met the bail requirements and you've signed the stipulations. And pay particular attention to the stringent travel restrictions. Mulvihill's order said to not leave Pennsylvania. What he implicitly said but will be very explicit in the bail order and remains paramount is not to leave Allegheny County nor visit any place that reeks of obvious temptation, like the Rivers Casino. You do know that the FBI will be tailing your ass from the grocery store to the bank, church, library, and any public restroom you enter. Don't try to evade them when you drive around because they will cover your ass like bad deodorant. Your Mercedes phone may even be bugged. Use your cell phone and be very cryptic. Mulvihill gave the prosecution thirty days, and that's very generous, to refile the formal charges with the Federal grand jury. This particular seated jury is only there for three more months. They're all anxious to go home. So they're motivated to return an indictment faster than you can turn out the lights at PNC Park after a seventeen-inning night game. We're fortunate he just didn't go directly to a preliminary hearing and assign it to a different judge. Mulvihill doesn't really want this case, but there is a host of others on this bench here in Federal District (court) who would salivate to stake your ass to the courtroom wall and make you a ward of the Federal correction system. You've managed to harvest a lot of bile over the years, so discretion is the paramount word. Do nothing sideways to give them the excuse for revocation. Am I very clear, Mr. Tsakrios?"

"This ain't my first rodeo, Randy," Tsakrios replied. "These Fed guys are all the same. Drab and predictable! I've dealt with them before. And as you noted, I have no convictions."

"Just because you think you're the mongoose," Shankle shot back, "doesn't mean you always beat the cobra. The FBI is good at what they do and they'll defend their fraternity with passion maybe unparalleled among law enforcement. Most of them really believe they're above scrutiny, and you represent a threat to their institution. You have no idea what the cliché 'circling the wagons' means until they turn their full light of attention your way. Just think Robert Mueller. He was on the president's ass like stench on manure until he finished. You'll relish a colonoscopy without anesthesia after they finish with you. The indictment will pile on so many charges that you may well die of paper cuts just reading the volume of evidence. They're awake and working 24/7 with no sense of humor. They don't do comedy. Never underestimate them and never provoke the cobra. So go see the court clerk right now and sign the bail docs… and remember to read them carefully before we go home. I'll wait and follow you.

"Capische?"

Capelli, the smartly dressed CPA, arrived as predicted and on time. Forty-five minutes later, the fulminating Greek began his way home with Veronica at the wheel of the Kraut through the Northside. His revenge factor hit ignition, and he already had a plan in mind to assure that he never went to trial.

No prosecution witnesses, no Federal case.

Shankle was in tow in one of firm's Mercedes, along with one of the firm's junior attorney, Emily K. Nelson., (the K as she was known to the firm's staff), along with the unmarked FBI car as inconspicuous as an outhouse on the White House lawn. Except it was a standard Chevy Impala. They made no pretense of evasion. The trailing agents were trail car number 1 in what could have been a three-car funeral. They were almost bumper to bumper with the Greek and Shankle. There was no pretense of coy. It was classic "in your face." In this case, it was "on your ass." The trick for the defense would be how to keep the Greek in check and have the bail and the firm's retainer remain intact. On the way to the Tsakrios house, Shankle said aloud what everybody in the defense team feared but politely never uttered.

"This son of a bitch has no impulse control. He's like Trump on Twitter overload, overwrought and flush with anger. Call both Olberfelt and Franklin before we get there. Apprise them of the situation. This guy is Mr. Volatility. But he's our son of a bitch."

"What exactly should I tell them?" Emily asked.

Randy exhaled perceptively and paused for almost a full ten seconds. He wanted to choose his words carefully but reverted to what he felt in his gut.

"Tell them I think we're about to get screwed by our most outrageous client!"

Chapter 20

MAIL CALL

The ride home was a mortuary visitation. No one wanted to speak frankly of the deceased, so mourners whispered in colloquy, with quiet, phony tones of condolence. The dead guy in the car with all the charm of a packed hearse was their mutual anger.

Angela said nothing; he was equally reticent.

They just seethed together. She wanted an explanation for the trauma of the warrant and subsequent search of the house. She felt violated, their privacy destroyed. At least, they didn't go through the humiliation of a cavity search. He, however, was beyond the spectrum of rage. Silence contoured the ride. Thirty minutes later seemed like a trip to Buffalo and Niagara Falls in January.

Chilly was too lame to describe it.

"When we get home, pick up the girls from school and go somewhere else until after dinner until about seven o'clock. I don't care. Take them to the mall, Applebee's, church, the park, wherever. I want to be left alone for at least two hours, understand? Don't give me any grief. I have business to attend to."

"*Si, amore mio*, I understand. But they still have to go back to Oakland for the rest of the week for class. They both have already missed twelve days this year for doctor and orthodontist visits, so they can't miss many more. The state limit is ten *consecutive* days before they might lose credit, although I'm not sure what the difference is between that and *inconsecutive* is. In Maria's case, how do you deny credit to a second semester, Senior? It's bureaucratic crap."

"They won't," he shot back. "Not with the number of checks I've written for tuition and school activities. This is a private Catholic school, so we're not dealing with the imbeciles from the commonwealth and the ton of public school fools. Money talks, even with that new wraparound they have in charge. Priests ain't businessmen. He'll back off. You don't deny a kid a diploma after some three and a half years over some petty crap like medical appointments. If he tries a stunt like that, I'll tack his ass to a legal wall. But just for today, I need some time alone with Shankle and some more uninterrupted time thereafter. If they took any of your stuff, we'll get it back. Just don't come home until later and don't make any phone calls about what happened Saturday to anyone anywhere. Keep your damn mouth shut, even with your motor-mouth sisters. Every cop on earth is listening, so tell the kids it's vital to lay off Facebook and all that social media crap they're into. That's a priority. Make it clear to both of them about this. This guy Oliver is out for blood—ours! Then tomorrow clean up the house from the mess made by those FBI assholes. And next week, I'll have someone sweep it for bugs on the two landlines and maybe elsewhere. They took the computer from my office but they missed the laptop in the crypt."

"And why did they take my jewelry box?" she shouted back.

He ignored her. There ensued a very pregnant pause. Her anger elevated the interior car temperature a distinct four degrees. "We clear about all this?"

The response pause leeched acidic.

"Yeah, but I'm still not happy about it."

"No one is. So just do as I say and don't say a damn thing to anyone about this."

Now the drive from the Federal Courthouse in downtown to Fox Chapel accelerated to low boil. She hated it when he slipped into his foul moods, but this time it was with good reason. There was no place to go to bury their collective anger. The FBI had pretty much thrashed their home, the office, the rec room basement, and all four bedrooms, even the empty guest bedroom. Why they'd even rooted through all three bathrooms was another mystery, along with the piles of dirty clothes strewn askew in the laundry adjacent to the kitchen. They'd taken everything from innocuous billing and household utility records, prescriptions in the medicine cabinets, along with their wedding album and both of the girls' laptops from school in their rooms. Their purloined collection of purported evidence also featured a host of black plastic trash bags that included the contents of their two backyard garbage cans and that of the rolling dumpster they put on the road once a week for trash collection.

"That fries my ass the most," Angela mumbled. "The kids aren't a part of any of your business. Why them?"

"They're Feds. That's what they do. I'll have to deal with it, so let it be! Stay out of my business."

Angela shot back, "Oh, my dear, really! This is your business? And when is it your goddamn business that which ruins our home, huh? Well, when your business screws up our home, it becomes my business too, Joseph, and I damn well will not tolerate this shit anymore. What the hell are you doing that prompted the raid? Huh? And don't give me that 'your business' crap because it's now our business. What have you made us a part of?"

"Just shut up and get off my ass," he said. "I'll deal with it!"

"Yes, you damn well better, or my paisan ass will burn yours down."

"Don't you dare threaten me, Angela. I don't have time for your whining. Just do as I ask you. Things will be all right. I've got too much on my mind right now."

"Well, your goddamn mind doesn't seem to have any room for the three of us, so I may just pack enough to take the girls to my sister, Gina, for the next week. Let the maid clean it up. After all, are you bangin' her too?"

"You know, sometimes you're just too much. And no, Angela, I'm not and have never banged your sister or the maid. That's low. Don't ever infer that again. Considering you're not into the bangin' thing lately, maybe I should consider honkin' your sister. At least, her ass is within playin' weight. You've eaten your way out of the welterweight division into the heavyweight one."

"Fuck you!" She slapped him with right backhand. He returned the compliment and backhanded her and then shouted.

"Just stop it before I really get mad!"

The thirty-minute ride ended shortly thereafter but not soon enough for Angela. The mood was bleak from door to door. She was vexed, frustrated, and not quite sure with whom to be most pissed—the Feds or her sometimes bully of a husband. She exited The Kraut, threw the keys onto the center console, and stormed into the house via the front door.

"I'm sorry I said that."

He just grunted. "Do you want a divorce?"

"No, we'll talk about this later. I'm not running away anytime soon."

But she contemplated it and packed the idea away for future consideration.

Greek waited for Shankle and Nelson following to pull into the driveway. A block away parked the FBI tail, open and obvious. They wanted Joseph to know they were there. They made no pretense of coy.

"Follow me" he said as he led them downstairs through the three-day garage down to the spacious basement recreation room. Nelson's heels stuck on the downstairs.

I shoulda worn pumps today, she thought. *Court dress isn't the same.*

Years of paranoia prompted Tsakrios to also build a huge alcove that abuts the basement where he ostensibly had a very expensive pool table, seldom played, in a crypt with a purpose. It was built for secrecy.

He had lined the top of the ceiling over it with a four-inch lead layer of protection against external surveillance sustained by steel girders that doubled as both an earthquake and bomb shelter. What he really wanted was a private conversation room, a soundproof extension of the basement. It was testament to his embrace of criminal paranoia. He would then close the awkward French doors to the room whose walls to the remainder of the basement were also heavily insulated but not with the triple-pane glass as the doors.

Conversation then became quietly absolute and absolutely quiet all at once. Greek was never known to do things halfway. Many of his business deals saw completion there. The total cost of his basement confessional originally ran somewhere between $75,000 and $100,000. If something's worth doing well, spare no expense. What seems like overkill to most only hyperventilates the criminal class.

Tsakrios was indeed making too much money. The little alcove was proof positive. Shankle and Nelson followed him into the crypt. Greek put his briefcase onto the pool table cover. Shankle did the same with his.

Then Greek dropped to one knee and slid under the table to a hidden niche in the underside. It was ingenious melded to structure with a spring latch that opened the shelf above that ejected a seldom-used laptop. Again it was a manifest of neurosis at its best. Justifiable, indeed, but it served its purpose. Who but someone imbued with complete distrust of outsiders would design such a room? The computer sported a key for a thumb drive. The C-drive was actually empty.

The FBI missed it, although they thoroughly ransacked the upper floors.

"So sorry," Greek said, standing back up and placing the computer on the pool table and inserting the thumb drive. "It's my insurance policy and their oversight!"

Neither Shankle nor Nelson said a word. "Upside, go!"

The attorneys dutifully followed as they went upstairs to his now thrashed office. No desktop, drawers asunder, but the printer remained, which they hadn't taken. Tsakrios first turned on the laptop, noted that the battery was still good, and typed the cryptic call to arms on the retrieved laptop and connected it to the printer:

> Gather at the preassigned checkpoint. The address is 13 Holland Road, Butler County. Leave no trace. If the wife and kids interfere, take them out too. Meet at the prearranged site the second Saturday in May at ten o'clock. Then

destroy, shred, and burn this letter completely, along with its envelope.

It was cold and starkly calculating. He did not share the contents with his attorneys. Shankle really didn't want to know but he suspected. That was deliberate. It enhanced plausible deniability and shielded both of them from the wrath of the Pennsylvania bar examiners. It's the approach you must use with all sideway clients. Accessory to felonies moved many an attorney from three-piece suits to orange jumpsuits. The rule was unspoken but perfectly understood between counsel and clients. Ethics were sometimes fungible with office of Oberfelt et al., although Shankle knew where to draw the line and keep his law license. Open those letters and he would fall under the penumbra of conspiracy to commit murder. You can't testify about what you absolutely don't know. Intuitively Shankle suspected what the contents were of the note and knew what his client had written…or something similar. The firm had Tsakrios on his client list for more than fifteen years, so he knew the letter must reek of toxic. He just didn't want to know, even if it was only remotely criminal.

How right he was.

Tsakrios ran off five copies on the printer, along with envelopes he hand-posted to five different addresses. He then reached into the desk drawer, retrieved the remaining roll of forever US stamps, sealed the letters from the computer, and handed them to Shankle. Then he yanked the thumb drive from the laptop and pocketed it in the left breast pocket of his suit coat.

"You're still two of my attorneys of record, aren't you?"

"Please, correction! Our firm represents you."

"Then mail these, please, on your way back to the office. Put them in a remote mailbox somewhere and make sure you're not tailed when you do it."

Shankle wouldn't bite.

"Do you want us to secure the thumb drive in the firm's safe?" Shankle asked. "That would be privileged information."

"No. Just do as I say. Mail the letters and go on with your day."

"No, can't do that," Shankle replied. "I also need to shield Nelson. None of our prints are on those letters. Mail them yourself. Remember, we were never here. It was just a social call after court. No business transpired. There are no billable hours here. Understand?"

Shankle closed his briefcase and motioned to Nelson. "It's time to go. We'll continue this later. But, Joseph, you'll have to see to your own mail."

He then pivoted toward the front door.

"*Hasta la vista, mi amigo*! We obviously will see a lot of each other over the coming weeks. Please be careful."

Emily remained in her thinking mode: silent but deadly.

"What just happened?" she asked after they got back into the car.

"Nothing," Shankle said. "I was just covering your ass, your law career, and you were doing the same for me. Concentrate on the defense of the case at hand. I have no idea what's in that ouzo-idled brain of his. And maybe it's best we don't know."

As always, however, the Greek had a backup plan. It was so simple that it reeked of sheer simplicity. He had Veronica drive into town on Monday with gloves and quietly put the letters in five separate postal boxes, including one at the mailbox near the FBI Federal Building on Carson Street, right next to and in plain view of the staff of the Federal Bureau of Investigation.

It was a two-word salute on a New York welcome. Veronica didn't have to lift a finger.

Chapter 21

LES CINQ

Some relish their family surnames. Sergei Romonov despised his. It brought him to the edge of retch. Although he spoke Russian as a child, he was a de facto Serb. The chaos of World War II pushed his grandparents to flee ahead of the Nazi swarm in what then became Yugoslavia. Refugee was a full-time occupation after the war. So 1945 found them accidental citizens of what is now the Serbian capital of Belgrade, also Yugoslavia's capital city before the collapse of the country into seven new ethnic states with Serbia, Bosnia, and Croatia the largest. The only thing that held Yugoslavia together after WWII was Dictator Joseph Broz Tito. Post mortem, what devolved were the Seven Countries that the average American couldn't identify if you spotted them five on the television show *Jeopardy*. Details about them were the staff minutiae of institutes like the CIA, the Defense Intelligence Agency, and the Department of State. Otherwise, it would challenge a geography major with a penchant for trivia to retrieve information savored only by wonks with obscure graduate degrees.

Few Americans in the '50s even cared about Slavic trivia.

Tito ruled by fear, iron-fist, Soviet-style that rapidly unraveled after his death with overlapping civil wars that prompted the North Atlantic Treaty Organization to intervene with years of air strikes during the Clinton administration to quell the rampant ethnic cleansing of the decade. The "cleansing" was mutual. Muslim

Bosnians hated Christian Serbs and vice versa. One of the Serbians' most morally repellant policies was to capture Bosnian young women of childbearing age and round them into rape camps. There they were detained and systematically raped until they became visibly pregnant.

Thus they had Christian sperm donors and carried babies with half-Christian identities. It was intended to both insult and impose a "scarlet letter" or stigma on them for life. The child would be the eternal reminder of Muslim impurity.

They would then continue to hold them until they were more than six months in utero and then release them, knowing full well they would not abort but carry those Christian impregnated babies to term. Abortion is anathema in both fundamental Christianity and Islam, so it was a kind of obstetric terrorism first popular with Genghis Khan and the Roman legions—dispose of the men, ravage the women.

The sojourn of the war weary pushed his grandparents and parents to become newly minted Serbians. But Sergei was indifferent to family history. The stories of Russian pride and past glory bored him. It was the material needs of the present that motivated him most. His childhood was replete with memories of war, hunger, meals missed, NATO air strikes, and multiple corpses rotting in plain view.

It created a kind of numb indifference to suffering. War does that to children. Immunity to death was Sergei's way to cope. He only knew he wanted to leave the chaos of the Slavic rampage of the 1990s and flee to what books and infrequent television images hinted as the celestial land of opportunity an ocean away. His parents' refugee status landed him and his family a United Nations visa to Ontario, Canada, where his high school years imposed two more languages. He already spoke Russian, along with a dialect perversion of Serbian/Yugoslav concoction. Now he added both English and French to the mix.

Thus he arrived in America in his late twenties with an accent no one could recognize. He botched his conversation with digraphs and diphthongs in English, French, and Russian. In high school, that accent evoked derisive laughter from his peers, but the teasing ceased after he developed his huge frame that served him well. He topped out at 275 pounds on a six-foot-five frame by age eighteen. Classmates rarely tormented him by that point, as he had a limited sense of humor and an even shorter temper. He had a "hockey attitude" without benefit of skates. Bored with school, he held a series of jobs after dropping out of the University of Toronto as an enforcer (aka bouncer) with a series of Toronto bars and nightclubs.

It was with one of them that he discovered how easy it was to kill smaller human beings. Offered $5,000 by one of his former employers to stifle a disgruntled business/drug competitor, Sergei discovered that an A-string piano wire, a dark alley at 3:00 a.m., and an unsuspecting ambush victim was easy money. Loping off heads is a cinch literally with a crushing knee to the back and a five-second A-string piano tourniquet to the neck. That became even easier over time as the Toronto police began to collect decapitated bodies bereft of sympathy melded to few other physical clues.

Except for the bloody piano wire! It was deliberately left at the scene!

They treated it as an aberration, but as all cops will tell you, there is almost always premeditation for murder. Homicide doesn't fester in isolation and hasn't from Macbeth to Charles Manson. You just have to meticulously flush out physical evidence and motivation.

So it was that Sergei became enthralled with the enhanced, adrenaline rush of the kill. Wrapping that piano wire around the neck of his first, quashing his weight onto the victim's spine, was more akin to a cocaine high, replicating the rush of orgasm. He hyperventilated as he finally dropped the body.

It had no name. He didn't care. It was just a payday.

Sergei had devolved, baptized in the waterfont of insanity. The hit was just a piece of trash needing disposal for an enhanced addition to his cash flow. The hits had no soul. They were more akin to hunted vermin. The ensuing contracts, therefore, became easier. After the third, he jumped into the river with his Canadian passport to Detroit where he met a "brother" of similar persuasion, Kamil Q. Dempsey.

They became a pair with a criminal patent on now the west side of the Detroit River that separates it from Windsor, Canada. It marked a two-year crime fest on both sides of the border. They were aspirant hitmen, who both loved high-end vodka and the thrill of human suppression. That began their circular journey to Western Pennsylvania.

Dempsey was the prototype, low-grade hood with enough sense to eschew misdemeanor drug beefs for the face of legitimacy. He first started out at nineteen as a Brinks armored car guard. Along the way, he acquired a low-level black belt in karate, along with an attitude and strict discipline honed by the lifestyle. He worked out incessantly and eventually cultivated a chiseled, alluring frame. But like his new friend Romanov, he also nurtured a love for exotic vodkas anywhere from Russia and Poland to France and the testosterone allure of multiple young, disposable women.

With gullible females, they were strictly "hit and run" men. As prospects for marriage and fatherhood, they were the antitheses. Amoral would stamp both their passports.

They originally met on a mutual protection gig for an Iraqi owner of a restaurant/bar near Dearborn to be the doormen at weddings and assorted parties for the local community. Their proficiency factor kept them employed virtually every weekend, as somebody always had some reason to throw a party for a wedding, funeral, birthday, or anniversary. Sergei's transnational good looks made him an instant sale to virtually any ethnic group willing to employ, and Dempsey (Q-Ball as he now preferred) was the complementary, dynamic "heavy." He was the head-shaven Mr. Intimidation, drenched in charm with a remarkable set of smiling teeth but no soul.

The money was easy, always cash, and often comingled with a proclivity for violence. Debt collection became part of the team's repertoire with service by any means necessary, no questions asked. Multiple broken ribs, arms, and ankles would so attest. Their business motto: "We only ask once; results guaranteed." That meant those unwilling to pay sometimes made short trips to sundry emergency rooms where memories eroded rapidly about how their injuries occurred.

Not surprisingly, victims magically paid their bills. Better late than never! Clients were happy, courtesy of the collection firm of Romonov & Dempsey. Although they both preferred not to do terminations as too riff with inquisitive police, four floaters, sans skulls, over the next two years in the Detroit River did ultimately catch police attention.

Cops may be a maze of many things, but stupidity is not part of their portfolio. Homicide dicks are not meter maids. That's why 70 percent of all homicides in most cities are cleared. Most of the time, they've solved them within the first seventy-two hours. They know who the perps are for the other 30 percent, but hearsay and temerity from prosecutors often prevail. Limited evidence, no indictments, not even for unpaid traffic citations.

Plainly speaking, police know the murderers got away with it, although the statute on murder and income tax evasion never expires. They just hope clearance occurs in the future, even after the pursuing detectives are retired or dead. *Exempli gratia*: O. J. Simpson!

The Detroit PD knew of and about the crime spree courtesy of Romanov & Dempsey, and they didn't think of them as members of the Detroit Chamber of Commerce. They even had notes and interviews with both to no avail.

The overworked homicide division had a caseload that would stretch well into the next decade. Seven of their very best pulled the pins on more than thirty years after the year 2000. Some of them left under a cloud of frustration. Too much overtime and exhaustion that precursed divorce were the order of the day. The job was not family-friendly, so the collective talent of experience quietly melted away.

The whole composite of daily death in what once was one of America's greatest cities left most of them with a WTF ("What the Fuck") attitude. Thus the loss of quality personnel precursed the slow pace of case clearance, the golden rod of success. Homicide work is relentless, immersed in detail, boredom, and necessary preoccupation with what seems the trivial. Cynicism prevailed at every administrative level in the Detroit PD for the better part of the '90s through 2010.

The motto on the plaque of Homicide Detective Eddie Boyd's desk said it all: "People are dying to see me. Who the hell are you?"

Boyd's division commanders ignored his lack of couth as his record of results preempted the temptation to impose politically correct discipline.

"Eddie is two bubbles off plumb," said one of his prior partners, "but how he manages to nab collars is almost mystical. Don't mess with what you know works."

"Romonov's the dangerous one in that tandem," Boyd mused to his current watch commander. "He'd off his own mother and sell his sister to the nearest brothel if he thought he could get away with it and pocket the change…as long as it was in large bills. It's a strange Russian thing, and we have yet to crack a credible undercover in that community. We also need some guys who can speak Russian or Arabic, so, Sarge, maybe you should work on that. We must have some younger guys who are not just monolingual. We are deficient in both counts. Those communities are a challenge, and we need cops who can speak their language.

"Q-Ball is more conventional, more like your standard, cautious hitman," he opined. "He's not an in-your-face type like Romonov and he fears the confines of prison, but he still had a proclivity for extreme violence. I interviewed him twice years ago after a fight at a Christmas party where he was hired as the doorman. Four guys hurt, two arrests, and we couldn't pin a parking ticket on him, even though we knew he provoked the confrontation. Witnesses all pled nothing. Every one of the more than two hundred guests was into the 'I know nothing' drill. He's a low-life dipshit but probably guilty of numerous assaults and maybe two murders. Skated on at least one I know of! He just struck me as that type, so polite in the interview. You know, kind of like an Eastern Diamondback. You hear him rattle and hiss but you wouldn't want to pet him. You knew he was the one who killed the family dog but you couldn't prove it, although he came from a den of snakes with multiple suspects just behind the barn on the property. So you just go for the shotgun and wipe the whole family out. You know, that kind of guy—not a Boy Scout!"

"Well, how come you didn't wipe them all out?"

"I was low on ammunition that day."

But Q-Ball also had a buddy in Wexford, Pennsylvania, with similar professional experience. He was soon to join them. All three received anonymous letters from Fox Chapel with stamp cancellations from three different post offices in Allegheny County. They arrived concurrently the next Wednesday. Romonov got his at his postal box in Ann Arbor where he slithered into the local student community. He was still a hitman and had the endearing charm of Eden's snake, but he loved the easy access to women on the party circuit. The university town of Ann Arbor fit the bill—good restaurants, easy coeds. Romanov wallowed in the sins of the flesh married to a vat of vodka.

Q-Ball got his letter at his mother's address near East Lansing, and Roger Allen Daltry received his at his PO box in Wexford.

Daltry was another piece of work who knew Dempsey from a leg-break they'd pulled off near Akron some two years before. Hired as out-of-towners by Tsakrios, they motivated a member of Greek's extended family. They didn't actually break the target's leg. It was just a love tap reminder to both shins with a Louisville Slugger that reminded the miscreant that talking to police of any stripe violated the Greek's code of malicious ethics. The next time the Louisville Slugger would be used would be as an ad hoc colonoscopy.

He complied.

Daltry's brother-in-law also owned a hunting cabin near Punxsutawney where he and assorted cohorts stashed enough weapons to topple at least thirteen of the smallest governments in the United Nations General Assembly.

The brother-in-law, married to Daltry's younger sister, was also a fervent member of the "don't ask, don't tell" policy of the criminal class. He didn't hunt. He just paid the rent. Daltry slipped him cash to cover it, but the bro could feign exquisitely stupid before any cop, or even the Pope. But two other letters also arrived, one in Johnston and the second in Erie. Daltry knew the recipient from Erie, but the second Saturday would be a union/reunion of the class of Low-Life U right there in Punxsutawney Phil's backyard. The five would reacquaint and strategize the job for which they were hired right there in the cabin in the woods under the purview of Pennsylvania's most famous groundhog.

Fewer than four months later, the quintet of sin would tally their scoresheets with the celestial judge. It was an endgame they didn't anticipate.

But their target was not Mother Teresa nor was her husband a disciple of Ghandi. Grab the bull by the horns and you might get the Southern end of an angry northbound, three-thousand-pound steak sandwich.

As Kathleen's mother, Eileen often berated her children with one of her six-pack of biblical bromides.

"Pride cometh before the fall!"

Vanity is its own empty reward.

Chapter 22

DEER CABIN

Daltry was the first to show. He rolled up in a bland rental from the Erie Enterprise office that replicated every undercover police prowl car west of Philadelphia. It had no distinguishing features, including the "fugly" gray-silver paint of the exterior. He reluctantly accepted the four-door Ford after an incessant sales pitch from the verbose clerk behind the counter with the stale personality. She rambled ad nauseam. Wouldn't shut up! It seemed the only way to cut her off was to consume the offer. Ten minutes into it, he waved the white flag of surrender.

"Yeah, it's okay! I'll take it."

He caved just to terminate the interminable sales pitch. Thirty-five bucks a day seemed like appropriate anesthesia, anything to shut her off switch.

"Yes, you could have this vehicle at a significantly lower rate for the weekend. It's part of our new promotion on midsize cars," she continued. "It's in the last parking slot and ready to go. It has four doors and an extra-spacious trunk, as I see you have a large luggage bag. The special on this portion of the fleet ends next week, and it's 30 percent off the normal weekend rate. And you won't have to return it until Tuesday. Does that appeal to you? You'll save a bunch."

"Okay, just do it!" he said. He assumed she had heard him the first time and shoveled the phony Andrew Shale driver's license allegedly issued by the state of Delaware over the counter, along with nine very clean $100 bills as a deposit. The fake photo ID only vaguely resembled Daltry, but she couldn't care less. The pitch worked well, even after her chatty persistence that rode the fringe of tedium. The ruse sufficed so she could get the vehicle out the door. He bought the Enterprise vehicle insurance because he had none of his own. She didn't even ask or didn't care if he had insurance of his own. It was just another sale addendum, merely an extra $35 commission. Back in five days, the car would generate no questions and no trail, just the roughly three hundred miles he would clock on the odometer. He opted for the unlimited mileage option blessed by the fake signature, signed left-handed by one predominantly right.

Her motif was "close the deal" and collect the paltry upgrade for a sale well pitched. That was her job. He would have it back by Tuesday, he assured her, but only after a very intense detailing at a local car wash. It would return pristine clean, ready to shove out the door again with another berated customer.

Romanov and Dempsey were the next to arrive, although they couldn't care less about hiding an incriminating rental. They were in Dempsey's four-wheel drive Chevy truck with distinct tires lawmen could recognize with a two-minute scan of the Internet. Very expensive, off-road steel belt-eds were an easy spot. Wide enough to resemble a military Hummer, they were the kind of tires that attracted state police attention on the highway both for their unique squawk and oversize diameter. They also had a noisy hum for the road warrior curious. Said tires call attention to the driver who might not want it. News is news by exception, and every cop knows a car with a putrid color, odd modification, or low trunk might require further scrutiny. It was, in fact, a Cadillac for special needs criminals.

And those two fit the bill.

Dumb! thought Daltry. *We'll have to take the box blade attached to the tractor in the adjacent shed next to the cabin and shred our tire tracks before we leave. That was a fuck-up on Dempsey's part.*

He immediately brought it to their attention loudly, rudely, and profanely.

"Could you just be slightly less obvious and indiscreet with your fucking choice of vehicles?"

"So what? There are ten thousand sets of these tires on the road, most of them here in deer country," Dempsey shot back. "So don't sweat it!"

"Well, I do sweat it, as you say, 'cause the hound dogs of law will eventually find this cabin and we need to cover our asses. So don't be dumb with clues!"

"Whatever!"

"How many bunks do we have?" Romanov asked.

"There are eight, so you have your choice."

"What about water?"

"There's an old hand crank to a well inside next to the sink. The stove is wood burning, but there's no hot water, so there's no shower. There's an outhouse out back, but we'll have to burn it before we leave 'cause even shit and toilet paper have DNA."

Sergovia and Bronson were the last to arrive; she was also sporting a rental with no distinct features. Only Daltry knew them both. Disposition of the rentals was their problem, he reminded them, even before the perfunctory introductions. If the FBI traced their cars, it was, in Daltry's words, "their pathetic, fucking asses!"

He obsessed over the evidence trail, but the others not so much. Arrogance was the group watchword that always prevails before the fall or the arrest. They thought it was an easy gig with few complications at $25,000 each. Romanov made the mistake of approaching Sergovia like a Russian playboy with a lewd suggestion in Russian the rest didn't understand. His appeal rested on very deaf, insouciant ears. She shot him down in English.

But he damn well better pay attention.

"I'm here only to do a job with you. If you wish to retain your testicles, do not play with me. Otherwise, you will take them home with you in a very small sack."

Her stare was enough. End of conversation. Potential romance extinguished. The promise of a gonad detachment is not an erotic encounter.

She punctuated her threat by laying out her array of carving knives on the upper bunk she claimed on the far west end of the cabin. She claimed both top and bottom bunks as her territory. The message: "Do not approach. I am armed!" There were three knives in all with sheaths she sported for attachment to her belt and/or boots. Romanov had no response and pretended he didn't hear her. Her Kalashnikov pistol had a fitted left underarm holster she supplemented with four extra clips. Those she also laid on the upper bunk were fully loaded. He moved to a bunk at the opposite corner.

Smart move on his part!

Romanov noted that she was most likely right-handed.

It was another mistaken observation. Unlike the other four, she was very ambidextrous with both knives and firearms. She was also wary of him, like she was of most Russian men, and only wanted the $25,000 each promised in their letters from the Greek. Like previous contracts with Joseph Tsakrios, she dealt only in cash. Unlike the others, she preferred a tidy cash exchange in advance. Greek accorded her that, as she truly was the only one of the five he completely and utterly trusted. She picked it up from her post office box near Homestead. Previously she would use the lockers at the Pittsburgh Greyhound Bus terminal, but new company policy opened each locker daily for security, now part of the post 9/11 protocol. So her letter came with cash in a small box that Veronica mailed during one of her trips to Oakland near the University of Pittsburgh to pick up the daughters. Housed in a small box, even one bought from the USPS, any mailed cash was a hazardous investment if discovered. But Sergovia insisted, and Greek reluctantly agreed as less exposure than the trace a wire transfer entailed. Paid in advance, she could have just collected the cash and run. But she knew Greek's memory bank ran from Pittsburgh to Palestine to Athens. To welch on a Tsakrios bet was a commitment that boded poorly for an employee's health record. Vengeance is mine, sayeth both the Lord and Joseph Tsakrios.

She clearly understood his vindictive nature and reputation, and she was not about to challenge it. To paraphrase a former Speaker of the California Assemblyman, Jesse Unruh: "Money is the mother's milk of crime." And money was the currency of the realm. That's all. There was no sentiment or true loyalty involved. The stereotype prevailed. There is no honor among thieves, derelicts, and assassins.

Homeland Security had yet to extend its tentacles to the lesser slovenly confines of most bus stations, either urban or rural. Bus security garnered very little bang for the buck, or so most Federal agents thought. New York they covered, but towns like Erie, Oil City, and Clarion less so. Budget priorities focused on air transport, trucking, tunnels, the Southern border, and trains. Terror groups, at this point since 9/11, saw limited value in bus sabotage. Maybe in the future, but the obsession with air transit was still king. Spectacular disaster remained their obsession. There were just not enough potential victims to risk that much exposure with intense preparation to target bus transit in the United States.

And there was insufficient Federal budget to cover all the threats. Too many fires, not enough firefighters. Although a problem in Israel, it had not yet seeped to the surface in the United States. It was that low visibility that caught the Greek's attention. Thus the slow exit of Moran and Laudergast and the low-tech money drops of a bus locker that Tsakrios abandoned several years after 9/11. But he reluctantly conceded that Sergovia had a point.

Send cash by mail. Tortoise wins the race every time. Greek would wire money to a bank in Israel for the fifth and lead assassin, Aaron Bronson, who had a phony account with a fake name. With his dual citizenship, the transfer needed little cover. Even the potential check of a hated FISA Court judge would not draw much attention. Federal agents were just overwhelmed with the whole spectrum of threats, and some FISA warrants were as sloppy as a rancid barrel of fish.

"We have to bat .900 to 1.000 in this league," groused FBI Agent Merrick Nash of the Brooklyn field office, "but they only have to bat .100. God save us when some of these fanatics acquire a nuke in a suitcase. New York becomes a distant memory. It's also why I moved my wife, kids, and parents upstate to Poughkeepsie. The weekly commute here isn't bad via train, so I'm just home on weekends. I just won't take the chance anymore with them here anymore in Brooklyn."

Bronson arrived with an engorged duffel bag with most of the prestaged ammunition for three AK-74s via an Uber driver for whom he offered a monster tip of $300 accepted for total silence. Inquisitive cops could examine Uber's computer records and note the mileage the driver generated for his commission, not necessarily the destination. That could be fudged. He could fake that and a phony description of the passenger. Sworn to secrecy, he could easily remain mute with a thwarted memory of the cash tip. Or he could just gin up a phony figure like, maybe, the tip was only $30. It was not a hard lie to cover. Bronson met the driver at the train station in Altoona after the burn phone he used to reserve the ride found a Dempsey Dumpster on its way to an Altoona landfill.

Standing silent sentry in the train station parking lot was Bronson's cheap Hertz rental. It would park there for the duration of the job. No one would notice how it huddled in the expanse of sedans blandly similar in style and color. Bronson would just pick it up after the job and nonchalantly drive away to Newark for the plane trip to Tel Aviv aboard El Al. It all seemed so simple. Like most plans, it all changed with the first rounds coming downrange.

Bronson, however, also had the surveillance toys they would use to reconnoiter the McShea property, two small but very expensive drones about the size of a large model aircraft. He had driven to Butler the day he received the Greek's letter and used the first early that morning to scour the property, the house, and the barn. He had the photographs on his iPad, along with four paper copies for the assembled hit team. The pictures correctly displayed both the house and the barn complex, along with both of the family vehicles and the goat fencing and front gate that only encompassed the house, the barn, and the surrounding fifty acres with an additional gate on the southern end of the property. When he finished, he also noted that the back (or southernmost) gate was wide open to the remainder of the fifty or so acres with no further fencing to adjacent properties. Although that made no logical sense, he wondered whether it was mere coincidence or a tactical omission by the McSheas. The property was wide open to an approach from the south. His instinct told him it was something of which to be wary.

He was strangely leery of the open gate. Was it just an oversight on the McSheas' part or an invitation to an ambush? He sensed a trap. It gnawed at him, but he eventually dismissed it as mild paranoia on his part.

So he derisively dismissed the open gate as irrelevant. After all, wasn't it just a farm? The drone disappeared somewhere over the southern end of the property but sent back the requisite signals with photographs. There was, however, no retrieval, as it apparently malfunctioned somewhere near the farmhouse itself. He attributed the loss to his own inexperience about how to operate it properly, as he already had the requisite pictures. He presumed on the fifty-acre farm that the drone would not be found.

"Okay, so what the hell!"

So he thus blew off the loss as a business expense. No big deal! That would become a terminal mistake.

Chapter 23

ASSAULT PLAN

After the random bunk selection, Bronson turned to address the others. Even gang members need a crew chief. This crew was more rabble than royalty, but their deadly proclivities were unassailable. That's why the Greek hired them.

Greek also anointed him as foreman. His letter was very specific. Aside from Bronson and Sergovia, the other three were disposables.

Bronson also purchased the drone toys and was the only one offered an extra $10,000 by the Greek for business expenses. Good drones with precision cameras aren't cheap or easy to master. It took him the better part of a week to locate ones appropriate for the task and another two days to practice controlling them in flight. He mastered the intricacy of remote piloting, but it took two days on both aircraft before they arrived in Altoona.

His brazen persona, however, needed no further stroking. Full of himself, cocksure, and supremely Narcissist, he easily remained the biggest ego in the room.

So Bronson was now the de facto, semi-anointed bully rabbi in search of a congregation. Also note that the Day of Atonement was never on his cantorial calendar. He hadn't seen the interior of a synagogue since his Bar Mitzvah. With a soul made for sin, the closest he came to a reformed, real Jew was lying on the beach in Israel near Israeli women with bodies of biblical persuasion. He was into that begettin' and begattin' thing so often described in the Old

Testament. Married, unattached, or betrothed, Bronson couldn't care less. Delilah was his favorite Old Testament character, and he needn't sweat the scissors of scorn, as he'd been shaving his head for more than a decade. He was Mr. Clean with a dirty mind and requisite soul.

Thus the two drones he bought would constitute a mere near-occasion of sin and a substantial tax write-off of more than $1,500, sometimes used for a legitimate business expense.

This venture was hardly that.

The FBI would eventually track the drone purchase to a legitimate hobby shop dealer in Newark in late May while Bronson languished on the beach near Tel Aviv, availing himself of the visuals of thongs and undulating flesh. The dealer remembered Bronson as odd. Otherwise, his memory of the sale was phony as a transgendered duck. Bronson's money was cash, backed by portraits of Uncle Ben. The shop dealer was a fervent member of the church of "don't ask, don't tell" with a fuzzy memory of customers or their quirks. Cash screams volumes and fogs the memory. His subsequent interview with the FBI so confirmed.

"If you won't ask, I won't tell."

The agents knew he was pulling their chains, but he did dig up the true receipt of purchase off his shop computer. The two young agents who made the call were brimming with sufficient professional courtesy to induce a torrent of vomit. They thanked him politely, dropped the alleged receipt in a kitchen ziplock baggy and quietly left. They knew his primary inventory was prevarication. The shop owner thought he conned them, but they already had him pegged as a potential accessory to a felony. He was an outlier to what was becoming a veritable shopping list of lying to the FBI.

"He's lying through his teeth, so I guess we'll be back," Agent Neil Rooney said. "That was a story straight out of *Grimm's Fairy Tales*, a phony receipt in search of a real story. These guys all think they're so slick. If he'd just told us the truth, we'd be done with him. But he insisted on peddling that story that he couldn't recall the basic attributes of his best customer that day. What a crock of shit! Stupid criminals seem to proliferate in this zip code."

They'd be back later to collect him for trial.

At the campsite, Bronson began, "I have laid out the aerials of the property so each of you can study them. There's a copy for each. Pay close attention to the details, all of you! The first drone didn't make it back, so some 'pucelage' of an FBI agent or cop will find it. I made paper copies at the local public library. Those will go into the hole. I'll take the thumb drive from the drone signal to my laptop and make it disappear along the way. Memorize the photographs because all evidence of our stay here is going into the burn barrel 'outhouse just before we leave, everything from scratch paper to toilet paper and tampons. That's everything you touch."

Daltry grinned and shot a rakish smile toward Sergovia. It was not well received. His fantasy of her unclothed body ran rampant through his lurid mind. If dirty thoughts were felonies, Daltry would already be in cuffs, convicted, sentenced, and on his way to the "big house."

"Fuck you, Daltry. My pussy's not for sale. Besides, your dick's too short and shriveled!"

And in the words of Cajun Marie LeVeau, "Another man done gone!" She slapped him down like a target horsefly.

"Daltry's cousin left five gallons of diesel, so we can soak the outhouse, including the diesel can itself." Bronson continued, "Then we'll light it up just as we leave."

"Pucelage?" Romanov asked, "What the hell is that?"

"It's an old term for *virgin*, because those are the agents who will be assigned to collect any physical evidence. But you probably are more familiar with the term *puke*." Bronson shot back, "Okay, the puke agents! The senior ones will not be the ones rooting through our remnants in their three-piece suits. The lowest on the food chain get the shit detail in scungy clothes just like the military, even in the IDF (Israeli Defense Force). So we have to destroy all signs of our presence here. Got it?"

The other four nodded in stunned, bored amazement at Bronson's unsubtle swipe at their lack of sophistication. The digs were not without warrant. His editorial did not endear him to anyone in the room, but Bronson embodied the classic Bronx attitude, the universal cheer of derision.

"I got two words for you, and it ain't 'Welcome to New York'! We're all here just to do a job, and I don't give a damn about any personality consolation prize. Your ignorance is none of my concern. Hopefully we will never see each other again after this, so stay out of my face."

The group feeling was mutual. Greed trumped fraternity.

"I agree," said Dempsey. "Those are my sentiments exactly! And I also brought a large box of latex medical gloves, and I'm sorry if you're allergic to them. Begin putting them on right now and use them for everything you touch while we're here. I don't think any of us want to fight extradition orders from our 'vacation' destinations if the Feds discover who we are. DNA is absolute and forever. Stay gloved with everything you touch from your groin to your asshole and everything else in between and in this building. And that includes prints on your returned rental vehicles and its paperwork. There's also a large box of baby wipes in the outhouse. Use them liberally. No trace, no DNA. Is that clear? All of it goes in the little round hole into the pit."

Again there was that group nod of yeah-yeah agreement from the hired idiot fire team. After all, this wasn't a meeting of Mensa alumni, so Bronson's popularity continued to plummet. The team plan for the pennant always looks good in spring training, but it was dubious in August that the assembled crew would make it to the World Series of crime. They were fortunate to have someone as lethal as Bronson taking the helm.

Bronx cheers work two ways. Logic did not make him more lovable, and the cold-blooded snake was not about to change into a furry puppy.

Daltry then jumped into the exchange.

"I also brought ten MREs (Meals Ready to Eat) for tonight and tomorrow morning. Eat them cold. No fires until we light the outhouse. Drink plenty of water from the well at the sink. MREs require a quart of water to properly digest, and I don't think any of you needs to be constipated on this gig. The well water is potable and cold. Everyone should pee and evacuate before we leave, as the fewer stops we make, the better. Put all the trash into the outhouse pit."

"Okay, so we all gotta wait in line at the outhouse before we leave," said Romanov. "What about the cars?"

"Well, we're not takin' Dempsey's police magnet to the step-off point that I noted on the photographs," Daltry said. "Leave that Detroit abortion magnet here. I'll rake the tracks with my cousin's tractor and box blade when we come back and then light the fire. Nearest volunteer fire department is almost seventeen miles away. Unless some curious hunter stumbles over this place, there's little chance of detection. You drop me off in Altoona where I parked, and we all leave and go our separate ways. We don't use each other's cell numbers or text. Use hand signals when approaching the target. Collect your personal trash, stash the trash, and disappear. Understood? You're all responsible for the ammunition for your own weapons. Hopefully you all brought flash suppressors for them. Despite how remote the farmhouse is, noise suppression is paramount. We'll be in Butler County, and this isn't deer season, so several dozen expended rounds will attract a bevy of unwanted attention. I have three AKs with 120 rounds, but they are to be used only on the extract if needed on the retreat back to the step-off point or if we run into some hotshot deputy sheriff. Got that?"

"There he goes again," Daltry whispered to Romanov. "What the fuck's a bevy?"

"Shut up, Daltry, and just listen to the man. I don't know either."

"Notice the winding road south of their property. I've scouted out a secondary dirt road off Sawmill Run that's not posted for hunters, and if we drive into the brush about fifty yards, we can easily hide the two approach rentals and move on foot toward the house about a half mile away. If we get there about 0300, we can slowly be on site about 0400, do the whole family, if necessary, and leave. But the male McShea is the principal target. If we piss off Greek by blowin' this, he will haunt us all to our graves. Finally, when we get the hell out, one car will go west and disappear south with three of you. But Sergovia and I first will come back here to the cabin, burn the outhouse, and split. Don't break any speed limits or draw attention.

We'll take Sergovia's vehicle back to the cabin. After we go back to light up the outhouse, we'll exit down State Route 8. The remaining three of you will take the other approach vehicle and go south on Meridian Road. Questions?"

"Yeah," asked Dempsey. "How accurate are these photos from the drone?"

"Very!"

"And are there any obstacles in this field leading to the house that we need to know about?"

"Like what?" asked Romanov "Like old farm equipment, holes, trenches, or old barns?"

"They have an old International Harvester tractor that they use. I don't know what the hell for. And they park it all over the place, but that's the only thing that may be there. The rest of the property is pretty much open space with a few trees, mostly removed over the years from near the house and barn. If they're asleep, we have the advantage. But if they're awake, they may spot us. There's no moon of any sort this week, so it should be plenty dark. So note the open land on the south end on the photos. The southern end of the property, our approach, is on about a 3-percent grade uphill. We'll not be visible to anyone at the house until we're about two hundred yards out. It was grazing and crop land for years, so there are few obstacles, only a couple of large trees. But dress ninja style, as it's a night with no moon. You all have dark clothing, right? In and out, quick and easy. One last footnote to your question, be alert!

"Yeah," Bronson continued, "they have two big dogs. Kill them if you must, but that might be dumb. That's why I asked if you all had flash suppressors. Noise will fuck up the operation. I've accounted for that with some ground meat laced with strychnine. I really don't want some hound responsible for my next arrest or a stint in prison. If they come near you, just feed them a treat. I'll give each of you a four-ounce sample. Use it only if absolutely necessary, when and only if the damn dogs interfere. If you don't need to use them, make sure they wind up in the outhouse because your DNA will be all over the little bags I dispense. Step-off to the site will be tomorrow night around 0200. So meantime, get your gear ready, sleep, if you must, and dispose of everything you touch. I know I'm being redundant but pay attention."

"There he goes again," said Romanov. "What the hell is redundant?"

The question hung in midair without an answer. The other four just wanted the briefing to end.

The hounds, nevertheless, and despite Bronson's foresight, would not be the problem. Bronson's plan ignored the married element and the fact that rounds and tracers work both ways. Five on two seemed like a perfect chance of success for an assault. Military math usually says assaulting a fixed target requires a 7-to-1 advantage.

But an M-14 has an accurate, maximum range in the hands of an experienced sniper at five hundred yards or more. Three of the assassination team would eventually lie very deceased fewer than 150 yards from the McShea house.

As noted previously, all plans descend into chaos with the first rounds downrange.

Sergovia and Bronson would escape and later meet more exotic fates.

Chapter 24

REALITY CHECK

Now it was time to punt in football parlance. Oliver had seen it multiple times, stretching back more than twenty years. What seemed like a slam dunk in the morning suddenly became the afternoon air ball. Tsakrios was out on bail, the shooter was in the wind, and a judge had scuttled their arrest. His staff morale wasn't in the proverbial septic tank, but they were all supremely vexed. Their professional irritation saw Mulvihill's gavel as a toxic weapon of legal suppression, better than a Federal sidearm. His ruling squashed all those months of prior work accumulating evidence on Tsakrios and tossed for a spurious bench harangue without merit. The tension between them was striking but directed at what they perceived as Mulvihill's judicial error, not some mistake on the team's part. They perceived it a swipe at law enforcement to be publicly chided by a sitting judge in front of their peers.

They fumed, but the judge prevailed. Their opinion and prior investigation died without any legal remorse.

Yet most of Oliver's senior agents were also attorneys or CPAs. That made the bail a kind of double slap. They knew judges were often mercurial, but Mulvihill grated their collective hides. It was all part of the game. They'd seen it and done it before, so it was back to kickoff, accrue new evidence, and avoid Mulvihill on the next warrant. "Shop your judges better," Oliver later told Weinstein. "Next time, pick McKay, Allen, or Alderdice, anybody but that prick

Mulvihill. He has the ass out for any warrant from a Federal agency, particularly us. Maybe one of our rogue agents banged his old lady in the past. It makes no sense. And I have no idea why. Maybe he wants an appeals seat on the Ninth Circuit. Beware of that appointment, but that's reality. We all know how the game is played. Just go back to the starting blocks and let's do it again…and get it right!"

"Obviously we crossed the Rubicon, not the Allegheny," Agent Lucinda Freese remarked to Oliver on the way out of the courthouse. "I thought Federal attorneys were better prepared than that. That was more like a second-rate ambush. We got hosed in there. Weinstein seemed lost, and Mulvihill seemed like he just wanted an early lunch.

"Did I miss something there, Chief, or did we get snookered?"

Oliver smiled but oozed with sarcasm. He was just too professional to say publicly what he was really thinking. Always reticent in front of a microphone, he was seldom guilty of shooting his mouth off in public. Private conversation, however, was a different story. His silence spoke volumes…in stereo.

"I don't think so…but," Oliver said as he stormed out and slammed his way through the courtroom door, "we had enough evidence, I thought, to at least keep Tsakrios confined until arraignment, but that is now a very public blunder. We need to reassess our approach this afternoon at 1500. Assemble the core team then and let's address the inventory of what we took out of the house. There have to be further physical links between Tsakrios, his shooter, and the GetGo on the Homestead Wharf. Did the store have cameras or any kind of monitoring? I mean every business open now has cameras, don't they? Even churches and convents employ them. And check in again with that Detective Murphy in Homestead. He really seems to be on top of it. I didn't notice any mention of anything electronic in the compilation of evidence."

"No," replied Agent Marvin Gillespie, returning to Oliver's question. "All four in the ceiling were phonies. They were there for show, not effect. They're worthless for evidence. But the two on the exterior got shots that confirm what we already know. Tsakrios and the shooter entered the store first, followed by McShea. Then two holdup guys entered last. Those pics are clear but grainy, but there are no interior shots. So the narrative of action is almost entirely built on McShea's testimony. Without his story under oath, we got squat, nothin'! The store clerk's a real ding-a-ling who'll be no help on the stand. Slick attorneys like the Greek has will shred her memory of the attack into eternal perforation in the witness box. Anything beyond 'I do!' after she swears to tell the truth, she will wither under Greek's sharks. We can't rely on her. She'll fold. So it's down to physical evidence that includes that big-ass handgun the shooter used. My bet is somewhere at the bottom of the Mon near the Homestead Grays Bridge. Chances of recovery—slim. Even Navy sonar likely couldn't find it. After all, they haven't even recovered the frame of that damn bomber that crashed there in, what, 1956? So our chances of finding the weapon are beyond remote unless we've got some crack scuba crew with sonar. Add that to the compendium for the expense account.

"So we gotta get the Greek's two henchmen and get at least one of them to flip on him and turn state's evidence. That's priority. Protecting McShea suddenly became paramount, so we damn well better keep him alive for the trial. We got a fuzzy facial rec of the guy pumping gas into the Mercedes paid on the Greek's credit card but a poor one of the shooter. It's all going to rest on McShea's testimony. The camera angles were so piss poor that they didn't even get plate numbers. I can't sometimes believe how cheap some chain store owners are. A little investment in cameras could save them a lot of money and legal liability."

"That's easier said than done with our primary witness! Notice how well he interviewed on Saturday. He's articulate and well educated," Oliver replied. "A reluctant witness is one thing, but a guy like McShea is absolutely visible in the open and will not go into witness protection. I mean, we're gonna have to put a clamp on him, arrest him, and maybe drag his ass into court. Reluctant doesn't begin to describe his attitude. He may barge into the court and grab the Greek by the throat all on his own. He's fearless and a bit of a very loose cannon. I mean, we can't protect him on the river while he's working without a phalanx of agents. We don't have the budget for it. And besides, what's to prevent a vengeance strike on his wife and kids. She's no one to screw with either, but what about the three kids?

We just can't put five people on lifehold and hide them in one of our safe houses indefinitely."

"That's right. There also is another issue, Chief, that you don't want to hear," said Agent Rory Beane. "All five of our witness safe houses are occupied with guests awaiting transit. Two are scheduled to testify in a case in Miami and another to a trafficking case in Phoenix. They don't have a transit date yet, so we may have to stash the whole damn McShea family out of state. Our money folks in auditing will go berserk when they see the request for that bill. This ain't goina be conviction on the cheap. Be prepared for the blowback."

Oliver exhaled perceptively as they reached the staff vehicles parked outside within walking distance. "Okay, class, any other blatantly bad news, my children? Tell me now so I can grab my antacid bottle when we get back to the office. I hate ambushes, and we seem to have two already."

He looked at all three and then threw his hands up. "Are we good? You guys have anything else? I've been blindsided with enough already this morning. Give me the whole magillah!"

The collective nods were a perfunctory group affirmation.

"Okay, the world's not coming to an end," he continued, "and we're not going to gaggle all our priorities on this one hood that some of my predecessors should have stuffed years ago. It is, my children, going to be a bit of a bitch explaining this to DC about how we could execute a warrant with twenty-eight agents, sixteen vehicles, and tons of overtime and then have a judge quash it with a public rebuke like we were a bunch of miscreant eighth graders. So string up an agenda for all active cases, prioritize them, and let's see where the Greek falls on the spectrum of importance. We need a scalp here. Can we get that done by 1500?"

The terse united reply came from the other three agents filing into the car.

"Hey, remember, we're the FBI! If we can't do it, it is the end of time as we know it. We're number one!" That cued the perfunctory unit laugh from all four.

"Fuckin' A," said Agent Beane. "We're the FBI, and this Greek guy is a piece of barnyard dung. And he's gonna' kick our ass? I don't think so."

But the reality was, round one went to the Greek and the FBI looked inept. Round two looked equally unpromising.

The meeting at 1500 promised to be a graduate course in management and leadership correction. None of the agents savored the confrontation on the horizon. It was like rewashing dirty laundry for the second time. They thought it was already clean. The group embarrassment was a shared conundrum. Tempers and time were already short.

"The new indictment will be the easy part, Chief. But what do we do with McShea now? You know their house is on that fifty-acre old farm site and virtually wide open from the southern end, and the only thing that will get Tsakrios off is to eliminate the two witnesses, McShea and that frantic clerk. We don't have enough manpower to protect both, so what do you really want to do? How are we going to deploy this reluctant Dirty dozen DC is sending? Lodging is the easy part, but I smell the haze of a pending disaster."

Oliver exhaled perceptively, slapped the car's hood in anger with his hands, and took a cursive look down Grant Street.

"I don't like it any more than any of you, but I got you guys covered. It wasn't your fault, so let's just go back to work."

"What now?" McPhearson said.

Oliver looked at his twenty-year Rolex, an FBI gift watch from his senior peers. Then he turned to the other three.

"It's just ten thirty. Take an early leisurely lunch, ruminate over some ideas. Have your minds clear…and address any remaining business on your dockets post haste. Then be prepared to rock 'n' roll at 1500. And then let's go bag the Greek!"

Convening on time, they went through the drill again, throwing out a random list of what-ifs for the agents to savor. The meeting lasted more than ninety minutes with the new panoply of problems: how to protect two witnesses with an insufficient staff. Oliver made the command decision to ask DC for more bodies. The response from DC was a call dripping with halitosis. He was put on hold for ten minutes before senior staff acceded, along with the requisite crass reproach that it not become a regular habit. Twelve more agents would pull temporary duty in Pittsburgh, but there was grumbling about the per diem needed to support them. Oliver didn't want to hear it, but he was pointedly told "not to muck it up again!"

"We thought we had it right the first time," Beane said. "I don't think we missed anything crucial. Does Judge Mulvihill really have the ass out for Oliver? They've known each other for more than a decade, and I'm betting his decision had more to do with past history than the merits of the warrant. Maybe this has less to do with Tsakrios and more with their interpersonal history."

But there was that fuzzy little matter of the wrong street address on the warrant and the broad, vague description of targeted evidence they sought. Mulvihill noticed; most of Oliver's team did not. But even clerical errors are offensive to due process. Defense counsels get a contact high when they spot such clumsy attention to detail. It just gave Mulvihill more ammunition to suppress the warrant and make Oliver look like the village idiot the judge always thought he was.

"How did we, and I mean all of us, screw up something as elementary as an address?" Oliver said. "That's totally unsatisfactory. This can't happen again over a perfectly avoidable mistake. I hate losing to a guy like the Greek. He reminds me of every mistake in evidence collection we've made over the last twenty years, minor or major. He sat there in court with that shit-eatin' grin of his, mocking the entire legal system. He mocked us. Rework every phrase of that warrant, every word, syllable, phrase and legal nuance. We can't make this blunder again. Now I really want his ass on a pike. He's insulted me and every one of you in this office, even Mulvihill. We need to crush him like the roach he is at the preliminary hearing next Tuesday."

Gillespie turned to Oliver just as the meeting ended.

"We haven't nailed him yet," said Oliver. "Let's get him before DC forces us to attend a McShea funeral. I'm not real good at lame apologies to a decedent's family."

Chapter 25

SUNDAY DINNER

The grandparents bought the grandchildren back after Sunday Mass and left to go back to McCandless. Ronk pulled five steaks from the freezer and dumped the hydrator bins at the bottom of their very full refrigerator with all the veggies and then spread them out on the kitchen prep island in the middle of their idyllic, very spacious kitchen. Today the remainder of the carrots, celery, and fresh beets would also be sliced and grilled. Ronk had a knack with seasoning that made barbecued vegetables a hit with his children. Even the Alvarez kids loved them. Let the carving begin. It was one of those little victories for parents in their campaign to get their children to consume, and actually like, vegetables.

"Do you want to add baked potatoes?" he asked very loudly over the bellow of music.

There was no response.

The second movement of Beethoven's Third Symphony absorbed Kathleen's full attention on the iPad circumventing the kitchen's milieu with the strains of Ludwig's best at high volume. He tried a second time. She was still too engrossed. Kathleen was in bliss and somehow absorbed with some unknown, creative baking production, so he made an executive decision without consult: four large baked potatoes at 375 degrees for seventy-five minutes and he would split them, as he knew each of their children would eat less than a half. Ninety minutes later, it would be chow time. Ten minutes before the potatoes finished, it was time to address the steaks—well done for the kids, medium rare for the parents.

With meat in hand, he moved to the large exterior grill just outside the kitchen to ignite the propane tank under the grill. Then he momentarily returned to the interior to try to quell the adolescent noise of their fabled three. At that, he was only mildly successful. The screaming and hollering tampered down for about five minutes, only to resume as before! Nine, eleven, and thirteen smacked down thirty-eight! Ronk just let it slide. He reminded himself it was the sign of life right there in his house. For that he was grateful.

When Ronk brought out the steaks, Jake and Rufus almost had nosebleeds with their patented sniffers going into hyperdrive. They wandered about the grill, just in case some of the steak morsels decided to escape the fury of the heat. Not a chance! T-bones were just too expensive, only for the most posh of canines. These were hardcore country dogs, but the odors still jacked them into nirvana.

But both knew they would get the after-dinner bones.

The buzzer on the oven went off just before Ronk bought the steaks inside, and they sat down at the large oak table that could seat eight. The kids and the food arrived almost concurrently in concert with Dad's rule that when the parents were seated, they must be also. After the traditional Catholic grace before meal, portions distributed, it was conversation time where the inspired sometimes intersected with the raucous. More often than not, raucous prevailed.

Seamus fired the opening volley.

"So what happened, Dad? Mom? Do we really have to stay at Grandma's house this week?"

"Okay," Ronan began, "I was coming home from work Friday about six o'clock when I stopped at the convenience store in Homestead on the river for some milk when I was caught up in a robbery by two bad guys. The robbers came in, but there were three customers, and one of those guys was a bodyguard for the oldest guy and he shot the two robbers."

"Did they die?" Katie interrupted. "And I thought you got beer too. I saw the horse on the six green bottles (of Rolling Rock)."

Anything with a depiction of horses caught Katie's attention. She loved horses and had long lobbied her dad to get one for her.

It's an obsession not confined to seven-year-old girls. Adult women sometimes went into hyperdrive over the same. To this point, the parents had deferred any decision until she was a little older, like the target date of fourteen.

"No, Katie, I bought those today. I dropped the milk I had at the river stop during the shooting.

"The bodyguard guy killed them both. Then they ordered me to go with them. I didn't want to go, but they all had guns."

"Did they kill the milk too?" Katie giggled. "Well, where was your gun?" Sean said. "I'll bet you left it in the truck, didn't you? And the bad guys had the drop on you," he added as he shifted out of his chair and mockingly hid behind it. "Dirty Harry wouldn't have made that mistake."

"Sean, Katie, this was serious business," Kathleen interrupted. "Don't make it a game of trivial pursuit."

"Okay," Ronk continued. "And I wasn't about to argue with the guys with the guns."

Once again: Katie.

"But you weren't scared, were you, Dad?"

"Yes, I was, sweetheart. These guys were very dangerous. They had just shot two people, and I was afraid I was going to be number three. But they did take me where I didn't want to go, so that makes their second big crime one of kidnapping. Even though they let me go about a half hour later and didn't hurt me, it's still a major crime. Remember me telling you the story of Charles Lindbergh and how his kid was also kidnapped long ago? So it's now a crime prosecuted by the Federal government in Washington."

"Well, why don't they call it adult-napping since you are obviously not a kid? Or how about dad-napping since you didn't want to go?"

"I don't know, Katie," Kathleen chimed in. "Why not? Ronk! Es-plain to us," she said mockingly, slipping into her patented Ricky Ricardo routine. "What would you call it? I'd call it spousal-napping.

Takin' my man anywhere without my consent makes me go into... what did you call it once? A red-headed-roid rage."

"I don't care if Katie calls it a green rooster, it still wasn't fun. These guys were not nice people. They still aren't. And when they catch them, I'll have to appear at their arraignment and trial to identify them. That's the problem here, Katie, the police think the bad guys are going to try to kill me now that I have reported them to Sheriff Malone and the FBI. We have nine days before I'll have to appear in Federal court in Pittsburgh to identify them, so you'll have to stay with Grandma until they put the boss guy of the three in jail where he can't hurt anybody else. Meantime, you and your brothers are safer with Grandma and Grandpa. Okay?"

Katie once again!

"What's an arraignment?"

"That's where the suspect, the bad guy, has to go before a judge and plead either guilty or not guilty."

"What happens then?" she persisted. "Can we just come home after that since they won't need Dad anymore?"

"No, Katie," Sean said. "Dad will still have to go back for the trial and tell the story all over again."

"That's dumb! Doing it twice! That's just like school. Don't they write it all down the first time? I mean Sister Veronica remembers all the assignments she gave before for us at school. Why do the same thing twice?"

"Yes, they do, Katie, but the second time it's before a jury of twelve other people, and the story of the crime has to convince them. So Dad has to tell it again for them, not just the judge. Got it?"

She slumped in her chair a bit because it wasn't the answer she wanted to hear.

"Katie, don't pout," Kathleen snapped. "Listen and pay attention to what your father just said. This is not a game, and you will come back to the house when it is safe again."

"Well, who's going to feed Jake and Rufus?"

"We are, honey, we'll stay here to protect the property and the dogs."

"Can I stay here with you then to help you?" Seamus said. "After all, I'm good with the shotguns."

"Absolutely not," Ronk replied. "This is not something like shooting groundhogs, snakes, or wild turkeys, Seamus. These are seriously bad people, and Sheriff Malone's deputies will be here to help protect us, the dogs, and the property. But the three of you must stay with Grandma until my court appearance."

He then looked at each of them with a stern gaze.

"Do you understand? Do not argue with us on that. Everything will work out, and you'll return here next week. Grandma will take you back and forth to school every day, and it's a long ride, so you'll have to be prepared to get up a half hour earlier at Grandma's and get ready for school. No lolly-gaggin' around in the morning. You're big kids now, so you all have to act like it. And one week or so at Grandma and Grandpa's house won't kill you. Besides, Grandpa's already told me he's going to take all of you fishing on his boat…on a school day. This isn't a democracy, so that's what's going to happen. Okay?"

"Yes, Dad," came the soft collective chorus surrender. "We understand."

It was a concession, not an understanding.

"But we still don't have to like it, Dad," said Sean. "It seems like you're sending us away to keep us out of the way."

"In a way, we are," Kathleen responded. "We love you and need to protect you from people who may harm you. That's what good parents do, so after dinner, go to you rooms and pack five days' worth of clothes for school, including underwear and your toothbrushes. Grandma has everything else you'll need. And take your rain jackets, as it's supposed to rain on Thursday and Friday. We'll check your suitcases before Dad takes you over there tonight."

"Do we have dessert after dinner?" Katie blurted out.

After all, kids do have their priorities.

"Yes," Kathleen said, "but only after you pack and put the suitcases into my Blazer. So finish the meal and let's get it done. You need to leave for Grandma's house by seven o'clock so you have plenty of time to pack and get it together. It's only four, and we'll be done with dinner by five." Fifteen minutes later, everyone finished eating, and Kathleen and Ronan were sitting quietly at the table, performing a requiem for one of their last bottles of local Chardonnay.

"Do you really think they grasp the enormity of this situation?" she began. "Katie's much too young to grasp it, and I think she's scared to death. What about the boys?"

"Well, Seamus is thirteen, and I think he's eminently aware of the danger," Ronk intoned. "They're both afraid for us and emotionally conflicted about what to do. Can't blame them! Remember how I told you about the sudden death of my grandfather, my mother's dad, when I was his age? It was super traumatic since I was really close to him, and the funeral put me into a state of real confusion, particularly the gravesite ending. No adult could adequately explain to me why it happened. He wasn't sick or anything. He just suddenly died of a heart attack without warning. I think it took me until I was a senior at North to reconcile it. When you're a very young kid, I think you recover faster from death. But adolescents have a more difficult time. I don't recommend death of a close relative for any high school kid as some sort of perverse way to grow up. So I think I understand how the boys feel. At that age, death is a kind of abandonment, and that's what they're afraid of. They're scared to say it, but they all imagine we're going to die and they're going to be left alone."

"Well, we're not going to let that happen," she sighed. "I'll call Securitas tomorrow and apprise them of the home situation here and take a quiet ten-day leave of absence. Mel Tapper will have no problem with it since we aren't scheduled to have any heavy-duty public appearances until sometime around Memorial Day. Most of our clients have no public appearances until then. Any administrative stuff I can do here from home. What about you?"

"I don't know," he mused. "The Corps does a lot of things well, but they have few backups for me. And the river contracts don't stop just because I'm not there. The only thing that's going to stall the dredging is weather, and it seems we're good with that until at least Thursday. This is the work season, and the rivers don't begin to get really angry until October. I can try to take leave time but I doubt it would be approved until sometime in May. And by then, this whole scenario will be done one way or the other. But I doubt we'll get an early trial date, so the threat danger may remain real for months, and we can't live in a state of constant siege here. The real danger might be at work. They don't exactly have any backup for me in the area, and I'm not sure the Feds are willing to babysit me with extended sick leave."

There ensued a very pregnant pause in the conversation. Thirty seconds became a dripping two minutes.

"This is truly fucked!" he continued aloud. His anger was palpable. "I know I have to testify in order to put this dirtbag away and out of business. In the meantime, he could literally sic his pack of jackals on us and kill me, you, or the kids. This Greek guy has the money and lawyers to string the kidnapping charge out for years. And since I ratted his fat ass out to Malone, I doubt he'll ever go into the confessional booth for the forgiveness business. He's not into the remission of sin. I don't think the bastard's into life everlasting. I guess we both have to go into combat mode motif again. Any suggestions, Major? We have all the gear needed to fight an intrusion here at home, but we can't control the place nor the time or extent of an attack. Advantage—offense! I mean, he could attempt to whack me at work, on the road, here, or at the parish during Mass. He gets to pick the place of the fight and its parameters. Again, advantage offense! Maybe he'll try to assassinate me at church, so I can die a martyr like Archbishop Romero in Nicaragua. Am I ready for beatification?"

"Please, Ronk, don't flatter yourself," she said. "I'll have Angelo, our Securitas guru, out here tomorrow to install our updated night-vision cameras on all four corners of the house and the apexes of the roof, both north and south. The beauty of these new models is their range, almost three hundred yards. We can tie them all into the computer at our bedroom and have full coverage from dusk till dawn, six shots of the property at a time. We have a sufficient number of screens. It'll provide 360 degrees of coverage on the house. It also helps that we're moving toward June 21 and longer days. I presume any attack on us will be early morning sometime just before dawn.

That's the way I'd do it." Their combat training and instincts were correct.

That's exactly how the hit team planned it. It was distasteful but logical. But their approach from the south would be their undoing.

Ronk and Kathleen had an ambush vortex into which the hired five would approach. Five would enter the kill zone., and only two would have the good fortune to escape.

Red-headed wrath awaited them later.

Chapter 26

PUBIC DISPLAY

"Okay, it's been a long day and is going to get longer tonight, so I'm going upstairs to shower," Kathleen said. "You all right here so I can take my time before you guys have to leave? Maybe you should take them earlier so you can be back by dusk."

"I got the scullery covered here, Major Hottie, so go clean up your raggedy Irish ass," Ronk teased. "Jake, Rufus and I have this evolution covered. Take your time, my dear! Shower and be inspection-ready for me later tonight."

"Just for the record…Ronkster…my ass has never been raggedy. It's yours that needed the overhaul. But I like the newer version. It was such a chore to housebreak you, but I'm proud of my work. I can actually take you out in public now. I consider you my finest work. It was ten years of a longer walk than that of Mao Tse-Tung. You've come a long way, baby!"

"I heard that line once before."

Ooh! Loving sarcasm override!

Before he could gin up a counter quip, she kissed him furtively on the cheek and gently snuck up behind him to grab some of her favorite Irish glutes.

"Yum-yum, ooh, I love this stuff!" she whispered in his ear. "It's so pliable. I have loved it ever since Ms. Rodriguez introduced Renaissance art to us at North in senior art appreciation class."

"And just how did she do that? You didn't have any clay to play with because that class had no pottery wheel. Besides, you couldn't trust the kids not to start a clay-pitching fight."

"You didn't take the class that spring because you were too busy with varsity baseball and those dipshits with whom you loafed senior year. Some of them just made the girls retch with disgust. Your foremost interest, I recall, was which of the cheerleaders you wanted to ask to the prom and bang. Those were the days when you were completely devoid of taste. You don't even remember Ms. Rodriguez, do you? I think her first name was Anita."

"Yeah, wasn't she that cute Latina teacher who used to be a St. Joseph's nun and wore a habit and then came back after Christmas vacation and she wasn't a nun anymore? I guess she quit over the holidays. Didn't know you could toss the habit that fast! It happened so fast that none of us asked how or why."

"She's the one. You couldn't tell how pretty she was in the habit, but she had really nice hair, and I'll bet all your nasty-ass friends made snide comments about her."

"Not me. She was still a nun to me. That's a super sin. Maybe Albert or Charles would. They were the anointed team jerks. You could see their tongues hanging out before they opened their mouths. They were into sexual harassment long before anyone could define it. And those two dummies couldn't even spell it, even if Vanna White spotted them all the vowels. So that art class explains your addiction to my ass, yes?"

"Well, the former nun now known as Ms. Rodriguez had this lesson on Renaissance art where she had all these slides she'd taken when she went to Europe some years before. One of them was of that immortal statue of David in Florence, and she was explaining how Michelangelo had to overcome the balance problem with the statue's extensive weight and how to make it stand erect. It's almost ten-feet tall. So right in the middle of her AP art history class, Regina Rossini blurted out 'Nice buns!' so everyone in the class would hear it."

"I remember Rossini. That sounds like her. She was as dumb as a sledgehammer. The team nickname for her was Pincushion."

"And without breaking stride, Ms. Rodriguez says 'Gee, Regina, nice to see you're finally awake. Been on vacation? Welcome back from your academic nap. You might even pass this semester. And yes, his buns are perfectly proportioned. The appropriate plural is *glutei maximi*, as I'm sure you're eminently aware. So glad you were paying such strict attention.' Then she casually continued, hadn't even turned back toward her, but Regina was still pelted with an array of class snickers as she put her head back down and pretended to go back to sleep."

"And the point of your parable is?"

"I liked David's buns too. It's an art masterpiece. But what I have here is the real deal. So can I just reach out and touch you here momentarily and get another squeeze?" she said as she put her head on his right shoulder.

"If you must." It was feigned annoyance. Ronk loved it all anytime. Like most men, tactile attention is always welcome.

As Kathleen previously noted: "Men are easy—food and sex." Then she slipped away before he could retort to what she thought was a private twenty minutes upstairs in the shower.

Downstairs, Ronk turned to Jake and Rufus, now at perfect attention, seated near the edge of the kitchen, close to the back door. Rufus was perfectly quiet, but Jake wined with that unique hound sound that conveyed impatience. Only dogs can do it well, and you have to speak canine to understand it. After all, Jake thought humans were put on earth to tend to the needs of dogs, and sometimes humans just don't get it.

"Like, when are you goinna be done with dem bones, Doc? We're here. Hurry it up!"

The drill was always in two stages. Give each dog only one bone at a time to avoid fights. Taking two, he went outside, made them politely sit, gave them the doggie dessert, and returned to the kitchen where he suddenly remembered the next task after finishing the kitchen patrol.

It was time to check the weapons in the gun safe.

Upstairs, Kathleen quickly stripped, threw everything into the laundry basket in the corner near the bathroom, and entered the shower. Since her hair still smelled like the indoor scent of the Pittsburgh police headquarters, she also elected a lengthy drench of her fiery locks with coconut shampoo. Ten minutes later, she exited to dry.

It was then that she noticed that their bedroom door was slightly ajar and a slight commotion just outside.

As she stood by her bed, wrapping a towel around her hair in a bun-like contortion, hands on her head, she suddenly realized she had just caught a pair of adolescent Peeping Toms at her doorway, cracked enough just to see. Now the Irish erupted. She dropped the towel on the floor, put on her bathrobe, and walked toward Seamus's room where both her sons were seated on his bed, feigning sublime innocence.

She didn't knock.

And she didn't buy what they were trying to sell.

They sat there in stunned silence as she bent over and yanked some of Seamus's anatomically correct magazines from under his bottom dresser drawer and threw three of them on the bed between the two. "Open it up," she yelled. "Pick out your favorite centerfold, Seamus, and show us!"

Both were shocked that she knew where Seamus hid them.

Seamus blushed but meekly complied and opened one. By sheer coincidence, the centerfold selected was a redhead with a full bloom of red pubic hair. Then she stood immediately in front of the two and opened her robe and yelled, "Take a good look!"

Their eyes rendered shock. Then the tirade began.

"You want to see what a real woman looks like? Seamus? Sean?" she began. "Well, take a long good look at this again. I am your mother and I carried the both of you here for nine months, birthed each of you in a great deal of pain, and I will not tolerate your intrusion on my body or privacy. Do you understand?" Now she was really into the strains of the fervent yell. "Do you understand?"

"Yes," they collectively mumbled incoherently. The robe on the flash suddenly closed.

"And yes, boys, my hair down there is the same as that on my head. Just like the woman in the centerfold. Did you see it? Did you notice? Take a damn good look," she said as she held the robe open again for another fleeting five seconds. "But the only one who gets access to this is your father. Are we clear? And you better not treat any of your future girlfriends like this. Women are not toys."

Another mumble came from the guilty parties in the docket.

"Our bedroom is sacred where your father and I conceived all three of you, and it is a private place where you are never allowed. Understand?"

Another mumble, followed by tears from Sean.

Peep show terminated, but the homily continued. The pitch of her voice accelerated another half octave. It went on for another five minutes. No swearing or cursing but an extended round of her public rage.

"All people, particularly women, have an expectation of privacy, and I'm your mother and I will not tolerate you violating it. Do not do anything like that again. You've both graduated from the Swat Club years ago, but Dad still has that sharpening belt hanging in barn, and maybe I need to ignite your little butts with it. Do you understand why I am angry with you?"

Further incoherent mumbling followed their lame response. They were caught between embarrassed and the need to run away. Adolescent boys may crave the sight of naked girls their own age but rarely think of their parents as sexual beings. After all, aren't their mothers the reincarnation of the Virgin Mary? And sex? No, not my parents!

"Now finish packing and we'll check what you have. And don't even think about taking any of the mags you've stashed. Otherwise, I'll show them to your grandmother. What will you two say to her if I show her these? Maybe you'd like to see her naked too? Sean, Seamus? We didn't raise you to breach people's privacy. I won't have it. So start packing."

Then began the litany of "Sorry, Mom" from both of them. It didn't quell her anger. Then came the weapon of choice—the wagging index finger within inches of both their faces. It was one of those behavior features they knew was a prelude to punishment. She was close enough, so they could smell her deodorant.

"This isn't over. Next weekend, you're confined to quarters, and I believe the weeds will need picked from the garden. And you will go to Reconciliation (Confession) with me Saturday to confess your little foray into sin. Now you two get it together before I drag your little butts out to the barn for some bottom inspiration. Don't think your mother won't light you up if you do this again. And you thought Swat Club was a joke. You'll remember this spanking when you're fifty."

Then followed the exit with editorial comment. "And you're both grounded for a month!"

The voyeurs just sat there in stunned silence.

Point made, she stormed back to the master bedroom, slammed the door so hard that even Ronk noticed from downstairs as he opened their gun safe.

Her threat was a bluff. She knew they were both a little too old to be treated like fifth-graders, but just the threat was sufficient to instill the appropriate level of "You damn well better heed and conform." Voyeurism was off-limits in the master bedroom, and they both knew they'd stepped in it big-time. They also knew she was serious when her facial color matched her hair. They'd seen that angry face only three times before in their younger years just before she lit up their backsides with a ping-pong paddle.

"Remember what she used to say just before?" Seamus muttered.

Yeah, I remember," his younger brother intoned. "One swat for each year of our lives. And this time it's with that belt? What should we do?"

"Well, first, maybe we should get rid of those magazines, you jerk breath," Sean said, "or she might do that threat to show them to Grandma. That would be even worse. Grandma can make you cry with guilt. Grandma has that way! And remember how Grandma used to use that wooden spoon. That stung!

"Do you think she'd really do that?" Sean whispered after he was sure she'd really left the room. The color faded from his face.

"I don't know," Seamus replied. "But I don't want to find out. I guess we really blew it."

"What's this *we* stuff, you bonehead?" Sean said. "You dragged me into it, and we made Mom mad because you wanted to see those naked girl pictures. Now what do you think. You owe her a big apology."

"I do?" he stammered back. "You were in on it too. I just hope she doesn't tell Dad."

"Fat chance of that," Sean said. "There goes fishin' with Grandpa. You manage to make everybody else feel guilty sometimes. It's one of your stinkin' gifts."

The commotion upstairs caught Ronk's attention, along with Katie who snuck up behind her father and gave him what she called a backward hug. So what's up my petite little spy?" Ronk said. "Mom seems pretty upset."

"Yeah," Katie said. "She threatened to spank their butts with the belt in the barn."

"Oh yeah? Why?"

"They peeked in on her when she was in the shower."

"They did what?"

Ronk turned around, picked his daughter up, hugged her tightly, and sighed.

"That's all right, Dad, I'll take care of you. Mom's already yelled at them enough. You won't have to do anything more. She even got Sean to cry. Just pay attention to me. I'll protect you against them. I've got your back, as you say all the time, just like this. Even daddies need protection from moms...sometimes!"

"Thank you, baby, but I've got to finish cleaning these weapons."

Just then, Kathleen came downstairs again, but now she was calm, back to just mildly irked.

"Did our little domestic spy fill you in on the upstairs trauma and my tantrum?" Kathleen began as she entered the living/office area.

"Yeah, was it mortal, venial, or trivial on the scale of sin?"

"It was more trivial than venial, but I had to stop it in its tracks. They crossed the line but they know it now and won't do it again."

"But what if one of them goes to school and tells other kids about it. We might wind up with a principal's phone call or some goddamn millennial social worker at our front door asking about possible child neglect or sexual abuse? You know how weird people are about disciplined behavior at home that doesn't make it to the *Dr. Phil* show. Did you have to flash them to make your point? I mean you know how to punctuate a point, but wasn't that a little extreme?"

"Trust me. They won't say anything to anyone. I brought out the nuclear option to show Seamus's mags to my mother in front of him. Stunned silence would best describe the both of them. The point was made, darling, and we will collectively counsel them before they leave for my parents not to brag about their little escapade."

"Otherwise, what? Mother of my children! I hope the barn trip was just a ruse. Social service morons take that kind of talk as gospel permission to take kids out of your home. The only place that sanctions rump raps is the country of Singapore, and we ain't there. Here it's brig time for parents."

Fifteen minutes later, Kathleen and Ronk had the talk with all three of them before they left. The boys just wanted it to be over. Katie grinned with delight as she watched her brothers squirm; she even giggled. She was so enjoying their discomfort. The parents didn't stop her. It was part of their punishment.

Public shaming has long-term benefits. Katie was the designated house conscience.

It seemed like the longest ten minutes of their young lives, particularly the needling by their little sister. Pacifying hugs and kisses finally exchanged, Ronk and the kids filed into the Blazer.

Sean whispered to Seamus, "I guess we dodged a bullet!"

"Yeah...no thanks to you, dufus! Let's hope they don't tell Grandma and Grandpa."

Forty-five minutes later, fears allayed. Ronk said nothing about the incident at first., but he did turn to Katie before he left to go back to Butler.

"Don't you say anything! Do you hear me? I've got to go back right now, so I don't want any phone calls from Grandma before I get home."

Katie nodded, but he knew Katie might have trouble holding her tongue, so he took his mother-in-law quietly aside, apprised her, and asked her to be alert to any eruption that might occur if Katie brought it up.

"This is kid stuff, Ronan," Colleen said. "If you get any grief from my daughter about how she handled it, either of you can just call me. I have enough dirt on your endearing wife to shut her up for a month. She was a kid who invented rude with her brothers. Ask her about the time she got drunk with the McCarron brothers and came home without bra and panties one night when she was sixteen. I was more afraid that she had gotten herself pregnant, but that bullet was dodged. There are things to worry about…and there are things not to sweat. This is fairly low priority. Remember, I raised four, including your three brothers-in-law who come from the same gene pool as your sons. So far, none of them has gone to state prison. Perspective is paramount if you're a parent. Kathleen is sometimes obnoxious, but she's not off the rail. Both of you are Marine officers and real combat veterans. Doesn't that say something about how you two approach life and its ascendant problems?

"Kathleen sometimes has the tendency to grab a problem by the throat, or the groin, and thrash it. Was she extreme with the kids today? Probably! But consider what she went through this weekend. Friday night she killed a woman. So if seeing their mother naked is the most traumatic thing in their young lives, they'll survive. How about looking at the good side of it? Unforced nudity is not the original sin. They have parents who love each other and are still together. That's more than what half the kids here in upper-middle class Cranberry have. Stepparents are the predominant breed here. Lighten up on yourselves. Here that raunchy term *blended family* prevails. You're not there. Most kids here have step-somethings. That's not one of your problems, so don't beat yourselves up!"

Her reassurance helped, but Ronk was still conflicted. It was enlightened mother-in-law wisdom. The hug from Colleen helped. Ronk hustled back and was home within forty-five minutes, just after twilight.

Back on the Butler home front, Kathleen had finished the weapons check Ronk started before he left. Reality returned. On the large legal desk table in the living room/office lay the arsenal: two M-14s with iron sights, four twelve-gauge Mossbergs, both their Walthers, and Kathleen's company .40-cal.

Then they tended to the cameras, wires, and trip flares stored together in, of all places, the laundry adjacent to the dining area. At least, the kids were safe.

Now it must be time to check the aiming stakes and set two sniper firing pads with the requisite distances and their overlapping fields of fire. What was formerly done in military practice was now sullen reality, and it made each of them tense, but their training prevailed.

Soon the word *incoming* would have a whistling reality right past their ears.

Chapter 27

COUNTER PREP

"Hey, I learned a new word yesterday in the Wally (*Wall Street Journal*) today," Ronan said as he barged through the kitchen door from the in-laws. Kathleen was still in the living room and den area with their arsenal, segregating the bullets for the pistols and rifles while loading the two rifle magazines and the two shotguns. Together they had more than 180 rounds for the three pistols and another 80 for the rifles with four standard magazines.

"And what was that?" she asked.

"Purdah!"

"New to me also. How do you spell it?"

"P-U-R-D-A-H."

"And it means what?"

"It's sort of a modesty curtain in Indian (India) homes that segregates the rooms of the house where women can have a modicum of privacy. Yeah, they used it in an editorial the other day on some drab economic topic, but it made sense. I thought it was a really creative use of language."

Kathleen momentarily stopped the loading.

"And its application here, my dearest and most astute wordsmithing husband?"

"Well, that's what we essentially have here. Surrounding the house is a veiled purdah that you can see through and will stop nothing. We're wide open and vulnerable to attack on all four sides, so we have to reply on stealth and clear visions of the fields of fire on both the north and south ends of the house and barn. The front gate we need to keep locked, as Malone's deputies can always crash through it. I think all their SUVS have gate-crasher bumpers on them. But the goat fencing is easy to cut. We essentially have to see them first. That's critical. You still do have those night-vision binoculars, don't you, among the stuff stashed in the safe or on the property?"

"Oh yeah, this is Securitas issue," Kathleen said as she showed him the pair with ability to convert to both day and night options better than the original Starlight scopes. They use minimal light to make targets as clear as day. They worked off moonlight. No moon, no light. We have the updated new ones. But there is only one. The company won't buy those Federal ones. These are slightly more precise and accurate up to five hundred yards. They're German design and manufactured by Zeiss. Their pedigree goes back to 1846. Germans don't make junk. This is top-tier optical, and I love them. And when is the last time we bought something made from Germany that was a returnable piece of trash? Go ahead! I'll wait for the answer."

"I guess you'll have to wait awhile. I can't think of anything… and I'm still in love with that '68 Volkswagen I had at Penn State. Wonder if it's still on the road. It must have six hundred thousand miles on it by now. I mean, I tire of all the stuff we are forced to buy from Walmart, Costco, or Sam's that's from China. I'm at the point where I'll even buy inferior merchandise if it's made here just to address our monster balance of trade deficit. But the Volkswagen and the optics on the glasses are testament to German quality."

"Well, whoever of us is on watch should have the glasses with him…or her," she said as she corrected herself. "We'd better not break the damn thing, however, as they will extract a month's pay from my riverine rat's Federal largesse. You break it, you own it. They're almost $3,000 a pop. They ain't cheap! Securitas spares few expenses. It just passes the costs onto clients. Their clients never bitch about it, as their lives exude paranoia and xenophobia. That's why they hire us. Money for them is literally no object."

"And what if you break them?" Ronk said. "Do you get a hall pass and a business expense write-off?"

"No, I'll weasel out of it with my charm and proprietary good looks."

"And the O'Rourke blarney bleeds to the surface again! Remember, talkin' Irish horseshit is part of your DNA. But changing the subject... Problem is, we're going to have clear skies through the work week Thursday but rain expected Friday and Saturday. And they'll probably have to make their move before then since the arraignment's next Tuesday, a mere six days hence. I think we'll be entertaining our homicidal guests within the next seventy-two hours."

"Well, I'm betting that our incoming visitors have little or no real combat training," Ronk mused, "as they rarely have a need for it. Real termination training requires stark discipline, time, and patience. I doubt these guys revere those qualities. The object is just to kill people and get the hell out. And I doubt Tsakrios hired guys who like to sweat and stomp around in foul weather like we tolerated. Mud and wet is our edge. Most criminal types hate discomfort. Advantage—us! My guess is Wednesday before the rain at the end of the week. Rain makes it more difficult to maneuver. Temporarily, our advantage is weather."

"So how about a four-hour watch from 2000 to midnight and a second to 0400? Then we both greet the new moon together because that is most likely when they'll strike."

"Okay, that's logical," Kathleen concurred, "but I doubt we're dealing with the upper quadrille of the Bell curve. My concern would be the number they send. If we have to deal with more than a half dozen, we might well be in a real firefight we can't win, a true world of hurt. And they'd want the attack to be as silent as possible to avoid detection with Malone and company. So the new lights will counter night-vision goggles, if these fools even have them." She then quipped, "By the way, have you gone to confession recently? We might well have a date with Jesus before the week is out! Did you clear the deck of all your randy thoughts about women other than me? And what about your less-than-splendiferous mouth? You still cuss like you did when we were in high school and on active duty. It's one of several bad habits of which I can't break you. You do know that you aren't back with your fraternity brothers at state, although I admit some of their obscenity was worthy of low admiration."

His reply was classic Ronk with a fake John Wayne accent. "Well, that's just un-fuckin' believable, Major. I hope that won't downgrade my quarterly fitness report. And have you checked your mouth lately? It's flat rancid! Well, you're also sometimes 'unsat' at the dinner table but highly recommended in the barracks upstairs.

Maybe it's the altitude change to the second floor that cleans up your shoddy mouth. The one phrase I remember from that brain surgeon, fraternity brother of yours, Mark Longfeldt, was when he called you a pinprick bug fucker. Now that's some low-grade, first-rate male gutter gross. How come you never came up with anything quite that creative? I would have expected you to respond with something very Shakespearian. After all, wasn't Mark one of those 'weinies' who majored in something worthless like social ecology or Tasmanian Art History," she shot back.

Now she was needling him with her special brand of humor.

"I wouldn't want you to have to go to heaven and have to explain your lingering litany of lewd thoughts of women other than those reserved for your erotically remarkable, saintly wife. After all, you've been blessed in feminine grace, charm, and beauty, but Peter might not give you any slack. I can vouch for you sometimes, but it might not guarantee your admission."

"That's great alliteration, my dear! Okay, St. Kathleen of Butler, how about your transgressions of the Sixth Commandment? And your ability to out-swear and outshoot any woman in Butler county?"

"Just how many other women Marines live in this county?" she shot back. "And I'm reasonably sure I'm one of the very few with a commission.

"So, darling…dear…Ronk! When I have you, there is no need to traverse the road of wandering ocular sin. My meandering eyes are only for you, not some vain set of beach pectorals at a Gus Brickner swim fest. You are God's gift to me."

"Please, I think I may heave."

"Fortunately for you, this woman has dibs on you. I don't share, as I mentioned yesterday. Must I mention it again—you're a bought man at the closeout sale. No more visuals of others like Jimmy Carter alluded. Lust not in your heart or with any other woman's bodily parts…except for mine, which, I must remind you, are completely compelling and alluring!"

"Oh, please, my dearest redhead, that's quite the press release. How many sentences did that pile take? And can I just look? It's a little hard for men not to notice. It's in our DNA. We're hardwired for it. We're terminally visual, you know. Dennis Prager told me so years ago on his radio show. So you're rackin' it up under the capital sin of pride. Such vanity for a skinny Irish waif from the Northside! That's one of the reasons you had the good sense to relent and marry me. Just to polish your slovenly girly act! It took you long enough to see the light."

"And who's into vanity now? Let's return to reality. Who cleansed whom? And who the hell says I'm skinny?"

"Would you rather be fat?"

"Keep it up and maybe I'll just shoot you. No, on second thought, you're too much fun to shoot. I'll just keep you chained to the bedpost, play with you, and whip your 'fondable' ass twice a day. If you even consider using that word *fat* again, it may be the most unforgiven sin of your life. And the spelling for women is *fatt*, and that's a four-letter, very dirty word for us, never to be uttered in this house. That's a mortal sin that I won't tolerate. Don't ever let it pass your lips."

"So finally," Ronk demurred, "what are we going to do with the dogs when these ass eyes show up?"

"I suggest we keep them inside," she said. "They'll alert us to any breach of the three doors downstairs. Out in the open, they'll just be targets. And Jake doesn't need a posthumous medal of honor. We need the advantage of height on the second floor."

"All right, I'll take the first watch and put the M-14s inside the doors to the front and back decks upstairs. Shotguns posted on each side of the bed with pistols in their holsters on the bottom bedposts, waddya think, Irish? Do we have sufficient artillery here to do some damage?"

"Good plan. The only thing left is to post my statue of St. Anthony in the corner of the bedroom."

"Why?"

"Isn't he the patron saint of lost causes or something like that?"

"Well, hell no! Then he's cut from the team. Don't we have one of Ignatius Loyola? He was a veteran soldier, and a badass Spainard to boot! And he founded the Jesuits, so he qualifies as an intellectual giant!"

"He's in the visitors' bedroom at my mother's house, a gift long ago from some Jesuit wannabe at North Catholic. No help here."

"Well, Tony's Italian, so he'd better get his pasta bowl together because we ain't losing this fight. And incidentally, Jesus can wait. He's very patient, and we needn't arrive early."

"Well, my guys will be here tomorrow before eight to put up the new lights on the house attached to a kill switch that will with a remote lead into the bedroom computer. That way we can suppress the lights on command so the night vision on the binoculars can work. Problem is they may hit the deck and start firing before we execute our ambush on the south side. I don't think they'll approach from the northern gate, as there's too much activity on the highway and we're only two hundred yards from that and the mailboxes. Remember, upon approach, they'd see the eight mailboxes just to the left of the southern side of the highway for our neighbors. Anyone with evil intent will want to creep up on us with minimum chance of observation. They don't want to be accidentally seen. Our Achilles is the south, so just leave the south gate untethered. There's no sense in having them wreck the fence line. Just invite them on in, and we'll terminate their evil ways. But Mama has the answer to target acquisition with a simple trip to Home Depot tomorrow. I'm gonna get four LED lights with back covers and set them up as range stakes in the ground at about two hundred yards out. Between us, we'll have the kill zone covered. Get some sleep. I'll do the first watch."

"Yeah, here we go, Steelers, here we go!" Ronk said as he put his boots in combat mode, laces down, ready to jump in by the side of the bed firefighter style.

Like all good battle plans, it always reads well at the evening briefing and turns sour with the first incoming. Plans were made to break and modify.

The dawn's early light on Wednesday morn, however, would so confirm. Except the McSheas would do most of the burstin' in air.

Chapter 28

THE PERIMETER

Kathleen's Securitas crew arrived precisely as ordered at 0800 Monday morning.

That mollified her morning mood. Punctuality was "one of her things." She was extremely pleased.

Kathleen demanded said from all her work subordinates. It was another one of her professional habits melded from years in military intelligence. One of the fastest ways to raise her ire and challenge her to fire your ass was to show up for an assignment or meeting abysmally late. The business with their client class demanded precision at all levels. Protection in the era of terror harbored not otherwise. Excuses risk injury and lives.

"On time or be gone!" said one of her office administrators.

She became almost obsessed with the meticulous when first hired by Securitas in 2009 and assigned to organize a security meeting for the Mohawk tribal council in Upstate New York. The agenda that morning was to address issues of money transfers from the tribal bank to five tribes within the old Iroquois Confederacy. Naively she called a meeting at 0900 on a summer Monday that year, thinking all the principals would attend and arrive on time.

Wrong. Oh so wrong! Think again. They sauntered into the powwow at sundry times over two days. The meeting agenda was not about the trivial but serious issues of security for the Confederacy's cash transfers from bank to bank. If still on active duty, she would convene disciplinary office hours, or captain's mast, as they call it in the Navy services, for said lapses.

But they were on Mohawk time. Kathleen was not and so conveyed the depth of her annoyance forty-eight hours later when she finally had the quorum of tribal elders in the same room.

"I am truly ticked off about the attitude of your tribal council," she told the then elected tribal president, Edwin Bedoy. "Pull that kind of a stunt again and we at Securitas walk. Try to weasel out of our contract money and you will drown in a lawsuit in Federal court that will tie up your tribal assets until the resurrected spirit of the great Mohawk Uncas returns from the great beyond. This is totally 'unsat.' That's not a threat, that's a promise. This is no game. So please do not toy with us. We are dealing here with real money reaching into the millions. You all signed the contract, so abide by it."

The ass-chewing she administered that Wednesday apparently failed to permeate the conscious of the conference attendees.

"Just another white squaw who didn't understand how we do business!"

"Remind me again," said one wag at the meeting. "Why did we hire these fools, anyway? We keep making the same mistakes again and again. Why rely on these outsiders?"

"You have a short memory, my brother," replied another one of the elders. "Indians steal from us as well as, or better than, some of our white contractors. Thieves know no skin tone. Have you checked the audit sheet at our casinos recently? Money has a strange way of disappearing, but our fools are the ones taking the cash. You can't legislate morality, either white or red."

They liked both her and her astute recommendations, but they had a very different sense of time. The word *hurry* was not in their business lexicon. That made security for the bank money transfers an unnecessary nightmare. They had too much money on float and paid too little attention to how it was transferred from place to place, particularly from the casinos. Lip service was the order of the day.

Her next step was to document the tribal failure to adhere to the provisions of their mutual security contract. She then recommended its abrogation to her bosses. The company honchos in Virginia concurred and reluctantly absorbed the lost revenue but vowed never to work with the Indian nations again.

The tech crew chief, Donny Ravelli, however, also knew her history and her "pique with punctuality," as he once told his crew. Her Mohawk rant later became urban corporate legend about how she addressed the Mohawk casual attitude toward time at the council meeting. One of the tribal attendees, a Marine graduate of Parris Island (Platoon 2145 of 1963), later said she "can chew ass better than a gunnery sergeant. I didn't think officers could do that. We dropped the ball. She's right. We can't continue to do business like it's 1789."

Everyone at Securitas heard the details with a mixture of humor, laughter, and dread. It began with the slamming of the contract onto the boardroom table to her description of their attention to detail as childish and pathetic. Her critique lasted a full ten minutes. It included no obscenity or profanity and wasn't bombastic. It was, in military parlance, a correction, not a rant.

Helluva correction! Bailing on the contract cost Securitas $1.2 million, but they swallowed it and absorbed the hit.

But it was close. It was just classic Kathleen: angry, logical, and to the point. No nonsense. Just get the job done.

But that's why the corporation hired her. Kathleen had two rules. They all knew rule number 1: Show up on time with all your gear, ready to work. If not, be prepared to lose some posterior weight at your own peril. One of Ravelli's team actually concocted the quote of the year for the company watercooler chat and posted it on Instagram.

"Man, that woman could dress down Mother Teresa, make her feel guilty, and drown her in a coffin of contrition." Rule number 2: Refer back to Rule number 1.

So Ravelli's team arrived fully equipped, just as mandated on the company work order with all their necessary requisite gear. The order included installation of a radio dimmer switch that they would install as an app on the upstairs computer for remote control of the defensive lighting around the corners and the apexes of the roof, both north and south.

It wasn't, heretofore, necessary at their Butler retreat. She normally directed this kind of protection for homes and businesses of the paying clients. Now the hazard and threat for other homes became the new McShea normal. She resented it but conceded it was a necessary evolution. Both of them could smell the vulnerability of the threat pending to their family unit. It was a hazard and danger imposed, so they had to summon the resources to confront it. But it didn't mean she had to like it.

The Ravelli crew finished the security lighting in about five hours, ninety minutes short of schedule. Kathleen loved that sort of efficiency and put a reminder note on her laptop to give Ravelli a letter of appreciation for his Securitas personnel file and recommendation for promotion.

Now it was time to set the aiming stakes with the grounded lights. She took her Home Depot haul out of the Blazer and called for Ronk.

"Ronk, are you upstairs?"

"Yeah, waddya need?"

"Go out on the back deck with the glasses and spot me. I'm gonna put these aiming stakes at about two hundred yards or so. Watch me."

"Suggestion," he yelled from the deck. "Get that standard length of climbing rope in the barn that the tree trimmer left. It's almost exactly that. Tie it to the west leg of the deck and run it out. That should be almost exactly two hundred yards or within a few feet or two. Okay? Then I'll throw down your headset, and we can talk it through. Go get the rope and I'll set up the headsets."

Five minutes later, she returned and tied the rope, and he tossed her the headset.

"Radio check, can you hear me now?"

"Ronk, please don't be a cliché. That line was bad when AT&T owned it. Yes, I have you Lima Charlie (loud and clear in military parlance), so position me first to the far left of the house when I run this as far to the south and right (southeast) as I can."

He watched her striding through the now ankle-high spring grass, both dogs in tow, just delighting at the visual of the walk-away backpack slung over her right shoulder, rope hanging over her left shoulder. His predicable, lurid mind slipped into venial sin. He signed heavily in visual delight.

What an ass! Goddammit, I'm lucky. That's two hands of heaven, he thought as she moved away. He briefly looked to the open sky to the south. *Hey-Suss (Jesus), you been berry-berry good to me!* When she arrived at the rope's end, she turned.

"Move it to your right about ten yards so we can spot anyone approaching toward the front door," he yelled.

Movement done!

"Okay! That's about right. Stake one there."

"Now move to your left about forty yards where you can still see the stake to your right."

Done again and the same for the final two. Now it left the de facto aiming stakes of the LED lights in the ground in a semicircular pattern that led to an imaginary vortex, the kill zone.

That done, Jake couldn't resist and he picked up the rope's end and began a long-distance tug-of-war with the anchored end of the back deck. It wouldn't move, so he took it to the right and tried again. He growled. He barked. It still wouldn't move, So he dropped it and barked at it as if it wasn't playing by the rules. So he barked at the rope a third time, picked it up, and yanked again.

The deck still didn't move. Jake was unhappy.

Kathleen then picked it up and moved left with the rope, placing a second aiming stake west roughly sixty yards away and then two in between. Jake picked up the dropped rope again and tugged furiously.

"Jake, it's not going to move, baby. Let's go back and see Ronk and we'll retrieve the rope from there."

Since both dogs loved to run, they led the way. Ronk came down the back steps from the southern deck. Together they scanned the positions of the LED lights before them to the south.

"Just right," he said. "I don't think we'll have to deal with any fog this week, so we will be able to clearly see any targets in the kill zone. At two hundred yards, we should have the advantage then of surprise. Waddya think?"

"If they come in on a spread formation, let's take out whoever is on the east and west perimeter and move them to the center."

"That might work if it's a mere half dozen. But what if they approach with more?"

"Think, my dear, this isn't the Soviet Army at the Fulda Gap. If this prick Tsakrios has more than six on the hit team, then Malone will never arrive in time with his deputies. All he'll have to do is call the Butler County coroner. Let's get real! Plan on six or fewer and panic if there's more. That's why God made cell phones. Tsakrios is not about to bring the Greek army to kill me. That requires too much tactical support planning. This is an assassination attempt, not Butler County WWIII."

"Point well taken, but don't you just wish we had just one artillery piece with something like an outlawed couple of old 105-mm flechette artillery rounds so that we could just blow all of them away in one fell swoop? That sounds like an adolescent male fantasy upon which you could salivate. No?"

"You know I love you, baby, but sometimes you make testosterone seem like low-grade estrogen. How does a dazzling mother like you come up with shit like that? Tsakrios may be afraid of me but should be terrified of you. I'd just kill 'em. You'd section him into pieces and feed 'em to the fish in one of the rivers one bucket at a time. I'd be satisfied with just stopping them. You'd make them prime chum, so I'm glad you're on my team. I'd hate to have you on the Greek's payroll. So what next?"

Now it was time to set the southern firing positions for the M-14s, one on the back deck and second east of the front door circa thirty yards from the house, but the area had no cover, so any shooter would have to fire from the prone position.

"So let's make one last adjustment," Ronk offered. "Let's move the tractor twenty yards to the southeast of the house and park it unobtrusively at an angle where one of us could assume an offhand or prone firing position in either direction toward either gate."

"Yeah, just like basic school and the rifle range. God, what would we do if we didn't have this fun gun training, all courtesy of the Federal government? Almost makes some of that imposed six months of misery worth it, particularly that segment on land navigation in the rain. Noah couldn't have ordered that much wet. I hated that more than anything else on the training cycle.

"I'd rather be in protective custody and cowering at some safe house with Malone's deputies and the kids. But this is the hand we've been dealt with, and I know we together can deal with it. I know I couldn't do this alone. This is better."

Then she blurted out, almost without thinking, "Ronan Patrick McShea, I love you more than I can put into words. But no way is this career criminal going to wreck our family. Who the hell does this pile of Greek garbage think he is?"

Now surveying the scene from the south-facing back deck, they hugged intensely for almost a full minute, exhaled, kissed deeply, and said almost in unison, almost on script, "No way! Our children deserve better."

Then they fell into the rifleman's creed.

"This is my rifle. There are many like it, but this one is mine…"

They finished and shared a laugh. They remembered all of it to their delight and surprise. After the recitation, they hugged again. Then Ronk turned toward the southern horizon.

"Bring it on, motherfuckers, and be prepared to see Jesus! I am now at my obscene and angry best."

Chapter 29

FOREPLAN

The bunks were hardly the caliber of the Weston or the Hilton but they sufficed. After all, this was a hunting cabin, decorated with desiccated deer heads and empty beer cans. They attested to the cabin's history. There was one spider-ridden shelf on the cabin's north end sporting empty Schmidt's cans, a brewery that left Philadelphia and fled to the Midwest in 1987. Guarding a corner in the cabin's southeast was a stack of Yuengling, most favored by the contemporary, suburban thirty-plus crowd. There was even a stack of Latrobe, PA's finest: *Rolling Rock*. The empty cans and bottles were circular epitaphs to the history of at least two generations of deer hunters, not wine connoisseurs. No Chateauneuf-du-Pape need apply here. Bottles of vintage French or California grapes are verboten in deer country. It was what it purported to be: a testosterone hangout for the working class with ammunition, augmented sometimes with a little whiskey after a successful day of venison hunting.

The hired quintet, moreover, was not the camping type favored by the literati of Guns & Ammo. Said campsites were an acquired taste repellent to New York's Upper East Side but coveted by the outdoor types upstate. Still the Greek's hired hands despised the choice of quarters. They saw no logic in their overnight stay. That's why the Tsakrios put Bronson in charge. Bronson was the brains. The others were the brawn but more like sidecars to a motorcycle, a necessary adjunct but not the driver. Their collective bad sense was just to go to Butler, do the deed, and collect their bounty. Collectively, they were slightly more disciplined than the Gang Who Couldn't Shoot Straight.

But not by much.

Only Sergovia and Bronson had the good sense to bring sleeping bags. The others slept in what they wore. Boy Scouts they were not. Even in spring, the Appalachian highlands could dip into Fahrenheit 30s at night. So they collectively bitched about everything in the cabin. By late Tuesday night, Bronson was already tired of the incessant carping by the male trio of grunge. Their negative griping annoyed him to no end. It only reminded him that never again would he work for the Greek unless he could pick the crew.

Bronson had also drawn handmade maps of the oblique route from the cabin to the site he preselected south of the McShea property the day before. There they could park unnoticed in the early spring foliage. Butler County, even today, is still more country than urban, but the southernmost creep of suburban Pittsburgh expanse through Cranberry Township was upon them. What was once purely farm country was now infected with the swill of suburbia. Brick and concrete bisected what were once pristine cornfields that precursed the invasion of the upper middle class. But Bronson selected the off-road dirt trail still well worn and obviously traversed mostly during deer season. It was about a half mile north of Pennsylvania Route 8, close enough to the McShea farm to affect a fast getaway, so he determined they had to do the deed before the projected rains of the coming weekend. Wet ground and tire tracks were not part of the plan.

"We'll have to go on foot toward the property, so pack all your gear accordingly," he intoned. "It's roughly about five hundred yards to the house from the where the vehicles will be. We need to be able to track one another, so I took the liberty of acquiring fluorescent, illuminating strips to put on your backs of your jackets so we can see each other from behind as we approach. Your shirts or jackets will have to go in the outhouse, too, when we return. That also includes you, Sergovia. Burn both your shirt and bra. If any of you guys have long johns, they also need burned. We'll approach, fifteen to thirty yards apart in a parabola. Once we step inside the property gate, hand signals only. No noise!"

"There he goes again," whispered Dempsey to Romanov. "What the fuck's a parabola?"

"Just shut up and listen," Romanov shot back. "We'll approach the house in something like a semicircle. It makes sense, so just listen. Ask Daltry. He'll explain it."

"And remember," Bronson continued, "our job, I remind all of you, is not to get into some sort of firefight with them or the cops. We sneak in, do the family, and hustle out before dawn. Daltry, Romanov, and Dempsey will have the three AKs. Do not use them except in an emergency extraction. Use your handguns once inside the house and don't use the damn strychnine on the dogs unless absolutely necessary. Bring it back, and that, too, goes in the outhouse. Got it?"

"There he goes…again! Strychnine?" Dempsey shrugged.

"Just shut the hell up and listen," said a now irritated Romanov. "You might learn somethin'."

The perfunctory negative nod followed from the Gang of Grunge. They giggled and laughed like adolescents exchanging dirty jokes. All they could dream about was easy money and an escape to some beach hideaway with a multitude of loose women just yearning for their bodies and dirty minds. The perils of the plan flew right past them like unwanted insects.

Attention to details was the knat collection that might scuttle the operation.

Sergovia was totally focused. She paid strict attention and was beginning to doubt the wisdom of it all but trusted Bronson more than the other three. For them, she felt nothing but contempt for their fake machismo. She had killed greater men than they in beds while she was nude. Her shaven groin was devolved of pubic hair, less evidence to trace. She did so with three others with both a smile and a sharp edge as she sent them to the afterlife with a straight razor. It was cold and calculating after a post-orgasm nap that would be the last sleep of their terminated, criminal lives. She was, in fact, an updated and much deadlier Elizabeth Borden. A quick shower and a double douche for her "mantrap" washed away as much DNA evidence as possible, even to laser away her underarm hair and any strains of hair from neck to ankle that left her completely shorn. Her fingerprints were not yet on anyone's database. She was, in psychiatric parlance, a true sociopath devoid of conscience, the perfect assassin. Nude, she was Helen of Troy with a straight razor.

That's why the Greek hired her.

Her script varied little with each of the three victims. They died efficiently, and she "cleaned up" without any semblance of remorse.

She took her time. All three contract murders: one in Binghamton, New York, and two others in Erie remained active police cases, withering with age and, as yet, no match of DNA on site that could connect her to them. All DNA evidence the police garnered from the bodies and their beds showed only body hair, mitochondrial DNA, minute traces that existed in the sperm of the decedent males, so they could only assume that the decedent was sleeping with either a male or female. It was no help and a cold trail. All they could ascertain was, the victims were entertaining someone of European extraction. Police assumption was that the killer in all three cases was female, as the victims had no previous dalliances with gay sex. The autopsies buoyed that analysis since there was no seminal fluid in either the tracheae or anal canals of the three deceased.

That profile became the assumption of their primary suspect: cold, ruthless woman, twenty-five to thirty-five, likely five feet eight to five feet ten and somewhere around 140 pounds with masculine upper-body strength.

On that score, they were right. Her soul was classic Dostoevsky. Her maternal instinct died with the Baltic Russian winter years before. That's why the Greek trust her most. She shared his most prominent trait, that of treachery. She belonged in Dante's Ninth Tier of Hell.

She employed a dark Russian soul, devoid of the capacity for empathy, perfect for a job like this. Killing the McShea children, if necessary, would just be a footnote to the mere perfunctory. She had very little empathy for any life from infancy forward. Money trumped everything, even adolescent life.

"We'll take the rentals brought by Daltry and Sergovia," Bronson continued. "That magnet of a police wreck you two brought"—he pointed to Romanov and Dempsey—"stays here until we return. It's too obvious on the road and noisy with that Hemi engine modification you put in it. Great for a camping trip, but this ain't it. That fuckin' thing screams 'Pull me over' to every cop on the road. Remember that going home. Obey the speed limits and don't do dumb shit! Police attention with weapons in your vehicle is a reservation chit to prison."

"Yeah," said Romanov, bristling with countersarcasm. "You're right. Your rentals are much more obsequious, far less likely to attract cops. You can just kiss my ass."

"There you go again," said Dempsey. "What the hell does that mean?"

"It means hidden, not obvious! Your truck is like a pink fire engine carrying the coffin at yo' mama's funeral. It's too garish to miss. We'll pick it up when we get back. Don't need to have some goddamn state trooper notice it at night. Bronson's right."

"There you go again," he whispered. "Garish what?"

"We're only going to be here until tomorrow and leave about three o'clock. We should arrive just before the onset of sunrise, so following me in the lead vehicle should by easy," Bronson continued. "It's only about ninety minutes from here to the farmhouse, but no Turnpike. Those folks keep records and photos of cars, so we'll use State Route 422 to the approach point. From there to the house, it's on foot, so check and recheck your weapons. Leave nothing to chance. Before we leave here, clear everything out of the cabin and your personal trash and put it in the outhouse pit. Meantime, sleep, eat, and unload. Even fecal matter is evidence."

"Why can't we just do it tonight? Why do we have to wait until tomorrow night," Dempsey said.

"Because the Greek thinks they'll send their kids to some relatives' house until the arraignment and he doesn't want them involved. Say what you like about our employer, but he does have two daughters of his own, and that's the way he wants it. And he controls the payroll," Bronson growled. "It has fewer complications.

It's just less than we have to deal with. May I remind you again why we wanted suppressors for your sidearms—limit the noise! We need to kill him and her as quietly as possible, so we're doing it the Greek's way. School is still in for the kids. That's why they won't likely be there. In an' out, quick and easy! Killing two should be easier than killing five. Remember the business McShea's old lady is in. Don't start an extended firefight with these two. I doubt the kids will be there. But between them and the Butler County sheriff, we need to move as swiftly and quietly as possible. Can't emphasize that enough! You won't get your money from the Greek if we muck it up. There's a projected three days of rain this weekend. Tomorrow night has to be it. Muckin' around in wet ground just leaves more clues to our identities, so that's the way it's gonna be. This ain't up for a vote."

Segovia sat on her bunk and just snickered. She concurred with what Bronson outlined. Trust the other three? *Not a chance. No fuckin' way*, she thought and then added out loud, "But I'll do the McShea kids myself, if necessary. No problem! It's this trio of clowns that worries me."

"Okay, sleep, eat, and outhouse!" Bronson concluded. "Are there any further questions?"

Boredom now became a continuing, contaminating factor for the next eight hours. Patience mattered but was in short supply with the three mutts, as Segovia deemed them. Her contempt for them was patently palpable.

Wednesday next, the mutt problem became moot. Their remains would take top billing as honored guests at the Butler County coroner's office. Some of their body parts would even go into the collection plate registry for patients needing transplants and medical school studies. They could go to hell with the assurance that some of their DNA would productively live onward in others.

They were about to become inadvertent organ donors.

It was Dempsey's prized vehicle that was the group's albatross and a later prize piece of evidence for the FBI's meticulous lab rats that would take its abandoned remains, disassemble, and reassemble it bolt by bolt.

Meticulous also applied to Bronson whose attention to detail included a child's loud Mickey Mouse clock with entreaties from Mickey, Donald, and Goofy to wake up to the still dark hour of 0300. Its annoying wake-up call from the Disney characters roiled the mutts, but Bronson and Sergovia were already awake ten minutes earlier. Trips to the outhouse secured, the abbreviated convoy began its deadly trek. They made one last early morning coffee run at a truck stop near the I-79 approach just south of Ellwood City. No one seemed to notice or care about the tall, nondescript woman in camouflage array who bought five large cups of coffee. After all, this was outdoor country, even out of season.

It also seemed slightly odd to the young female clerk that none of them exited to use the restroom except the woman. These hunters all appeared to be men broaching forty or fifty, and she knew from experience they all likely had impinging prostates. She wondered aloud why they stayed in their vehicle. Guys like them peed incessantly. Minutes later, she blew off the incident until weeks later when a junior FBI agent out of Pittsburgh came into the station and asked about them.

"Yeah," she told him, "now I remember. The woman came in, but all four of the others remained outside in two cars. It just didn't seem quite normal. Five people stop and no one uses the restrooms?"

It wasn't, and Special Agent Sean McCoy then told the store manager that they would have to have their monitoring tapes for the last thirty days immediately.

"We only keep them here for ten as per our corporate attorneys," she said. "After that, they're shipped to headquarters for disposition."

"Thank you," McCoy said as he whipped out his .40-cal cell phone to get Oliver.

"Patch me through to wherever he is. I need to talk to him… now…for an immediate warrant."

Chapter 30

THE ASSAULT

Small talk permeated the trip and became the order of the day with Bronson at the wheel of Romanov's rental. The conversation was short on the personal but long on opinion. Bronson shared very little of his inner self, so he and Sergovia were a match made in hell. The rest of the crew, *au contraire*, ran their mouths like elementary school kids.

As per his own admonition, he actually wore medical gloves to cover everything he touched, including the pages of the pulp novel he was reading. He suspected that a copy of his fingerprints was somewhere on myriad files in cyberspace since he had served in the Israeli Defense Force (IDF). Given an arrest for petty theft years before in Marseilles, he also presumed that a copy of said hide in the bowels of Interpol somewhere since they save everything of evidential value, particularly since 9/11 and the deadly incident with the staff at Charley Hebdo in Paris. He was, in fact, the very epitome of a low-grade, professional criminal with a pliable conscience that embraced the nuances of sin. His ego knew few bounds, along with his penchant for the lewd with any woman, but Sergovia he trusted because she was the foil to his satyr. His thoughts about her swarmed in the marinated filth of lust, but he knew not to express them. At the core, he feared her violent streak and didn't want to provoke her presumed response.

Yet his instincts were correct. Gloves sheltered the prints of suspicion throughout the stay and subsequent drive. His prints were not for police display. The sloppy attention to detail by the others fell on deaf ears.

As did those of Daltry! Bronson had to remind him several times of the glove and DNA protocol. Dempsey, consumed by boredom, spent most of the previous day on his chosen bunk that he covered with one of the clean but dusty sheets and an army-issued blanket that Daltry's cousin had left in the stock closet. Both Dempsey and Daltry's literary taste ran from old copies of *Outdoor* magazine to *Maxim* and sundry porn mags with forgettable names now sliding into oblivion with the advent of the Internet. Those, Bronson reminded them multiple times, were also grist for the outhouse fire. Daltry's cell phone, moreover, was now the center of his information universe. Like millions of others, the addiction was overwhelming, and he traversed the universe of XXX websites with high gear, creating an inventory of cyberspace evidence. The FBI cyber nerds later would salivate, digest, and unwrap every website of his pornographic allure.

Most slowly ate their two allotted MREs, except Sergovia. One was sufficient for her, as she duly noted it took about a quart of water to properly consume an MRE and leave its remnants in the outhouse. Bronson reminded all, at least three times until dusk, to download before they left. Around 1900, the treks to the outhouse began. Romanov didn't even bother to close the outhouse door.

His lack of class or polite sensitivity even offended all three of the other men.

Sergovia had a different problem: her period was in full swing. But she also had her own sanitary bag in which all her tampons and cleaning wipes that she would collect in one container of which she would dispose herself. She put all her used tampons and wipes in that personal baggie, wrapped it in a second paper bag hidden in the toiletry bag, and stashed it all in the trunk corner of her rental. She didn't trust the perverted instincts of the men in the team, especially Romanov. Making them aware of her "moon" would only ignite their adolescent fires. Her placement of the disposables in the trunk of her rental just before they left, however, would later become a tactical blunder. She should have just dropped them in the outhouse. Forgotten placement would be her demise.

When the team shoved off just after 3:00 a.m., Bronson and Sergovia took the lead in Romanov's rental, and the other three followed in the second, the one she rented. They arrived slightly earlier than expected and followed Bronson into the bush.

Bronson put the team into a linear formation where he led from the rear.

When they arrived at the open gate, dawn was fewer than fifty minutes away. He put Dempsey and Daltry on the wings with Romanov in the center, Sergovia on his right, just behind the lead three. They could not yet see the house, as it was not yet visible on the upward slop until they were within two hundred yards. They checked one another for a tight fit of their ammunition and knives. Bronson gave one of the Kalashnikovs to Romanov and the other two to Daltry and Dempsey on the wings. At the open south gate, he gave his last instruction.

"Silence from here on out until we get inside the house," he whispered. "Do not fire until we get inside. Is everyone accustomed to the darkness now?"

Night vision acclimation acquired, they collectively assented and moved forward.

"Stay within ten to fifteen yards laterally from each other and look to the center as we approach. If you spot anything wrong, raise your fist and slowly tell the team to drop to the ground and we'll assess the threat. Don't do anything stupid like fire off rounds prematurely. Once inside, use your pistols and let's get out as quickly as possible. Is that clear?"

The following four vocal grunts were an affirmation.

"Okay then, let's do it."

Through the gate, they dispersed and moved forward, not knowing even their foot movements were now already under scrutiny. Even the silent footsteps transmitted signals to the bedroom computer. The buried detectors on the property functioned perfectly, a rare feat in detection technology two generations removed from the primitive ones of the Vietnam era. Earlier variants couldn't discern a human footprint from that of a coyote. The new ones could tell you the weight of an intruder within five pounds and likely even his or her height and possible gender.

Updated cyberwarfare works.

Bronson felt even more emboldened when he found the two trip flares Kathleen had set. He alerted the other team members via hand signals. They all then carefully stepped over the connecting line, but he was wary. "What is going on here?" he said in whisper to Sergovia. "These folks are not fools. We need to be extra cautious from here to the house."

"Calm down," Sergovia replied in muffled tones. "We're not yet exposed."

His paranoia was not assuaged. *Why had they set them out in such an obvious placement near the open gate?* he thought. *This is just too convenient to be random. These folks aren't stupid. Why is this so damned obvious? This is no lapse.*

He was nervous now but dismissed his own reservations, still unaware of the buried ground sensors. Round one to the McShea defense.

The decibel level of the speakers in the McShea master bedroom began with a mouse-like squeak and then amplified to a louder alarm as the five approached, now spread out in tactical formation. Then it elevated to concert level.

"Ronk, reveille, they're here! Coming through the south gate! I'm going to kill the lights inside the house," she screamed as he almost jumped directly into his boots from a prone bed position. Thirty seconds later, he was alert, hugged Kathleen as she grabbed her M-14, and darted down the steps to the front door.

"Got your headset, baby," he yelled.

"Yeah, what about yours?"

"Radio check?" she replied as she turned her headset on and quietly exited in stealth mode through the front door toward the family tractor parked roughly thirty yards away to the southeast of the front of the house.

"Signal affirmed!"

"Gotcha! We're Lima Charlie!" he replied.

The front wheels of the tractor were turned directly southwest into the kill zone where she assumed an off-hand position, leaning on the rear right wheel of the old Harvester International, now poised as more than just an icon from the days of the Great Depression. Ronk had the night-vision glasses, but three minutes later, she could also plainly see the outline of three lead figures approaching. All three on the approach line had what appeared to be rifles with banana clips strung over their backs.

"Must be AKs," she whispered into headset.

"Roger that," replied Ronk. "They came for bear. Nothin' like overkill. And these guys make no pretense of guile. They're blunt, obvious, and tactically stupid, so I guess we have a genuine gunfight on our hands. It's the okay corral right here in Butler County! You ready?"

His view from the back deck rang with clarity.

"Yeah, three up front, two in the rear—a total of five. These shitheads are clueless. And you're right, they have Kalashnikovs. That makes it an even-up fight," he said. "I'll start the countdown and you take out the one on my left and I'll take out the one on my right. Then we both drill the center prick."

"Roger that, *mon amour*! Let the countdown begin."

They breathed, exhaled, and squeezed their triggers: sight alignment, sight picture.

Ronk leaned his chin into the stock over the railing of the deck. They were slowly coming into plain view. Kathleen did the same from the left, back wheel of the tractor pointed northeast. They didn't need scopes in the early morning light. Then a minute later, he began. The targets were now within 150 yards. It was like their first day on the rifle range. They didn't even have to snap in for prefiring practice. Their assassins could not have made themselves better targets unless they lit themselves up with neon or strobe lights.

As per the very antique cliché, they were the proverbial fish in the barrel.

"Ten, nine, eight…five, four, three, two… The shots rang almost simultaneously.

Dempsey was on the approach right flank. Kathleen dropped him with a shot to the sternum. Daltry was on the left, to Ronk's right. It took two shots to neutralize him—one to his shoulder, a second to the head. The remaining three dropped to the ground. The hunters suddenly became the prey. What followed was minute lapse of moribund silence. To the prey, it seemed like an hour. Then Romanov lost it, his composure and his miserable life.

The Russian panicked, came to his knees in the center position, and indiscriminately unloaded almost a full forty-round clip in the direction of Ronk on the second deck with four different bursts of fire. But then the weapon jammed, and he began to clear it. Even updated Soviet crap requires a modicum of maintenance. He panicked and yelled something in Russian. It wasn't enough time.

"*Dosvi danya*, motherfucker!"

At that moment, the furious flurry of 911 calls began from neighbors. The Butler County sheriff's phone computer lit up like a 1950s, old-time pin ball machine.

"Party's on at the McSheas'," the dispatcher said ever so nonchalantly. Her voice elevated not a decibel. It was like she was ordering groceries over the phone. "Multiple gunshots fired at the McShea residence!"

All five patrol cars on watch knew what it meant. Lights! Sirens! Action! They were all five to fifteen minutes away from the farm and apprised earlier about what might happen next at the shift briefing. And into the fray they went, playing out all the potential scenarios, none of which had a happy ending in the now hyper adrenaline drive of their minds. Cops are genuine adrenaline junkies, and this was the kind of fury that fed it. It's a special kind of energy reserved for the few.

The Butler deputies all had it.

Romanov, meanwhile, had taken the first magazine out, cleared it, and, in a nervous panic, tried to replace it with another loaded one. He came back to his knees to insert the new one. That time breech was his death warrant, granting just enough lapsed seconds for Kathleen to spot him and place two well-aimed rounds center mass to his chest, just as he blurted out another Russian phrase. He fell backward. Threat extinguished, but he was still alive. A short three minutes later, she ran to his position, oblivious to the retreating two in the rear of the ad hoc formation. He was still alive. Butt-plate strokes from Kathleen's M-14 to Romanov's head, jaw, and throat ended the threat. Multiple strikes later in anger to the neck, chest, and shoulders were noted in the autopsy report. Seven in all!

Then she turned to search for the other two when her mission abruptly changed.

"I'm hit," said Ronk over the headset. "Lower back, I can't move my right leg. Help me!"

The short jog back to the house could have been the victory race from Marathon to Athens. Her legs paralyzed with fear. The return should have taken a mere two minutes. She ran, but it played out in her brain as twenty. Sprint exhaustion overcame as she reached the base of the steps on the west side of the second-floor deck. She screamed his name in panic for what became the most feared moment of her life. Ronk had passed out from the pain and couldn't reply.

"She let out all her anger on this one dirtbag," the coroner later told Sheriff Malone the next day. "You could probably even charge her with desecrating a corpse," he continued. But the coroner's cryptic humor flew past Malone.

"What are you going to do, Randy?"

The sheriff finished reading the report, dropped the autopsy summary of the center cadaver, looked at the bodies on their parallel slabs, and sighed.

"Nothing!"

"What about the DA? Does he have to see this opinion?"

"Waddya mean or what are you implying?"

"Can you legally or ethically edit any comment suggesting corpse desecration, please?"

"Yeah, it's not essential."

"Then do it!"

Chapter 31

CLUSTERFUCK

In the lexicon of military vulgarity, the term *clusterfuck* has a storied place in semantic, military mythology. Think *snafu*, a slur from the annals of World Word II. How many under forty could correctly identify the acronym that originally meant "situation normal: all fucked up!" or the updated Iraq Wars era *fubar* cited earlier. Now *snafu* is a common usage, a legitimate word promoted from colloquial to Webster's acceptable use. *Fubar* will soon join the colloquial lexicon, along with its newest twist, but maybe shortened and softened to Charlie Foxtrot.

Just don't ask about its derivation. It might embarrass your mother-in-law's refined sense of etiquette. But again, she might tell you to stuff it. Some mothers-in-law do have foul mouths and short tempers.

Better to soften the acronym with something more synonymous than offend the sensitive of a public now berated with variants of four-letter words in multiple contexts. The boundaries of good taste in language are now as rare as the cloth diaper.

Although combat lore spawned a host of such acronyms, the Charlie Foxtrot best describes the unanticipated chaos that prevails during an ambush or an unplanned collision of people and events. Think train wreck with a school bus or helicopter crash halftime at the Super Bowl on the fifty-yard line. That would be more of a scandal than the Janet Jackson wardrobe malfunction of prior lore.

The US Navy is the champion of acronym acquisition in a thick, hardbound blue logbook that would take you hours to read. Thus cluster-fuck has also permeated and defiled genteel American slang, taking its place among choice obscenities.

And yes, the phrase does conjure the image of random group sex. Maybe that accounts for its affinity with males thirty and under. It's kind of a fantasy everyone knows will never replicate in real life except in the pornographic mind of some lurid filmmaker.

Whenever any group initially confronts an external threat, the response is often sudden, initial panic. The plan of the day devolves and challenges any semblance of order whether to advance or retreat. Vocal commands become screams, responses descend to cognitive dissidence, and the situation planned so assiduously becomes nightmare. Group fear often vetoes an appropriate response.

That was the classic clusterfuck not quite fully arrayed for Kathleen and Ronk right on their doorstep. It now breached the sacred serenity of their Butler homestead, but it was the aggressors who panicked. Between the screeching of the fire battalion first dispatched, the sheriffs, and the EMTs, the discordant noise was the paean of help, confusion, and threat suppression. She mounted the stairs to the back deck, her legs trembling with the surge of adrenaline, secured their two rifles near their shower, and then bent over a moaning, pained, now semiconscious husband. He had arterial bleeding from two spots, one just above the right hip near the spine and a second on the lateral side above his right knee. You could count his pulse rate with the ejected squirts of blood. First-aid instinct: stop the flow! She ran inside to their bathroom, grabbed two small washcloths, and returned and stuffed them into both wounds. It wasn't gentle and defied the essence of sterile offensive in any ER milieu.

But it was effective.

He screamed in agony at the insertions that forced him back to full, pained consciousness. "Goddammit, woman, was that necessary?" he said as she jammed both wounds separately with her right index finger and pushed hard.

"Yes, it stopped the bleeding," she screamed back at him. "So don't give me any shit, Marine. I'll be right back."

Back inside, she thrashed through the base of the sink where she thought she'd left the emergency medical kit. It wasn't there.

"Where the hell is it?" she wailed at the top of her lungs to the cavernous master bath. The walls had no answer. Their silence was deafening.

Jake and Rufus had moved quietly to the southwest corner of the adjoining master bedroom. They sensed when Big Red was either angry or upset and they knew not to aggravate her. Furiously she ransacked the towel cabinet to the left of the sink. Scrambling through it in a heated frenzy, she found the kit's surgical scissors, returned to him just feet away, and completely cut away the camo pants and Duluth Trading skivvies he was wearing to completely expose him so she could assess any other wounds. Random gunshots can be just as deadly as sniper hits as she gently moved him onto his left side. Luck works both ways, positively and negatively. Only two bullet entry holes were evident and plainly visible. Not so any exit holes on his hip, leg, or back. That could be good news or bad. She finished cutting the right pants leg completely away and surveyed the damage.

"Do I still have my nuts?" he cried softly. "Never realized bullet wounds could hurt so fuckin' bad. I can't feel a goddamn thing. Excuse me, Jesus, for my foul mouth!"

After all, to paraphrase the character from the movie *Dirty Harry*: "A man's got to have his priorities."

"Yes, dearest, your toy box is intact," she said as she gently and slowly checked his nether region and groin. "Don't worry. Just let me see if these guys hit you anywhere else." The wounds staunched, but blood still slowly oozed over his midsection and onto the deck. Seconds later came her affirmation.

"You have two bullet holes, Ronk. I see no exit holes, so you still have them as souvenirs. I've stopped the bleeding and you're conscious, so stay with me! You're not going to die. That's an order. Hear the sirens. Emergency help is crashing through our north gate. They've trashed it but they're here. Don't move and I'll stay with you until the EMT guys get up here. Understand?"

He nodded a weak affirmation and quietly said, "I can't feel my right leg. I can't feel my right leg. It's completely numb."

"Ronk, listen to me! Stay focused. Help is here. I'll stay with you."

Then the flares on the front gate popped before he could answer, and Malone's deputies had crashed through it, along with one of the fire battalions. It tripped the flares she had set nearby. Now everybody knew where everybody else was. It lit up the property like a night game at PNC.

Welcome to the muddle.

The EMTs were almost instantly on the stairs with a spine board ready to stabilize him and collar and tape him down to prevent further damage. The crew of three, along with one of Malone's deputies, then slowly hoisted him down the steps and onto a stretcher to await transit.

Assessing the severity of the wounds, Chief Emergency Medical Tech Emmet Boudreaux of the Butler County response team then "called an audible" and changed their normal routine and evacuation route via ambulance. His next call was to the University of Pittsburgh Medical Center-Mercy with a code 3. UPMC is one of four trauma centers in Allegheny County located on the site of the old Mercy Hospital on the bluff next to Duquesne University overlooking the Golden Triangle at the confluence of the three rivers. All four were available this morning for medevacs, but Boudreaux had a long history of personnel connections with staff at the Mercy site, and prior history dictated his choice.

"Yes, HQ, I need an immediate medevac chopper at my location off Route 8 south of Butler. It's a farm with complete open acreage on approach from the South. There are no overhead obstacles or power lines. We will set up landing flares on a direct approach from your pos. How copy, over?"

"Roger that! Need us an approximate grid on a county map."

Seville ran to the ambulance, pulled out a grid map of Butler County, stretched it out on the ambulance hood, hurriedly calculated the grid that encompassed the farm, and then rattled off the eight-digit coordinates nearest and south of the farmhouse.

"As best I can ascertain, it is 8437...3674. Break, how copy, over?"

The operator replied and repeated the numbers that confirmed the transmission and site of the medevac. Dead radio static followed with what seemed to Kathleen an agonizing break of a mere fifteen seconds.

"Roger that. Evac 2 will be on station in fewer than ten mikes ready to pick up. Break, how many wounded on site?"

"Only one, but he's a spinal."

"Roger that. Stand by for incoming!"

Malone's deputies ran forward to set out a landing zone with large road flares in a square pattern approximately thirty yards apart. Later in the summer and fall, this would be a fire hazard. Since the spring dawn reflected the spring wet, it presented little danger to the flight crew and attendant first responders. It was humid with no morning breeze and temperature in the mid-sixties. The spring rains made any danger of fire remote. The EMTs and the deputy then very carefully walked Ronk to the northern edge of the proposed LZ and gently placed their now sedated victim on the ground.

The wonders of the administered opium extract worked in Ronk's favor. He quietly slipped into la-la land.

Malone then ordered the remaining five deputies on site forward with the command to exit their four-wheel drive vehicles with lights on near the three bodies now lying laterally to one another, fifteen yards apart and very dead. The modified four-wheel drive, Ford Explorers, he convinced the Butler County Supervisors to buy was a concession to the unforgiving spring and winter weather that Lake Erie often imposed. Sheriffs everywhere knew summer always descended into winter that demanded response vehicles so prepared.

Ford and GM were more than happy to supply the requisite chariots of law, but even Toyotas could be found in some jurisdictions, provided they were all adequate to challenge mud, snow, and ice.

Now they were worth every dime of taxpayer money. Between them and the flares, the chopper pilots had a clear vision of the emergency landing zone with the Explorer headlights. Those unfamiliar with the noise that helicopter blades make included some of the deputies. Malone yelled at all of them at the extraction site to remove their uniform covers and secure them away from the wash of the rotors as it approached. In aviation parlance, hats and cloth headgear could become FOB (flying object debris) sucked into an aircraft's engine, propeller, or rotor that could stall it on the spot. It was an avoidable hazard.

After a short brief of the firefight from Kathleen, Malone was more afraid that his deputies might suffer the curse of an ambush, a fear that became moot within ten minutes.

They all correctly surmised that the remaining two assailants fled the scene and the arriving dawn let the deputies begin the mundane inventory of collecting physical evidence. It was a tedious process that would take several days as they moved carefully south toward the back gate of the property. They did a cursory search of each body, finding no ID of any sort, just the pistols, the three rifles, and the knives of combat variety readily available on the open legal market.

"Great shots on these two chuckleheads on the ends," one deputy yelled aloud. "The McSheas are the real deal. What did they hit them with?"

"I'm goinna guess a .30-ought-six something," said a second. "But they were definitely rounds big enough to drop a deer or an elk."

Then the medevac came on station.

The chopper's arrival stirred vivid memories of the sound ingrained in the head of any combat vet from Vietnam to Afghanistan. Kathleen was on the verge of panic. Most could identify the chopper type and model merely by the rotor wash and sound that Kathleen knew was the whisper of life. The bird was a reinforced, heavily-modified Sikorsky, and at first, she felt relieved.

Then she tried to get on the chopper with Ronk, but the crew flight chief stopped her.

"Only enough for medical personnel!" he yelled over the deafening swirl.

Backing away, Chief Malone wrapped his arm around her and pulled her back. She began to sob with a mixture of frustration and consummate anger.

"Kathleen, hold it together," Malone yelled. "We need to gather your shells and mark your shot positions, so come back with me and show me. When the FBI arrives, they will lay out the field of fire precisely and demand that it be absolutely correct. This is all necessary to cover both you and Ronk from any accusation of impropriety. Got it?"

"Those bastards shot my husband! Those bastards shot Ronk!" she screamed again. Her voice crackled as Malone held her and slowly moved her away from the yawing and pitching of the chopper as it lifted off to the southwest. Without comment, they watched the hovering medevac fade forward with the angelic throb, along with its Doppler effect that bled into the early morning light. The decibels diminished in articulate steps and finally into the monastic morning silence toward the Duquesne Medical Campus overlooking the Monongahela River.

Kathleen's boiling rage only seeped to the surface. Her children and her husband were under the threat of death.

"I ain't havin' it!" she yelled at the chopper. "You will not take the father of my children."

Randy grabbed her again.

"You're here and God is with you," he said. "This, too, shall pass!"

At the moment, she just didn't believe it. "Vengeance is mine," sayeth the Lord. This morning, however, Kathleen wanted a chunk of it for herself.

Chapter 32

ESCAPE & EVASION

The firebreak road leading to their vehicles was traversable, even in the wet spring, but they left enough footprints that even a platoon of tenderfoot Scouts could follow. Panic breeds sloppy; thus, the hasty retreat was the model of slop, replete with abundant physical clues that included some ripped clothing shreds and footprints. Bronson left the AKs with the newly deceased, but Sergovia retained all her "carving knives of sin" and pistol as did he with his sidearm. But they both knew the dead members of their hired fraternity carried enough evidence through imputed DNA that would link them together. That alone would warrant prison time for both of them, even if it was only for accessory after the fact. Time was of the essence and counting down. Bronson later unloaded the extra AK ammunition left in the cabin into the elegant woodland toilet, knowing that the rounds would loudly cook off and perish in the coming evidence fire.

So they didn't tarry on site after Kathleen's final shot that sent Romanov to wherever he was destined to go after death. Likely it wasn't to heaven. The only point—at that point—was to get the hell off the McShea homestead. "When we hit the hardball, Route 8, I'll go west and you go east," Bronson stammered with winded breath after they returned to their vehicles. "Can you get to the cabin on your own?"

"I know the way, Bronson. Don't sweat me. See you there."

Bronson sped out first, but Sergovia had a sudden immediate menstrual emergency. She jumped from her rental as she felt the immediate need to change her tampon. Her choice was to move about ten yards to the west where she crouched, released the old, and inserted a new. Hurriedly she threw the used one onto a nearby bush and, just in a momentary panic, forgot her original bag of disposables in the trunk of the rental car.

Wrong move! That slight indiscretion would eventually be the precursor for the assignation with Kathleen and the eventual termination of her amoral life.

Both shed their hunting gear and doffed more conventional attire they brought, paying attention to shoe changes for eventual disposal of the boots they wore, and bagged it all in two plastic trash bags. Now he looked like the morning dufus of a husband going for some coffee at the local caffeine café and she a sleepy-eyed soccer mom. Carefully maintaining the speed limits, they each took the two meandering paths back, five minutes apart in initially opposite directions. Ninety minutes to arrive became more like two hours as they arrived back at the hunting cabin shortly after 0800.

Quickly she and Bronson began the task of evidence destruction. He gathered every speck of paper within the cabin with medical gloves and a small plastic bag and began to toss them into the outhouse. Then the ammunition! Four trips around the interior were sufficient to seemingly erase any remnant of a recent stay since 2016. Sergovia arrived later and assisted with anything in sight they remembered might contain any residual evidence. The nasty books, the sleeping bags, even the sheets with possible DNA residue hit the hole for disposal, particularly their bagged change of clothing and boots.

They were both mildly frantic but stuck to the original plan.

"What do we do with Dempsey's piece of junk?" she yelled from outside.

"Don't touch anything on it or in it for starters. They're dead," Bronson yelled back. "So don't take the chance of a loud explosion if we torch it. Cops will instantly trace it to Dempsey, not us, so let's just light up the outhouse and get the hell out of here. They'll know where and who the three of them are. What we don't want them to know is us."

Thus, the evidence compilation went onward for another ten minutes, everything they touched from the MRE package wraps to even the bar of soap on the cabin's sink.

Then Bronson intoned, "Time to go!"

He grabbed the diesel gas can and poured the five gallons over, on, around, and into the pit. Then he carefully lit one of Daltry's "nasty mags" and applied it to the fuel after he threw the can into the little house behind the house, along with the ignition paper. A crude sign attached to the privy door paid tribute to William Shakespeare carved with the word "jakes."

At least one previous hunter had a sense of humor and more than a perfunctory tenth-grade education. Now the "jakes," first immortalized by the Bard of Stratford-on-Avon, was to become part of the embers of literary outdoor history in central bumfuck Pennsylvania.

Shakespeare would have flashed a smile. It would be just another one of the lewd humorous breaks he always inserted into his tragic plots.

Two minutes later was their cue to exit. No further words needed exchanged. They left concurrently—Bronson first, trailed by Sergovia.

The fire blazed fiercely for twenty minutes with smoke visible for miles, along with the noise of the expended rounds. The 911 call summoned the volunteer fire department from Hollidaysburg who arrived with nothing but the foul odor to extinguish. Their arrival avoided the fleeing felons just in time, twenty-five minutes after ignition. The sheriff's deputy routinely dispatched from Blair County at first saw nothing amiss.

Oh my, this is just a goddamn outhouse fire! What the hell! But why burn an outhouse and not the cabin? he thought. *That's weird. But again, hunters have their own brand of strange.*

Curiosity turned to inquisition when he approached Dempsey's open truck and noted the license plate and vehicle identification (Vehicle Identification/VIN) number with keys in the ignition.

"Somebody obviously had to drive this piece of junk here," he said aloud to one of the volunteer firefighters calmly drowning the scorched outhouse with water. His call-in to dispatch would describe the incident as an anomaly, "suspicious" in cop jargon.

"Stand by as we run the vehicle plate," came the cryptic response from the dispatcher. Two minutes later, it came.

"The car belongs to a Roland John Dempsey with a Michigan driver's license and a Detroit address. No current wants or warrants on either the vehicle or Dempsey, but he has a lengthy arrest record for misdemeanor assaults and petty theft."

"Then I have to assume," the deputy said, "that Dempsey now qualifies as a person of interest in this arson case and has now graduated to felony fire school? Yes?"

"That's affirmative! Scour the immediate area and apprise if anything seems amiss."

"Roger that," replied Deputy Tom Haggerty as he entered more information into his handheld phone/computer for the perfunctory written report on scene mandated for later publication and record. He loved the technology of the handheld and then he laughed out loud.

"God, we used to have to do this crap by hand and we even had to print it like a third grader!"

Turning to another one of the volunteer firefighters, he said, "I could use some help here around the immediate area of this vehicle. We may be looking for a body or anything that seems out of place, like the very presence of this thing, this hybrid jeep something or other."

"This whole episode is out of place," shouted volunteer firefighter Glenn Wilson. "Why the hell would you burn down an outhouse? There must be something in there for someone to hide. That's a lot of trouble just to make shit disappear."

But Wilson couldn't resist the lowbrow humor to follow, like low-hanging fruit on a tree: easy to pick.

"But you know, deputy dawg, shit happens!"

Then the first of the cook-offs began. *Bang, bang, bang!*

"Thank you for the perceptive insight into the vagaries of human waste this morning," Haggerty replied. "But you'd better move back until that batch of ammunitions expends itself. Ain't this just bad humor central! I think we've already garnered that. So just have a couple of your guys fan out about thirty yards from the vehicle and walk counterclockwise in a circle, east to south and then west. I'll walk clockwise in the opposite direction. Holler if you find anything. We should meet to my left, facing south. If you find a body, try to stay completely away from it. Just alert me and I call in the MEs folks. I'm sure the county coroner will be happy to take any body off your hands. His interns drool over scatology like that."

"Scat what?" said Wilson. "Body? What joy you bring us today Haggerty. Now that it's a burn pile, I guess that's a no-shitter conclusion. That'll be a new training evolution for this crew. We haven't dealt with any charred bodies lately, just traffic accidents. Burnt bodies are not nasal friendly and not normally our purview. Arson we ain't trained for."

The low pops of the ammunition continued for another forty-five minutes and then less frequently.

The preliminary search around the circumference of Dempsey's dumpster was fruitless, so Haggerty returned to Dempsey's off-road toy. He gloved and carefully opened the passenger door, thinking the most viable prints would likely be in and around the driver's side and steering column.

His instinct was correct.

Haggerty was savvy and experienced enough to have a portable dust kit (at his own expense) that he used on the steering wheel and driver's door. He garnered at least one partial set of prints that were likely the driver's left hand on the door and partials on the wheel. Those he photographed with a personal camera and inserted the images on the chip into the computer phone. But it was the back bench seat that confirmed the registration.

Amidst the predictable mountain of camping and hunting trash were empty bottles of the resurrected Stroh's Brewery in Detroit that Haggerty vaguely remembered from his college days at Edinboro State (Pennsylvania) in Erie. What he would later discover was that it was Pabst Brewing Company (of Pabst Blue Ribbon and their historic sponsorship of boxing) that apparently bought Peter Stroh's iconic brewery in 1985, so noted on the back of the multiple empties in the back seat.

"What we have *heir*," he said aloud with a mocking Southern voice borrowed from the Paul Newman film *Cool Hand Luke* with George Kennedy, "is connection to a Detroit crime spree. Why I's reasonably certain what we have *heir* is a pro-fess-shun-al criminal (accent second syllable) who may even be in the burnt outhouse."

"You ain't right!" Firefighter Wilson said. "That's sick!" he muttered to Haggerty and moved away to complete his assigned dousing.

"You just ain't right!"

Turning to another one of the volunteers, he wanted an editorial endorsement.

"Wilbur, that boy just ain't right, is he? Just tell 'em. He ain't fuckin' right!"

Wilbur shrugged. "Yeah, cops are sometimes like that. Otherwise, they couldn't function with all the ugly they're forced to see. Give the guy a break. Just stay back until these cook-off rounds finish."

Haggerty followed with a call to Blair County dispatch over his cell phone rather than the open police frequency. No clutter of junk information need transferred on the open air.

"I'm bringing some prints I snatched from the interior of the truck here that must have something to do with the fire, but no trace of that guy Dempsey. The rest of the scene here seems secure, 10–4? Maybe we can send some of our crack arson specialists from county fire here to follow up on this fecal felony."

"We don't have any crack arson specialist in Blair, Thomas," was the sarcastic response. "You gotta go to Harrisburg for intrepid Smokey Bears like that. The state guys have the lock on the nerds of fire. That's their bailiwick. It's like a made-for-Internet film. I can already hear their first response. What? Say again, an arson fire of what? A what-house? Please?"

"Sounds like good humor and entertainment for somebody's central fire station. Better than a *Saturday Night Live* skit," Haggerty replied. "I'm sure our guys here will have a field day with all the intimate details of this dastardly deed. Unless you've got something hot, I'm secure here and back on patrol."

"Roger that, Big T. I'll relay your sitrep."

As he returned to his prowl car, he replayed all the nuances of the scene over and over. And then a third, fourth, or fifth time! The more Haggerty mulled it over, the less sense it made. He transferred the information on his handheld into the Internet computer mounted on the car dash just to see if some squirm of relevant "cyberbytes" emanated from the depths of the Internet. Roughly two thousand police websites responded. He scrolled down some of them for almost two minutes and caved to exasperation.

"Good God, I could be here for weeks!" he muttered.

And reached the very logical conclusion!

"It's not the trash in the outdoor privy," he yelled aloud to himself. "Whatever happened here or elsewhere has to do with that damn white-trash vehicle and someone with a Michigan driver's license who probably has his or her fingerprints posted somewhere else. So what's the Detroit connection with an outhouse fire in central Pennsylvania?"

Haggerty had a buddy from Altoona Area High School who worked for the Pennsylvania State Historical Society who often led teams of "skullions," as he called them, through the remains of outhouses in older rural areas to inventory what people threw away seventy-five to one hundred years before the advent of indoor toilets. He found it fascinating that the former classmate once regaled him with the inventory of collectives they would find that accurately detailed the way people actually lived before the indoor toilet. They culled a mountain of information from what people threw away. There was more than just a little DNA in what they found during the digs, but it ranged from toys to tools, household utensils, and glass bottles of museum quality. Everything they ate, including those foodstuffs in cans, made it to the outhouse, one way or another. Before the indoor potty, the outdoor privy was that which also doubled as a garbage pit housing a family's unwanted personal history. Before garbage collection, disposal was personal, private, and rarely subject to public scrutiny.

"I have no clue about outhouse history, but it sounds like somebody in Detroit does. There's a crime spree here somewhere. I just haven't found it yet.

"That's my take," he said to the computer screen with the spring screen saver. "I predict it's a felony about to erupt somewhere else."

The screen was silent.

There was no audience response.

Enter the sleuths, stage right, of the Federal Bureau of (fill in your favorite blank insult).

Take your pick. Like it or not, they were now in charge.

Chapter 33

SERGOVIA

Galina Elena Sergovia grew up in Homestead, and her parents were faithful members of St. Gregory's Russian Orthodox Church on Fifteenth Street. For reasons never quite articulated, she hated her baptismal birth first name and went by Elena. Like a lot of first-generation immigrants, it was not about where you were from but where you are in the present tense. The old country was a secession of memories, many of those mostly bad. The new ones were the adventure, often fraught with rebellion. Parroting many American adolescents, Elena often did exactly what her parents found abhorrent. It is an ethnic story often repeated with pain among all immigrant groups. Progeny preferred to shed the skin of their heritage for a new identity that offended their parents.

The Irish, Italians, Jewish, and Hispanic parents of previous generations all had anecdotes of similar trauma.

She attended Steel Valley High School and graduated with a mundane grade point average of 2.1 in 2000, punctuated with a compulsive need, in her words, to "just get the hell out." Her description of her time at Steel Valley was more often couched in vulgar obscenity. High school for her was a purgatory of mind and soul with adolescent boys who had only one function, adoration, and service. None of the rest of anything curriculum piqued her interest, except a metal shop class where she secretly made her first hunting knife, handle, and blade and sold it to the father of another kid in her class.

The $75 he paid her for the original piece was her first incursion into the world of the dark entrepreneur.

Friends at Steel Valley described her as a cross between seductive, amiable, crass, and nasty. She touched all four bases on that spectrum. That underscored the collective of her sometimes strange social behavior. She bragged that she had a tattoo just above her pubic hairline of an open-mouthed snake poised to enter the love chamber below. Female classmates were put off by it and her titillating bragging but curiously poised to see it in the locker room during gym classes. But it was the stapled tongue pin she would use to tease the boys that almost universally elicited the ultimate teen putdown: gross. A select few boys would be accorded dynamic fellatio, replete with said tongue pin, in her senior year, but she intimidated most of her male classmates. Unlike her high school classmates, she was not enthralled with the rage of social media. She preferred face-to-face, or more often, in-your-face contact at school. She was adept at swearing and obscenity in both English and Russian, using a perverse concoction of Russian-English used by street kids. Referrals to school counselors came in bunches for her plethora of classroom disruptions. It was not uncommon for her to have two to three sessions a day with staff counselors. Defiance was her blood type. Staff tired of the constant referrals from teachers. Even in her senior year, she accrued a full ten days of suspension for sundry offenses, mostly ranging from obscenity in class to outright defiance, a rarity among seniors who most often saw the goal line in June.

Not Elena.

In the words of one of the girls in her senior class: "If it wasn't about what she wanted, she would just blow you off. She was flat-out weird. I think half of the boys just wanted that exotic blowjob and the chance to brag about it. I'd describe her as just plain disgusting. I know of at least one guy who paid her $20 for the experience in the school parking lot. She gave me the creeps."

Two of the four women counselors on staff were more than mildly afraid of her. Whenever possible, they sent her to the two senior vice principals for discipline disposition. They all universally described her as strange. The staff psychologist said she was a fringe sociopath. She was, in fact, a walking estrogen minefield. All in all, the faculty shed no tears when she graduated, even with a stash of D grades in her junior and senior years. Her SAT scores were barely triple digit.

Ambition for college entry never entered her mind. It's what her parents wanted, not she.

As her senior English teachers noted before graduation: "A D in your senior year means we just wanted you ass out the door! You were a pain in the ass while you were here, so go flaunt your ugly persona on the rest of the known world."

Among her favorite movies as a teenager was *The Fast and the Furious* series, and it reflected her outlook on life. She wanted it *now* and to consume it whole, as long as there was a stack of Uncle Benjamins.

The piety of her first generation Russian-American parents transferred little to the second of their four children. She appalled their religious sensibilities with the brusque announcement in her junior year that attendance at any church function was a "bogus tribute to Russian culture in which I no longer participate."

It was the permanent breach that dug the chasm with her whole birth family. Her siblings were equally offended by her lack of sensitivity toward their parents and gradually moved away from her, both physically and emotionally. The invitations to weddings, baptisms, and Easter reunions gradually evaporated. Bottom line: they just didn't like her for a host of venial transgressions she imposed upon them throughout her adolescence.

And she cared even less about their lack of filial affection.

Although conversantly bilingual, like many second-generation ethnics, she could only write or read Russian with great difficulty. What she really wanted to do was make money, legally or outside the bounds of ethical behavior. Lust and avarice were her cherished virtues. That made her an eventual prime target for recruitment into crime by Tsakrios in her late twenties.

Driver's license at sixteen coupled with a work permit from Steel Valley High allowed her to work up to twenty hours per week at the Lunch Bucket owned by the Greek on the Southside. There she started as a busser/waitress/dishwasher but was lured away to the seedier side by the Son of a Greek (as she affectionately called him) who assured her that she could "fuck and suck" on her own time for money with the many sleazy married steelworkers who patronized the family bar business. His only further caveat was "don't get caught. I won't back any illegal play. I don't give get-out-of-jail cards." Joseph slowly lured her into his budding crime syndicate with errands like breaking the hand of a graduate woman student piano diva at Duquesne University who "welched" on a Tsakrios's backdoor student loan. She previously auditioned with several orchestras in the Midwest and looked to a budding career with a symphony orchestra.

After her hand "accident," those offers drifted away. Auditions became disasters. Her proficiency on the Grand '88 was never the same, and she eventually became an elementary school music teacher.

As always, the Greek got his money back…with interest!

And she kept completely quiet about her encounter with Galina Elena Sergovia. She was warned that the next breakage would be just short of her skull and relegate her to a wheelchair. Elena just oozed that kind of charm.

The threat worked.

After graduation, she also bled through a series of other jobs as both a cocktail waitress and bartender that allowed her the freedom of the self-sufficient with time to develop a proficiency in karate and an attraction to the allure of female professional boxing. That morphed her interest by age twenty-five into MMA (mixed martial arts), a craze with an addicted audience with free-flowing cash. She hooked up, literally and financially, with a Russian ex-patriate, Vladimir Dyschinsky, as her mentor, manager, and sometimes love interest in a single package. Unlike many of her previous connections as a cocktail hostess, Big D, as he was known, was the profile of honesty and integrity. He fled Russia for the west after Vladimir Putin's first term as the Russian president in disgust over the rampant corruption of the oligarchs that seemed ubiquitous after Putin's ascension. For a short time, they were indeed the odd couple of the sport. Team Sergovia trolled the boxing circuit, culled their winnings, and by age twenty-eight, she had legally stashed away more than $250,000 when lust converged with greed to enter the more nefarious world of contract murder.

She never turned down an offer from the Greek but drifted away from his employ during the MMA years. But he welcomed her "retirement" from MMA, as he knew they would once again cross paths.

Sergovia also rejected the advances of several Russian mafia types to do seductive undercover work. It wasn't until a businessman named Sergei Rachmaninoff (yes, just like the famed composer!) after one particularly brutal MMA match in Las Vegas. He approached her with the clichéd criminal offer she couldn't refuse. Losing the match, along with a monster shiner over her left eye, pointed the way directly to retirement. Although competent in the ring, her professional fight record was fifteen wins speckled with five losses, and she lost her fury for battering other women legally fewer than fifteen minutes after the last bell. Vanity and pain trumped continuation.

"Nothing is forever, and I have better things to do with this beautiful face," she told Vladimir. "Enough!" Thus, in one fell swoop, she walked away from a circuit on which she could have made a million by age thirty-five and dissolved Team Sergovia.

After her last fight, vanity and common sense finally prevailed.

"When it's time to quit, it's time to quit," she said to Vladimir. "And now is the time. I can't do this anymore. I just don't want to do it anymore. You'll have to get another fighter to sponsor."

He couldn't even get a *but* in edgewise yet he understood. Her frustration was clear. It was the end of the line for the team, yet they parted on amiable terms.

Although Vladimir accepted her decision reluctantly, he also had a pressing family problem with a brother-in-law who physically abused his younger sister. Even after a warning from him and an eventual arrest by the Binghamton, New York police, the sister refused to prosecute, citing the trauma their three young children would suffer if he went to prison. He did not want his hand on any retribution but decided the sister's abusive spouse had to go. She wouldn't divorce him, so he recruited his friend Sergei as a surrogate and asked him to devise a plan to "terminate the fucking bastard."

"I don't want to know any of the details. I just want him away from my sister. Whatever it takes to get him away from her and the kids permanently! Do what you have to do."

Sergei was in the audience that night in Las Vegas in the winter of 2017 on what became Sergovia's last fight. After the fight, he approached her in the locker room and offered to take her to a late-night dinner.

"I have a job offer that doesn't involve boxing where no one will hit you or force you to do anything you don't want to do. See me outside after you've dressed. Please, no manager. I've already talked to Vladimir. This is just between you and me."

Curiosity drew her to accept. Twenty minutes and a short downtown cab ride followed. Destination: the Four Queens and an extended dinner at Hugo's Cellar where the specialties are exquisite seafood offerings.

She was always hungry after each fight and loved lobster, so there it was and so she indulged, fully expecting Rachmaninoff to pick up the tab. She disavowed him up front about seeking any post-dessert recreation.

He did…pick up the tab, that is, and assured her he was not there to hustle for something else.

After the four courses, she posed the obvious question that lay on the table after the evening wine and coffee.

"So why, Sergei, why are we here?"

"Tell me," he asked, "what's your cut for this fight tonight? I know it's not what the men make."

"Our standard contract spelled out $25,000 for the winner and $15,000 for the losing opponent. My purse was obviously the latter, as the referees gave it to that bitch McBride on points. Fifteen and a messed-up face! My decision to dissolve Team Sergovia is final. We'll go through the formal legal dissolution when we get back to Pittsburgh. I just don't want to do it anymore."

"Well, Tsakrios, Vladimir, and I have known each other for a long time as well. I understand you knew the Greek's old man also since high school, correct? While you worked for Joseph, right?"

"Yes, I met him working at his bar and worked with him. His old man had a bakery business several blocks farther East on Carson Street, and I heard the legends and stories about some of the girls from his son's high school, South Hills. Joseph obviously closed down that business long before I met him. Those bitches are all thirty years-plus older than me now, but everyone on the Southside knows about the Greeks' vaunted pimping. It's urban legend. I think about half of it is pure Greek goat shit. And no, by the time I met them, these old broads were just older bartenders somewhere north of 50. I don't buy half of that bogus crap they peddle to drunken customers."

"Well, I know all about your past history and your skill set and I need someone like you."

"Like me what?"

"What if I said it was $25,000 before and another $25,000 later for neutralizing a violent one who needs to see Jesus pronto?"

"So I presume for this much cash, we're talking about a termination, right?"

"That's correct!"

"So are we just dancing theoretically, or are you asking me to do it?"

"What I am hiring you to do—"

She interrupted him, "Okay! Plain English, Sergei! You want me to off some dirtbag. I get it. Tell me who, when, and where. Then convince me why I should take the risk of life in prison if I fuck it up. Is it a man or a woman? I can seduce either one. I will need to know all the details about the person. Need a good picture and the first half of the money up front and I decide the timeline. First installment is in cash and the second sent to my bank in Costa Rica. Understood? If not, thank you for the dinner and I'll see myself to the street."

"Why," he demurred, "don't we just order dessert first? The Cherries Jubilee served here are splendid."

And so they were. Total tab for the night: $143 plus tip followed by contract acceptance.

As he hailed a separate cab for her to leave, he opened the door and held it momentarily for her into which to step.

"The target is Vladimir's brother-in-law, a dumb-ass white boy named Everett Kant. He lives in Binghamton, New York and he's a legal drug detail salesman for Pfizer Pharmaceuticals. But he's also a complete asshole! I'll leave a picture and details about him for you in the package at the front desk tomorrow, along, of course, with the first installment. Included will be my business card with cell number. Call and tell me where you want the second installment to go after you finish. He abuses Vladimir's sister and can't keep his pants on for a seductive beautiful woman. Like you. Need I say more? I believe you know the rest of the script."

"Yes, I do. And I won't even charge you extra for the castration."
"I'll throw that one in as a bonus…on me."

Thus, Everett Kant became Sergovia's first.

And the Binghamton Police duly noted the detached gonads but never made it public. It eventually would become the "calling card" for two more terminations in neighboring Erie, none of which yielded an immediate suspect. But they knew it was the same perp in all three yet had no idea who she was. The motif was the same. A straight razor was the weapon in all three with a left-handed twist. That's where the evidence trail ended.

Until April of 2019.

Chapter 34

THE CHASE

Mostly every FBI field office cultivates a pristine model of work efficiency with furniture and motif similar, much like the final cut of a good Hollywood film. It moves in a paced, logical sequence leading to the denouement.

The Pittsburgh field office was no exception.

Although the Federal workday officially begins at 0730, case tasks at hand dictated the agents' work schedules. They began filtering into work by 0600, sometimes earlier by those on the trail of nocturnal felons. Those agents were generally the younger ones classified by their older peers as adrenaline junkies. The young'uns loved the hunt and chase that bring older agents to a collective yawn. They knew, in the Internet era, that capture and arrest more often depended on fugitive identification and location with patience and website search proficiency. And if they couldn't get it done immediately, there were the patient arms of the US Marshal's Service whose memories rambled through decades of fleeing criminals. Their persistence was legendary, including one recent collar of a convicted sex offender near Pittsburgh that they nailed after seventeen years on the run.

"You can run but never hide was a cliché never truer," mumbled one FBI agent. "The FBI and the marshal's service often ran out of many things, but time was not one of them."

It was Monday after the Mulvihill disaster of the previous week when Chief Oliver sauntered into his semiprivate office. He fired up his computer and then perused the deluge of daily e-mails, along with the morning reports from his field agents that noted no red flags demanding his immediate attention. Unlike his younger agents, he had no use for a laptop, which he compared to a dog leash.

"Are you the mutt or the guy with the leash?" he always droned to anyone who would listen. "I and all of you," he once opened at a morning briefing, "are on the front line of defense in this country, and all of us here in supervision don't want to waste time cleaning up mistakes that were perfectly avoidable. We trust you to do your job professionally and we won't ride your ass with trivial requests or questions. Security of Federal property in your trust must be absolute. Don't lose it or misplace it."

He disdained portable devices because he loathed what a security risk they've become with WIFI everywhere and an occasional dunce agent who would leave them unattended in their car or car trunk. The reporting paperwork for a lost or stolen laptop or handheld, compromised intelligence and mandatory ass-chewing all too often was a major distraction from their missions. Such mistakes reverberated all the way to DC and the revered, or feared, Committee on Professional Responsibility. His solution: "Use your phones issued to you, but if you must take your laptops home, it is mandatory that you have a secure safe in which to lock it if not in use. The safe is at your own expense, but you can write it off your income tax. Secure it and never lose it."

But he also had a front office on the fourth floor with a view of the Monongahela River, sometimes a spectacular one, depending on the season. Spring evolved into summer that slid to autumn and the eventual gloom of winter. Those were the only times he noticed the aura of the parkway vista across the river.

But he loved watching the bald eagles who have repopulated the cliffs overlooking the river in the Duquesne Heights and the Hays sections of the city. In moments of meditation, when he closed his office door to think through a notorious problem thrust on his desk, they provided him with clarity and peace when he watched them fishing, particularly in the spring. The American icon returned to the cliffs above the river fewer than twenty years before with help of the EPA and the Pennsylvania Department of Fish and Game. The majestic symbols of American democracy are now back to a home where industrial pollution once either killed them or drove them away in the twentieth century. Their presence daily reminded Oliver that the FBI's mission was a sacred trust.

It took the better part of a generation to bring them back since 9/11. The birds have now reclaimed what was rightfully theirs as far back as the French and Indian War fifteen years before the Declaration of Independence was signed. The French first laid claim to the Three Rivers point and named their military position Fort Duquesne, later to be supplanted by the British who renamed it Fort Pitt after then British Prime Minister William Pitt.

Ergo, the evolution of the city of Pittsburgh, Pennsylvania, the only Pittsburgh of the more than twenty variants strewn out through nineteen other states spelled with the digraph "-gh" at the end. Its unique spelling makes it the only true Pittsburgh in the entire United States.

The eagle now stands as the unchallenged bird of prey along the river at the top of its food chain again adjacent to the Golden Triangle. Otherwise, when he turned away, there was only the unchanging cherry mahogany of his desk, laid out much like the desktop on his computer. It was his very own chicken-and-egg conundrum—which came first: the desk arrangement of stacked files or the desk-op file on the screen?

It was hard to tell. The files were the original compilation of the icons on screen, as they waxed and waned from week to week. The most annoying icon this week was a picture of Tsakrios noted with the number of caseload hours assigned to him: 45175.

"That irritates the hell out of me," he yelled toward a young eagle on a sortie just to his immediate front on an unsuspecting fish. "Maybe you can work for us. You certainly are more productive than some of my agents. You always get your prey!"

Now he momentarily got his frustration out of his system, and the eagle got his morning catch for return to the nest. *I wonder if this is a male or female,* he thought. *They both hunt for their chicks, just like my staff. Our females are sometimes more focused, just like these magnificent birds. River fish should never surface when you're around, although I guess God designed them to be food for birds or Homo sapiens.*

When the workload depressed him, the eagles were his momentary therapy...at no charge.

He turned to finish his second cup from Dunkin' Donuts, sans doughnuts, as he distrusted the BUNN brew in the office that ranged from acceptable to fire hose wretched, depending on the skill of the first agent in the morning. That was the staff rule: first in gets the coffee detail. No exceptions. Even senior agents had to brew for juniors. Now it was time to address the cattle call morning briefing at 0800. In sauntered his two most senior/junior agents, Joel McKnight and Kevin Duke, as they unceremoniously barged into his sparse but adequate office at 0730.

"Helluva view this morning, Chief," said McKnight. "What's your priority for the titillating staff powwow at 0800? We've whittled the national portion of the brief to seventeen items. That should take less than forty minutes. What do you want to press on the local scene? Agent Presley has a real juicy one on a gunrunner named Duarte who's also hockin' some funny money. He's identified the bills as Uncle Bens of North Korean origin. He says the bills are of high quality and hard to spot. Picked them up near Grove City! Secret Service Agent Melanie Batch is the lead for them and is on it like stink on shit."

"Stink on shit? Can't we just have a new metaphor? That one's a little old," Oliver snorted. "Mark-fucking-Twain you ain't. And who is this Agent Batch? Will she be here today, along with the rest of our Federal brethren?"

"Yes, she will," said Duke. "She has the ass out for this cold case from around 1982 in Seal Beach, California. That's why she's here in town on a follow-up for some potential witness. A Secret Service female agent, whose name now eludes me, was following some suspect in another forgery case and found murdered outside a Jack-in-the-Box on Pacific Coast Highway that summer. At least, I'm reasonably sure it was '82. They found her body behind the store's Dempsey

Dumpster but never cleared the case. It remains unsolved and is still open. Batch is here on that but Pittsburgh rather than LA? I dunno. You'll have to ask her. The dead Secret Service agent was apparently trailing this suspect alone from somewhere near the LA harbor area. She then apparently tried to arrest him, but she died with two mortal chest wounds after an obviously violent struggle. Don't know anything else about the case. but Batch is messianic about solving it."

"And this is what? Thirty-eight years later?" Oliver snorted. "That case is more than cold it's etched in stone. Will Batch be here this morning? I think I'd like to meet her. She's either a superstar or somebody who will never see the White House detail. Wonder if she has a guardian angel mentor up the totem pole or she's on somebody's shit list, you know, one of those who's out of sight…out of mind…and out of state, just the way they want her!"

"What else is new and intriguing?"

"Well," McKnight replied, "we're trying to reduce the local agenda down to the top ten most pressing cases to keep the whole show under an hour."

"Thank you," Oliver said, heaving a long sigh. "Sometimes these guys ramble on with the sequel to *War and Peace* when a simple paragraph would do. I'm not impressed with agents blabbering onward, awestruck with their own briefs. I prefer succinct."

"We also have seven surveillance reports on the docket as an appendix," Duke said. 'One on that strange cult up near Oil City that's into the illegal transit of Asian women for prostitution, another on a law firm near Johnstown that's laundering phony real estate docs to the tune of about $40 million and a third about some local union election irregularity in Beaver Falls."

"Uh! What's real estate have to do with it all? Are these connected or separate? Besides, isn't that a parody on some old Tina Turner song, 'What's Real Estate Got to Do with it?'"

He looked to his two lieutenants for a laugh. They didn't get the joke; they were too young.

"Separate, Chief! There's a lot of smoke but mostly embers. It takes time for us to unravel most of it, particularly the real estate deals. No arrests on the horizon. Embers I like, no immediate three alarms today."

McKnight and Duke took the hint when Oliver leaned forward and stood.

Meeting adjourned. They grabbed their briefcases and turned left to the main conference room.

"Oh, before you leave, one final note!" Oliver said. "Where are we on the new Tsakrios warrant? This guy's in my dreams and my head. I really want to shut him down."

"Well, the arraignment's tomorrow," Duke reminded him. "And I think that idiot Weinstein managed to get it on the docket of Judge Owens' court. We should get a more fair hearing with him, and maybe even a bail revocation. Keep your fingers crossed."

"Luck should not be the wild card here, gentlemen. This should have been an easy out call with the first warrant except for that bonehead Mulvihill. By the way, when's that Neanderthal slated to retire?"

"Sorry, Chief," McKnight said, suppressing an obvious grin. "He's only fifty-three, even though he looks seventy. He'll be an ongoing nightmare for another twenty years. You'll likely be retired and fishing in Utah before he steps down. He still has three of his five kids to get through college. There's no incentive there to retire."

"Joy, joy!" Sarcasm redeployed!

"You've already twisted my Hanes into a knot."

Then he laughed. "Maybe God will intervene and take him out early!

"Remind me to piss all over your next quarterly eval. I'll be sure to downgrade it to excellent with potential for advancement to field office supervisor for you in the Fargo office or better yet." Then he paused. "To Reykjavik, Iceland. It's nice this time of year. Waddya think?"

"I think my wife just scrubbed you off our Christmas card list, along with the invitation to our wine-and-cheese Christmas party at our humble abode in Mt. Lebanon."

"Is that it?"

"For now!

"You two ready to convene?"

"Yeah, time for a head call," Duke said, "before more hot wind from our august audience in the auditorium and more caffeine!"

"Which comes first, the coffee or the download?"

Duke turned to Oliver. They laughed in unison.

"God, we've all been here for too long. It's corrupted our sense of humor. Your cynicism is rampant."

"It's not corruption, Duke," McKnight said, "but extending the long arms of bad taste to the staff rookies. Some of them really think you walk across the Mon and never get your feet wet."

"If we have any of those who truly believe that," Oliver rejoined, "remind me to fire them by noon. How many newbies on the Pittsburgh staff do we now have fresh out of Quantico?"

"Just four, Chief—me and McKnight…and the two we sent last week to Butler to irritate the yahoos of the sheriff's office there. Everyone else is appropriately cynical, crusty, and socially obnoxious…just like you want us."

"You two don't qualify as rookies. After fifteen years, you're just yesterday's used Federal whores."

"Oh, wound my heart with a piercing arrow!"

"I'll just pierce your ass, Duke, if you give me any more grief."

Ending on that loose note of jeer, the three headed to the ecumenical brief that would include the FBI guys in town, reps from the Secret Service, DEA, the US Marshals, along with, of course, the mother of all mothers—Homeland Security.

And so it began with the perfunctory intros, but all the forty or so in attendance knew each other either remotely or by reputation. They were all on the same page, at least for the next hour, with petty rivalries shoved to the back bench. Junior staff designated all their places, outlets for computers, copies of the agenda, and door security before the call to order. The four doors to the auditorium were locked with a guard assigned to each: standard protocol for discussion of sensitive or classified topics.

Late arrivals would suffer the scorn and indignation from their cohorts. Serious security demanded serious punctuality. That was Oliver's rule number 3 in the food chain. No one ever asked him what rules 1 and 2 were. Else, they might suffer a blistering array of his most potent obscenity. FBI Agent Ron Watters, on loan from the Atlanta office, took the mic center stage and began the national summary review first, locals second, questions and concerns last.

Forty-five minutes later in the Q&A set, the question erupted about Tsakrios from one of the agents TAD (Temporarily Actively Deployed) from DC for the Tsakrios raid.

Oliver responded, "His arraignment is tomorrow, and the Federal attorney will seek revocation of bail. Sorry, *amigos*, the wanton morning attack on the McShea family in Butler last Wednesday now takes precedence. Our primary witness, Ronan McShea, suffered two serious bullet wounds, one near his right knee and a second above his hip, too uncomfortably close to his spine. Although he's clearheaded, he remains in intensive care, and the actual arraignment and trial may have to trail by maybe as much as three months. He can testify, even from a hospital bed, but we will have to provide some protective cover for him and his family, as they have adamantly refused to go into witness protection.

"Please carefully read the attack summary report before all of you. Three of the decedents come to us courtesy of the McSheas. Two others fled. As yet, we can't connect them to Tsakrios, but we will. He's the only one with the reason, the motivation, and the money to pull this sort of thing off. Next step," he concluded, "track and nail the remaining two suspects."

"Dismissed! Thank you all for coming. Let's go to work."

The clapping briefcases and laptops swing into full MACH-3 mode as Oliver motioned Duke and McKnight back to his office.

"Well, guys, let's go after 'em. Two should be easier to find than five."

Then came the intercession from heaven coveted by Oliver. As former Pittsburgh Pirates icon broadcaster, Bob Prince, once said on air, paraphrasing Branch Rickey, "Sometimes I'd rather be lucky than good!" and "We had 'em all the way!"

Today would be their lucky day, and Bob Prince would be cited again.

"Chief, you have an urgent call from the Blair County Sheriff," said his secretary, Allyson Grief, who took a ton of jocular "grief" from staff for her surname.

Oliver slowly and deliberately picked up his office phone.

Three minutes later, he sported a bodacious smile that Duke later described as a shit-eatin' grin and put the phone on its ancient cradle.

"You, my senior children, are going on a road trip to Altoona. Stay as long as you need. *Per diem* already approved. And don't forget to take your dirty orange suits and booties."

"What's so pressing in Altoona?" McKnight asked.

"Lotsa shit! Enough shit to last and inhale for your whole career. The last two apparently convened at a hunting camp and burned the outhouse, likely, I'm guessing, filled with evidence through which you may sift."

Duke and McKnight looked at each other and then at Oliver.

Then in unison, they said, "You're shittin' us!"

"*Bon aperitif,* my children! Leave as soon as possible. Make sure to shower before you return…and I want the Federal vehicle of your choice impeccably clean when you return it to the motor pool."

Chapter 35

SHIT DETAIL

Any road trip order to his first lieutenants always had the antecedent adverb that comes before *now*. They understood that explicitly. Like, when should they leave?

The adverb was *immediately*, followed by the question, "Why are you still here?"

It didn't mean this afternoon or tomorrow or next week. It meant they should have anticipated the order and left ten minutes before he issued it.

McKnight and Duke both understood and kept a ditty bag, actually an airline suitcase, with three days of clothing, including two suits and toiletries for said contingencies in the trunks of their personal vehicles. When the ghost of J. Edgar summoned, it required instant response. Excuses were like everyone's, veritable "flaming gaper." "Everybody has one, and most of the time they stink." Oliver only rarely found excuses rising to beyond risible.

"If you've got an excuse, it damn well better be good." It had best be something like a terminally ill spouse or an emergency with your children. Otherwise, FBI orders he dispersed for his road warriors were set in concrete. The operative word was always to anticipate it before he issued the order. They all knew how to score the odds of the expected next.

McKnight went to the motor pool while Duke collected two evidence bags, along with the requisite chemistry kits, overalls, hiking shoes, and rubber boots for the trip. They'd done these trips so often that they both knew each other's shoe size and coverall preference. Dead bodies were not something new. Their seemingly infinite training classes on evidence collection gave them a wealth of knowledge sometimes more vast than most county medical examiners and coroners with whom they often dealt. Although McKnight's undergraduate degree was in accounting and Duke's in biology, they both could dance around forensic evidence as well as most doctors, DO or MD. This detail, however, was a seismic shift for both. But by 9:00 a.m, they were on the road and on the phone simultaneously with the Blair County Sheriff's Office. This time, McKnight drove the selected Chevy Suburban, and Duke placed the requisite phone calls. It is almost a ninety-eight-mile straight shot, even in inclement weather, from Southside Pittsburgh to Altoona.

"I presume you guys have prearranged lodgings here," said Sheriff Ron Hayden via cell phone, "but our staff will help if you need some input. Do your field offices in either Johnston or State College need a heads-up?"

"Nah," said Duke, "we notified them online of our departure and arrival time and we already have standing rooms at the Hampton Inn because they have a quality safe we can use to secure evidence and weapons, so we're good there. Would appreciate it if you could meet us around noon," Duke said. "Brief us on the fire and hook us up with anyone deployed on site, either deputies or fireman."

"Roger that, can do," Hayden said. "I'll have Deputies Tom Haggerty and Veronica Menendez link up with you here, and they'll take you out there to the burn site. Hope you brought your nasties because it's fugly there."

"Yeah, we're cool," said Duke. "We'll be there in about six-zero!"

"See you then."

"Is there anything else I can get you two?" Hayden asked.

Both thought for a minute.

"Yeah," said McKnight. "Can you hook us up with a guy you trust who has a backhoe? We'll hire him, or her, on the Federal dime!"

"Yeah, that's a piece of cake. I'll have somebody ready for you by the time you arrive. I've got several reputable guys we use for digs. I'll have one of them on deck by noon."

Then came the perfunctory two minutes of silence! Both men were mentally sorting the elements of their coming task.

"I know we're going to need a backhoe to lay it all out in some sort of visible strand where we can sort through it logically. Did you throw face masks into the gear bags? We might even need oxygen packets if the smell is that bad," McKnight asked. "The last fire I sorted three years ago for some fugitive druggie had an odor I'll take to my grave. Meth can bring you to heave, so we may need the masks and plenty of bottled water."

The rest of the trip left both men with their private thoughts, reservations, and projections about what they might confront. Although it was part of the job, it was not one they found appealing. Just the thought of it was a cross between vile and comic.

"Imagine that," McKnight finally proffered, "burning down an outhouse to cover your tracks. This is a first for me."

"Same here! Let's put on some road music until we arrive"

"Yeah, how about some raucous country rock?"

"You go for a little Travis Tritt?"

"Yeah, please! Anything! Make it loud, rude, and distracting!"

McKnight always traveled with his raucous CD collection.

It began with the cut of Tritt's "Down in the Bible Belt," a song originally appended to the early '90s film, *My Cousin Vinny*, set in Southern Alabama. Although Central Pennsylvania is dramatically far north of the south, the rendition was appropriate for central Pennsylvania. Altoona can swap places physically with any town in the old Confederacy, but it had a Yankee pedigree, more mainstream Catholic than Southern Baptist. Yet the buildings' history and visuals replicated much of the Old South with its post-bellum architecture. But it remained unshackled by the South's odium of slavery. Ethnic Germans and Irish came and settled and worked the railroad and the mines. Like many small towns throughout the United States and central Pennsylvania, its population drew upon those of rural persuasion but also those outside the rim of the law. It was a culture as hostile to urban as anything you could find in Tennessee or Georgia. One hundred miles from Pittsburgh, another two hundred-plus from Philadelphia, replete with the drinking, carousing, gambling, and whorehouses tolerated as the lesser of multiple evils.

But it culturally may just as well be a hundred miles west of Waco, Texas.

It was almost Knoxville-north in the middle of Keystone, Pennsylvania.

"Criminals and the addicted," Duke once said, "crave the obscurity of isolation where they could fuel their perversions without oversight.

"Think about it. Marry that to the Internet and what do you have? The perfect medium for festering evil! So there remains no dearth of business for us. Duly note our office in State College, Pennsylvania, the home of Penn State University where scholars and Internet derelicts plying the Dark Web with threats and conspiracies to Western civilization and flouting drug laws. They shave their beards, infest our graduate schools in the most remote places, and hide in plain sight. They purvey their swill right out in the open.

"State College so qualifies!"

Railroad was king in Altoona in the nineteenth century, and today is still a town of roughly fifty thousand. It garnered fame as a nineteenth and early twentieth-century railroad hub with the winding track around the city's reservoir where, if you were on a passenger train circumventing the famed Horseshoe Curve, and the train had sufficient passenger cars, you could see the opposite end of the same train across the water as it rounds around the municipal lake west to east…or east to west. The curve around the reservoir is that pronounced. Today Amtrak trains have fewer cars, but the ride is still dramatic where you can see the train at points front to rear in one view.

Its professional baseball team also is now known as the Altoona Curve, a name applied to its Eastern League minor league AA team affiliate of the National League's Pittsburgh Pirates. But McKnight and Duke weren't there for the spectacular train ride or the baseball.

"At least," McKnight said, paraphrasing one of his favorite lines from the film *Patton*, "you won't have to shovel shit in Louisiana!"

Exemplars of punctuality, they arrived as projected at exactly 1201. But Sheriff Hayden couldn't resist.

"You're late," he bellowed as they strode into his office. "Lost a minute here in transit, eh? Not up to snuff for Feds. But I forgive you. Step into my office and note the spectacular décor. You guys want lunch first? My deputies are the raging connoisseurs of the Altoona restaurant scene. They'll steer you right."

"Nah, we'll pass on lunch right now. So this is what constitutes local 'spectacular décor'? Makes me glad I'm a Fed."

Then turning to Duke, McKnight continued, "Oh, man, we've got to turn Sheriff Hayden onto Martha Stewart. This cop shop seems very police officer mundane with paint just two barfs above yuck. And the furniture, '*Oi vey!*' It couldn't pass muster in a Nevada bordello."

"I dunno," said Duke. "Lunch before this assignment may cause us to *hurl*."

"Gentlemen, gentlemen!" Hayden retorted. "You have no idea about taste. This office motif is straight out of *Country Living*. Our coffee could even wake the dead. We call it Altoona Resurrection Brew. You're welcome to try it!"

At that point, Haggerty and Menendez arrived. Exiting their sheriff cruiser, they entered the building and barged into Hayden's office without invitation. Menendez opened up the taunting session by flipping into her fake Southern accent.

"Are we goinna havta takes these city boys from the Burgh and teach them the realities of flyover country?" she began. "I understands these FBI boys might get sum-e fecal on their city shit-kickers this field trip. We will watch your technique so we hillbilly-types can pick up some pointers on manure-maulin. The crime scene in question is odiferous. Do you think these DC types can handle it?"

"It's what?" Duke interjected.

"Smells like shit, darlin', 'cause that's where your evidence is, so follow us. It's about twenty minutes away. We've even managed to coax a unit of some of our volunteer fire suppression heroes to come out…just in case. They love playing with their toys on the taxpayers' dollar. Otherwise, they're bored. All of them just love the sound of the summoning county siren. Now the chief has them all on cell phone response. It takes away some of the drama of the old days. The responding fire unit to that scene only has forty volunteers on its roster, and not all of those are always in town. I mean, these folks do have other lives. The unit came out of Hollidaysburg with the literary label, the Phoenix Unit."

Then she paused.

"Get the inside joke?"

She looked directly at Duke and McKnight.

"The Phoenix Unit?" Duke asked.

"Yeah!"

"So what's going to rise out of the ashes at our destination?"

Then she flashed both of them her best wide-mouthed, brown-eyed smile.

"It's your graduate exam in ER, excremental remains, guys! We'll be there with you throughout the process as proctors for the test with our Nikons to give you your final grade. We watch but do not touch."

"Hey, Menendez," McKnight interrupted, "where are you from originally? You don't sound like a local country girl. And you're much too flippant!"

"Well, actually, I was raised in South Philly, so I'm a very sophisticated, urban transplant with a country bent and a diseased sense of humor."

"Waddya you think, Haggerty?"

"Diseased, uh? Oh yeah! Good description! She's all that wrapped into one, but I ain't goin' there. I gotta ride with her for the next thirty days. She's irrepressible. Besides, she's a better shot than me, so I have to treat her right. She might be useful in an emergency. She might even shoot me.

"Get your chariot. Follow us. It's a short haul."

The ride was as promised—uneventful! The scene was as described, a pile of blackened lumber shards atop an outhouse land-fill. What surprised both McKnight and Duke was the lack of damage to the hunting cabin itself, fewer than thirty yards removed from the fire itself. They also both knew that the fire and chemical suppressants the Phoenix contingent put on the flames would contaminate almost all of whatever evidence remained. As promised by Sheriff Hayden, a backhoe local arrived on site fifteen minutes later. He was a local small dairy farmer named Emmet Stead, who had obviously traversed the better part of eight decades, at least four of them with his backhoe and six of them with local whiskey, the moonshine variant. He was just another living stereotype that would feed either your most endearing or your most wretched pre-image of a country hick.

He and the deputies were all veterans of the "manure movement" scene and knew the entire range of jokes about digging up dead bodies.

This, however, was quite different.

He shut the backhoe down about twenty yards from the scene, spit out a wad of Red Man chewing tobacco, and peered suspiciously at Duke and McKnight.

"You must be them city Feds. You ain't dressed for the occasion. So how would you like to utilize my services, and to whom should I give the bill?"

"I'll take the bill," McKnight said, "and give us ten minutes to put on our grubbies. Since the evidence we want may link to an attempted murder scene in Butler and our suspects were here for only about thirty hours, anything of interest in waste product was probably hidden in less than three feet in the pit. So move the burnt wooden remnants to the north and then carefully dig out about three feet of the entire pit dirt and spread it out in a linear formation where we can carefully rake through it."

"Gotcha," said Stead. "Just don't forget that check. I bill out at $35 per hour."

Stead moved the backhoe into place as the agents moved to the rear of their Explorer and began to dress for the occasion, replete with oversized hip boots and two nifty rake contraptions that folded out into light fan rakes to skim the surface of the pit remnants.

"Ooh," ogled Menendez. "We gotta tell Hayden to get us a bunch of these for all the local volunteer suppression units. They're quite functional."

"Yeah," Duke added. "They are, except when you have to clean them! That's less than delightful."

Stead then very tactilely spread out the outhouse droppings as requested. He had a touch with the backhoe that broached artistic. The two half-burnt sleeping bags were the easiest to spot, supremely thrashed by the diesel.

That bundle of cloth looked least promising.

Stead then very lightly strewed the waste product out over about twenty linear yards, careful not to run over or crush whatever may be significant. There were unburned strips of paper and assorted other seemingly worthless items in the tossed salad of feces and urine now in full sunlight view of the morning and mostly lying on the surface of extruded remains.

And the unmistakable odor it inspired whiffed upward.

McKnight and Duke had done this before and carefully began at one end with the fan rakes opposite one another and moved down the line. Forty-five minutes later, they had bagged, at that point, about nineteen pieces of unidentified stuff for further review and evidence analysis, including both the sleeping bags.

It took another fifteen minutes to work their way to the end when they came across the coup d'grasse: a small baggy which appeared only partially burned, with something reddish-brown inside.

Duke held it up to the morning light with Menendez peering over his shoulder, camera in hand.

He turned to her. "Does that look like what I think it is? I do have a wife and a fourteen-year-old daughter."

Menendez sighed.

"Yes, Federal Agent man, it appears that one of your five suspects is a menstruating female. That's a recently used tampon that eliminates immediately more than half the female suspects in North America, those forty-five and older. I'll bet you've just bagged the DNA, blood type, and ethnic type of one of your five assassins in one small ziplock container. And if she's one of your contract hitmen, you guys have your work cut out. That's freaky! Women who murder for hire are a special minority of evil. We don't ordinarily deal with them. Not bad for an afternoon walk in the woods. I'm impressed. You both get an A on your test. Now go get this babe before she goes on another rampage. We'll defer to your judgment on this. After all, we country types don't need some psychotic female type contaminating our bucolic home here."

Duke nodded and turned toward Haggerty. "Menendez is a real piece of work. Oliver would love her."

"Yeah, she's about as irreverent as they come, but aren't most of us in this profession? I mean find me a cop not drenched in cynicism. Murder victims and their assailants will do that to you. They sear your very soul."

They checked the inventory sheet for the collected evidence, made sure the tags were properly labeled, and finally packed it all in an airtight box for overnight shipment to the lab in Quantico, Virginia. The boots and work coveralls all went in a separate airtight bag and assumed the remaining space in the back of their FBI Suburban. Until now, it was scrupulously clean.

"One night here and we can return to Pittsburgh tomorrow," McKnight said. "We should have the analyses of this stuff back within the week."

Priorities reset. Then followed the pleasant surprise! The good news report of the detail was back on Oliver's desk by Thursday afternoon, even before they reported back into town.

"I love it when a plan comes together," Oliver gushed on Thursday after their phone call, "especially when I devised it."

And the Senior FBI agent of the Pittsburgh field office continued to bellow onward and outward.

Except this time, there was no audience of note and the eagles still didn't care.

Chapter 36

PURSUIT

What seemed like a rain-out on Tuesday in court suddenly looked more like a walk-off home run Friday afternoon. Oliver perused the hard copy of the ten-page report four times, highlighted certain sentences, and screened every last nuance of the lab numbers and their ancillary suppositions. It was the Quantico lab summary of the Altoona Outhouse, as it became known around the fourth floor, along with the spectrum of evidence garnered on the McShea property. Oliver just sat there for a full five minutes…gloating…aloud.

His gloat ended with an extended conversation with all four walls. The final sentence: "Gotcha now, you idiots! Criminals always think they're the smartest dudes on the block. Most of the time, they ain't even in the upper quadrant of the bell curve. Never think you can outsmart the talent we assemble."

Then he screamed at the top of his lungs, "Fuckin' A, you toads! Your ass is grass and I'm the Federal John Deere!"

Agents in the main office outside noted his absence of professional restraint and descent into glee. Rancid emotion was not normally Oliver's forte.

"It's always a good thing to have your boss enveloped in the happy," said Agent Bethany Ross. "It just makes our day that much less stressful. This thing with the Greek had become his 'great white whale.' I expect to see the resurrected ghost of Herman Melville with his peg leg right there in his damn office. Be glad the Monongahela is fresh water and not ocean. His obsession whale would wind up hanging from the rafters in some goddamn Southside bar. I'll be glad when June gets here. I'm already approved for two weeks of leave and I'm going to get as far away from this Tsakrios shit as I can. Jim and I are leaving the kids with my mother, and we're going to disappear north of Banff, Canada, with no cell phone towers in sight. Maybe our Captain Ismael Ahab (Oliver) will get this Greek guy out of his system."

"Are you kid'n'?" replied Agent Garrett Lloyd at the adjoining deck. "That addiction won't end until the Greek gets fifteen to twenty for something. I don't care what the hell it is. Just get him out of our line of sight. Send him to prison, any prison. Just get him out of our hair and morning briefings."

The report also included the grainy picture retrieved from the coffee shop camera his agents seized off Route 422 of a woman with sunglasses…at 4:00 a.m. who entered and ordered five coffees while four others remained outside in two nondescript sedans. The waitress thought they were completely out of place because they did not fit the mold of hunters. Although the morning light and camera focus was dim, you could discern one car was red and the other silver. *That only covers about 40 percent of all the cars on the road*, Oliver thought. *But it's better than nothin'.*

"Why can't store and franchise owners just invest in more than just Walmart Chinese junk equipment," Oliver muttered to himself. "Color doesn't help much. I need plate numbers. Obviously these are Pennsylvania colors, but a little focus could go a long way. Yeah, the cars were obviously registered in Pennsy, but that only eliminates forty-nine other states and the ten provinces of Canada. Color is helpful but not so much."

The exterior shots did not pick up the license plate numbers.

The interviewed waitress said that there were only five other customers in store at the time, and as the only one of three servers that morning, she relished the thought of the five more tips that would follow breakfast.

Hope, however, ceded to disappointment. As the strange woman entered alone, an oddity the waitress said, she noticed the clock above the door was almost at 4:00 a.m. Then she only ordered five cups of coffee to go and spoke not a word further. She just handed her a twenty and awaited the change.

But she only made one egregious error at the cash register by removing her sunglasses to retrieve her wallet from her purse. The waitress noted that sunglasses at 4:00 a.m. "was a bit odd."

The interviewing FBI agent agreed.

Yet the picture covering the register was low quality but enough to marry with the blood and DNA report later to create a composite with her almost exact height of five feet and eleven inches as she went out the door with the five Styrofoam cups of coffee.

As yet, they had no name with the collective profile, but the lab report was detailed enough to soon put a face to their suspect, originally dubbed as Ms. Hot Coffee. The net was closing rapidly on Elena Sergovia, but the FBI's best counterpunch was yet to come.

The Quantico dossier became the working nexus that the photographed woman was likely both at the hunting cabin near Altoona and on site that night at the McShea homestead. Marvelous tech enhancement at Quantico then produced a scary accurate picture of Sergovia.

Both location suppositions later proved to be correct.

The partially burned blood evidence from the outhouse matched the tampon she threw away during her hasty retreat from the McShea residence. The analysis gave the FBI a full panel of her DNA, along with her B-negative blood type that occurs in only 5 percent of the world's human population. Even in the United States, therefore, that only reduced the narrow list of potential suspects down to about sixteen million women of menstruating age.

"Well, it's a place to start," said Oliver to Agent McKnight. "At least, we know we're not looking for Diane Feinstein, Elizabeth Warren, or Hillary Clinton."

So suspect number 4 was apparently female but also a deadly update of Lizzie Borden. The police reports from Erie and Binghamton confirmed that. If she was the woman in the photograph, she also likely was the one who sliced the three male victims from behind in bed with a straight razor in Erie and Binghamton. The cuts in all three cases went through their carotid arteries from the victims' right side to their left. That supported the conclusion that she was left-handed with extraordinary arm strength for a lean woman of her apparent weight.

But that wasn't the bonus about which Oliver was most excited.

IRIS, the FBI-DNA/fingerprint computer also matched her DNA with the three unsolved murders in Erie and Binghamton. She (as staff referred to it) was the inspired update from HAL, the computer with a life of its own from the Stanley Kubrick film *2001: A Space Odyssey*. Oliver could barely contain his almost adolescent joy for the next 0800 staff cattle call Monday morning. IRIS hit a proverbial home run for any and all zealous baseball fans in the Pittsburgh field office.

"This is almost a first in bureau history," he screamed at one of the diving eagles on sortie above the river. "Clear three murders and one attempted in one fell swoop. Sorry to steal your metaphor, big bird, but even you can't nab more than one fish at a time."

The eagle flew directly toward his river view window, fish in talons, looking directly at Oliver. They saw each other. Their eyes met, but the eagle didn't flinch. He ignored the irrelevant human.

It was "another fish done gone" to metastasize the lyrics of country singer Bobby Bare's "Marie Laveau." But Oliver's mood now perched on the limb of giddy.

The Pittsburgh FBI office, nevertheless, lost their quest for a second warrant and the appeal to restore the bail. The new judge in the Federal Court case (Abraham White) rejected the government's motion and acceded to the Tsakrios's attorney's demand to return all items seized during the original raid on the house. Then to amplify the insult, he reduced the Tsakrios bail to $250,000. It only had one caveat.

He gave Oliver and the FBI one week to verify the collected inventory with him and Tsakrios's team of attorneys before the return of it all to the Tsakrios family, sufficient time for the agents to examine the "stash" for incriminating evidence. If nothing else about garbage collection, the FBI was monastically patient. After all, that's why they hired the new guys. Rookie agents were most often tasked with the "trash" details.

They did find a veritable lifetime of the Greek's financial and business records but no connection to the attack on the McSheas. Oliver would gladly copy said collection to the IRS, DEA, SEC, and the rest of the Federal alphabets so their bean-counting snakes could go through it.

"I want his ass for the Homestead murders and the McShea kidnapping thing. That's our primary goal," he screamed to the indifferent eagle. "Let someone else wallow through the eternal spectrum of his previous financial sins of moral turpitude."

Then he added, "Come back here, bird. I'm not finished with you! You know it's a felony to lie to the FBI. You can lie to Jesus or Yahweh but not to us."

The eagle came back, gave him a two-squawk, piercing shriek, the two-word Monongahela version of "Welcome to Pittsburgh! Now get out of my beak!" He didn't even drop the fish to deliver the insult. It was an aviary screech of distain for the human presumption of moral superiority.

The next step was to identify, retrieve, and impound the vehicles that led the assassins from Altoona to Butler. Oliver suddenly jumped from his desk chair and scurried to the open main office room where his phalanx of agents worked and thrived.

"Who wants overtime?" he yelled. "I need four agents on deck, two teams to saturate the rental car market in Altoona. It should be no more than a one-day gig. *Per diem* and lodging included. Volunteers first, draftees second! You have twenty minutes to volunteer and think about it. Then I assign. McKnight, in my office, please!"

Before his lieutenant could muster an objection, the boss' palm shot up.

"No, I'm not sending you or Duke. You've already done the Altoona Tour. Just assemble the teams from here and stand by this weekend. Try to get all the single agents to volunteer first. Most of them suck up the overtime, and I want the teams to hit every car rental agency within fifteen miles of Altoona."

"Why fifteen miles, Chief?"

"Just a logical hunch! If you commit a crime with a vehicle, what's the first thing you do to effect your escape?"

"Dump it."

"So a radius of fifteen miles within and around Altoona seems reasonable. It's logical because you could safely park your own car, say, near that large train station lot or the baseball field parking lot or"—he paused—"at one of the many hotels there for a couple days where absolutely no one would notice or give a damn. Since there are two of them, I'm sure they'll pair up to return the rentals and split. I'd start with the rental places nearest that train station. Bus stations have too many derelicts for them to chance leaving their personal vehicles there. Get two teams ready, spun up, and have them on the road by 1900. If you can't get enough volunteers, get me the remaining list of agents who haven't worked weekends in a while and I'll order them. You've got thirty minutes to put this together before I start to draft. Get on it."

Overtime, *per diem*, mileage, and a (Federal) company car was the penultimate platter of succulent red meat. Some loved it, others found it totally unappealing. The FNGs often jumped at it, particularly the single ones. Older, married agents were less frenetic about weekend gigs. "We don't volunteer," said one. "I learned that in the Army at nineteen. Wait until ordered."

Eight agents volunteered.

McKnight could barely contain his good fortune. Ordering nonconsenting agents around always created staff disjoints and personnel irritations, so volunteers were always positively noted in their quarterlies, the evaluations that either elevated or decelerated their Federal careers. Even artificial fawning on the boss had its place in Federal ass-kissing. Everyone pretended to do it with maximum joy.

No one pretended to like it.

McKnight first assembled the eight volunteers for a short briefing and parried them down to two teams. The first two, whose enthusiasm waned with the weekend parameters, immediately bailed. A third agent, Emily Seville, was lukewarm to the ascension and also declined the mission. She feigned a dying grandmother excuse. That left everyone apparently happy. The remaining agent was happy to un-select himself as multiple social commitments to in-laws provided a convenient fiction to whip out the "visiting in-law" excuse. He opted out with a sufficiently lame pretext with which McKnight didn't want to deal.

"Okay! Fine, just go."

He now had his two teams, as per Oliver's request.

"Take all day Saturday and Sunday, if you need it," McKnight ordered. "You have my cell and that of Duke's. Please check in with either one of us at three-hour intervals beginning at 0900, Saturday. Take both you primary and backup weapons, including the M16s and the shotguns. This should be just a standard interview process, but remember, if you encounter either one of these two, particularly the woman, approach with extreme caution. She is now the prime suspect in at least three other contract murders, and he is some sort of rogue assassin for hire. Use all standard precautions because missing one of the check-ins, for example, will bring the Federal world down on you, us, and the ghost of J. Edgar in every zip code around Altoona. The check-ins are crucial at all the rally points. Apprise us immediately if you spot either of the suspects. Understood? Don't muck it up by missing a simple phone call. Got it? I'm deadly serious here. Let me reiterate. It's a safety and security issue. You guys all know that, so follow the protocol."

Their silence was golden. No agent dissent tainted Oliver's plan. Take the OT, pocket the money, hit the motor pool, and find the vehicles used in the Butler shootout.

"Okay, get on the road ASAP. After you get settled at the Hampton, apprise us of your position, hotel rooms, and status. Then get to work first thing Saturday. I believe most of these rental places open at 0800."

"Roger that!" came the group affirmation.

"Curtis, you're with Edwards as Team Alpha. Bishop, you're with Lester as Team Bravo. Get rollin'!"

The teams did indeed shove off shortly after 2100 and were in Altoona an hour or so later at the Hampton, convening in Curtis and Edwards' room to divvy up the range of car rental sites the next morning, most of which were within ten minutes of Interstate 99. They put three rooms on Uncle Sam's dime, as Emily Bishop was very married with a husband and children in North Hills. Ed Curtis and John Edwards had paired up before and had known each other for five years. They agreed to convene at 0700 in Curtis' room, have the hotel breakfast thereafter, and be on the job by 0800.

When Bishop and Lester arrived, sporting coffee from the breakfast bar, Curtis had already Googled the relevant information on the two Enterprise outlets, both the Hertz outlets, along with the Chariot, Eastern, and Budget franchises.

Curtis and Edwards agreed to cover the Enterprise and the Chariot, while Bishop and Lester took the Hertz, Eastern, and Budget ones. They presumed to finish no later than 1600 and convene again. Curtis reminded them all of the check-ins at 0900, noon, and 1500.

And they all had a copy of Sergovia's grainy but now enhanced FBI restaurant picture and the Quantico report, convinced they could find both escape vehicles and be back in Pittsburgh Saturday night.

They hit a eureka moment just before noon and reconvened to telephone the good news to Oliver. Again quoting long-time, deceased, iconic, Pittsburgh Pirates Hall of Fame broadcaster Bob Prince: "Sometimes I'd rather be lucky than good!"

This Saturday, they would wallow in sudden good luck.

"Damn," Oliver said. "I knew you guys were good, but this is a true shit-howdy. Remind me to gussie up your fitness reports. I guess I'll just have to promote you to water-walker status. Good job, agents!"

Chapter 37

WARRIOR WIA

Kathleen was obviously too rattled to think clearly, so Malone offered to take her to Mercy (UPMC), lights and sirens active. She conceded and, after a short trip to check on the two dogs, came out the kitchen door and didn't even bother to lock it. Their property abode was replete with sufficient law personnel to guard the White House and most of the UN. She did remind the senior sheriff deputy on site, Kevin Goss, that Jake was not stranger-friendly, although Kevin knew him and Jake trusted him. Kevin had two German Shepherds of his own, and Jake seemed to sense that he was a true dog lover. There was just only so much trauma that she could now absorb.

At least, the kids were safely stashed.

"Dogs have a sixth sense about humans they should avoid," she said. "If you don't like them, rest assured they are wary of you and have much sharper teeth. Never come above Jake with your hand. Always come from underneath. Remember, Jake has a limited sense of humor. Don't let any of these FBI guys or deputies go thrashing about the house without Kevin or someone near Jake that he trusts," she warned. "They can use the first-floor bathroom, if necessary. But just take your time when you need to scour for evidence. Both M14s are just inside the master bath and cleared. Jake and Rufus are on the second floor, and you can let them out but kindly don't shoot them if they approach the scene of your dead bodies. Rufus won't care. He's mostly indifferent to things dead. He likes his prey alive. But Jake's a military dog and his training is to sit and guard the deceased. It's a detail he did in Afghanistan. Do you have a dog handler here?"

"Yeah, we've called in the State Police handler, but she likely won't be here until midmorning."

"Please don't muck up this trauma with a dog tragedy. If somebody shoots my dogs, I'll be severely pissed, followed by an angry lawsuit. Got it? I'll want somebody's ass for it. And that lawsuit will go so far up Butler County's anal canal that the county supervisors will think they have an adjunct appended to their livers. Please be careful with my animals. I already have enough to worry about sequestering our three kids."

"Understood," Malone said. "Give me five minutes to align and brief my deputies here and talk to the now arriving senior FBI agent, and then we'll split to the Bluff as soon as possible."

The Bluff is actually an elevated section of the city just above the Golden Triangle where the Mercy UPMC and Duquesne University share adjacent space. The six thousand students there on the fifty-acre urban campus is a Catholic university founded in 1878 by an order of Catholic priests called the Society of the Holy Spirit (aka the Spiritans) next to what was, for more than one hundred years, Mercy Hospital now a part of the University of Pittsburgh Medical Center. UPMC is one of the two monsters in health care in Western Pennsylvania, along with Allegheny Health Network, that controls most of the hospitals in the Greater Pittsburgh area and Western Pennsylvania. It was the most available trauma center to which Ronk could be medevac'd.

With Sheriff Malone at the helm, the sixty-minute commute became forty-five. Malone could push his police cruiser to the max, but its regular abuses augured poorly for its longevity. It already had more than 220,000 miles with an engine and frame merely two years from purchase.

One of the attending physicians, Dr. Aaron Lipsky, apprised of their arrival in advance, met them at the ER and escorted them to the ICU where they could see the sedated Ronk through the observation glass but could not enter. As badly as Kathleen wanted to touch him, his condition at that point was too grave. The heavy sedation administered did not allow for visitors of any sort.

"The inflammation around the spine will take two to three days to quell," Lipsky said. "Then we will attempt to remove the bullet, maybe next week. The bullet above his leg is out, and we anticipate no long-term, residual damage to the knee or leg, but that wound will likely still require extensive therapy and at least four to six weeks of formal rehab. The bullet nearest the spine is the tricky one. We won't be able to correctly assess the damage until then. We hope he can recover much like Ryan Shazier, the Steeler linebacker injured last year, but *patience* is the operative word. For whom does he work?"

"The Army Corps of Engineers," Kathleen said. "I think he has only about twenty-five days of accrued sick leave left on the books. He's been with them fewer than five years. How much rehab do you anticipate?"

"I can't estimate until after we remove the bullet near the spine," Lipsky said. "But two to four to six months is reasonable. Again, it all depends on how the nerves surrounding the spine heal after we remove the offending bullet. That's the simple explanation, obviously not as technical as what we will likely encounter. The medical jargon would make your head spin, but the bottom line is, if we can remove that bullet safely with minimal damage, he can likely fully recover in six months and return to work."

"I just want him to return home and be a father again," she said in a soft sob. "His Federal job and status with the Marines can adjust. The Marines will probably be less flexible than the Corps of Engineers, as their work rules don't have a mandate for an annual physical fitness test. What I need to know immediately is, will he be able to climb up and down stairs? We have a two-story old farmhouse from the nineteenth century that we renovated, so I presume that will, at least for the immediate future, be a problem. Correct?"

"Well," Lipsky replied, "if you have the assets, I'd recommend a stair lift chair for him and one of those elevated toilets to put less strain on his lower back during the recovery period. Can you manage that? We know a couple of charitable agencies that can help you with that through UPMC."

"I don't want to outthink myself on this yet," she said. "The VA will help, and I have excellent company coverage, so let's just take it one step at a time. The surgery first. Then let's address the immediate recovery and the nuances of therapy second!"

Then there was another one of those uncomfortable pauses where neither party knew what further to say. Both the doctor and Kathleen knew what to say next. The situation was bleak, but the prognosis was pretty simple. Dr. Lipsky reached out to shake her hand.

"Good luck with it all. We'll do the absolute best on our part here. This is the best staff on paralysis injuries within two hundred miles, but my prediction is, he will walk and return to full viability. I understand his Reserve commitment but I don't know how they will evaluate his injury. I obviously wouldn't recommend running, basketball, volleyball or any activity sport that jolts the lower back."

Then he paused.

"That includes motorcycle riding. He doesn't have one of those, does he?"

"No, that's not a turn-on for him, but he was 'jump-qualified' on active duty and is a pure adrenaline junkie when it comes to occasional skydiving."

"No way," Lipski continued. "He's got to put that in the rearview mirror forever. The threat of permanent wheelchair confinement will be too real with this injury."

"Well, it's an injury that may terminate his military career at seventeen years, the end of his current contract if he can't pass the Physical Fitness Test mandated for all Marines until age fifty-five. But right now, that's almost trivial. Just get him well!?

"Thank you, doctor, for the time."

"I'm sure we'll talk again later."

Then returning her focus to Sheriff Malone as Lipsky returned to surgery, she leaned on Malone and hugged him.

"Thank you ever so much....for everything! When can we return to the house? Will your guys be done with the bodies by then and the accumulation of evidence by at least the weekend?"

"Can you wait until tomorrow, at least, to return home?" Malone said. "I'll have Deputy Goss feed the dogs. We just will need about another twenty-four hours for unimpeded access to the property for my guys and the FBI."

"Okay," Kathleen said. "The dog chow is in the far cabinet nearest the south exit door of the kitchen. I'll call my mother and have her pick me up and I'll stay with them until tomorrow afternoon, if that is all right?"

Now it was time for Malone to refocus. The big picture for him was now on the three dead visitors to his county morgue and the extraction of all their remaining secrets. So he returned. A contingent of four of his deputies remained on scene and worked with the FBI lab personnel who arrived around 1000 and stayed for the rest of the day.

Lights and sirens for the return trip also were *de rigeur* for Malone as Kathleen made the call to Cranberry for her mother. His return trip was a blue-light special.

He made it made in thirty-seven minutes.

Meanwhile, the FBI team began the slow walk about noon from the shooting site to the back gate midmorning. There were eight of them spread out in a linear formation along with four of Malone's deputies as they meticulously walked in unison toward the back gate. They did notice and make multiple photographs of the five intruders' footprints and replication casts of the same, and also located the LED lights Kathleen had placed in the arc just beyond where the three bodies fell. One agent harmlessly tripped the flare trap that Kathleen set near the back gate.

There was "no harm, no foul" on the accident, but it did release a litany of profanity from Agent Jake Duval and the required derisive laughter from his fellow agents and deputies.

It would take several weeks for Duval to recover from the incoming barrage of insults from his peers. The jibes ranged from hazing about his clumsy feet to his diminished visual capacity. His peers were unrelenting.

"Dammit, I screwed it up," he said afterwards. "It'll take weeks to put this into the rearview mirror. These guys don't forget. I guess I'll just have to suck it up but they'll remember this until I retire."

But the eureka factor came into play as they carefully examined the not-so-obvious path down the dirt road from which the five assailants entered the property. The path may have been either a firebreak once upon a time but now seemed only there for seasonal deer hunters. It was about one hundred or so yards from the back gate that they came upon the clearing where the attackers parked two vehicles and moved toward the house.

There wasn't much beyond the tire tracks of two vehicles they apparently brought to the fray, but the circumvention of the place where they temporarily parked their escape was cluttered with depressed, clumped grass but no other obvious signs of human activity.

Then came the vaunted eureka moment.

Deputy Emil Carter spotted it first and alerted FBI Agent Phillis McGuire.

Carter put on sterile gloves and picked up what he thought might be a used tampon.

"Is this what I think it is?" he asked McGuire.

"Yes, Emil, it's truth in a tacky, disposable item used by menstruating women only. Most of the time! Although I must tell you that medics in Afghanistan, when I was there, carried them to stop immediate bleeding of soldiers who suffered bullet or shrapnel wounds," she replied. "Isn't it amazing how creative you can be under duress? Some of the most innovative procedures in medicine are the unintended consequence of combat. This is one of them. So what we have here," she continued, "is likely one of our two final suspects, as this is obviously a fresh extract from a female who was here and apparently in a hurry to leave. Do you buy that, Carter?"

He held the bagged key piece of evidence up to the morning light.

"Amen! Yes, ma'am! Amazing! She was in such goddamn hurry to get rid of it that she practically gave us a DNA profile. Up to this point, these guys have all been pretty good about concealment and covering their asses. What else can you guys find from this?"

"Well, among other things," McGuire replied, "would be her blood type, approximate age, and what day it is on her period. Heaviest flow is generally day three. And, if she's anywhere in our data base, we may even get a partial print from it. See, all that CSI shit on television in the '90s is now just ordinary procedure. We might even be able to tell her ethnic background if the blood type is rare enough."

"That would be the ultimate irony," he said. "Conviction of a felony with evidence you offered by yourself. That's a remarkable piece of self-incrimination. I wonder what other crime spree she was into."

They were very soon to find out.

Chapter 38

MORE EUREKA

Division of labor was abjectly simple.
Curtis checked out the standard four-door Ford from the motor pool while Edwards killed another tree at the armory. Paper is the mother's milk of government. No Federal movement occurs without deceased wood pulp, and the FBI gets no pass. The IRS and the Social Security Administration are the kings and queens of paper, but the FBI also masticates the protocol. It's their version of publish or perish.

Sign here on the highlighted portions…at least five more times.

Two shotguns, two M16s completed the requisite paper chase for the trip. They had done this so often before that Edwards almost forgot to count the exact number of rounds issued for each weapon. It was a trivial slight of mandatory oversight. But this was the clerk's domain, and he wasn't about to relinquish the undersize importance of his assigned post as the denizen of the armory swamp.

"Don't you want to count the rounds noted on the invoice, or should I?" the property clerk asked. The sarcasm was thicker than a molasses sandwich. "We wouldn't want to lose some of our taxpayers' firepower in a maze of uncounted arithmetic now, would we?"

Edwards ignored the comment in a building already drenched in an array of classic snark. So he loudly and deliberately counted each and every round, much to the clerk's delight. It gave him a sense of the real imploded importance of his job. But it did nothing but irk

Edwards and remind him that the clerk should be accorded some of his undivided agent attention in the future.

"Okay, we done here?" said Edwards, dropping the last shotgun round into the metal ammo can. "Wouldn't want to make any mistakes now, would we? Misplacement of ammunition is a serious peripheral felony, is it not? God forbid we should miscount."

The nameless clerk just smiled. It was the glee of the verbal spar. He loved to pester agents at whatever level. Petty harassment was one of his more esteemed supreme virtues, and he was very good at it. He had no idea of the residual drool it caused with the agents.

Edwards slung the two M16s over his left shoulder, grabbed the shotguns with his right and the ammo can with his left...and left.

"Remind me to fuck with that little weasel running the armory first chance we get when we get back," he intoned to Curtis. "I tire of his imperious attitude. He's a piece of detritus without manners. Wonder how he got the job!"

"Well, he's a low-level Fed," Curtis replied, "so he, at least, passed the piss test and presumptively is not a druggie. The job doesn't require royal etiquette, humor, or a warm personality. It's repetitive and dull. That's the crowd it attracts. I mean, would you do what he does for that miniscule salary? Isn't he pretty low on the totem pole on which to waste any anger? So why do you let this kind of pettiness get under your skin? You know half the new hires in this building barely have a room temperature IQ. Let it go. Hell, there may be a new guy there by the time we get back from Altoona, and he or she will be just as much a flaming gaper as he is. You know, the standard Federal issue!"

On that dubious note, Edwards slammed the sedan trunk, and their focus shifted.

Curtis drove and Edwards began reading aloud the incident report on the firefight in Butler, the hunting cabin in Altoona, and the apparent gang of five about which Oliver obsessed with the connection to Tsakrios.

"So we're apparently looking for two rentals from the Altoona area for the remaining two, at least one of which was driven by some sort of deadly femme fatale that we should handle with extreme caution. Right?"

"Yeah, I think that a violent connection to three contract murders in Erie and Binghamton plus the attempted one on the McSheas qualifies," Curtis said. "I mean, Oliver was more than his usual paternal, deadly serious, ego-driven self when he described her. She appears to be the perfect DNA intersection between sociopath and psychopath. He didn't have to say 'handle with care.' Although I understand those two terms are out of vogue with the daytime television psychobabblers, isn't it? I mean this bitch is the paradigm between sordid and pure evil. Serial and contract killers have no soul, and she is very apparently on the varsity roster of both. I mean, that's why we hire those eggheads at the Quantico FBI lab to dissect. She's a behaviorist's dream…or nightmare. What else is in there?"

"Just the standard blood work, summary of the three autopsies that the McSheas whacked, the purported picture of her from the coffee shop off '79, and that workup of her used tampon from the Butler site with her blood type. What we apparently have here is a contract female killer with B-negative blood, so our suspect list is at least narrowed down to some thirty million women of menstruating age in North America. Okay, you take the first fifteen mil, and I'll take the second bunch. We should be through our interviews with them in about twelve more years, just in time to retire."

Curtis grunted an assent. Then he laughed.

"If this was a careful contract killer, who apparently was able to elude the local gendarmerie in three previous hits, why suddenly so sloppy with personal evidence on site in Butler?"

"Panic maybe! Incoming gunfire can do that. It changes the whole composition of your mind and body. I haven't been shot at since Afghanistan, but I know it changes your whole outlook on life. I suspect the five of them never fathomed the idea that maybe the McSheas would open up on them first, much less drop three of their crew. Criminals almost always overestimate their own prowess. My guess is simple panic, and, thereupon, she had an immediate personal emergency and made a dumb mistake. After all, haven't you ever known a woman who suddenly excused herself to scurry to a john at that time of month without explanation? I mean, with your Joanna, was she ever part of the 'never ask and I won't tell' about a sudden trip to the restroom?"

"Not that she ever admitted—and trust me, I never ask—but there are some things men should just clam up about. It ain't none of yo bleeping business! So don't embarrass your woman by bringing it up, especially in front of her friends. I've already had this conversation once with my thirteen-year-old daughter, but she was teenage blunt about the whole process. I'll never ask her again. Bright middle-school girls have a profound ability to embarrass even their own parents. Diana is one of those. Sometimes what exits her mouth has no premeditation and just spews out without thinking of its consequence. So our suspect must have been in a real panic. So now we know her blood type. It's an identity start. The guy with her might have rented from the same agency, so we might get double lucky."

"How long have we been in this business, Jake? Since when has pure luck ever solved a case? Luck is the by-product of the intersection of 'prepare meets the opportune.'"

"Oh, please, Jack! This would be too easy. I mean, we're almost tripping over this babe. All we have to do is find her rental, take some prints, and wrap this all up for Oliver by noon. Since when in our twelve years together has any case been that easy? I'm bettin' this will be an all-day, mundane round of interviews that may yield nothing. I'm not wrapped in the department blanket of optimism. Let's see. I'll call Bishop and Lester. They left before us and should already be there."

And so it was.

The next morning brought them together at 0700 in the room with Curtis and Edwards where, as noted previously, they quickly divvied up the search quadrant that promised to be an easy morning with only six rental outfits in town. Coffee and a continental breakfast later, they adjourned with the admonition to check with each other at 0900, 1200, and 1500.

Curtis was the senior agent on site and, thus, in charge.

"Heed Oliver's warning. If you spot either one or both of these two, call us first and we'll rendezvous. Don't take them on by yourself, especially that strange female. I'm not in the mood for any burial details or visits to your next of kin. Does everyone have their .40-cals and backup?"

Group assent followed.

"I know," Curtis said, "it was a dumb question, but I had to ask. And park your vehicle in an open street or a busy restaurant parking lot if you must exit. The last thing we need is some amateur poppin' one of our trunks in a back alley and helping themselves to Federal firearms. Let's hit these agencies and meet back here by 1700."

"Roger that," said Elaine Lester. "We're on it. Check in at zero-9."

First stop for Curtis and Edwards was the "cheap" Rent-a-Car outfit just off Interstate 99. The woman clerk who greeted them seemed steeped in seven levels of drab and almost choked when they flashed their FBI badges.

"No shit! So this is what an FBI agent looks like! You guys seem much more like our company auditors. You're a little dressed down for Feds. I expected more three-piece formal, along with an attitude."

"If you like, ma'am, we can cop an attitude," said Curtis, "but it's not our preferred approach. We're actually just in search of a couple of suspects clients who may have rented from you. So can you help us?"

"Suspects in what? We're very busy today."

"Murder and mayhem," said Edwards. "We do not toy with suspects like these, and neither should you."

"Okay," she replied, "if I can help!" Now her tone changed. It seemed the word *murder* yanked her back into polite conversation and she changed her flippant tone.

"Well, we're looking for a man and woman tandem. We have no description of the man but a grainy picture of the woman," Edwards said. "Please take a look and see if you can identify her." He handed her the eight-by-ten grainy photograph. "She would have rented it within the last week or so. Did you have anyone even remotely fitting this description rent from you this last week?"

"Well, that's easy," the clerk said. "We haven't had a woman rent a car here in more than a month, and you can go through all the pictures of the guys who rented. They're there with pix of their driver's licenses and credit cards in the applications. All of them seemed to match their signatures with the license. No red flags there for us."

And so they did…all thirty-two of them. Nothing seemed immediately amiss and rang no bells with either of them. Ten minutes later, it was time to move on to Enterprise.

"Thank you very much, ma'am. We appreciate your cooperation, and if you can think of anything else, please call us."

The clerk took Edwards' business card, snorted, and gave the pro forma. "I'll call if I remember anything."

Exiting toward the Ford parked on the front street, Edwards was never one to restrain a negative opinion drenched in sarcasm.

"Well, she was as helpful as tits on a boar," he chimed. "Don't you get the feeling that her previous encounters with the law were less than positive? We weren't nasty with her, but she went out of her way to be petulant. Did you notice the tattoos? Waddya think?"

"I think we should go on to Enterprise. File her in the 'No Help' column. I'll bet their employees have a better sense of public relations. It's less than ten minutes away on this same drag. Hell, we might be done by the 0800 at this rate. And our per diem covers the whole day!"

As promised, the staff at Enterprise was much more corporate savvy about public relations as was Evonne McGraw, the branch manager who greeted them.

"Good morning, gentlemen. What can I do for you?"

McGraw was not intimidated by the Federal agents and was much more cooperative than the first clerk.

After their introduction, Edwards showed her the photograph.

Then what followed was the eureka moment.

"Oh, that one!" McGraw said, rolling her eyes. "What a piece of performance art she was. Very creepy woman! She had an attitude galore for no apparent reason. May she never darken our door again!"

She went to a file cabinet to her left and pulled the file on the rental.

"The name on her Pennsylvania driver's license was Elena Sergovia. She wouldn't take off her sunglasses, but I insisted for the company photo attached to the left side. She wanted any car, seemed in unconventional hurry, and was really irritated when informed of the company policy of a backup credit or debit card. The signatures on both the license and the Visa card seemed to match, and I had no reason to doubt their authenticity, but there was something very weird about her. She rented it Friday, ten days ago, and then returned it this Thursday and paid in cash. Most women renters are chatty. You know...the standard stuff, kids, husbands, paramours, and such. But she had all the personality of a viper. I'm just glad we got the car back intact. We haven't even had a chance to clean it yet."

Before she could say anything more, Curtis leaped into the fray. "Where is it?"

"Parked in the back, near the cleaning rack. Do you need to see it?"

"Well, more than see it, Ms. McGraw, the Federal government has just impounded it as evidence in a series of Federal felonies. Show us where it is and do not let any employee touch it until we finish collection of any evidence on or in it. We will tow it to our lab in Pittsburgh, and it will be returned, sparkling clean, after we're finished with it.

"So my suspicions were not unfounded," McGraw said. "Glad I didn't engage her any further. She was just a little too bizarre. The whole staff noticed. I'll clear this with corporate headquarters, and they'll replace the unit if we need something for a new customer. Take your time with it."

"Trust us, we will. Just show us where it is now so we can begin gathering any forensic evidence she may have left."

McGraw grabbed the keys from a back rack and led them to the Ford. Edwards had gone to their car and retrieved his portable print dusting kit. They gloved and very carefully opened all four doors.

There were collectible prints on the exterior driver door, the steering wheel and around the console, and a second set on the driver's side door.

"I can't find anything else, so apparently the two of them were in the vehicle together at some point," Edwards said. "Let's just pop the trunk and call for the tow."

Then came the unexpected Eureka moment.

And there it was, lying in a stuffed kitchen baggie in the near corner or the trunk on the passenger side.

"I don't believe it," said Curtis.

"We can't be this lucky," said Edwards. "I mean...really?"

Then they both laughed aloud and wandered into the pool of relevant sarcasm.

"I believe this bag of evidence has your name on it, Agent Edwards."

"To again quote the immortal Bob Prince, I'd rather be lucky than good!"

Then they both laughed. "Really, who's going to be the bag man?"

"She was here in Altoona. She was there in Butler. She couldn't have picked the worst four days of the month to self-incriminate. What was she thinkin'? She's going to wind up going to prison for being a menstrual moron. This is a new level of stupid for me. Wait 'til I tell Joanna! This bag likely will match the stray Butler tampon."

"Yeah, numb nuts, just don't bring it up over dinner. That topic is an appetite suppressor. Oliver's going to hyperventilate over this chain of evidence. We'll have to peel his ass off the ceiling."

"Can't wait for that visual! Wait 'til it gets on YouTube. My kids will alert us."

Chapter 39

TIGHTER NOOSE

By the check-in at noon, FBI Agents Bishop and Lester had run through Budget, Eastern, and Hertz with no "possibles" and no hint of either suspect, male or female. Meanwhile, Bronson had no intention of returning the Romanov rental car that arrived with the trio from Detroit that might shine any penumbra of suspicion over him. No sense in providing the FBI or anyone else with help to place Aaron Bronson at the scene of the Butler debacle. Once he got to Newark, about to board a plane for Israel, he would call Tsakrios, take the risk of a wiretap, and give him the bad news. Meanwhile, the FBI wouldn't find Romanov's rental for more than a month, as Bronson drove it directly to the Altoona train station, parked it, wiped the interior clean, and locked it. He made sure there was nothing in the trunk, threw in the keys, and slammed it shut with gloved hands. It was just another parked vehicle innocuously molding in the station lot, indifferent to the curiosity of equally indifferent humans.

It would take another three weeks gathering dust and grit on its windshield to garner the attention of any station employee. Parked cars mattered not, unless they belonged to those employed there. It was only until the windshield became a mockery of vernal debris that anyone noticed. By then, the cold tracks of Bronson's retreat to Israel yielded few clues, just a presumption that someone drove it to the station and abandoned it. Bronson had already dumped his rental in Newark where it was cleaned and re-rented at least a dozen more times. Degraded DNA has no relevance when pilloried by the spectrum of household cleaners. The tracks of his escape eroded into prehistory. Bronson melded into modern antiquity where he retreated to the beaches of Tel Aviv and his main obsession: the allure of seminaked women lying in the sun, awaiting his full attention.

The two auto recon teams quietly returned to Pittsburgh on Sunday cheered by the knowledge they had likely nailed the final piece of evidence sufficient for an arrest warrant on the suspect identified as Elena Sergovia.

Oliver even interrupted his Sunday baseball game at PNC Park to spread the good news with a group e-mail and a Twitter feed that "it was now coming together in an aggregate complaint that would snare Ms. Sergovia and the yet unidentified fifth suspect. See everyone tomorrow morning!" All agents within his purview and Twitter spectrum received the text percolating with the unctuous tone of "I told you so!" It was classic Oliver, never one to let a victory lap shine on its own.

He just had to brag about it and cheer his own incisive input. His vanity always required a modicum of gloat. The text received mixed reviews when the sullen receptors gathered for the Monday briefing. Oliver then began the predictable.

"There he goes again," said one of the rented agents from DC. "Is this guy always that vain? Or does he have some sort of pervasive retribution thing that I don't see?"

"Both," whispered Agent Beth Dupree. "She's not the one he's after. It's this Greek guy that's his career addiction. Remember Ismael in Herman Melville's *Moby Dick*. He'll just use her to turn state's evidence because he couldn't care less about her insidious past. So he'll avoid any talk about the prior three murders and maybe put her away on a Federal beef for seven to ten for conspiracy or accessory and negotiate with her. That won't sit real well with the cops in Erie and Binghamton. Tsakrios, however, is the one he wants to put away for life with her testimony for his litany of Federal and common law crimes that run from here to Milwaukee over four decades. So he really doesn't give a damn about her priors. Witness protection for her will be quarters in a separate Federal facility for a proposed seven years. She might even get Club Fed, Long Beach, CA, or Miami. He couldn't care less if she gets out on good behavior in less than the proposed because she may not get immunity on the suspect murders of her previous resume. They may prosecute her now or later, but evidence from mitochondrial DNA is a slim thread, and it degrades rapidly over time. Then add this to the mix. Time and staff inertia will further degrade the ability to prosecute. So if she gets one of those dumbass Simpson juries, she may just walk completely.

"Juries roll their eyes at some of this opaque science. They'd rather have some TV wonk like Bill Nye explain it to them in junior high school terms. It's a close call. Prosecutors may beg off the priors as lacking in evidence because none of the local cops can absolutely place her with the three victims on the nights of their murders. I mean, she was either super slick or the detectives were super sloppy, so the locals may just blow it off. After all, the three upstate victims were not exactly paragons of virtue. Citizens of high repute they were not. Either way, they will have difficulty pinning motivation on her, although the book on her resembles the biography of the angel of death. She's a piece of work. Just remember, she's not the target, Tsakrios is."

Oliver's first phone call on Monday morning was to Deputy DA Weinstein, inviting him and his staff to the 0800, where the details of the case would then need Weinstein & Co. to gin up a Federal arrest warrant.

"And bring a deputy Federal defense attorney with you to act as her counsel. This isn't going to be a standard interrogation, just an Oliver homily and summation of charges with an offer to roll her as a Federal witness," Oliver's secretary, Allyson Grief, said. "Don't need to sweat her as we have all the evidence we need to pack her away on the Butler attack. She can either listen or just keep her mouth shut. Just hope she's smart enough to take the deal. Seven with us or upstate on murder charges! I think she'll go with us."

All the usual Federal, state, and Pittsburgh police showed for the *Oliver Show* and, by 0850, had all the red meat they could chew that implicated Sergovia. They anointed an ad hoc task force and prepared a raid on what was likely her last known address in the Mt. Oliver section overlooking the Monongahela River. By 1000, they were already rolling. She wasn't home, but they had a de facto, "no knock" warrant in hand and crashed into the apartment on Arlington Avenue across from Mt. Michael's Cemetery.

Aside from a small hoard of pistols and knives, there was little to link her to the earlier murders. The apartment yielded no straight razors, but she made her final unsubtle and terminal mistake, however, discovered by Agent Rory Duquette as he carefully rooted through her office desk and its contents.

And there it was—the third nail on her cross!

Duquette carefully gloved and opened the letter sent to her with a North Side Pittsburgh Post Office cancellation. It was slit open and had no return address. Just like the unsigned ones sent to all of the other four, it now was the manna from heaven that would tie her to the Butler attack and justify the pending warrant for her arrest, along with the physical blood evidence at both the hunting cabin and onsite at the Butler property:

Gather at the preassigned checkpoint. The address is 13 Russellville Road, Butler County. Leave no trace. If the kids interfere, take them out too. Meet at the prearranged site the second Saturday in May at ten o'clock. Then destroy, shred, and burn this letter completely, along with its envelope.

It was another incriminating, gross error on her part not to destroy it, but the FBI now had the proverbial dragnet out with sufficient information from her backup phone book in the desk extracted by Duquette to start knocking on other doors of friends, acquaintances, or cronies. Forty-eight hours later, she fell into their hands by returning to the apartment, yet unaware that the FBI had almost restored it to its formerly neat and pristine state. The apartment manager, however, almost "screwed the pooch." He saw her exiting and alerted her to the FBI's intrusion the day before. Realizing what the manager just revealed, she bolted back toward her car only to be greeted by a maze of FBI in no mood to swap spit or conversation. She smartly offered no resistance.

The arrest was the paradigm of appropriate. The fact that she had a knife longer than four inches and her favorite Russian Kalashnikov pistol hidden in the small of her back only added to the savory of felony they would hang around her neck. She said not a word to the agents as they whisked her away to the assignation with Oliver and maybe another one of those offers she couldn't refuse.

Although they made her arrest at about 1400, Oliver couldn't wait to squeeze her. She was only given a quick head break to relief herself and then whisked down the hall to be accorded some "Oliver prime time."

Less than an hour later, the senior Federal attorney in Pittsburgh drafted one of his staff newbies to meet with her. "Advise her to say nothing and apprise her what was about to happen. Then further advise her to acquire her own attorney henceforth. That's it."

"Roger that!" He then entered the interrogation room where Sergovia was handcuffed and leg-shackled to pins on the floor. After he introduced himself as a Federal defense attorney, he launched into his short admonition.

"If you have no attorney of your own, the government is obliged to provide you with one, but most of those guys won't want to take your case," he said. "So my advice is to listen and say and admit nothing. Listen to Agent Oliver because he wants the man who hired you and will make an offer you really should really consider. Oliver doesn't give two hot counterfeit twenties about you. He has you by the short hair. The evidence of your complicity in the Butler case is clear on all six elements of premeditated or attempted murder. Take the seven to ten years with the chance of parole with us or be thrown to the wolves in Erie or Binghamton. They will attempt to put you away for life with little chance of release until your hair on both your head and groin is very gray. You'll be a very old lady accustomed to the joys of pudendal sex until you see the sun from the outside again. So I strongly advise you to listen and take the Federal offer or be shipped Upstate 79 tonight. There are two other jurisdictions just pining for a chunk of your ass."

Sergovia thought for a moment, pursed her lips, and cleared her throat.

"I want that in writing. Otherwise, it's no deal!"

"What you're offered will be formal, in print, and cleared through the Federal Court and signed by a judge. When Oliver comes in here, just listen. If you have any questions afterward, save them for me. I'll be here the whole time. Please don't say anything about any facet of the Butler incident. You know nothing other than your history with the Greek. Silence is golden here, and that trite cliché about 'anything you say may be held against you' is not a line out of Grimm's fairy tales. This whole thing will be recorded. If you are unclear about anything, just say 'On advice of my attorney, I decline to say anything that may incriminate me. I invoke my right to remain silent under the Fifth Amendment of the US Constitution.' Am I perfectly clear?"

"Yes," she replied, nervously twitching in her chair.

"Okay, I'll call for him!"

Three minutes later, the cocksure Oliver entered with his executive officer, Joel McKnight, and a third nondescript woman that Sergovia assumed was some sort of clerk, and they all sat down across from her.

Oliver began. He didn't even bother to introduce himself, just launched into his diatribe with his best intimidating posture. But his demeanor moved her not a diastolic. She was unimpressed and shot him a look of absolute scorn. Unable to rattle her, he said, "Okay, Ms. Sergovia, here's the deal. The government is prepared to offer you limited immunity from prosecution if you plead guilty to one count of attempted murder and a second count of conspiracy to commit murder for hire. We have sufficient evidence to convict you in Federal court on both courts. In return for that and full cooperation and testimony as a Federal government witness against George Tsakrios, confirmation of your witness to his crimes on the witness stand and under oath, we are then prepared to reduce the complaint against you to one count of attempted manslaughter with a maximum sentence of seven years in Federal custody with chance of parole after one and a half years. Your current bail, moreover, will remain, however, at $1.5 million cited in the original complaint. What happens next will depend on your full cooperation and testimony against Mr.

Tsakrios. During this time, you will be remanded to Federal custody during the pretrial process, interviewed extensively in preparation for your testimony against him. Mr. Tsakrios will be unable to touch you, and you will be under consistent armed guard at a nearby location where we will prepare you for the event. Any of his attorneys who interrogate you will confront Federal attorneys in the room to protect and advise you.

"Your required testimony will be here in Pittsburgh in open court, subject to cross-examination likely by these same Tsakrios defense attorneys. It may be brutal, as his attorneys have to deflect your testimony by attacking you. Be prepared for that. They cannot bring up any inference to alleged crimes in either Erie or Binghamton. Upon his conviction, we will return you to a secure Federal facility where we are then prepared to recommend a reduction of the Federal complaint against you to six months and admission in court of guilty to attempted manslaughter. It's a Federal felony offense that will follow you for the rest of your life.

"The government, however, will also follow your eighteen months with an offer to put you into the Federal witness protection program and move you thereafter to a permanent location of our choosing and provide you with a different identity and documents that so portend. Should you commit and be convicted of any crime, either common law or Federal statute, at any point in the remainder of your life, the government will reinstate the remaining 5.5 years of the attempted manslaughter conviction and you will serve every day of it. Your new identity will include everything from a new birth certificate, driver's license, and work history in your new community. Zealously guard and completely forget every element of your past life from now until the time you were born. Do not attempt to reconcile or connect with any member of your birth family, as that will also violate the program. That is the government's offer. Consult with the attorney provided or one you hire yourself. Time is short, so we need our answer within seventy-two hours. Meantime, you will remain in custody until we receive your response."

Then ever so nonchalantly, he closed the thick folder from which he read, got up from the table, and left, along with the other agent and clerk. He left two copies of the proposal, one for her and one for her assigned defense attorney. It was resplendent with legalese, but Oliver's summation was correct.

Give up Tsakrios under oath or maybe spend seven years with the girls in some Federal warehouse not of her choosing.

She didn't need seventy-two hours to contemplate her answer. Her birth family was a shredded scar from her past. Forgetting them would be easy.

I took a mere two minutes to decide. She signed G. Elena Sergovia on four different pages.

"If it were done when 'tis done, then t'where well it were done quickly."

Lady Macbeth had moved Sergovia to the next act.

Chapter 40

VENGEANCE UP

Kathleen awoke Monday shortly before sunrise yet unaware of the sudden weekend FBI chain of events. UPMC called shortly after seven. It was a phone com with the good news that Ronk was out of the ICU, downgraded to progressive care, and expected to be home soon where he could begin in-home therapy for the lower back injury. The bullet stabilized sufficiently so surgeons could contemplate removing the lodged threat sometime within the next two weeks. His knee was healing well and not a chronic issue. The nurse who called said they would retain him after surgery for a final week of therapy in hospital until assured he could walk erectly on his own and with no lingering nerve damage at both bullet sites.

That was the good news.

What came, however, was one major caveat of the necessary next and her newest household project: no stairs and some sort of recliner for him in which to sleep until the extracted bullet wound completely healed, a process the nurse said would take six to nine weeks.

Now almost fully awake with the phone check, reality was on deck for their morning formation. Jake and Rufus gently reminded her of the morning agenda. Dogs outside, chow up!

First, she had to do some interior watering of her own.

Seated and contemplated, the cobwebs dissipated with the flow. She grabbed her robe hanging on one of the bedposts and caught a glimpse of herself bare-assed and full-throttle naked in the bedroom's full-length mirror.

"Not bad for an old broad with three kids. Thank God for red hair and good DNA. Ronk has a point—I guess I am sizzlin' hot. But high school was a no-go! We were definitely not ready for each other then."

Followed by the apropos pause…

"And please, God, excuse my lapse into vanity!"

She then looked to her left for the holster on the western bedpost nearest the head of the bed. Removing the Walther from its assigned sheath, she checked it, assured it was still on safe, and returned it to the holster. The kids were still at her parents, so she released the dogs downstairs via the second deck southern utility door and went to check on the other three first floor exits. Then the routine shifted to the den and office to open the weapons' safe. Normally the kids did the morning dog feed.

Today that task fell to Kathleen.

All of this was part of the security routine they replicated daily, even before the trauma of the assault from their southern flank.

But now it yielded to the scourge of coffee. Both she and Ronk were not yet complete caffeine junkies, but they came perilously close before 0900. Unlike Ronk, whom she once said would drink MRE instant spiked with battery acid, she was very particular about caffeine and scoured the many diverse coffee outlets in Northern Virginia for novel imports. Today's selection was one from Costa Rica but a full pot not required for her when home alone. She didn't have what Marines called the gunnery sergeant hook on her right hand, that permanent tilt of the index finger replicating a fish hook designed to hold the heaviest of coffee cups all day long.

Maybe in the distant future! Not now.

So fortified by the morning joy juice, it was time to return upstairs and dress for a day confronting home issues like the remaining bullet holes on the southern exterior of the house.

Thus, Monday became a "jeans and no bra" workday with a chambray shirt and her favorite decades-old cowboy boots. She could still do the *nota bene* (no bra) thing at her age with little hint of Cooper's droop that affected an array of women this side south of 50. Ronk's fraternity brother, Mark Edwards, invented the "NB" phrase at Penn State where they were on constant watch in those post-pubescent days for university coeds electing to go braless. That was a phenomenon normally confined to the spring semester with young women of minimal adipose and light superstructures. Winters around the Mt. Nittany campus demanded the full spectrum of cover in January. In common parlance, University Park, Pennsylvania, was mostly butt-fuck cold from December to Easter. No cold-chisel nipples, sans bra, need apply.

Since the weekend rain cleared, next on her checklist was patrolling the fence line. Taking one of the Mossbergs from the safe, she relocked its haven, retrieved her cell, and set the ponytail and favorite Pirate baseball cap in place to do the forty-minute walk of the family perimeter with two very happy canines, Señor Moss, and a vat of coffee. The walking path with its high grasses around the fifty acres took almost that long to traverse. Her first stop was the front gate that Randy's deputies thrashed the previous week and would become the first call on the morning schedule to their Allstate agent. She needed to put the Mayhem Man to work! She knew Allstate would deny the claim on the gate, but the Butler County Sheriff's office would get the bill.

And she knew they would pay, however reluctantly.

Moving east around the fence inspection, she noted about every sixth post needed either removal or repair. Most of the previous wooden posts suffered dry rot and needed replaced at $10 to $12 dollars per, so the walk around the fifty acres began to look like a $7,200 homeowners' claim. She assured herself in advance that Allstate would also reject that, but the work still needed to be done. The back gate needed limited attention, partially because they left it wide open. Although the nearby DNA remnants of the three dead bodies would probably yield attractive scents for months, there was little ground damage from the fight to the property itself. That would disappear with just a flurry of new grass and the onslaught of spring. The site certainly made Jake and Rufus eternally curious, as their noses were forty times more likely to hover over the ground where once three bodies lay and decipher information no longer obvious to human investigators.

They just weren't givin' it up, that is conveying what their noses detected there.

If dogs could talk, she thought as they walked up on the back gate, *what would they reveal? How much could they tell us about the world around us? Ours are so limited and theirs so gifted.*

So much for the morning daydreaming and visuals of the lush spring resurrection! Ten-thirty crept up on her like a morning ambush at the end of the walk. Now the workday shifted to the very mundane as she headed back to the office.

Her first call was to Randy Malone. The guard at the gate, Mrs. Hobbs, was on duty, on guard, and summoned him immediately. She was better than Hamlet's drunken bridge guard but a lot less humorous! Kathleen and Ronk had priority access and never had to be put on hold, but Hobbs would cut them off if the conversation lingered too long.

"Good morning, Randy. Do we have any news of which I should be aware? Ronk is sedated, progressing, and should be home in two weeks, but are your guys and the FBI finished rummaging for evidence so I can start the damage repair on the house?"

"I think so," he replied. "I believe we've collected all the expended shell casings, brass in your parlance, and the FBI report indicates all those rounds came from the same Kalashnikov rifle with the one they identified as this guy Romanov. The other two that you and Ronk nailed never got to fire their weapons, either the AKs or their pistols. They both became guests of the county before they could draw or load. And by the way, thank you two for that. It's less bullshit for us to process. Dead bodies give straight answers with no Fourth or Fifth Amendment evasion. Congratulations on your enduring range skills. Your collective first three shots dropped those two. I managed to persuade our coroner, Jed Nelson, to omit the post-shot trauma administered to Romanov's upper torso in his report. Remember that when you talk to the FBI again. He was still alive and resisting when you encountered him. Got it! You were putting down an active shooter and threat to your lives when you engaged him. Okay? Otherwise, you might face some blowback. It's just how they operate."

"Understood," she replied. "It all was the heat of the moment, and I really feared for my life and Ronk's. I have no qualms about the confrontation."

"I don't either, but they might," said Malone. "They shouldn't pursue it, but some Quantico lab rat might look at the photos of the deceased and call it extreme beyond the necessary bounds of self-defense. Just be aware of that. That's all I'm sayin'. Watch how you parse your verbs with them. They seldom delve into spurious humor. Got it? It's called job justification. Hell, I woulda just shot the son of a bitch again and be done with it."

That cued a set-up, pregnant pause. Five seconds later, came Malone's wry wit.

"Twice! Just to make sure the fucker wasn't twitching."

Her next call was to Allstate. At first, it seemed perfunctory with the initial acquiescence that they would pay the damage on everything more than the standard $1,500 deductible they had on the house.

"This wasn't an act of God," Kathleen said, "but it does qualify as an act of man. The bullet holes on the main house, our home, will likely require complete replacement of the exterior and most of the interior dry wall adjacent to the master bedroom. Romanov must have put the better part of two dozen rounds into the exterior before I capped his ass. At this point, I have no idea what it will cost to repair. It's a pain, but we have no previous claims, so all those five years of premiums better yield sufficient cash to cover the damage.

"Otherwise, the Mayhem Man may get some of my specialized attention, and he won't like it."

The call from Kathleen was detailed and assertive. The agent was humbly supplicant and listened intently.

Just as he was trained to do!

Appease the client with the requisite sympathy and just make the claim go away as cheaply as possible. So he promised to have an appraiser to their address within the next forty-eight hours.

Just as he was trained to do!

He goddamn well better, she thought. *After five years at $1,000-plus premium annually, these guys had best deliver on policy.*

She refrained, however, from verbalizing her irritation. No sense in insulting him without good cause. After all, he wasn't the one authorizing the check to cover the repair.

"It's always some dipshit further up the food chain, even if he is a 'dwizelle.'"

But she held her tongue so as to not muddle the claims process.

The next call was fraught with tension. She wasn't quite sure if she even trusted FBI Agent Oliver, but she did know she didn't like his condescending attitude that saturated the debriefing after the shooting in which he bled questions about both the incident on Carson Street and the home assault. Unlike all the other law dogs at the meeting, he had a detached, almost deprecating attitude toward both her and Ronk. It was "all about him and not the crimes he was investigating."

Unfortunately, she was right, but he was the one with whom she had to deal. Just like the insurance adjustor, Oliver was the FBI head honcho in charge, even if he acted like a four-foot speed bump suddenly imposed on Interstate 79.

Although used to it when dealing with multiple Federal agencies and cretins therein, she still hated the arrogance that seemingly permeated the upper layers of civil service. The Federal pyramid, in her opinion, was too often fraught with limited imagination and a spectrum of rules and policies that moved like setting concrete on a hot lava bed. She knew what to expect but still had to make the call.

Quite surprisingly, Oliver answered the phone call almost immediately, much to Kathleen's surprise. She didn't want to manufacture a fight or alienate him, but she coveted any information below the fold.

She already knew the headline.

"Good morning, Ms. McShea," Oliver began. "Glad you called. I think you'll be happy to learn that we have apprehended and arrested the fourth of the five suspects, that woman whom we have identified as Elena Sergovia. She's from the Mt. Oliver area, and we think we can connect her with the Greek and have charged her with multiple felonies related to the assault on your home and maybe has some information on your husband's kidnapping. She is in Federal custody right now, but both the cities of Erie and Binghamton have claims on her for murders in their jurisdictions. But they will have to wait. The Federal government is assuming primacy in the kidnapping case, and she will remain in Federal custody and has agreed to turn state's evidence against Joseph Tsakrios where we will then put her into the witness protection program. We've offered her a seven-year sentence with parole after eighteen months in prison where we will hide her in a secret location and give her a new identity."

Kathleen moved her cell phone away from her ear at arm's length and quietly muttered, "Well, kiss my red Irish ass! The bitch is going to get away with murder and kidnapping, and I won't be able to confront her."

"Agent Oliver," she then asked, "is this a done deal?"

"Yes, it is, Ms. McShea. The Federal prosecutor has already signed off on it."

"So, when will she appear in court?"

"Unfortunately, only at the trial for Tsakrios for the prosecution! Then there will be a sentencing hearing for her later."

"May I appear as a witness in aggravation of the charge of kidnapping?"

"That won't be necessary, as she will only appear in the separate testimony in the assault on you, Ronk, and your home. There will be no witnesses at this hearing. It will be just for a sentencing plea. Since she has already pleaded guilty, the judge will impose the negotiated seven years confinement with the possibility of parole. You may appear there in the public gallery only. The entry into the witness protection program is a separate administrative addendum, so the good news is that she will plead guilty and be permanently out of your hair and your lives while she is permanently under Federal supervision."

"Well, she's not out of our lives or my hair," Kathleen yelled into the phone. "She assaulted me, my husband, and our home. It can't just be wished away by making her disappear to someplace like

Billings, Montana, or Deming, New Mexico, or Anal Gap, Nova Scotia."

"Well, I'm sorry, Ms. McShea," Oliver said, "but that's the way it's going down. I'm sorry if you can't accept that. Is there anything else I can do for you?"

She hung up without a perfunctory goodbye. There was only one consolation.

Four down.

One to go.

Inside she sizzled. She would be denied the privilege of confronting Sergovia in court…but she could legally track her through the Federal prison system until she escaped into the vortex of witness protection. Securitas had computers as dazzling as any in Homeland Security.

"One thing about the Irish," she once demurred to a close friend, "we have the longest memories of abuse from an overbearing English culture and we don't forget. They stole our land, enslaved my ancestors, and imposed their language, but it didn't erase the memory. Don't get mad. Get even. Wasn't that the Kennedys' motto? *Even* it shall be…even if I have to wait the full seven years on Ms. Sergovia."

Chapter 41

RE-AZMITH

Thirty days post discharge ushered a mixed transition. Ronan was home but still had the "Ronk" attitude tethered to either a walker or a cane when in public. He hated the walker but reluctantly employed a cane.

His sarcastic consolation was that he qualified for a disability parking sticker for his truck that met VA criteria now that he could employ either device for walking assistance. "Bravo Foxtrot Delta," he said. "You gotta have a damn walking device to get a disability sticker for my truck from the VA. To quote comedian Dana Carvey, the church lady from SNL, 'Isn't that just special?'"

UPMC assigned a home therapist who came to the house three days a week to continue the strength and stretching training. The surgery left a minimal lower back scar, but the promised recovery protocol was tedious in form and execution. It was yoga, along with a matador with bull whip and chair. On him!

His hostile bent toward disability rendered him a reluctant and sometimes irascible patient. Not surprisingly, his "joy" with the healing regimen was underwhelming.

Two Marine Corps tours in Iraq, moreover, did little to mollify the entry of Jolene Ann Zinzer from Norman, Oklahoma. Like an Oklahoma tornado, she showed up on time, ready to deploy. Zinzer was the physical therapist anointed by UPMC for thirty-six visits to their Butler homestead for the in-house physical training after the back surgery that removed the offending bullet. Although she was a registered nurse in three states with an added PhD in Kinesiology, she appended the persona of a Nurse Ratched to her vita sheet. Recall that film character Randle Patrick McMurphy, played by Jack Nicholson, couldn't handle her protégée in *One Flew Over the Cuckoo's Nest*. Neither could Ronk quite handle Ms. Jolene, although spared the lobotomy McMurphy endured.

Zinzer was professionally relentless but measured. She pushed him to his limits and demanded he perform, almost always with a smile on her face.

Unlike the spectrum of drill instructors with whom he once dealt, she never gave orders laced with occasional obscenity, although she had piercing eyes and a stoic countenance. A session with Zinzer was a full ninety minutes of business. No trite conversation, just the required protocol. Like Kathleen, Zinzer was slightly taller than he with—to quote singer Travis Tritt—"a body made for sin." That could have been an unnecessary distraction, but she wouldn't allow it. She'd encountered the problem before with multiple men but turned his unsaid visual around to force therapy compliance. The stretching routine of the opening twenty minutes couldn't camouflage the inherent pain of muscle and cartilage that screamed not to separate. Ripped from their previous moorings, they crackled with pain. He could hear it tear within, and occasionally she would too. It was "necessary to complete the mission" in military jargon.

No one, however, ever insisted he had to like it. "Pain in the ass" was often the phrase he applied to her. Several other abrasive insults were deep forays into insult that he dared not utter either to her or Kathleen. Yet deep in his manacled psyche, he knew he needed to follow her lead precisely.

Zinzer heard the quiet crunching tissue as a measure of success. It was necessary to return his body to stasis. It was the litany of agony on a rosary of pain. Ronk conceded but wasn't convinced that abuse had to be that arbitrary. He groused about it but could never break her concentration on the task at hand.

Like the grind of his workday, his problem with authority percolated to the surface. Zinzer, however, was both his professional and emotional equal. Calm under patient duress, she knew how far to press and when to decelerate. Multiple patients had tested her before and resisted. Eventually they all surrendered to either her charms or demands.

Soft motivation or brutal insistence completed her portfolio, just like a drill instructor.

Kathleen, on the other hand, loved watching every minute of it as they turned their office/den into a de facto gym in which Jolene imitated a torture chamber mistress that pushed her reluctant husband to heal with the mandated range of exercise.

"Oh, c'mon, Ronk," she said. "Don't be such a douchebag. I didn't marry a pussy, so don't insult my choice of men. You have obviously faced more dynamic challenges than this. You've looked death literally in the face in the Middle East, so get it together, my love! Yes, this is a real challenge but not something you can't handle. Besides, your whining gives me the chance to massage your back and neighboring anatomy. And I just know you hate that attention. I'm such a sucker for your naked buns. You'll be back to jogging again before Labor Day. I insist."

"And the beat goes on!" to quote a long-forgotten song by a long-forgotten '60s duo, Sonny and Cher, previously cited. The business of healing, nevertheless, also heralded the return to domicile regular order.

The kids returned home, although Kathleen's mother and mother-in-law switched days to help with household chores, and Cecilia became a de facto, full-time domestic complementing the home team's squad of help. The rental of the electric chair in the den with variable positions so he could either sit or sleep was easy, but the required elevator chair from the first to the second floor was a major renovation project. Although it took two days to install, it gave Ronan the mobility to navigate about his own house on his own without dependence on Kathleen, Cecilia, or family. Now permanently stationed on both floors were two walkers to assist. Those he sometimes chose to ignore. In a pique of anger one day at some nebulous irritation, he once just threw one of them crashing down the stairs toward the front door. Sympathy factor from his wife: zero!

What ticked him off was a letter from the Corps of Engineers confirming the scheduled end of his allotted Federal sick leave days. Although the walker rage was volcanic, Kathleen quelled it with curt words and an abrupt stare.

"Ronk, you're not twelve again. You have two sons. You're their parent, not one of their rowdy classmates. Just what the hell was it that ticked you off? It can't be that important. I know you're frustrated, but this recovery is long term. Don't take it out on the rest of us. We're the support team, not the enemy, so knock it off."

The doors throughout needed little modification since the McSheas made both the interior and exterior ones wheelchair-accessible during renovation of their homestead five years before. They did that as a projection of buyer appeal for sale after their projected geriatric years when their kids left. It was an insight that paid dividends now for his recuperation. The trauma of today trumped the promise of tomorrow.

Two days later, after Sergovia's arrest, Sheriff Malone called with what he thought would be good news well received about her status. It surprised him that Kathleen seemed either insouciant (acidly indifferent) or hostile.

She already knew. Her mood: unhappy and testy.

"That *Bozo* Oliver called me and told me the whole story," she said. "That bitch is going to get away with attempted murder of my family. Maybe there is some justice in the Federal court system, Randy, but right now, I don't see it. She's going to slide on criminal assault, conspiracy to commit murder, and a host of other crimes that I cannot even pronounce. And I have a graduate degree. I'm outraged, and we're all hung on the cross of Oliver's obsession and ego with that damn Greek. Well, screw him and his whole miserable staff! I am not impressed with the FBI's threat response to our family. They're essentially going to let her ride the easy train into a plea and make her disappear into witness protection. All she has to do is run her mouth and testify against Tsakrios in open court? That's a crock, and you and I both know it.

"She gets a pass on criminal assault with deadly weapons and attempted murder. That pisses me off intensely and will not abate."

Her angry response took Malone by surprise. It was unlike her and certainly anger he rarely saw from a disciplined, professional, and mother of three.

"Well, I just thought you'd like to know. Didn't realize Oliver got the jump on me and obviously crawled under your skin. He does have an ego and rampant dismissal for those of us outside of urban America. The rookies he sent up here to brief us after both incidents thought they were dealing with a bunch of country rubes. Feds don't smooze you unless and until they need something. Maybe we taught them a lesson."

"I'm sorry to unload on you, Randy. It's not your fault. This is a travesty perpetuated by a bureaucrat with a personal agenda. I just don't know where to pack and stash my anger. I just am not wrapping my head around this decision to protect and hide her."

She put the phone down and thought for a minute, but it took several seconds for her to regain her composure. Randy Malone was not someone she wanted to insult. Good friends are hard to find, and she didn't want to push him away. She called him right back and apologized.

"No need," Malone said. "I understand your anger. It doesn't affect our friendship."

"Well," she continued, "you know that bad old cliché about the lead dog in the sled team? He gets the forward view, while his staff sucks up the view from the rear. It's amazing the FBI is as efficient as they are with guys like Oliver at the helm. He wouldn't make it long in the private security sector. We demand collegiality and leading from the bottom up. Dictation purely from the top doesn't work anymore. He can take his damn obsession with this Greek character and stuff it up his moon shoot. I'm appalled at the deal they've given Sergovia, so I'll just bid my time for confrontation."

"And then what? She's going to be out of all your lives and never threaten you again."

"Remember, Randy, I'm Irish with a memory bank that spans centuries. My nickname on the basketball and volleyball teams at North Catholic was Morrigan, the female Celtic warrior god of war and fury. I had it sown on all my jerseys and my Letterman jacket. That nickname, given by my teammate, reflected my attitude. I had it on my team uniforms in volleyball, basketball, and track, not O'Rourke. I loved to stuff a basketball in taller girls' faces and make them eat leather on the court with volleyball spikes, and I especially enjoyed trashing those arrogant bitches from Mt. Lebanon and Upper Saint Clair in any sport. It jacked me up to stuff it into their cocky faces. So it is what the name implies, and I am what the name says—fierce and relentless! Note that Morrigan O'Rourke-McShea is consumed with fury at this punk woman my age. I want to kick her ass from here to Belfast. We'll meet again someday to her eternal regret. She will regret she ever set foot in Butler County."

The call ended when Mrs. Dodd interrupted with what she perceived was a more immediate crisis. Malone was just glad and wanted to end Kathleen's tirade. Dodd was the lifeguard to his drowning repertoire of consolation. He agreed with Kathleen but wanted the conversation to wane. It was wadding into therapy. Like Charlie Brown and Lucy in the comic strip *Peanuts*, the sign was out.

"The therapist was not in!"

He didn't know how to assuage her anger or appropriately intervene.

"Gotta go, Kathleen," Malone finished. "Butler's finest, low-life criminal class once again demands my undivided attention, along with Mrs. Dodd. I promise we'll talk soon. Later, my friend!"

***

Four years and a seeming lifetime later, Malone forgot Kathleen's last comment about the Irish until vividly reminded by a random published coroner's report of a floating corpse in the Mon almost at the northern mouth of the Youghiogheny, identified originally as a Jane Doe. Ms. Doe's identity caught Sheriff Malone's attention at the end of the autopsy summary floated to all police agencies in the Tri-state area.

It was then the summer of 2023. The read jolted him. He flashed back to Kathleen's angry tirade of 2019.

Normally such reports routinely filtered throughout local jurisdictions only for information, case study, and maybe identification. Mostly they gathered collective yawns and dust before placement in the cold case morgues of sundry police agencies for proper burial, available for perusal later but rarely perused. Every department had one, along with the plethora of inert cases that interested few but the most inquisitive of detectives with too much time on their hands to investigate the cold ones.

***

Not this time, not this one. The report was a time warp with a ghost returning to haunt. Withered prints identified the body as Galina Elena Sergovia, along with the B-negative blood samples and DNA taken from her fish-racked body and rib cage that year for further confirmation. The fish had treated themselves to the menu of her internal organs and the eyes. Her liver was their particular favorite and virtually gone. The Pittsburgh coroner's office fixed the time of death as five days before her corpse surfaced, dredged up from the water by a couple of local fishermen. They dragged it ashore but declined to touch it. The skull and thorax remained remarkably intact, but her throat was slashed.

The cut was from right to left.

Then it hit him. "No, please no! This can't be. Sweet mother of Jesus, this can't be it. Not the same woman in the 2019 incident. She's supposed to be in witness protection. What the hell is this?"

Reluctantly the memory of Kathleen's caustic comment bubbled to the surface. It made him sick to contemplate. He didn't want to believe it, but there it was, sitting on that heap of pervasive cop skepticism about random things that seemed to coincide with logic. They don't believe in them. The story seemed too wrapped in fantasy to swallow.

Except for the reality of explicit and implicit facts!

Wasn't Sergovia one of the five suspects on the assault on the McShea house back in 2019? he thought. *This can't be true. That might make sense.*

He answered his own query in the affirmative.

Leaning back on his chair, it hit him like a sledgehammer with an insight he didn't want to entertain. "And now she was dead, just like the three upstate that Sergovia allegedly whacked? What kind of morose karma is that? Oh, fuck…nooo! No, no, please no! Dammit!" he muttered aloud.

His chair bolted forward and he remembered, but he didn't want to remember.

Malone knew but didn't want to admit or blurt it out.

Kathleen O'Rourke-McShea, his longtime friend, is left-handed.

Chapter 42

FIFTH TARGET

Solving murder cases descends to atrophy after ninety-six hours. If you don't at least have the person of interest or suspect by then, the trail of clues and the scene fade to black.

Murders rarely close when they morph into ancient history. Forget the Internet stories of cold cases suddenly being solved through detective persistence. That's fantasy posed as rare reality. Every cop knows it. Fast-forward to 2023! The Butler shootout followed a similar script as police exhaled with the assumption that four of the five suspects were either identified or thankfully dead. But Numero Cinco was in the wind!

Rewind to 2019.

Oliver strongly suspected their fifth and final would surface via the myriad of aggregate clues they'd painfully tracked. The procedure to find and collar suspects had a storied history with the FBI. They essentially wrote the book on it, copied by police agencies worldwide.

They had a name, Aaron Bronson, and little else they'd dug from Tsakrios's telephone records and texts. That would change rapidly. Their computers were already collecting the zeros and ones into a coherent profile, along with dynamic photos that Bronson's mother would cherish. The brand-new world of public security cameras followed and identified people by the millions.

The Israelis, Brits, and Americans were good at it, but the Chinese were the best.

Bronson had no criminal record in the US but apparently had dual US-Israeli citizenship that allowed him free flow between the two countries without suspicion. That didn't exclude him from the criminal class.

He just wasn't yet on anyone's police blotter or had an arrest record, except that foray into crime years before in Marsailles. The reforms following the trauma of 9/11 were imperfect. Closeted criminal characters like Bronson flowed freely between here, Europe, and the Middle East. Oliver suspected Bronson had modified his real Israeli family name but apparently had a legitimate New Jersey driver's license. He had an agent on that lead. The arrest record from Interpol would follow.

The lottery of dual citizenship, however, was what Oliver's father called a racket left unchallenged since the Eisenhower administration.

How profoundly right he was.

"Why should certain select ethnic groups get a priority double for entry into the US?" he often railed to his son. "Dual citizenship is a perversion of the privilege of American law. Either you're committed to one nation or the other, not both. That's a crock."

He also had other more profane descriptions often shared. The childhood rants became part of his son's spectrum of bias. It made no sense to Oliver too. Chasing citizens with an out to a second country made extraditions painfully complex and most often impossible. If no iron-clad extradition treaty existed between the US and another country, the net result was flight without possibility of return. That is especially if the reciprocating country disavowed the death penalty or the openly hostile to the United States…like Iran.

Try that extradition suit on. It's two sizes too small.

Effectively, an airplane ticket for a suspected homicide felon was a cover to flee un-harassed outside of the grasp of American law, the FBI, or the US court system.

Oliver despised the "knothole in the wooden fence," as he once described it, that allows such felons to flee. Now he feared that knothole, now large enough through which to drive a truck, would check the chase for suspect number 5.

Cited earlier, Interpol had Bronson on their "Less-Than-Distinguished" guest list, but Americans not so much. His slimy association with the Greek never made headlines or stoked an appearance in Federal or Superior Courts. What gnawed at Oliver most was that Bronson had no American criminal record, not even speeding tickets. Whatever drove him to couple with the Greek's hit team made no superficial sense.

"Why would an apparent low-grade criminal Jewish-American expatriate hood append to an open pond-scum criminal like Tsakrios?" he railed. Something was missing. It was a proverbial burr under his saddle. Bronson had honorably served in the IDF. "What motivated him to move to a darker side," Oliver asked, "that's the connection we need to make to plug into his association with Tsakrios. Good Jewish boys don't just do that without motivation."

Etch the facile answer: cash! Money was the mother's milk of crime and corruption, and the Greek had a ton of it spread around to a willing and depraved audience. Money precurses all other sin. It is the human addiction stronger than drugs or sex because it bought all the others and their adjuncts thereafter. Find sin, download the money.

Kathleen, nevertheless, cultivated connections rarely massaged by Oliver and his local FBI staff. Unlike Oliver, Kathleen's multiple overseas travel assignments went to places on itineraries Oliver couldn't even bother to spell. She had a deep cover and covert friendship nurtured by multiple security operations with Mossad. Over the seven years she'd been with Securitas, they'd cooperated on a number of sensitive protection details. Through those, she'd developed a professional, personal relation with a number of agents, several of whom owed her favors. They were paybacks for at least three instances that Securitas helped "pull their butts out of the Sinai camel shit," as she so graphically described it once, on operations to protect visitors at resorts on the Red Sea south of the Suez. Kathleen and Securitas were among the few private contractors that Mossad trusted, as they suspected the twenty-three agencies of American intelligence were too riddled with hacks who couldn't keep a secret if you shoved it northward for a liver biopsy.

The sad fact was that it was too often true. The exceptions all too often infected the general rule. Now it was time to "call in a marker." The one closest spy with whom she felt akin and trusted was Ephraim Ben-Artzi, an agent with more than forty-five years in Mossad now encroaching on seventy and purported retirement.

But, if you are Mossad, retirement is an obscene word, rarely a real option. Unlike Americans, Israeli military commitment is for life. Geography demands it. Surrounded by Muslim fanatics determined to destroy you, you are a Jewish warrior until death. Ephraim was an infantry officer in the Six-Day War of 1967 and almost immediately transitioned to Mossad in 1970. She nourished a professional relationship with him over the years that worked well for both Mossad and Securitas. Ben-Artzi was a committed defender of the Israeli nation, willing to work with anyone so committed to the same, including Arab, Muslim, Christian, or…American. His trust for Securitas was absolute. Kathleen's was the same for him. Now the cultivation of mutual admiration was about to bloom some fruition.

Her call was unexpected but warmly received. The Securitas issued cell phone line, which was moreover secure from intruders.

"Ephraim, I guess you've heard about the trauma of the last ten days, and I've earned some time off, so I've elected to take some vacation on your magnificent beach near Tel Aviv. Would love to see you again in a social context! What's your upcoming schedule?"

"Trauma, old friend?" he said. "I would love to see you, but bad news doesn't travel quite that fast from North America to the Middle East unless it's projectile vomit from Washington DC. What are you talking about?"

The next twenty minutes of conversation became a recital. Ephraim did not interrupt but took pointed notes and asked probing questions as she recanted the entire sequence of harrowing events.

Finally he stunned her with a glib array of anecdotes about Bronson to which the FBI was likely not privy.

"We know about this guy Bronson. That's not his family name. I believe his parents were Cohens, a Tel Aviv family heavy into the export-import and construction business. Their money is legally earned, and their projects ironically parallel the extended Bin Laden family's in Saudi. They have their money tentacles all over the Middle East. He legally changed his name after his stint in the Israeli Defense Force and managed some aspects of the family business overseas in Europe and North Africa to cover his Jewish roots. No one seems to know why he changed his name, but he hasn't run afoul of Israeli law enforcement. I'd have to research how he managed to manipulate American citizenship. Maybe it's through his mother, who, I understand, grew up in Yonkers. He's a pure playboy now with enough family wealth to support the lifestyle. He has an apartment near the beach in Tel Aviv but spends most of his time on his garish yacht anchored in the harbor. His parents seem to tolerate his excesses, as he's a real mama's boy. She's been covering for his delinquent ass since he was a teen. The yacht, however, you can't miss. It's painted some strange, racing variant of aquatic blue and gold, I think. I think it's as ugly as a Persian whore, but the family money is 'quite legit,' to use an American colloquial expression. But he's somewhere shy of forty-five, and his primary addiction is beautiful women on which he preys with abject zeal. He's a fervent man-slut with tons of cash to buy sex until eternity.

"Does the FBI have enough on him to indict?" Ephraim asked.

"Don't know," Kathleen replied. "I only heard his name for the first time from our county sheriff. He tells me the extradition process is laborious, and the head of the local FBI detachment wouldn't give me the time of day if he had the last wristwatch in Pennsylvania. So I don't know how they made the connection with him and the attack. But the FBI seems quite sure he was the last of the five suspects, so expect a request to extradite him now to the US. Although I won't hold my breath on that."

"It is not as easy as it seems, my friend. Remember our Knesset has as many *tachats* (asses) as your Congress. And Bronson, or Cohen if you wish, has a family flush with money and enough lawyers to represent every Jew in Brooklyn. Corruption is not confined just to Gentile nations. Your FBI had better have a mountain of evidence. Israeli judges are loathed to hand over Israeli citizens on a whim. Remember, previous American administrations sometimes gave us the back of their hand on a variety of issues, particularly that dickhead Obama. We may be the best of friends, but like all marriages, there are issues. This is one of them. Remember we swapped you for that prick, Jonathon Pollard, and he's now living the good life in Israel. He did a great deal of damage with his revelations, even if it was only to us. I suspect he also sold at least some of that info elsewhere. He's not exactly the pristine Jewish boy patriot. But he was the exception. We took him off your hands after you rendered him a life sentence. At least, you didn't have to feed him kosher for the rest of his life."

"Yeah," she said. "My father, for instance, has never forgiven Israel for the attack on the USS *Liberty* during the Seven-Day War. That was a cover-up long before Nixon made it a household word. The payouts and payoffs to the sailors' families did little to redeem American anger. There's sadly a growing strain of anti-Semitism in our country that I hate, and it directly affects our business at Securitas because it makes recruiting touchy. Our Human Resources department gets mildly paranoid if we have too many American agents on staff with authentic Jewish surnames. I find this residue offensive but I am forced to deal with it on almost a daily basis. But let's get to the core reason for the call," she continued. "I'm going to take seven to ten days of vacation by myself under the guise of company business and just get away from recent history. I would love to see both you and Esther so you can introduce me to your passel of expanding grandchildren."

"Well, who's taking care of Ronan and your children?"

"That's already covered by my mother, mother-in-law, our magnificent maid, and a physical therapist assigned to Ronk three days a week. We're okay there. I just need some relief from the barrage of law and media types constantly calling and sniffing around our kids and Ronk-like bloodhounds. What I really need is a public relations officer like we have at Securitas. All that will have to wait. I just need time to myself, and Ronan needs some space where he can heal without me on him 24/7. He doesn't need prodded to do the right thing, and sometimes I don't help with my hectoring.

"I just need some time off, so recommend a favorite hotel near the beach and I'll be in touch with you and Esther sometime after I arrive, sometime in the next week. I need the time to myself."

"Well, they're all good near the beach and…trust me…security is tighter than an Orthodox Hebrew virgin before her wedding night. You'll be safer here than at the White House. We don't tolerate much of what you allow in America. Remember we daily face a host of religious fanatics that want to drive us into the sea and an almost daily barrage of individual assaults against our population. That will not happen to you but use one of the rampant surge of Internet sites to book. Then let us know when you arrive. Shalom, my friend. Esther will be happy to see you."

"Thank you, Ephraim. See you soon!"

Now it was time to plan a trip soaked in vengeance and lie a lot to everyone she knew: husband, children, Ephraim, and family. She had a mission, but the sins of her mind were about to become mortal. Vacation was the cover.

Termination of a threat took precedence. Biology trumped ethics.

Bronson must meet Yahweh and account for his multiple absences at synagogue.

Kathleen would be the devolving Catholic girl to deliver Yahweh's message.

Chapter 43

ISRAEL

Direct flights from Philadelphia, Newark, or New York to Tel Aviv are eleven hours or more, give or take normal delays, weather, and intense security precautions. It's a trek mandated by the hostility of Israel's hostile neighbors who would sooner eat Kentucky-style hog barbecue during Ramadan than allow a Jewish airliner landing rights. Accorded few options for intermediate stops en route, El Al flies directly from Europe and the USA but not on the Jewish Sabbath (Friday). So Kathleen's chosen itinerary first went to Philadelphia from Greater Pitt on Friday with arrival in Tel Aviv with United Airlines early Sunday morning.

The trick was to lie to Ronan and family about the extent, pretext, and length of the commitment. Ronan was the easy part. He knew and accepted the sometimes erratic postings from her bosses because he tracked the money they handsomely paid her along with a very generous per diem. They valued her. She valued the salary.

"This is one of those professions," Ronk once told his father, "that's very much like a professional athlete. The travel time demanded is obnoxious. You're sometimes rarely home. It's a limited career fraught with the pressure and demand to sharpen shooting skills that never relent. Remember, Dad, she has to pack heat everywhere she goes now. And shooting is a perishable skill. It wanes with age and eyesight. She can't continue this gig much beyond forty-five, so we'll milk it as long as possible. The only real downside is the intermittent times away from the homestead and the kids. It's an adjustment we've both made that I hope will provide sufficient support to get them all through college and beyond."

His father listened. He grunted and mumbled something incoherent.

He wasn't convinced. The paternal skepticism never abated, even after her seven years with the corporation.

Her next goodbye was a loaded rationale in a leaky wineskin bota bag for the trip. It only takes one lost or injured client to scuttle a company's reputation. Up to that point, she'd batted one thousand with her charges, but potential failures were an ever-looming disaster, not an option either now or in the future. Thus, she chose her cover story very carefully.

"I'll be gone no more than seven to ten days," she said. "And I should be back no later than May 10 under any circumstance. I've connected with Ephraim. You know his number in an emergency. Either that or call Esther at home and you'll be able to track me, although I anticipate this client's trip will be nothing more than a lecture presented for a medical symposium near Tel Aviv. It will address a new vaccine for measles within an oral protocol modeled on the Sabin polio one. The kids can e-mail me, but the Twitter account is for business only. This particular doctor we're protecting, however, is semiparanoid about security despite what we've told him. He thinks he's walking into the sands of eternal war, and to say he's uptight is an understatement. I may even be back sooner if he can conclude his pitch early. He doesn't want to linger in town. He's safer there than he is in New York City but he doesn't believe it. He's a first-class *putz*, but he's our *putz* and writes a big check. That seems to be the one area where he doesn't whine."

Her kids were less consoling, particularly Katie.

"Mom, why do you have to go away again," she pouted. "We need you here."

"Baby, you'll be fine," she consoled. "Granny Mac and Ma-Ma O will both be here, along with Cecilia. Mom will be home before Jake and Rufus are even aware I've been gone. You need to take care of your brothers and dad. His therapy trainer will be here three days a week, and you have to make sure none of you leaves junk on the stairs to the second floor that impedes Dad's use of the chair lift. Don't let your brothers put any of their stuff there that might block Dad's ability to get up and down. Do you understand? That will be your job, along with taking care of the dogs."

"Okay, but I don't like it," she replied, stomping her feet for emphasis.

Kathleen's cover story was a misdemeanor tale. The doctor would have Mossad draped all over him upon arrival. She would hand him off like a preheated football. His health was assured. All she had to do was get him on and off the plane, so Ephraim couldn't even lie to cover it. Ronan, however, never assumed nefarious intent with Kathleen. He loved her and presumed total honesty. And she never allowed him to breach the inner dark content of her inner intent to destroy the fifth and last assailant. All couples have some secrets. She didn't share this one with Ronk.

Or anyone else.

It was Kathleen's penultimate slide into the dark side.

The essence of the O'Rourke family motto on its historic crest so reflected: "*Facta, not verba!*" Deeds, not words. "Do not threaten me or my family. Or I will obliterate you."

It all melded together in a collaborative family income of more than $180,000. He had no reason to suspect that she was on nothing more than a standard security trip to coordinate with a Mossad peer for protection of a client traveling to Israel with a reluctant attitude. She'd done it before. Half of that was true.

The so-called client and the rationale were not. She was there to terminate, not defend. The New York doc would be surrounded by security tighter than a tick on a redbone hound. She pegged him as a pampered mama's boy, a breed of dependent men that never tipped her applause meter. But he was an epidemiologist, who had written three books, a spectrum of important papers to become renowned in his narrow field of medicine, and married with three children.

"Apparently along the way, he forgot to grow a set because he whimpers like an infant. Katie has better social skills than this *smeckle*. I'm just glad," she said to one of the Mossad agents on the protection detail, "that he didn't bring the whole *fam-damily* with him. He'd better pay his protection bill, or I might get some of our collection termites to eat his Scarsdale house. Why do some of these intelligent, seemingly well-educated guys seem to have no balls? I can't handle them. This guy wouldn't make a pimple on a good Marine's ass. It's an assignment like this that sometimes makes me wish that I was still on active duty. Sometimes! But that's only momentary insanity. It fades in a hurry. I'll let you guys handle this goat pen in the desert."

The agent nodded in agreement and said something in Hebrew that Kathleen didn't understand. She presumed it was some variant of obscene.

But his body language showed that it was derisive, not directed toward her. She was not the object of his contempt.

He reserved that for the doctor.

The flight, like most of that length, was almost like an arduous hump up and down the hills of Camp Pendleton—long, sometimes bumpy and boring. The conversation with the physician was merely perfunctory. The trip to Kabul she took years before was a wretched fifteen hours "over the pole" (i.e. North Pole) via Germany, so this trip was a proverbial piece of cake. The bathroom facilities, food, and access to alcohol soothed whatever the cramped space a multi-million-dollar aluminum tube could impose. The military flights to Afghanistan were a trip to Purgatory with shared and limited head space (not just for your noggin). This would have been a relief to catch some sleep, but turbulence over the Atlantic interrupted her nap. Exhaustion was the deboarding pass.

The twenty-seven-minute early arrival, thanks to a tailwind, was limited consolation after almost sixteen hours in airports or onboard. She had booked a room at the Carlton Tel Aviv, adjacent to the four major boat marinas just north where she would find her prey, begin the process of seduction, and send him to the afterlife. She brought her snorkeling gear and correctly presumed Bronson might have a similar proclivity for the water.

"Why else, then, would he buy such a large yacht just to park it at a marina? My, my, my," she whispered to herself, "said the spider to the fly. Come into my lair and expurgate your tarnished, vacuous soul. After sin, my dear, there is always redemption…even for bad little Israeli playboys. Come hither and I will cleanse it of its roster of sin."

Kathleen wasn't sure if traditional Jews believed in a hell, but she did know that Christ once described it with a comparison to the Jerusalem city dump of the first century AD as an era where every form of garbage, vermin, and carcass gathered for decay. She thought the Hebrew word for it was something like *gehenna*.

"If that was it, I'm about to punch Mr. Bronson's ticket on the descending train to the nether region. Aaron Bronson, G*ehenna* awaits your arrival. Your room will have a warm spa on the upper tier floors. Satan will be the maître d' and you'll be surrounded by an army of naked Jezebels begging for attention, wanting intrusion. But you will be unable to perform. That will be your personal hell for eternity after what you wrought in life from the Middle East to Butler County."

She just wasn't sure if that was a prediction or meandering fantasy. She was not having the requisite theological moment. What she really thought melded a loose confection of irritations with refined lapses into cursing metaphors.

So she checked it all off in the fantasy column. Reality was less romantic, harsh, and unforgiving.

Her complement of the weapons of man destruction included choices of two bathing suits, both bikinis with exposure skin max allowed for Israeli beachgoers governed by the rabbinical code of public exposure. You may ride the rim of allure on an Israeli beach but not disrobe entirely. Her two bags were also packed with the appropriate business attire to placate any Israeli custom officer hypnotized by her stunning visual and flaming red hair. To accentuate the image, she deliberately let it all out to shoulder length. No ponytail, coed, or cropped look this trip. As she slowly removed her sunglasses, the two young customs officers meticulously searched her luggage, quickly, quietly, but efficiently. The younger of the two, however, was obviously so distracted that Kathleen could have hidden a plutonium baseball inside her cosmetic kit along with a .44-Magnum.

He reveled in the lucky visuals of his job...but would have bypassed the plutonium. His gaze bordered on the intersection of rude and salivating. Like most young "salivators" his age, he appeared to be just shy of twenty-five.

The older woman agent, however, scoped out Kathleen's frame from head to heel with military precision, noticed nothing amiss, and summarily dismissed her through the line of the disembarked. It helped that the passport e-scan showed numerous trips to Ben-Gurion over the years and that there was a long line behind her.

Again, there was no hint of suspicion.

When asked, Kathleen stuck to the stock, standard reply that rang no bells and raised no flags, neither red nor checkered.

"I'm here on both business and a short vacation. I'll be here about a week."

Again, no warning klaxons on any horizon, east or west.

Asked to open her laptop from Securitas and present Company ID, she completed the process and immediately hailed a cab to the Carlton five minutes later. She stopped at the hotel pharmacy for the final accoutrements of her plan, a vaginal douche kit, along with two Fleet Enema bottles.

There would be no evidence or lingering reminder of what she was about to do. Four days earlier, she had most of her pubic hair lasered away at a medical cosmetic group with a nurse named Rhonda Wilhelm in Butler so certified to remove. All except the teaser patch at the apex. Rhonda's tagline business model was "Go where no woman has gone before; dare to be all bare down there." The clientele were mostly women under thirty-five, and gaggles of them stormed her office before the baring season: summer. Rhonda rarely saw flickering gray hairs at the Southern sites of exposure. Bare bottoms were the Venus flytrap of the young. Cash, check, debit or credit cards! They were all welcome. Kathleen was the apparent age exception to the obsession coupled with the excuse that she was doing it as a surprise birthday present for her husband.

It was a miniscule, micro lie Nurse Rhonda was used to hearing. The women who solicited her service often juggled the truth. She presumed little else of her clients' motivation. Inquisitive interrogation was bad for return business. Like many others in her industry, Rhonda Wilhelm was into the "don't presume, don't ask, don't tell, don't insist, and never gossip." Lips can easily seal for the $735 per session, along with a jaw tighter than a Chase Manhattan bank vault. Business discretion provided an easy and enduring income with a packed client list and appointments almost thirty days in advance of the summer season. At about sixty minutes per, she could book six to eight clients per business days…and even some Saturdays.

"Ronk hasn't even seen it yet, and then I'll drown him in bliss."

She arrived mostly shorn and completely clean. The shearing included her underarms and some wandering hair at the base of her back.

She planned to leave that way with no angry traces of DNA, either foreign or domestic acquired on the Eastern Mediterranean shore. Seven days later, mission complete, Kathleen boarded a Lufthansa flight to London for the return trip to Dulles and a check-in at company headquarters. From there it was a short commuter to Pittsburgh and a drive in her rental back to Butler, along with the relief that it was all over.

It wasn't.

Chapter 44

VENUS FLYTRAP

Along with her aquatic gear, Kathleen also bought a box of medical gloves at a nearby Tel Aviv pharmacy to erase any trace of her presence either on Bronson's yacht or the hotel room. She kept a pair in her purse and a second cache of a half dozen in her large beach bag for sojourns on the sand. She also had a cover passport and Virginia driver's license with the moniker Jane Doe McGurk. That's the name under which she registered at the Carlton. No one overtly questioned it.

Much to her delight, no one at Ben-Gurion caught either the joke or the second ID at the airport. Although she entered the country as Kathleen M. McShea, she would leave for London as a Ms. Jane D. McGurk.

"Sometimes the Israelis and Mossad are so wrapped around the axle with the obvious threat from Islam," she once told her mother, "that fundamental police work falls by the wayside. Isn't it strange that the cradle of Western civilization was sometimes blinded by what obscured the real threat from a hostile subculture? Common law crimes occur in Israel also. Cain and Abel recirculate throughout the ages."

With a fifteen-to-one, Arab-to-Israeli population advantage, Shiites and radical anti-Semites have a regurgitating, frothing pool of vile upon which to recruit from Syria, Lebanon, Jordan, and Saudi. Kathleen's trail of evil intent hoisted no blip on Tel Aviv radar.

She had been to Israel so often that her Mossad profile featured her weight as well as shoe and bra size. Safety always trumped privacy in the land of Moses. Pharaoh lied millennia before, and so do most of Israel's neighbors.

Moses knew Pharaoh was a liar and ordered the caravan northeast.

But Kathleen was not the threat about whom they obsessed.

"If you thought your personal privacy was in jeopardy here in the States, thanks to the poorly written Patriot Act, note the thorough security in Israel," she once said to Ronk. "Intelligence is the core for their survival. What they know about every aspect of your life is security essential. They're surrounded on three sides by hostility. It amazes me that they they've forged alliances with some in the neighborhood who publicly refuse to accept their very existence. Privately they know Israel is the best friend they have in the Middle East, given the intransigence of Iran. The Iranian Mullahs only want the destruction of Israel and the elimination of Judaism. Thankfully these old bearded, jaded bastards will eventually die. Then maybe a new generation of the more enlightened business class may replace them."

Then she exhaled.

"At least that's the hope, unless the new jaded bastards repeat the mistakes of the old jaded bastards wallowing in their pit with prayer beads of anti-Semitic hate."

Now in the light of midmorning at Ben-Gurion and the routine of his assigned job, her arrival only distracted the male customs officer days before. Under the duress of time, he never bothered to scan the second passport blatantly within view in the kitchen baggie in her second onboard handbag.

He was too unfocused on her braless upper body with the tight blouse wet with teasing perspiration.

It was almost pure theater. Two customs agents rummaging through her luggage saw the fake second passport and never questioned it. The long line of deplaning passengers evoked loud ongoing rebukes from a senior supervisor. That took precedence. Lines were long and the shift was almost over. Kathleen knew the protocol and the cracks within it, so exploiting it with distraction was easy.

As she collected her two bags and headed to catch a cab, she again thought of the deadly cliché that at some point in life traps all male humanity—"Men are easy: food and sex!"

Promise either or both and women almost always get want they want. Think Delilah and Samson. In this case, it was the oversight of the phony second passport for which she had a prepared cover under the aegis of Securitas International, Inc. Glorious wet nipples shining through the blouse on a warm Middle Eastern day even saved her the pig shit story upon which she might have to rely for any salivating inquisitor.

"God, men are so predictable, and this kid was so male," she muttered to herself on her way to the cab, "and I have two sons that I hope won't fall prey to the obvious addiction of the flesh. It snared their father, so I guess I'll have to concede the biblical. Here I am in the heart of Christianity, but the veil of Salome still covers them all. Please, God," she prayed, "save my sons from what I know that to which they will eventually succumb."

She made her reservation at the Carlton Tel Aviv nearest the marinas where she knew Bronson would dock his yacht. Her quiet inquiries with select friends in Mossad confirmed its noxious color scheme and size noted by Ephraim Ben-Aertzi that made it easy to spot. The yacht mingled blue with gold striations along both the port and the starboard sides. It qualified as ugly, even by nautical standards, but Bronson obviously loved it. The boat and his ego enmeshed. She spotted the target yacht immediately on her walkabout near the second of the parking slots on the first of the four marinas.

Obvious, indeed, it was.

Now she knew where to lay the bait. She checked back into the Carlton with four more hours of daylight left to complete her reconnoiter. The beach south of the marina featured the full throttle of religious insanity with Muslim women draped in "bur-kinis" and some in full hijabs languishing on the beach and in the water next to minimal thongs wrapped around undulating thighs and mounds of adipose tissue. It was what one female Mossad friend described as "exposed buns craving the touch of biblical hands of exploration. It's estrogen slapping the face of misogyny right there on the beach."

The clash of culture with Islam was grossly apparent where the sea met the shore. She once told Ronk that "it was the shame of the female body colliding with the shamelessness of the West." She remembered Ronk's description of Iraqi personal computers his Marines confiscated during the second Iraq War from suspected members of Saddam's Imperial Guard.

"These guys had collections of pornography collected on CDs that featured every variant of human sexuality from hetero to off-the-wall types of sadomasochism," he said. "The males apparently start to masturbate at a very young age, often at the behest of older doddering family women. And despite Islam's condemnation of homosexuality and their public treatment of gay men, sex between male adults and young boys is implicitly ignored. We had to catalogue this shit for higher commands, and it seems this whole culture is preoccupied with sex, unlike even the more bizarre stuff that surfaces in the West. It's almost like anything goes as long as it's not public. Abuse of young women is almost a blood sport. When adultery warrants the death penalty, there is something terribly skewed and wrong with any culture. This is the ninth century regurgitated. Its perception of women just has to change. Just be happy you grew up Catholic in Allegheny County and only exposed to gentle souls like myself."

"So that's what you're goin' with?" she shot back. "Maybe you need to edit that position, my dear. I love you but maybe you should see yourself more from the perspective of '*su mujer favorita con cabello rojo*'! You are more male than you admit publicly, although I admit you have infinitely more class than most pedestrian men. You just camouflage your proclivity for concupiscence of the flesh so much better. And you hide your unsavory thoughts in a lockbox to which I have the only key."

His reaction to her comment: a sneering grunt!

"And there's *another* reason I didn't date O'Rourke in high school! She didn't have sufficient class to appreciate me yet."

It was an endearing exchange in which she now indulged on her beach walk that was today's vacation. Tomorrow is mission. She loved Ronk but was about to cross the thin line of morality. Thus, came the construct of a mortal lie to the man she loved most to cover the upcoming collage of sin.

Returning to the hotel room, she mulled over her plan that would start midmorning the next day. Although always an early riser, she allowed herself the luxury of a 0800 wake-up call and a light breakfast through room service. It entailed less exposure to hotel security cameras. She knew she would catch Bronson's attention with accoutrements that screamed lust. It was a purple semi-thong bikini with monster sunglasses shielded by a large straw beach hat that she knew would ignite his inner satyr.

Isn't it strange, she thought, *that Bronson will succumb to the color of sin but likely wouldn't know why and what it signifies. Purple is passion and passion is what I will deliver.*

It was almost noon when he spotted her walking the marina with some sort of old thirty-five-millimeter camera that he thought "quite quaint" from twenty yards away. In a digital world, the use of film was a flashback art form. He was on the stern of the yacht, along with two other men and a woman, and they all seemed to be saying their appropriate goodbyes as she approached.

She first pretended to ignore him as his morning guests exited the short gangway from the yacht to the dock. Afterward, he followed her toward the end of the pier as she pretended to take more photo shots of the boats and the Mediterranean horizon. There his approach became conversation.

She deliberately bent over, took off her sun bonnet, and pretended to rumble through her beach bag so he would get the lascivious visual from behind. He took the bait like an adolescent schoolboy.

"Good morning," he said. "I've not seen you here before. I often live on my boat here and you're a new beach visitor. Where are you from? My name is Aaron. How do you do?"

"Well, *bonjour mon ami*. My name is Jane. I'm American and I'm here on vacation and ever so enjoying it. Aaron, is that it? Your name? Is that also your boat?"

"On both counts, yes, it is. Would you like to take a tour?"

"Absolutely, how is it that you can afford such an affectation? I'm jealous. My estranged husband has a fishing boat that he seldom uses. It just drains money, merely fills another damn hole in the water. Congratulations on your success. It is really beautiful."

"Is your husband here with you?"

"No, we are in the throes of divorce settlement, and it's turning ugly. So I am here on my own for a respite and without chaperone. I need time and space away from him. Don't I look like a big girl? It's my time alone. My choice! Please let me see your yacht. Yes, Aaron, I'm interested."

He gave her the ten-shekels guided tour while visually undressing her and noted the new growth of red pubic hair creeping above the bikini line, just as she planned it. The bikini bottom was a size three. The fit was tight with deliberate pubic exposure.

She was a size six or eight in all other venues.

The creep of groin hair matched the mane on her head. Kathleen had just set the mantrap, stage one. She had him in the kill zone, and he was oblivious to the snare of his own lust. Then she set stage two.

"I'm sorry, may I use your loo? I had much too much coffee this morning at breakfast."

"It's the first door on the starboard side just ahead below on the second deck," he said. "Please make yourself at home." She descended the three steps, opened the door to the head, unlaced the bikini bottom, knowing full well he was watching. Stage two of the trap.

He made no pretense of personal decorum. The stare was pure voyeur.

"Are you okay?"

"Yes, I am." The door remained open as she stretched her legs, relieved herself, and stood to readjust. Now he also had a frontal shot of what he thought would be his latest conquest.

He exhaled deeply. *Yes, indeed*, he thought. *There it is—flaming red hair all around, top and bottom.*

"Do you always use sterile gloves when you relieve yourself?"

His lack of class about any bathroom privacy was part of the trap.

"When I travel, yes! It's a habit I formed on active duty in this part of the Middle East."

Stage three. Now it was his turn.

"Jane, I hate to be so forward but would you be interested in dinner this evening. I am eminently familiar with every upscale restaurant here on what is the Israeli Riviera. I would consider dinner with you an honor. Where are you staying?"

"At the Carlton."

"That's perfect. They have a kosher restaurant that I often frequent. It's quite a cross-cultural experience. The menu is a testament to all things Judaic and you will love the selections, particularly the fish. I presume you're not Jewish but you will find the cuisine exquisite. Would you please be my guest this evening? I can cover everything, and maybe tomorrow we can do some scuba diving from my yacht. Have you ever 'scuba-ed' before?"

"Yes, I became dive-qualified when I was on active duty with the American military and I would love to indulge again. It's been a while but I am checked out on scuba gear. And no, you are correct. I am not Jewish but enthralled here by the culture."

"What time should I meet you?"

"Does seven o'clock sound appropriate? At your room or at the restaurant?

"At the restaurant or on the veranda?"

"But what if I miss you?"

"You won't. But if by chance you do, then go to my room."

"What number is it?"

"It's 315."

"The veranda has a stunning view of the sea. I will make the reservations. I know the maître d' personally. You will enjoy both the meal and the view. Will that work for you?"

"Yes, I'll be ready. Please, see you then."

She had already checked the restaurant's veranda outside, overlooking the Mediterranean. The view was worth the evening. It was the one place where they had no security cameras.

"Perfect!"

Now her plan accelerated into action upon return to 315. First, she posted the "Do not disturb" sign on the door handle. She purchased full-length under pad from the same nearby pharmacy to place below the sheets to trap any remnants of recreational DNA. No leaks or bodily fluids need remain as evidence of sin within. No interruptions needed by the maid service. Then she ruffled the sheets and threw the perfunctory blanket aside so their conjuncted bodies would have a significant target area on which to fall. It was all calculated to seem random.

Dinner was the opening gambit. Aaron arrived exactly on time. She was already seated outside the purview of the interior cameras on the veranda.

Conversation was correctly minimal.

"May I order for you? I suggest the fish vegetarian entree he cited on page 3 of the menu." The view from the veranda melded with the setting sun. He didn't ask why she was wearing sunglasses this late in the day.

He didn't care. That detail eluded him. Kathleen in the nude was.

But he did order for both of them—fish for her and a kosher beef dish for himself. She pretended to like his choice, even though she didn't like fish much beyond salmon. The dish he ordered for her had a name she couldn't pronounce. That mattered little with the agenda at hand, so she laid stage four of the trap.

Thirty minutes later, the waiter presented the check. Sunglasses still posted on the bridge of her nose.

The meal was superb, but she left most of it.

"Would you care to share a nightcap of cognac with me upstairs? Shall we go? It's the least I can do to thank you for this very exotic meal. I promise not to get too drunk."

He fell for it hook, line, and sinker!

"I will pick up a bottle of Hennessey in the hotel liquor store and meet you at your room. I'll be there in ten minutes."

She hustled to the elevator and began the prep. The entrapment negligée was a deep blue that matched a pair of seductive panties. The remainder of her nondescript skirt, bra, and blouse she wore to dinner immediately packed for departure. The less of her clothing he touched, so much the better.

Arriving with the liter bottle of cognac, he first went to the hotel room minibar and drew two brandy glasses, poured them to the half, closely sniffed his, and offered her the second. After consumption of a second round and more filler conversation, he reverted to the vulgar lothario he was.

He unbuttoned his shirt, undressed quickly, and moved onto her with a deep, passionate kiss. Unlike Ronk, he was overly hairy, all the way down the back. She found it unappealing. His dental hygiene also left something to be addressed. It was all she could do to accept the tongue lurching and swashing down her throat.

And it almost made her gag.

His left hand moved slowly down her back and, without notice, ripped the panties and negligée away. He then let out an almost satanic growl, pushed her onto the bed, didn't even bother with preliminaries, and forced his *gladius* into a very reluctant *vagina*. Consensual was absent. For her, this was merely a chore.

The Roman sword sought its sheath.

He was ready; she was not.

So much for foreplay, she thought. *But this bastard is predicable!*

She pretended to like it, but the irritation was palpable. The lack of foreplay hurt. The semidry thrusting went on for another five minutes, followed by the shock.

Kathleen didn't realize how strong he really was, as he was only about two inches taller than she but a good sixty pounds heavier. With his clothes now finally discarded and with him grunting, he grabbed her right arm with his left, rolled her over, forcefully spread her legs with his thighs, and entered from behind.

She was almost too stunned to resist but felt completely limp as he sodomized her without benefit of lubricant and laughed aloud. He cupped her mouth to stifle the cry of resistance. Romance morphed into rape.

He was in the throes of passion; she hadn't even begun.

It was over in less than two minutes more before he rolled over, redressed, sat on the edge of the bed, and nonchalantly put on his very expensive loafers.

She seethed and said nothing.

"We still good for tomorrow?"

"Yes," she said weakly. "What time?"

"Be at my boat by seven. You'll enjoy the day!"

Then he got up, thrust a seedy smile toward her, slowly shut the door, and left.

Still shaken from the attack, she went to the shower with both the douche and the Enema bottles. Using both, she showered away any perceptible trace of Aaron Bronson's DNA from her vagina and rectum, emptied the cognac bottle wiped any prints from it, the glasses, and wiped the bathroom clean. Gathering any remaining evidence in a bland hotel laundry bag, she dressed, went downstairs, and found a dumpster almost full. She calculated correctly that it would be emptied the next day. Thus, the negligée and panties, along with the under pad, cognac bottle, and cleansing bottles disappeared into antiquity.

When she left the room in the morning before the anointed checkout time of noon, she left the "Do not disturb" sign in place so the maid service would not enter until late afternoon.

Her flight to Heathrow was at 1535, Tel Aviv time.

The dumpster was cleared by midmorning, and the maid service found nothing amiss as they changed the sheets, dusted the room, and cleaned the already sterile, disinfected bath.

And on the third day thereafter, Aaron Bronson did not arise from the dead like a Jewish predecessor two millennia before. Instead, he quietly washed ashore early Friday, head badly mangled by scraping the sea bottom with eyes and extremities that became small fish food. Beachgoers scattered when the body belched from the surf. The Star of David tattoo on his left arm remained intact.

But his throat was cut from right to left.

Apparently his previously circumcised, favorite body part was also an *hors d'oeuvre* marine delicacy. You couldn't tell if he was Jewish or Gentile.

It was almost gone.

Chapter 45

CORPUS EXANIMIS

The 112 call came from the Tel Aviv Chief of Lifeguards on the scene: "Floater on the beach, apparent murder victim. Throat cut. Body maybe from a yacht anchored four hundred meters offshore. Have sent two guards to retrieve the boat and re-anchor it here.

"How copy? Over!"

The response was bereft of commentary.

"Unit on the way with EMTs and coroner for transit. Crowd control paramount. Secure site for evidence. Any further victims?"

"None at this time."

And so it goes. Dead bodies are not an unusual event on public beaches. They arrive mostly because they can't swim or underestimate the power of the ocean. Accidental drownings in Israel used to be rare. The number, however, accelerated the last ten years, mainly on beaches without lifeguards or after permitted swimming hours. What used to be infrequently rare has become more commonplace with more than two hundred such deaths in 2018. But security and lifeguard personnel are so well trained that floaters remain unique events despite their upsurge the last decade.

This one today, however, was very different.

Israeli Constable David Barach and Sgt. Levi Elman drew the short end of the goat stick this morning. The floater washed ashore near the southern perimeter of their Tel Aviv station jurisdiction about 0600, near the end of their shift. They parked nearest the sand and hitched a ride with a lifeguard jeep to the scene cordoned off in a perimeter approximately thirty yards from the beached body. The requisite plenty of early-morning gawkers were still there, but the lifeguards had covered the body with a tarp. Barach and Elman flashed their badges for the crowd with the appropriate command to "stand back and let us do our work."

As per most crowds with perverse curiosity, they ignored the admonition. The conversations on the rim were muted but transfixed on the dead icon. Dead bodies remind all viewers of their own mortality. The view is almost hypnotic. It terrifies as well as attracts. To police, it's a major hindrance and annoyance. Crowds impede investigations and degrade physical evidence.

Barach lifted the tarp, noted that the body came ashore, and landed on its back.

"Well, he appears to be Jewish, Star of David tattoo on his left arm," Barach said, "but any evidence of circumcision is gone. His *smuck* just became a fish *schmeckle*. Hope he wasn't alive during the piscatorial. Where the hell's his bathing suit?"

"No, I think his conscious state subsided with the throat slashing," said Elman. "What we have here is a perfectly dead floater with a Jewish pedigree. If that's his boat they brought in, then we don't need to wait for the autopsy.

"My bet it's Aaron Bronson, although you can't tell from his masticated face. The head likely banged around on the sea bottom while the fish were enjoying the free food. The yacht I know. The body, I'm not so sure. His face is about gone."

The ambulance crew finally arrived twelve minutes later. They didn't hurry for the dead. That was the purview of the medical examiner's office who had all day to dissect the deceased and render a verdict. Elman had more than twenty years as a member of the INP, long enough to call it the coroner's office.

"So I guess we wait for the autopsy report, although we probably can identify and coble any evidence on the yacht if you don't mind getting your feet a little wet."

"I guess that's the next step, even if it's a wet one," replied Barach.

"Let's wade out to it and see what we can find."

The two lifeguards remained on scene, summarized their survey of the vessel before they attached a towline, and swam back to shore, boat in tow. It's a common procedure called a boat rescue for which they train often to remove stranded boats and boaters away from swimmers near the beach. Barach and Elman boarded the boat aboard the stern ladder, popped medical gloves, and began to search the bridge and the interior below.

"Nothing amiss up here," shouted Elman. "No clothes or dive equipment. If they were scuba or skin diving, there should be some remnants of that activity like face masks, fins, diving gloves. Something!"

"Well, there are a couple of unused full tanks with regulators that are down here in the rear well near the stern well, so this wasn't a group activity. There's a woman's sun hat and a pair of sunglasses. But this is the beach, so that tells us next to nothing. With Bronson's social life, they could have been here for weeks. So why does the dead body have no swim trunks? Did he wash up on shore nearby? You can conceivably swim naked out here, but the boat and Bronson would have been in full view of early morning spectators. You know that would attract some peepers.

"I checked the engine room and nothing seems amiss. The requisite tools are there, and there appears to be no evidence of a mechanical failure."

"Where's the anchor?" Barach asked.

"The lifeguards retrieved it before they dragged the boat here. It's under the unused tanks at the stern."

"Okay," said Elman. "Then I'll call in some help and let's begin interviewing some of these early morning star witnesses to the body's arrival. Maybe somebody saw something. I think four extra constables should be enough and I'll call the station for that. We'll also need a dive crew to assess any evidence on the seafloor that be already drifting either out to sea or toward shore. What time are high and low tides today?" Elman asked the station com chief over his cell.

"Wait one," came the crisp reply. "Low tide should already be underway. High tide about 1535! If you're looking for evidence to wash up, it should be there for your examination, perusal, and amazement within the next thirty minutes."

"Roger that. I'll have our interviewers scour the beach."

Comedians even in the INP, Elman thought. *That wasn't proper police radio protocol. It's a little morning, end-of-shift flippant.*

Elman called for a dive crew to scour the seafloor in the area where the lifeguards retrieved the boat. The sea depth there was about thirty-five to fifty meters at the point where the boat was anchored, approximately two hundred meters offshore.

Police Sgt. Ezra Weiss radioed Elman on the beach as he briefed the four new cops on scene about the incident. The dive crew arrived within ten minutes after Elman's request. They had the full complement of gear, including underwater cameras, and began their search.

Thirty minutes later, they surfaced with photographs of two dual tanks and two weight belts strapped together with a set of fins, a face mask, and a snorkel. Back on the boat, they reported the cache. The station sergeant major ordered them to tie and retrieve all of it with a tether and grappling hook.

They returned to the bottom, hooked the gear, resurfaced, and pulled it all to the surface with a wench on the bow of the dive boat. The catch seemed standard. He radioed Elman.

"Everything here points to maybe just two divers," said Sergeant Ezra Weiss. "There are no particular identification markings on any of this, but the weight belts are distinctly different in waist size. I measured both, and the larger one looks like that for an adult male with a ninety-five-to-one-hundred-centimeter waistline. The smaller one is for a waist of seventy to seventy-five that's likely a lean adolescent or a woman. A guy with that small a waistline is highly unlikely. I also noticed that's the Bronson yacht you have there on the beach, so my guess is, it's a woman. If there's a second body, it'll be female. Also saw one spearfishing gun down there, but it was far removed from the site of the tanks. Do you want me to go get it?"

"Nah, not right now. Spear divers all wear gloves. Are there any gloves or wetsuits floating around out there?'

"Negative. Has a second body shown up yet in the last five days?"

"Negative on that too," said Elman. "Well, Bronson obviously went down there with someone. And given his reputation and proclivity, it was probably a woman. So no trace of a female floater anywhere out there?"

"Roger that. Just the two tanks with the gear we brought up. Do you want us to remain on station? We have a priority call farther north on the beach, so we'll have to come back if you need us. Right now, that call takes precedence. Potential injury from a boat collision in the water! We'll remain nearby if you need us later."

"Roger that, we'll call again, if necessary."

Elman and Barach wadded back to shore to greet the ambulance crew who were loading the deceased into their vehicle for transit. His thorax and abdomen were bloated as was common with drowning victims after three to four days in the water. Aside from damage from hungry fish, the body's internal gases inflate the victim, which is how most drowning cases resurface.

It's simple biology. Methane prompts the body to bloat, rise to the surface, and meet the local coroner.

Staunch Jewish tradition mandates burial within twenty-four hours. The tradition is accession to the Pentateuch and the often harshly hot weather in the Middle East. Jewish law and tradition also forbid embalming a corpse as a desecration, but the Tel Aviv coroner's office would hold Aaron Bronson "on ice" for five to six days to do an effective autopsy—standard modern practice, in this case, of obvious foul play.

Coroner David Weiss (no relation to the Israeli National Police officer) had a sometimes morbid sense of comedy when dealing with the dead. He would take a chair in the morgue, sit on the deceased's left side of the autopsy table, and "interview" the body on the table. It was a technique much like what attorneys do with a list of questions on a cross-examination. He would sit there, pose the questions, predetermine the answers, hold a one-way conversation with the deceased, and handwrite answers on a legal-size yellow pad. Unlike most of his peers in the department, he disdained the use of handheld computers for his "interviews." His cohorts and team members in the IPD thought David was more than a little strange, but his work was meticulous and his reports rarely questioned in court. Like many Israeli doctors, Weiss went to medical school in the United States at Johns Hopkins near Baltimore. In his second year where the standard curriculum provided students their own cadaver to dissect, he developed the strange habit of conversing with it. Very often medical students were alone with *their* cadaver while they did the assigned tasks required throughout their academic year with the dead body. Some would freak out, while others would approach the work with quiet resilience and resignation.

Many even enjoyed it.

David had heard the circulated tale of an American medical student at UCLA who immediately dropped out of school when presented with his body.

The story pivoted about that of American popular singer of the 1960s, Bobby Darrin, who alleged donating his body upon after his death to the UCLA medical school. Weiss didn't know whether the story was true or not, but it made good conversation at social gatherings among the medical fraternity in training who sometimes nurtured a ghoulish sense of decedent humor.

It was a way to cope with the discomfort of extended time with the dead.

He had three other bodies in class upon Bronson's arrival, two of them were Muslim. A local Palestinian imam was slated to take those off his hands today, so Weiss could give his full attention to his star floater.

His summary was pure David Weiss.

"The body of the decedent exsanguinated rapidly after a violent right-to-left cut of both carotid arteries. There was also an extremely high level of carbon dioxide in his bloodstream likely from either a defective regulator or tank or something possibly introduced by a third party. The decedent had visible bruises about his neck and upper body that indicated a violent struggle of some sort that precipitated convulsions and almost sudden death. There was less than two pints of blood left in the victim's body, and whoever attacked him used an industrial strength cutting device, likely a straight razor of some sort. The victim likely lived less than a minute after the attack.

All other damage to the body was likely the result of convulsions on the seabed and foraging by the marine life."

The constable who interviewed the beach gawkers came up only one viable lead. A young surfer described a tall redhead coming up from the water with face mask and fins that morning at around eight thirty. He remembered that because she was only one of a half dozen or so women on the beach that early. His description exuded pubescent joy.

"Man, she was hot," he said. "I mean smokin' hot. I'm almost 186 centimeters tall, and she was almost my height with red hair and a purple bikini. She was hard to miss. She'd stand out on any beach any day. The most interesting part was, she was about my mother's age. She was a real MILF. Do you know what that is?"

Back at their office, Barach and Elman read both the autopsy report and the rash of interview summaries collected by the constables.

"Levi," said David, "you're more familiar with American English and standards. How does this kid's height compare to our potential suspect? And do you know what a MILF is?"

"Well, if it's a woman, she's damn close to six feet tall in American parlance and, with red hair, stands out in a crowd. And yes, David, the vulgar street expression is 'Mothers I'd Like to Fuck.' The kid was obviously in the age group for whom that is some sort of Freudian fantasy. That, however, could likely describe 10 percent of the women on the beach here this morning. Red is sometimes confused with auburn coloring and blonde in the morning sun. It's so hard to tell these days because hair color camouflage is a practice to which half the women of the world subscribe and every woman I know here in Israel."

"Well, we'll just have to interview all our redheaded suspects naked to check and see what their real hair color is," Barach said with a leering smile.

"As much as I know you would like that, David," Elman replied, "I'm afraid your fantasy is already dead with Aaron Bronson. Unless we get something else, this case is already colder than a fat Persian whore."

Chapter 46

SUDDEN DEPARTURE

It was Friday, the Jewish Sabbath, and Ephraim and Esther had just returned from Beth David Synagogue in their neighborhood northeast of Tel Aviv.

Their children, Miriam and David, were bringing their spouses and children to Sabbath dinner at their parents' home, a rotating ritual that both shared intermittently with their in-laws. Everyone related got the chance to be with all seven of their grandchildren throughout every month, three from Miriam and four fathered by David.

"Esther," said Ephraim, "did you hear from Kathleen yet? She's supposed to be here all week. Well, there's an item here in the Thursday *Jerusalem Post* in which she'd be very interested. It seems that the body of that playboy Aaron Bronson washed up on the beach. He was murdered, but police are not saying how. They're being very quiet about it. That's odd. But he is apparently very dead."

"So why would Kathleen have any interest in his death? I know I don't. His family is a stain on Judaism everywhere."

"Well, the United States FBI thinks he may have been the fifth assailant at the home of Ronan and Kathleen in Western Pennsylvania last spring. It's odd if he drowned because he is obviously a very accomplished swimmer. He had to be good in the water because I also heard he was heavily into scuba diving. But that yacht of his is the ugliest in the marina."

"Well, no, I haven't heard from her," Esther said. "That's unusual. Maybe you should call her if she's still in town. I was very much looking forward to seeing her again."

"I think I left my phone in my car. I'll be right back."

Seven minutes later, Ephraim returned to the kitchen.

"That's very strange. It went directly to voice mail. I'll try her again later."

But Kathleen had already switched planes in London and was on the way home to Butler with a rental vehicle from Pittsburgh International.

"That's so unlike her," Esther said. "Keep trying. I hope she's okay."

But Kathleen had already left Israel.

Morrigan left with her.

Mission complete for her daughter.

Chapter 47

RECKONING TO RECONCILIATION

There are many things from which you can run and hide. For pious and fervent Christians, God is not one of them. If you're susceptible, guilt is second on the list. It will hunt you and eventually devour you.

Now the verdant spring season drifted into late summer, almost four months since her last trip to Israel. The case against Tsakrios seemed closed with the death of the Butler assailants and the pending Federal charges against him. Good lawyers can keep your felonious ass out of prison sometimes for years.

But not forever.

The mountain of evidence against the Greek slowly accrued. It cued the slow strangle that involved months of presentencing negotiation. It was a veritable lava flow, slow but unrelenting. Like all charging prosecutors, they threw everything at him, including the proverbial kitchen sink, the first-floor toilet, and grievances that rolled back to petty crimes of the '70s. The litany of charges included warrants for avoiding traffic tickets and a spectrum of financial misdemeanors. It was more than subtle overkill. The Feds wanted not only to confine his ass for a lifetime of crimes but to crush and break him financially.

They succeeded with aplomb and wrapped it all up with a bow: a fine of $250,000 for an aggregate spectrum of transgressions only understood in the world of CPAs.

Shankle's firm fought the mountain of charges with more than $100,000 in billable hours and managed to whittle down forty years of possible confinement at a Club Fed to sixteen, with possibility of parole after seven. Plea deal accepted in Federal court, Oliver went onward with his team to cull other criminals on the Federal ranch of malfeasance. Oliver was in ultimate glee mode. Sixteen years for a seventy-year-old may just as well be a death sentence. Even a parole after seven would leave him destitute, without resources and effectively on the dole. The irony of the American prison system is that senior citizen convicts more often have better health insurance than their peers on Medicare and Medicaid roaming freely on the outside.

In prison, there is no deductible, and unlike private insurance, the government has no 80/20 split either. Federal or state prisons, thus the taxpayers, cough up every dime of the convict's care.

As Oliver once opined, "taxpayers can't have it both ways." He would rail, "If you want these people off the street so they won't commit heinous crimes, then you must have a system to either track or confine them. All of these cost big-time money. So if we decide that the imposition of death is too drastic and unconstitutional, then you'd better find a place to warehouse some of these vile human beings somewhere."

Then he went on a further rant with Agent McKnight, the morning captive audience.

"Remember that film with Sean Connery years ago called *Outlands* where he was the sheriff on some distant mining planet and the only law enforcement officer? Well, his jail was to confine his prisoners in suits floating in space where they couldn't escape without risk of instant death. I'd love an option like that."

"Dream on, Chief," said McKnight. "I think we're stuck with eternal confinement in this millennium. Maybe we should try an underwater solution in the middle of the Pacific?"

"I like that. I'll have to mull that one, McKnight. But that's a damn good idea, an underwater prison. Right now, we're stuck with confinement, but that's a primo idea to consider. Right now, it's just confinement, even until their dying day! Then if necessary, taxpayers cough up the bill to plant you. It's all so perverse."

But the prison term was less harsh a sentence than breaking Tsakrios financially. He had to liquidate most of his assets to defend himself. His house was up for sale. Veronica had moved out and filed for both civil divorce and annulment of their marriage through the Diocese of Pittsburgh. His daughters became permanently estranged and refused to even talk or communicate with him.

He bathed in the ruins of his life, contested neither of the separation proceedings, slipped into depression and contemplated suicide.

At the same time, Kathleen, tortured by the memories of what she had done, wallowed in a Christian vat of guilt. She relished the sentence and justice imposed on Tsakrios but floated in her own sewer of self-recrimination. The aftermath of the last five months, fueled by vengeance that propelled her rage, was the daily reminder that she allowed it to consume the core of her ethical and moral *ens*. She succumbed to the ultimate sin of premeditated homicide. The unanticipated aftermath shredded her psyche. Guilt can corrupt your innermost beliefs about yourself and your relation to the transcendent. She felt "I have to get right with God. I should have just left it all alone. I let my anger take complete control and committed murder. I was out of control."

So she turned to expiate that guilt through the Catholic sacrament of Reconciliation, long misunderstood and long ago rejected during the Protestant Revolt/Reformation. Contrary to most Protestant theory and misunderstanding, Catholics do not "confess" their sins to a priest in the confessional. The confessor is acting as "Christ in the person of the priest," the conduit to God, if you will. He is witness to the conversation, the exchange directly with God. That's the actual theology. It's an important distinction poorly understood by the general public.

The penitent is admitting his or her guilt directly to God via the ordained priest in a private setting. It can be in a confessional box, as understood by most, or face-to-face. Either way, the priest is bound legally and by Catholic Canon Law to keep the exchange completely private. The conversation is between you and God, and that conversation is a formula, not just a casual conversation in an open setting.

The priest acts more like an umpire or referee.

The technical title imposed on all priests is the "seal of confession." Revelation of any sin admitted during reconciliation will subject the offending priest to excommunication and defrocking called Code 983 of the Code of Canon Law. Police and legal agencies from sundry countries have tried unsuccessfully over multiple years to compel testimony about an accused based on a confessional admission.

They have always failed.

Over the two-thousand-year history of the Catholic Church, even the most repressive and hostile dictators have attempted to coerce information from priests they thought penitents revealed in a confessional setting. There are several confirmed priests martyred for refusing to break that absolute seal.

Joseph Stalin tried that coercion on multiple occasions.

He executed many but failed on that count. Likely it precursed his probable ticket to hell. Priests truly committed to their ordination vows will die or be incarcerated rather than reveal anything said to them by a penitent in the confessional.

There are seven major sacraments historically part of lifetime Catholicism practice that starts with Baptism, the Eucharist (communion), Confirmation (performed by a bishop or his official designee), Reconciliation (Penance), Holy Orders (ordination), Matrimony, and what used to be called Extreme Unction (last rites).

Depending on your point of view, Henry VIII and Anglicans kept most everything but confession.

They dumped, however, any allegiance to Rome or the pope.

Lutherans kept most of the seven in their liturgies, while Baptists junked everything but Baptism and Matrimony, including the entire ritual of the Mass which daily, and every Sunday, replicates the ritual of Christ in the Upper Room and the Last Supper with the twelve original apostles during the Thursday of what Christians call Holy Week. Baptists merely flog you every Sunday with sermons bordering on theater that moan onward too long.

Muslims only admit Jesus to a long line of prophets, but Mohammed is still "the man" and the only acceptable pipeline to

Allah. The rest of the spectrums of religion emanating from Asia take very different and divergent paths to the hereafter.

They all, nevertheless, have congregations with hefty demands on collection plates.

Atheists and agnostics don't quibble about any of this. Unlike adherents who profess Western faiths, like former lady Nancy Reagan, they just say no! They're unbothered by the Western philosophies and arguments from Aristotle to Friedrich Nietzsche. Marxists just have no clue.

To them, it's all just cacophony and distraction.

"To break the seal of confession is, in fact, an act of utter betrayal to Jesus Christ," said Chad Pecknold, associate professor of systemic theology at the Catholic University of America in Washington DC. "No reasonable person would give their lives up to protect a child molester or a serial murderer. What they're protecting (during Reconciliation) is the seal, which is their obedience to Jesus Christ, who is the agent of absolution in the confessional. To break the seal is to break trust with Christ."

So Kathleen decided to expiate her expanding sense of guilt with a Reconciliation where she was unknown. She deliberately chose the St. Mary's of Mercy Church near the point of the Golden Triangle where complete anonymity would be assured. The parish was first founded to serve an Irish working community in the 1930s during the Great Depression. Formerly a Methodist Church, Catholics took over the building in 1893 and still has a unique, active ministry where the parish serves lunches through a Red Door to the kitchen of the church building where they even today serve one hundred or more bag lunches midday to those homeless or in need.

Confessions there are held daily, Monday through Friday, from eleven to noon. She had Cecilia come over for the day for the kids. She had also hired Jolene Zinzer for extended therapy with Ronan. He had adjusted better with her, and Zinzer had him walking around the perimeter of their property. Progress was still gradual but actual. His attitude was also modified so that he now had a rapport with her, a kind of ceasefire where they both seemed to understand the necessary compromise to stasis. Kathleen made some slightly phony excuse about having to go into town to meet with the chief of police about private protection for a National Rifle Association convention to be held at the David Lawrence Convention Center. The drive on a Friday remains an hour or so with traffic going both ways I-79. It abates a little on weekends, but today the Pirates were in town in the midst of a rare pennant race, so the real challenge would be parking. The Wharf Lot was up and open and the river was down, complemented by a short ten-minute walk to the church.

As per vintage Kathleen, she arrived ten minutes early, sat in a pew near the back of the church, and collected her thought.

The priest was younger than she. He approached the box, kissed the purple stole used for the sacrament, put it around his neck and entered, turning on the lights on the tripart confessional. It turned on a red light above his own center seat and green lights above both sides for the penitents. Once inside, penitents on each side would kneel, and it would automatically switch the green lights to red. One woman entered to the priest's right. She was the first penitent.

Kathleen was the second.

She entered to his left, knelt, sighed heavily, waited for the sliding privacy door within to open.

What seemed a long five minutes later, the door opened. A kneeling, shaken Kathleen began.

"Bless me, Father, for I have sinned!"

Epilogue

2029

The spring was relatively dry compared to the previous cycles of wet, cool weather that pelted Western Pennsylvania the previous decade. *Farmers' Almanac* did a better job of prediction than the National Weather Service. Although the Almanac began publication in 1782, every year backyard gardeners relied on it rather than the hysteria of The Weather Channel with its daily focus on the most extreme in both of the world's hemispheres. You could live in a constant state of fear if your spectrum of weather information was Internet-exclusive.

Local farmers, however, loved the challenge of 2029 and the chance at an early planting season. Two crops by September 30 was the goal. October was too fickle for most gardening, unless you had an addiction to pumpkins or cabbage. By then, both the McShea sons had graduated: Seamus (now going by Jimmy or James) from Penn State like his dad, Sean from Carnegie-Mellon. Katie was a sophomore at Duquesne University. This was an early spring to relish. McShea kids launched or semi-launched, while Mom and Dad lurched toward something like retirement.

Seamus's degree was in something like mass media ecology, to which his father once abruptly asked, "What the hell is a major in… what did you say….media ecology…what on God's green earth is that? Did I miss something here? Is that for which we wrote all those checks? Wha' cha' goin' do with that...son? Mom and Dad are a little confused."

His flippant answer pleased neither his father nor his mother in the adjacent office.

"Drink beer, party, appreciate beautiful women, and make a ton of money as a New Age blog site journalist with a global readership. I'll already have a following on social media sites. I'm on three of them. Be patient with me. It's graduate Internet time, Dad, and the old way of going to school is obsolete. It'll take a little time, but I got it under control. I mean you guys actually used keyboards in the old days when we were kids. All I have to do is just speak it and the magic writes itself. I'll correct the robot's poor grammar later. It's almost like having a secretary that seldom makes a mistake."

The sudden entry of the offended Kathleen into the dining room stifled his self-flattering conversation. She heard but did not like it.

"Here's my eldest and most unperfected son on the road to perdition. You're almost twenty-five years old, Seamus. Playtime is over. I know you write well and you're just like your father but kindly remember the $35,000 in student loans over, and above what we shelled out was not a grant or a gift. You're getting away cheaply compared to what some of your friends' parents have paid. You'd better figure it out quickly because your tenure here in Butler is about to expire. Vague degree, no job, no future doesn't cut the mustard, the cheese, or even the front lawn. It's amazing you even graduated given your fraternity affiliation. Your mother belonged to a different kind of sorority that espoused learning and service, not party. And may I remind you that your father is a decorated Marine officer and civil engineer. That doesn't happen without commitment and discipline."

"Mom, Mom! Lay off me. I was just kidding. You don't give Sean and Katie all this grief. I'm getting it together. I realize my next moves will not be easy or normal, so just gimme a break."

"You lounge around here much longer, Seamus Patrick O'Rourke-McShea," she shot back, "and that break will be your nose. Try explaining that to your harem of girlfriends. I need a scorecard just to track their names. Much of your party time is out of vogue with your advanced adolescence. You need to grow up and out. We've given you a range of freedom here appropriate for an adult. We rarely see you for dinner anymore while you're out carousing. We seldom see you here more than once a week. So I gotta' ask, like Ronk's mother once asked him, haven't you had enough sex this week? Stop by for dinner sometime. Your parents would like to see your smiling face occasionally and not on the back of a milk carton of missing progeny. And get a full-time job! You're in possession of a degree and a massive student loan debt and are sporadically employed. Please address those issues before I go completely off the rails with you."

"Damn, that's gross," he replied. "Mom, I'm your son. Please!"

"Hey, Dad, can't you just get her to lighten up? I mean, she won't give me a break."

"On what or why? I agree with her. You're working on almost two years removed from graduation and you're moving out of the house at darter snail's pace. In fact, I believe you haven't moved at all. Your ship needs to launch, my dearest and first. Sean's a senior with a degree in economics on the horizon. He's already on the road with three job offers, including one from the Commonwealth (of Pennsylvania) and another from British Petroleum after the summer intern work he did for them. They were righteously impressed. Even Katie outpaces you with her projected degree in political science. The Navy is already courting her for Officer Candidate School and later law school. Maybe a little more hustle in your career choice would be appropriate.

"I won't harangue you anymore about it, but Mom might, so kindly get it in gear, or Mom may just burn down what's left of your House of Shining Personality."

Interruption terminated the parental rants. It was the phone call on Kathleen's cell back in the office.

"Excuse me, gentlemen. We'll talk more about this later, and we will address said issues. You are going to stay for dinner, right? It will be the first time in three weeks we've had all three of you here. Sean will be here about dinnertime, and Katie's already on the way, but I have to take this call."

Kathleen scrolled through the litany of previous calls that she saved for years. She didn't recognize the number at first. Then it made her sit up very straight in her office chair. This one she remembered like a bad migraine.

"Lo and behold, a blast from the very distant past!" She wanted to delete it but realized he would just keep calling again. Back again like an unwanted case of herpes.

She touched the screen.

It was the retired Detective Joseph John Duffy, replete with an updated photo. Now he had flickers of gray in his receding hairline.

And probably that same noxious attitude! she thought. *All right, J.J. Duffy, lay it on me!*

She put the phone to her breast and sighed to herself. "I think I know what it's about." After a five-second, very pregnant pause, she began, "Detective Duffy, how are you? Glad to see you're still upright. What can I do for you this fine top'a tha mornin' to ya?"

"And to the rest of the day to you, ma'am!"

She waited for the perfunctory answer but already knew what he wanted as she put her left hand to her face.

"Mrs. McShea, as you may already know," he began, "I'm writing a book compiled about my years as a Pittsburgh police officer and detective. I'm focusing on twenty of the most interesting cases I pursued, and that includes your run-in with that gang George Tsakrios hired to assassinate your husband. I'd like to interview you two to complete the chapter, if I may, with a few quotes about the encounter."

"Well, maybe you should interview Tsakrios," she retorted. "It was his hired hands whom we dispatched. I don't think I can add anything more than the public record that's already there. I presume he's still in Federal prison somewhere and hope he dies there. There's nothing about that night I want to revive or relive. I think we've said everything we knew about it. But you're welcome to recount the evening. What did you have in mind?"

"Nevertheless, I wasn't there for the gunfight at your place and wanted to fill in some of the more subtle nuance of what transpired that's not in the official FBI or Butler County Sheriff's reports. Those details merely reflect the dry nature of police after-action summaries."

Subtle nuance? she thought. *Like most cops, he still has a way with jargon that reeks. That's not what he really wants, and now we both know it.*

"Okay, Detective Duffy, whadda want and how can I help you? Ten years ago warps a lot of ancient history. What's you angle?"

"All right…I'd just like to interview both you and your husband about the details of the incident to complete the chapter. That stuff missing from the official record. I've also asked retired Sheriff Malone to join me. I'd be remiss," he continued, "if I excluded both your firsthand impressions to complete the story. After all, you two were the prime actors who thwarted the attack."

Kathleen paused.

"Ronk, come in here. Lieutenant Duffy wants to interview us about the attack in 2019. I'll put it on speaker." Ronan entered from the dining room and sat down.

"How are you, Duffy? I presume retirement allows you more sleep time, no more 2:00 a.m. calls from folks 'dying to see you.' Did you ever marry?" he teased. "You were the bachelor cad of the decade when I first met you. Is there any woman who would have you?"

"As a matter of fact, Ronan, I met a great woman whom I married shortly after 2020. Turns out she was a photographer for National Geographic and I met her at another retirement party, one for my former partner, the piano man, completely by accident. It wasn't a setup. Turns out she'd done a lot of work for the department years before. I discovered we have shared interests in photography and fishing. We married in 2021 and now have four kids. It's also helpful that she's a gym rat, so she's on my ass all the time about working out. So I'm in the best shape of my life."

"Well, how the hell did you do all that? Is she your age?"

"Nah, she's ten years younger, and our kids are all now in elementary school, all four of them. Good lady. I'd love to have you meet her. Her name is Analisa Ramirez, now Duffy or Ramirez-Duffy, depending on her mood."

"Four! You are one fertile son of the old sod. Maybe later," Ronk said. "When do you want to meet for this reunion of sorts?"

"I'll come up anytime that's most convenient for you. I have a post-retirement security gig with New York Mellon Bank, but I can adjust that. What's good for you?"

Ronk looked at Kathleen. The look on her face gestated only one adverb, and she silently mouthed it: Never!

"He's also invited Randy Malone along for this confab," she said.

"How about next Saturday morning at 1000?" Ronk chimed into the exchange. "We have great coffee. Our three kids will be preoccupied with the grandparents O'Rourke, and we can work with you for the rest of the morning. Our kids won't be back until early Sunday morning. Will that work?"

The subsequent look from Kathleen was etched in sour, like "What in God's name are you thinkin'?"

"No, no, no! Please don't encourage this moron," she whispered. "Now that you've stuck both our feet in it, cut it off at noon!"

"Well, Duffy, let's call it at ten to twelve this Saturday, as we have commitments from shopping to church work at the parish that afternoon. Can you work with that?"

The white lie was intended prevarication. She just didn't want Duffy to think it was an open-ended invitation to a marathon query. But she also had that sinister, dark reason she'd never shared with her husband. The hostility of the past encounters with Duffy still simmered. Less Duffy, more peace!

"That should be sufficient for the interview. See you two then!"

"Roger that!" Ronk said and pressed his cell to end the call!

She exhaled perceptively and threw a Securitas file on which she'd been working across the room.

"Ronan, you know what he wants to probe, don't you? This is all about his ego and the death of those other two dirtbags who survived the attack. He thinks there some connection between their deaths and us. Some of his questions will incriminate us both. It's a probe, not an interview. That's why he's bringing Randy along."

"Well, there isn't any connection that I see, just fortuitous luck," Ronk replied. "Maybe this will just make him go away. I mean, this isn't a meeting with his publication lawyers. Let's just see what he wants. After all, we did kill three of those knuckleheads who attacked us. That's public record. I don't see what the problem is. This ain't like he's showing up with a subpoena. And Randy probably has a different tack on all of this. Let's just give them their two hours and hope Duffy goes away forever. This isn't like he's writing a book about the O. J. Simpson trial."

But some things really never change. Duffy, Malone, and punctuality were among them. Both showed up between 0955 and 1000 in separate vehicles just as advertised.

"At least, these law dogs are on time, not like that parade of newspaper shills who hounded us in 2019," Ronk said. "Isn't it strange that Duffy is collaborating with Randy? I mean, that's a classic pair of snoop dogs of opposite persuasion. Ten years ago, you couldn't pair them together as paid mourners in a trail car behind the hearse. I don't get it, but that's just me."

They parked just outside the newly renovated barn that Jake and Rufus once patrolled and which now sported a woodcraft shop and an extra guest bedroom. They also updated the canine crew with two German Shepherds roaming their Butler paradise, mostly indifferent to the presence of strangers.

The knock on the kitchen door was perfunctory. They didn't wait for a response. They just entered and announced their presence. It was presumptive. Malone had history and proprietary rights to visit any time of day as a longtime friend. That friendship, however, cooled over the last decade.

"No shit! *Entrez*," barked Ronk. "Glad to see you two derelict dicks again. Glad you both made it to retirement without any added lead fragments!"

That was more for Duffy, less so for Malone. Randy in retirement still remained a friend with an encroaching separation Ronan didn't quite understand. Somehow the warmth of earlier years faded, but Duffy remained on the shit list with his snarky attitude toward

Kathleen a decade before. Ronk didn't know even why they showed up together.

Ten years still did not erase their perception of Duffy as Kathleen once said. He was "still a designated punk devoid of class." Her hostility over his approach then and now didn't quell her distaste for his attitude. She didn't want him in her house but conceded to the meeting reluctantly.

They met in the kitchen and adjourned to the adjacent dining room. Ronan noticed Duffy came fully prepared with computer and a briefcase crammed with reporters' notepads and the police reports from Pittsburgh, Butler County and the FBI.

Malone just brought his good looks and a very detached attitude, not one nurtured by more than twelve years of friendship, and a copy of some sort of official police file marked "Confidential" that he never opened. And nothing else!

Kathleen was on guard while Ronan smelled an ambush. "Why now? Why so many years later?"

The rambling ninety minutes next defined circular and repetitive. Ronan still didn't get the point of it all until the last fifteen after a fusillade of questions that finally unwrapped where they really wanted to go.

"You do know Sergovia is dead, don't you?" Malone announced. "And Bronson too?"

"So are we holding a wake here for their demise?" she said. "Yes, I knew. I'm still with Securitas for another four years, Randy, and am aware of their passing into the netherworld. Should I bemoan their deaths? Neither one of them is on my prayer request list. And shouldn't be on yours too! Absolutely not, so what's your point?"

"She died here somewhere in Western Pennsylvania. Her body was found in the Youghiogheny River down in Fayette County, almost in West Virginia, and his on the beach near Tel Aviv. Both had their throats cut with the same type of knife."

"That I knew. Actually, Oliver apprised me just before he retired, just to punctuate the finality of our trauma in '19," she said. "Apparently her entry into witness protection was closer to home than mandated by normal policy. Maybe the FBI is running out of places to hide people. Don't they normally send them to places like Opossum Trot or Monkey's Eyebrow, Kentucky, places teeming with nondescript culture to conceal them?"

Her sarcasm went underappreciated and flew right past him.

"I think they actually stashed her somewhere near Morgantown, West Virginia. I wasn't aware that you knew," Randy said. "You can get lost in a big university town just as effectively as you can in Throckmorton, Texas."

"Throck what?" she said. "That's as obscure as any question on *Jeopardy*."

Malone was quiet most of the session until those last questions. Duffy looked at his watch as he noted she did the same to the clock on the dining room wall. It was that uncomfortable moment when both parties wanted the conversation to end but didn't quite know how.

Then Duffy awkwardly broke serve.

"Thank you both," he began, "for both the time and the coffee. I think I have enough to complete the chapter. If you remember anything else, this is my new business card. Please feel free to call! I've appreciated your time."

That cued the phony goodbyes and handshakes. After the kitchen door closed, Kathleen turned to Ronan and said, "I'd rather have an iced water enema than deal with Duffy again. He's such an annoying, braying goat."

"Well, I can help you with that enema thing, if you want," he teased.

She grabbed a kitchen towel and slapped him upside the head.

"Ou-owl! That stung!"

"Don't be a smartass, Ronk"

Then she chucked the business card into the kitchen trash can.

As they approached their vehicles outside, Malone turned to Duffy as he opened the door to his truck. "Did you know that Sergovia and Bronson both died from slashes through the throat, just above the larynx? In Sergovia's case, almost decapitated! The slayer cut both of them from right to left. In your years of homicide work, what did you look for in a suspect, Duffy?"

"Motive, opportunity, timing, and weapon! What are you saying, Randy?"

"We both too old to believe in coincidence, right? What we have here is motive, opportunity with a panoply of coincidence. She's still in the security business. As such, she's a world traveler. And both of them are weapons proficient, and at one time, both acquired black belts in Tae Kwon Do."

He slammed the truck door, started the engine of his semi-antique Ford 150, rolled down the driver's side window, started the engine, and yelled back at Duffy, "Did you see the sign that they've put on the front gate, there for about nine years now?"

"Nah, I didn't notice it coming in. What's it say?"

"Morrigan's Estate."

"Okay, I give," said Duffy. "What's the reference?"

"Kathleen's nickname at North Catholic was Morrigan. She had it on all her varsity uniforms and varsity jacket.

"And?"

"Morrigan is the Celtic goddess of war!"

"What else did you notice about her in the interview? Kathleen took some copious notes."

"Yeah, so what?"

"She's left-handed."

About the Author

This is the author's first trek into fiction.

The characters are all drawn from events and people he met throughout his life. Although the characters are fictional, they draw their profiles from his father, along with myriad US Marines with whom he served. His previous works include *The Ten Commandments of Script* and *The Forced March from Vietnam to Kentucky*. He grew up in Pittsburgh and graduated with degrees from both the University of California (Irvine) and the University of Arizona. He and his artist wife, Anita, live near Lone Oak, Kentucky, where she teaches art history classes at Western Kentucky Community & Technical College. Their oldest daughter, Adriana, is a graduate of Thomas More College and lives in Lexington, Kentucky. Their son, Sean, graduated from Murray State University (Murray, Kentucky) and works in retail business in Paducah, Kentucky. Patrick remains a hardcore Pittsburgh Pirates and Steelers fan and still remembers the long road since the last time the Pirates won the World Series—that is, when he was in graduate school in Arizona (1979). He welcomes comment on his works. His e-mail is patfitch@vci.net.

CPSIA information can be obtained
at www.ICGtesting.com
Printed in the USA
FSHW010848180920
73786FS

9 781646 288021